Academia Draconia

Seven of Stars

Also by Mae McKinnon
(credited as M. Aei)

DAWN OF THE WINDS

WOLF'S BANE

Academia Draconia

Seven of Stars

Mae McKinnon

DRAGONQUILL PUBLISHING

Academia Draconia
A DragonQuill book

Cover art by Juliane Völker, Nightpark Art
nightpark-art.de

Edited by Ashley Lachance
scribecat.com

Title font: RM ALBION by P2pnut
Creative Commons Attribution-NoDerivs License (CC BY-ND)
1001fonts.com

First pinted by Amazon, City of Luxembourg, Luxembourg 2016

ISBN 978-91-983535-0-1
A CIP catalogue record for this book is available from the National Library of Sweden

DragonQuill Publishing
Stenbocksgatan 26, Simrishamn, Sweden

dragonquillpublishing.com

Contents

Acknowledgements

This story has been with me for many years, been poured over many times and has, by now, probably worn out more eyeballs than a simple novel has the right to. But between the feeling of being in charge of a cast at the theatre that has clearly been given a whole different script than you; the characters choosing the most inopportune moments to re-invent themselves and the resident muse taking a vacation at the drop of a hat, it's safe to say that it couldn't have been done without Mal.

A more constant source of encouragement, boundless ability to see beyond my mere scribbles and a better friend, you'd be hard-pressed to find in any universe. I am truly fortunate to have been allowed to share the journey of this story with you and I hope that many more adventures await us both. It goes without saying that this book wouldn't have been half as good nor nearly as enjoyable to write without you: my wonderful fellow Wrangler of Words.

Prologue

The sun was colouring the world in red and orange, its light dancing across the heavens. One moment it illuminated, the next it returned to shadow or as close to shadow as could be, up here.

At this very moment it was busy disappearing beyond the horizon and the cloudbank that was about to shelter it looked as if it was being set on fire.

Up here, above the clouds ... far above the clouds, would be the last place that fell into the embrace of the night. With its colour rapidly draining through it was a spectacle that, while repeating every day, rarely looked exactly the same.

It was tranquil. The kind of tranquillity that was brought about by simply being where no one, or nothing, else was. The only companion here was the wind, and while it could sometimes be a bit boisterous, it was only one thing. More importantly, much more importantly, was that it didn't berate you. There was a kind of give and take to it, but it remained aloof and distant even as it carried you across the world.

The world itself, seen from this height, seemed almost as quiet. From the great oceans and lakes to the continents and islands, it too was distant, and yet, it felt almost as if, if only you would reach out just a little bit more, it would be enough to touch it.

At least, that was the impression it had always given him. Of course, he knew that *technically* that was impossible, but it was more about the sensation than anything else. This was the one place where he actually felt connected to the world. Not just connected either, but a part of it.

That rarely happened down there, on the ground. Unfortunately, that was where he spent most of his time. Sometimes he laughed at the irony of that. How typical really…

Bursting out of a wisp of cloud quite a bit below, a flock of jingo birds turned sharply as they caught sight of the shadow against the sun. They decided that this airspace wasn't for them after all and that taking the long way around wasn't such a bad idea when you stopped to consider the options.

Not that they needed to worry. Not really. He didn't mind sharing this space *that* much. The birds, too, belonged up here – somewhat more so than he did actually, he had to admit. After all, he could not, in any sense of the word, be accused of being native to this world. None of them were.

Another good thing about being up this high, well, two good things really, was that not only did you get a great view, but once you'd managed to get here, it required almost no effort at all to remain. And so, his wings fully extended, he drifted lazily across the heavens, content for the moment to just *be*.

To the birds that had just veered off, the shadow he cast would have been scaled somewhere beyond enormous and a word that hadn't even been invented yet, had he been a bird too. Even as a dragon it was distinctly larger than you'd have expected.

Not that there was really anything to judge against up here. Not now that the birds had vanished. The bits of water vapour that made up the occasional cloud here and there didn't really care much what size he was or wasn't.

But he knew, and perhaps that was enough.

A New Beginning

There were great 'oohs' and 'aaahs' erupting from the crowds that happened to be on the esplanade and approach-roads as a whole wing of red and black dragons shot over them at high speed.

They felt almost close enough to touch. They certainly felt close enough for you to duck – and there were more than one person down on the ground who did.

Almost immediately after passing the main entrance to the Dragon Research Centre, the dragons broke formation. Splitting into their respective colours they banked sharply to left or right, dancing in between each other as they did so.

The display didn't last long – only five minutes or so of winged acrobatics showing off some of the skill of the centre's resident dragons and riders for the new arrivals.

Even so, a whole set of people who'd already gone through the doors and entered the front auditorium trickled back out again as word quickly spread.

Not that there weren't plenty of people out here as it was already.

Gaile looked around, craning her neck to take it all in; from the white, or at least pale ochre, structures that made up the DRC up ahead to the smaller buildings that were scattered around as well as the pale stone-paved courtyard in front of it all.

Not that "paved" here meant "filled in and covered with concrete". Not by far.

As her eyes drank in everything she could see, they were filled with the imagery of green plants, both potted and planted, growing here and there;

from small shrubs to flowering vines that climbed up the pillars. They lined the marble tiled path closest to the main entrance, sort of like a miniature causeway. They weren't the only ones either, as all the pathways converged on the main courtyard and all of them were filled with life.

Long, shallow, pools added their decoration to the scenery – ranging from turquoise to bright blue to almost transparent. The welcome sound of moving water traced back to several small, and some not so small, fountains interspersed among the rest of the decorations.

'Where do they get all the water for this?' Gaile wondered.

Her feeling somewhat perplexed by the whole thing was easily understandable. For if you let your gaze travel just a little bit further, in any direction, they'd not be able to fail to land on the distinctly arid existence that made up the actual landscape in these parts. It was hard to miss. Impossible you might even say.

Whoever had decided to locate the DRC, or Dragon Research Centre if you wanted to feel formal about it, out here had obviously *not* done so because of the spectacular lush forests, rolling grassland hills and sparkling streams, Gaile thought.

You could in fact have been forgiven for thinking that they might even have had a direct aversion to those things – or to anything at all.

There were two things that could be used to describe this place, if you were to know the mind of the young woman standing on the edge of the planted area, where the shuttle from the closest city had dropped her off.

The first word was flat. There wasn't anything even resembling a hill from what she could see. In fact, it was difficult to imagine anything being flatter and not being a body of water.

The second word was hot. Gaile fanned herself with her diom, which was sadly inadequate at its new job.

It wasn't the steaming heat of a jungle, but the dry heat that accompanied the vast impression of nothingness … every single mile of it.

Admittedly, the reason you thought it was flat was because you didn't see the canyon that ran for miles and miles nearby. It was the largest canyon on the planet. That didn't make much difference though, not if you weren't seeing it.

Just breathing made your throat parch up and Gaile was already thinking longingly of cool creamy sundaes and sparkling iced drinks. Something that was only serving to make her even hotter than she already was. She'd grown up in a far more temperate climate and had, when travelling, chosen places that suited her better. Coming here, there had been no such choice, not really.

The air brushing against her skin, touching places on her arms and face with only the memory of its passing to prove its existence. It wasn't the least bit cooling either – and on top of that, you could actually only feel it when you moved. If you were standing still so did the air. You were left on your lonesome in a tiny little private world slowly being depleted of life giving oxygen. Or so it felt anyway.

'Is there no cursed wind in this place,' Gaile grumbled to herself. 'Even a tiny breeze would be nice right about now.'

The air didn't seem inclined to listen though, so she sighed and started off for the main entrance along with many of the other hopefuls that were arriving today.

There were both more and less people here than she'd expected.

Admittedly, there was only a limited time that the yearly matriculation for the DragonCorps opened. One day a year when, for a few hours, people of all ages and abilities, physiques and inclinations, could sign up to join the Academy.

Yes, getting in, provided you managed to hit that small window of time, was the *easy* part.

Enduring through the years of training – first alone, then with your new partner, was the part where most people fell down and didn't get up again. And that wasn't always metaphorically speaking either.

'Whoa,' Gaile suddenly exclaimed as the doors into the auditorium swooshed open as she approached. That's what she got for walking about, daydreaming.

Turning her head first this way then that, she blinked. It took a while for her eyes to adjust after the bright light outside, but when they did she saw that the combined atrium, auditorium and reception, was *huge*, but that wasn't what had caught her off guard.

Despite its size, it was filled, absolutely packed, with people. People were milling about in groups or rambled around alone. Some had managed to find a quiet spot where they just sat, with an expression that said they'd defend their precious seat with tooth and claw if it came to that. They were everywhere. And so was the luggage they'd brought (hence the lack of space for additional people, Gaile figured).

Between the ornate pillars, on seats in the holding area or stacked (in the case of the luggage, not the people) against the reception and lurking behind large and expressive greenery there were people. Everywhere there were people.

'Great! And I who don't actually *like* crowds.'

Gaile could see that even the areas closest to the large, arched windows were packed – and that just had to be hot, with the sun shining in like that, she thought.

'Blimey! I knew this was popular, but I didn't think it'd be *this* crazy. There's even kids? Isn't that going a bit far?'

Admittedly, though never admitted by herself, kids were, at the moment, anyone younger than she was. However, catching some snatches of conversation, Gaile realized after a while that quite a few of those were friends and family of the applicants. Here for moral support no doubt, or worrying, and as such were *not* prospective dragonriders.

Besides, the fallout from the course, especially in the first month or so, was reputed to be disastrous, it was *that* huge. The number that actually went on to become riders was even smaller – usually only a handful every year and that was if they were lucky. Sometimes, there wasn't anyone at all that passed that final gruelling test.

They were probably here should the chosen few (or the chosen many in this case) not actually make it in time and having to go back home … hopefully being able to be dissuaded from trying again next year by anxious parents who'd rather see their sons or daughters do something more "sensible" with their lives.

Well, that wasn't an option for her. Gaile set her chin firm. She'd taken too much of a chance coming here. It was either going home a rider or not going home at all. Knowing herself, she knew far too well that anyone placing a bet on the outcome would be unlikely to lock the odds in her favour.

Despite this, she squared her small shoulders. Yes. This was it. The moment she'd been waiting for ever since making up her mind. There was no going back now, none.

At least, that's what she tried telling herself as, with a loud 'dong' the first hour of the afternoon was struck ceremoniously. The sound rolled out over all those assembled. It emanated from a wooden contraption in which was suspended a metal disk several times larger, and rounder, than a man's head.

Before the echo had died away, the large doors through which they had entered clicked shut. The locks sliding into place did so more for dramatic effect than out of any actual necessity. Though it did prevent latecomers from rattling the handles (there not being any) or banging on the windows (of which there were a lot).

And, by the looks of it, not everyone *had* managed to arrive in time.

Turning around, Gaile surveyed those around her, her curiosity getting the better of her.

So, these were the people she was going to be "working" with from now on, was it? Well, it wasn't as if you could pick and choose right from the start (that would kind of mean you didn't need to bother with the trials after all) and it was a bad idea to judge by appearances anyway. She knew that. Still, some of them looked confident with themselves. Very confident. She wished she could say the same.

Gaile was brought out of her reverie by a voice, amplified as it was, that asked for their attention.

She couldn't see the speaker, and neither could most others, but they sounded official, so Gaile tried to pay attention in case it turned out to be important later. From what she was hearing so far, it seemed to be some sort of speech.

'…to have passed the first of the challenges now set before you on your way to becoming the next generation of riders. I assure you that there will be many more challenges in the years to come for those of you who will remain with us and none of them will be as easily navigated as this one.'

There was a quite a lengthy pause and Gaile had nearly turned her attention to trying to find somewhere to sit when the speaker started up again.

'Now that we have identified those that have passed this first challenge …

or, to speak more plainly, those who have arrived on time, I believe that we can begin this year's matriculation. As you, in the front, can see, several of my colleagues are standing by ready to assist you, after which you will pass through these doors behind me and be on your way in your new life.

Please note that applicants only will be allowed past this line at this time, so for those who have been accompanied here, please ensure that your parents, guardians, siblings, friends, children or pets do say "adieu" *before* then. There are five members of staff on hand, so if you could all form a line and we will deal with everyone in a prompt and efficient manner. This is your first day at the Academy, ladies and gentlemen. Please ensure that it is also not also your last.'

The speaker, now revealed through a gap in the crowd as a small somewhat round fellow, took a deep breath and plunged on.

'Also, to forestall the question I am sure many of you are already waiting to ask. No, you will *not* be allowed in the parts of the buildings belonging to the DRC proper as students, except by special exemption or classes. There are however many areas that both the Academy and the DRC share between them as part of the DragonCorps. And so you will not be isolated from the presence of those whose ranks you have come to join. Welcome and I hope you will enjoy your stay with us.'

Dr Cosgrove breathed out. Giving these speeches always tired him out. He could only hope that some of the young ones actually got something from it. It wasn't as if they didn't already have a million things clamouring for their attention right now.

That was why he preferred to keep these things simple and not ambush the new students with any amount of information on rules, which they weren't likely to remember anyway.

He ran a hand through his grey hair and put the spectacles back on. He didn't really need them, not in today's world, but he'd always felt they lent a certain credibility to the position as the Head of the Academy.

The moment he stopped speaking, a small wave of human bodies surged forwards.

Gaile had few memories of the next few minutes … or the next few hours for that matter – apart from a moment here and a moment there.

Here, she had to supply her details. There, she had to pick up a uniform. Here, someone set all her access codes, downloaded all the maps, room-assignments and schedules. There, they put you through a medical. And goodness knew what else they'd come up with to pass the time.

By the end of it she was thoroughly exhausted, milling around with the rest of them in a state of bewildered confusion.

It wasn't as if they got assigned to rooms at this stage anyway, so why bother? There were just too many of them. At the moment, all any of them could hope for was a decent bed in the barracks and by the time Gaile, and a fair few others, had gotten that far, they were too exhausted to care about anything other than that they could finally stop dragging their luggage *and* their new gear around and could instead opt for flopping over the nearest vacant soft surface in sight and refuse to ever move again.

New Retmia wasn't that big a planet and it hadn't been settled all that long, less than a century, so it wasn't like it had a huge, dense, population. With the DragonCorps being a large part of both planetary exploration and maintenance and involved in opening up new worlds, it wasn't surprising that the DRC and the Academy together weren't just among the oldest structures on the planet, but also one of the biggest.

It was still small compared to the original Dragon Research Centre back on Casticia, judging from the layouts that Gaile was looking at, but for a frontier world on the forefront of the boundary between the fledgling Empire and the cold dark unknown space it was sizeable enough.

Technically … she flicked the screen, causing the map she was looking at to zoom out and instead display the star field that made up the region, it was more accurate to say that New Retmia was on the forefront to the boundary that belonged to the large galactic cloud that shielded this region of the galaxy's spiral arm.

As such, if you wanted to move between here and the rest of the galaxy, you either had to have some very impressive machinery (the region of space that it bordered being rather unfriendly towards their current level of technology) or take the *long* way around – leaving the galaxy altogether, swinging around and coming back down on the other side.

It did make a very pretty background though – which was why she always enjoyed looking at it; all swirly colours and bright lights.

Switching back to the images of the DRC, which wasn't nearly as nice to look at, she had to admit that it held the post as one of the most imposing and impressive artificial constructions around. Here.

It wasn't so much out of anything but necessity – including the very simple fact that even an ordinary cottage built for a pair of dragons would have to be on an entirely different scale than if built for your average *Homo Sapiens* – at least if you wanted more cottage than dragon.

The DRC played "permanent home" to almost every single dragon on the planet, including those few that worked and lived elsewhere. It was to be expected that it had been built accordingly.

It was now, also hers.

Gaile thankfully didn't have much trouble claiming the lower end of a corner bunk bed, appreciating that that way there'd be a nice wall to one side and not another student. Most people seemed to be wanting the top ones – except for those too tired to do anything as complicated as climbing up a ladder and who just opted for falling over the nearest vacant lot.

She, herself, settled for watching the ensuing ruckus between a number of her fellow students who *weren't* drop dead tired and definitely weren't in the mood to give up on the bed they'd set their eyes on, despite several others having done exactly the same thing.

Yet others had taken up a stationary position on their already claimed beds, some happily tapping away and punching up directions and schedules on their dioms.

They'd been told they had an hour to themselves to get sorted before they should be ready for dinner.

That was the only part Gaile was interested in right now. She'd missed lunch and all the "arrangements" over the last few hours hadn't exactly allowed her time to stop for a snack somewhere, assuming she'd even know where to find one. She'd already eaten all of her own on the journey here.

So, couldn't the clock tick just a little faster?

It had another bright point as well. Going to dinner would get her away from these maniacs who were, in her eyes, causing far more havoc than they needed to. In places around her were the loud voices of some of the more alert students.

'Let go!'

'That's mine!'

'You can't do that!'

'Oh yeah, you're gonna stop me, are you, twerp?'

'Put him down, Drak!'

'Don't want to.'

Gaile longed for some earplugs. This was going to be a nightmare, staying like this. A pure nightmare – and without even having the benefit of being asleep at the time. She pulled her pillow over her head and wished that the day would end already.

* * *

A few days later and Gaile was still getting her resting periods disrupted, maybe more so now that everyone wasn't dead tired anymore. If it wasn't because people were arguing, it was energetic students playing around and getting excited over something. Probably something silly. It was beginning to seriously get on her nerves.

Maybe that was why she was still getting lost in this place?

The maps helped, a little. But getting from A to B in the peculiar layout that made up the complex and the separate buildings and where, in some places and only some of the time, the maps suddenly didn't work – or, more accurately, worked, but wasn't showing what you were seeing – could get a bit confusing.

She'd learnt to not rely on them too much. That meant trying to commit the entire place to memory.

So far it wasn't going all that well.

For someone that was prone to being absentminded and wandering around in their own thoughts it meant she was still late for classes, meetings and nearly everything else. Even dinnertime was something that was troublesome to meet, depending on where she started off from. It wasn't, after all, as if the cafeteria was very hard to find, being rather large.

As a first year in their first couple of weeks of term it wasn't exactly a lot to remember. Most of the areas in the complex lot of stand-alone buildings, connected buildings and general structures and mish-mash that didn't seem to have a point to it other than just being there, were off limits. Many of them would stay off limits until she passed, *if* she passed, the Final Exam.

That was the big one. The key to this whole future. It was reputed to be beyond compare or understanding. One thing was sure though, those that took it never spoke of it. Even those who passed it only alluded to that it was where they had met their partner.

There was probably a reason for all the secrecy, but she wished they hadn't bothered. She was nervous enough as it was. And *that* exam was a whole three years away. If she was going to be like this the whole time, she'd go mad, wouldn't she?

Gaile shook her head. No, wrong thought, there was no *if* to it. She'd definitely do it. So why was it so hard to memorize the few bits and pieces that she, and so many others, moved about in?

There were the dorms or barracks as they were sometimes referred to as, as unimaginative on the inside as they were on the outside. There at least she felt some vindication for getting confused. They all looked identical. The only thing that separated them was their numeric designation. Would it hurt them to at least paint the walls in soothing colours, or essentially anything other than institutional grey or green? Would that really have been too much to ask?

'Miss Ashworthey? Miss Ashworthey?'

It took a moment before Gaile realised that it was her they meant.

'Umm ... yes?' she replied hesitatingly.

'If you can deign to remain with us for a little while longer, Miss Ashworthey, perhaps you could answer the question I sent you?' Their teacher for the day gave her an unamused look.

Tall, dark and with a physique more suited to a wrestler, Saranon Duchamp cut an imposing figure. Where most teachers they'd seen so far were wearing a uniform, albeit not necessarily the same one, Duchamp wouldn't have looked out of place at some sort of heavy concert. To say that this made the students a bit weary of him was to say the least.

'Right ... question ... umm,' Gaile cast around desperately before looking down on her screen to find it blinking insistently at her. She felt her heart sink to a new low somewhere below ankle level.

'Sorry. I don't know.'

'You don't know?' Saranon tapped the desk theatrically. 'Well then, Miss Ashworthey, you have obviously not been paying attention for the last twenty minutes or so.'

He switched her off, turning instead to the remainder of the packed auditorium. 'Class! What is the Final Exam?'

'Trial by Dragon,' came the massive answer as everyone of the three hundred or so throats rose to the challenge.

'Right,' Duchamp nodded. 'Trial by Dragon. And can anyone tell me what that means?'

This caused a somewhat hesitant mumbling issuing forth between the students as they tried to work out what answer he was after.

Quite a few of them had wondered about it too – there wasn't really a whole lot known about the Final Exam. And what happened it you failed? It wasn't like the dragons were going to eat you, was it? They weren't allowed to do that, right? Right?

One member of the front rows raised a hand gingerly. Unusual as it was for him to volunteer information, today was apparently an exception.

'Yes, Mr Drak.'

'No one knows, Sir. Only those who have passed the test is supposed to know what it was. And it's supposed to change every year,' came Drak's slow drawl.

Duchamp grinned.

Rather than improving his features this display of teeth made much of the class wish they could back up a bit. Sitting firmly entrenched in their seats in the auditorium that wasn't really an option. They settled for making a sort of crouch, hunching down behind their desks-chairs. There was something distinctly predatory about the way his lips parted.

'It means, Mr Drak, that you could fail every single test we set you. Fail every single exam. Knock yourself blue and green in the practical lessons from lack of aptitude and *still* be accepted into the corps. The only choice that really matter … is your dragon's choice of you as a partner.'

He leaned forwards for emphasis, treating them all to a cold stare, before continuing. 'Doing so would mean that you'd be a danger to yourself, your partner, your teammates and everyone else in the vicinity. Never in the history of this Academy has that been allowed to happen. So for you, who thirty seconds ago suddenly thought that this was going to be an easy ride. Don't!'

Someone in the midsection raised a hand imploringly at this point.

'Sir? Has it ever happened at all? Somewhere else I mean?' the young man who'd introduced himself as Kalim to all those who asked, wanted to know.

Duchamp frowned. He'd hoped that he'd have deterred them from asking *that* question. There always was someone, wasn't there?

'We are a frontier world. Our Academy is one of the youngest ones in the Empire. Yes, it *has* happened before. Yes, it will happen again. But it will not, understand this, happen on my watch! Dismissed.'

The class dissolved into the various mobile components as they all set out for whatever they had next. "Philosophy & Methodology of Dracology" was one of the few subjects that they all had together as it involved, judging by the outline, no practicals what so ever. Because of that, getting so many of them into one place wasn't a problem. It was just stuffy.

From what little that Gaile had heard before her mind had tuned out, it was also proving as boring as she'd expected from skimming through some of the set texts. With that kind of teacher though, not taking it seriously might prove fatal – though hopefully only metaphorically. He looked like someone had, in the past, used him as a battering ram; successfully.

The next two hours proved much more interesting, despite her having a hard time hearing what the emancipated figure in the centre was talking about, thanks to the group of girls in front of her who kept talking incessantly throughout the whole lesson.

Trying to ask them to be quiet only earned her a glare from them all, before, with a flick of their hair, as if she was something best scraped of their boots, they returned to their favourite occupation – talking; if possible, even louder than before.

Gaile didn't know who this "Sera" was that they were talking *about*, but she was already beginning to dislike them.

Complaining to the teacher at the end of the class didn't help much either.

'It's every student's responsibility to ensure that they gain the necessary knowledge from these classes, Miss Ashworthey. Therefor it is up to you to ensure this is the case rather than blaming others for your failure to do so. You are, of course, free to leave at any time, should you so desire.'

There was a brief pause, in which Gaile chose to keep her mouth shut, least it get her into even more trouble.

'Incidentally,' the teacher, a certain Clarissiia Bookman, added, almost as an afterthought, 'all the classes are recorded to audio and accessible for up to one year after their recording.'

Turning on her heels, the woman stalked off down the corridor, hoping to catch some lunch before another repeat of the same lecture with a different class.

Gaile on the other hand, after checking her schedule, had to hurry off in a completely different direction if she was going to have a single chance of getting to her next class on time, and not be late, as usual.

What was with this place and running so many things back to back anyway? Did they do it on purpose? Did they know full well that it was next to impossible to get from, say, one end of the Academy to the other in the allotted time? Was there some sort of secret to the whole thing?

Maybe, should you be able to get there on time, the teachers would know that you'd discovered some of the hidden places and passages in this peculiarly designed building? As it was, it'd be a million years before she'd find that out, that was for sure.

Gaile sighed and narrowly avoided running into a corner. Usually, that only happened early in the morning.

Speaking of mornings … tomorrow's was one that she dreaded. The first true practical – and what a theme they'd chosen? Yikes…

It was a lucky thing that she'd overheard some of the teachers. It was definitely not something you wanted to be having sneaking up on you unprepared. It was bad enough if you *were* prepared.

She'd have been happier, had she'd been able to skip it – but it was kind of important. After all, you couldn't go around avoiding dragons forever if you wanted to become a dragonrider.

* * *

And now that morning was upon them. Oh, to be able to be elsewhere… At least it wasn't raining, that was something. But then, could it ever rain in such a place as this?

'Ok, gather 'round people, gather 'round,' the lean man beckoned encouragingly at them.

One by one, or in small groups, a number of the students taking part in today's practical lesson trickled in to an amphitheatre roughly hewn from the pale brown rock-face around and above it. Needless to say, this *wasn't* their usual classroom. A lot of necks craned here and there to take it all in.

The place had a distinctly crumbled look – like something that hasn't been used much and for a very good reason. Pairs of eyes watched it warily.

If they went and sat down in this place what would happen? Was it likely that something was going to fall on them? Like, maybe, they were going to be getting crushed under a huge boulder shaped like a face or maybe one of those strange looking demonic masks coming loose and shattering into a thousand pieces while at the same time crushing them flat like bugs on a screen?

Shuffling along the blocks of stone that made up both seating and footrests none of them were particularly enthusiastic. There were several barely stifled yawns scattered haphazardly among them. It was one of those that were started by one person and, as soon as they'd finished, another person would follow suit, and then another, and another.

Why did they have to come all the way out here just to sit down? Sure it was supposed to be a practical, but couldn't they have used one of the special rooms back at the Academy for that? It was such a pain…

A few of them cast glances around, trying to see if there was something else in this place but old bits of stone and sand dust. The students found it distinctly lacking, *all* of it.

It *was* their first practical "outdoor" lesson, but, frankly, they'd all expected something a little more impressive. If the locale was anything to go by, the lesson itself couldn't possibly be as dry, could it?

The stone beneath them was still chilled from the night's passing. The sunlight was distinctly absent from the shadow cast by the immensely tall rock-wall behind them. It would be several hours until the sun rose high enough to illuminate this side of the canyon and it was distinctly cold to sit on, judging by the amount of squirming that was going on.

And it wasn't just the stone that was chilled. Their enthusiasm wasn't exactly red hot and glowing either.

They shifted uncomfortably. The uniforms weren't meant for this, were they? Surely they had to be a strictly indoors type?

Not that you really needed much protection from cold in this place, during the day, quite the contrary.

Gaile wasn't all that much happier about the time of day chosen for this, but, judging from the look of a lot of her fellow students, she could count herself lucky. At least she'd been spending the night asleep.

Several of the students that had been assigned to Green Group were bleary eyed and slightly unsteady. They moaned loudly at having to be awake so early, or at all. Whatever they were doing today, it had better be good, they thought. Staying in bed had seemed like such a better option.

In fact, quite a few students *had* opted for doing just that.

While there were many that suffered less from last night's impromptu party in the barracks, they couldn't be said to be much happier about it.

It was barely after dawn. The damp of the night still lingered in the air. This was an hour that many of them might see from time to time, but never from *this* direction.

Whatever today's lesson was, it had better be worth it. That was a thought that echoed from mind to mind. It wound almost unanimously through the people gathered as they gazed down upon the man occupying the centre of the semi-circular area that made up the stage.

That had to be today's teacher, they figured. The teachers tended to change around a lot depending on the classes, so it was sometimes hard to tell. Especially since so many of them weren't wearing the same type of uniforms and several of them so far hadn't been wearing a uniform at all.

The fact that they seemed to come in all ages, shapes and sizes, didn't make it any easier to call either. This one they hadn't seen before.

He didn't look like someone you wanted to cross. It wasn't just the scar, jagged as it was. His erect and stiff posture, squared shoulders and no nonsense cut to the uniform didn't exactly flag him as a friendly either.

'A teach you can actually tell is a teach. Well, there's a novelty in this place,' someone quipped.

Teacher? No, some of the students disagreed with that. He looked more like someone whose features should be plastered all over one of those old fashioned "Wanted" posters – possibly right underneath a ridiculously high bounty. To call his eyes intimidating was like referring to a summer gnat as a "big bug" – it didn't nearly do them justice.

'Yeah. How're we supposed to tell them apart if they won't wear a friggin uniform,' another one grumbled.

Several nods in the vicinity supported this.

'You're just saying that because that means you can't just go ahead and bully anyone you like – having no idea who they are. Most of them *do* wear their uniforms you know. But how long did it take for that little lesson to sink in, eh? Two, three times, five maybe?'

The girl's voice, coming from the row above, was scornful.

'Shut up!'

A vicious smirk played on Robin's lips. Like that was going to stop her. 'Truth hurts, doesn't it, little brother. Kay, dear.'

'I said, Shut Up!'

'Ooo, are you going to make me?'

The argument was just getting into gear when the people next to the both of them nudged them cautiously. The siblings turned around to find the teacher looking their way and he wasn't looking too happy.

The students involved straightened up and returned their somewhat sleepy attention to the centre of the stage.

It was true that it was sometimes hard to tell the teachers apart from the many others that roamed the DRC and the Academy, including the students. Uniforms were mandatory for all students and technically for most on-duty official staff – but it was a rule that some people, for various reasons, seemed to be able to get around. Or possibly they just ignored it and dealt with the consequences.

Maybe there was a difference between those that worked on the Academy side of things and the ones with the straight DRC? The students weren't allowed over in the Dragon Research Centre so they couldn't exactly go and check.

There was also the little fact that people of all ages were eligible to apply – and therefore able to eventually join the Corps – so students weren't necessarily all youngsters. Same went for the teachers for that matter, only there it was the other way around.

While it was true that the majority of the student body tended to be made up of younger folk, simply because so many vied for the positions as soon as they were able to, it was by no means a fool-proof way of telling students and staff apart. There were plenty of younger riders as well and many others whose actual work the students had no knowledge of, scattered among the rest of the non-students, supporting personnel and everything in between.

Also, if you saw a person in, say, a lab coat – how did you tell the doctor apart from the assistant anyway? You could guess, of course, and, if the age was in your favour, you were probably going to have a good chance of getting it right, but it was by no means a certain bet.

That lead to that it could, at times, be hard, not to mention down right hazardous to your health if you got it wrong, to figure out who you were talking to if you didn't already know them. Same went for the person that might be telling you off for that matter. More than one first year had already fallen foul of that and they were only in their second week here.

The upside of the matter was that people from all walks of life mingled, if not recklessly, so certainly freely. It all came down to the type of person you enjoyed spending time with, not what they might be doing for a living or what age they were.

Not that the man down there looked like he socialized with *anyone*, many of the students thought.

'Alright people, listen up. Are you all sitting comfortably?' Turing's voice was carried excellently by the theatre's acoustics without any need for electronic amplification. Even those at the very back had no trouble hearing him. Well, not for those reasons anyway.

A lot of them squirmed in their seats under his fierce gaze. Was he trying to be funny? Was he serious? Did he expect an answer? What would happen if anyone of them actually laughed?

Tam Turing surveyed them, hands clasped behind his back. He had quite the presence. And from his lack of props, he evidently didn't need a diom to remember his presentation either.

'I trust that you have all been diligent in your studies so far? I know that you've been receiving quite the crash course in basic theory. Today is, however, going to be your first practical *draconic* experience,' Turing said.

At this, several heads swivelled around as the audience refocused their attention. Some rose sharply, alarmed at this unwelcome news.

Practicals? *Real* practicals? So soon? Weren't they just going to have one of those outdoorsy sessions where they played around with tools? No one had warned them about *this*. They hadn't had any time to prepare. What if they did something wrong? Was it going to hurt? What were they going to do?

Turing made a sweeping motion, encompassing them all. 'As you can see … this class does *not* comprise the entire year group who will be taking this lesson today. They will instead be taking it at a further hour. You people are the first. Now, before we begin, I would like you to arrange yourself in your assigned groupings.'

Several hesitant glances passed between the students at this. There were plenty who didn't particularly get along with the others in their groups and they hadn't even had them for very long. Whatever criteria that had been used to work out whom to include in what grouping, the students themselves had clearly not been consulted.

As a result, perhaps intentionally so in the minds of the suspicious, it was far more common for those within a particular grouping to be more at odds with each other than the other way around.

It certainly created a whole new meaning to the words "Team Dynamics".

The groupings themselves had been announced one afternoon about a week ago, along with simple instructions to "get to know your team".

Today was the first time they actually had to use them. There were plenty among them who hadn't bothered doing more than just glancing at their assigned colour and then continue with more interesting things.

Who made up these team-names anyway? Couldn't they have come up with something cooler? Who used ordinary colours for this kind of thing in today's age?

'The teachers in this place…' some mouthy character had quipped at the time – which had promptly set off another disagreement about what actually was a cool name anyway.

Now, it looked like they were stuck with them whether they liked them or not.

'Come on people, look lively there. We haven't got all day.' Turing clapped his hands at them for emphasis.

A few minutes of disorganized chaos ensued before the students once more settled down. Many were looking, if not outright unhappy about the new arrangement, then at the very least distinctly uncomfortable. Some even bordered on rebellious.

'Now, let's see,' Turing looked around. 'For this session we should have all members of Amber, Mauve and Azure Groups present. We're missing several from Crimson and I do believe that only a handful of representatives have turned up from Viridian. It looks like the first couple of weeks have already taken its toll on your numbers, I see. Tsk, Tsk. You need to do better than that people.'

He gesticulated at them, elbows stiff and formal.

'I know some of you believe that because it is yet early days that you won't miss anything important by not being in class – but I can not stress how much of what you will learn from here on will build on things you pick up during these *easy* early days. And if you fail to attend, especially the practicals which are designed to give you an idea of what to expect if you pass the Final Exam and to give you an idea if this is really something you want to pursue, well, if you fail to attend, you will be at a distinct disadvantage.'

Turing paused to see what effect his words might have. Good. Some of them looked a little less sure of themselves.

'Now, for today's exercise we will be assisted by five of our active duty riders...'

He didn't get any further, because at that point an excited babble broke out among the ranks of the students. A real rider? Here? *Five* of them? Wow!

'Sir. Sir!' One of the younger ones nervously raised his hand. 'Does that mean we'll be working with dragons today? Already?'

'That is correct,' Turing gave an affirmative nod.

The student who'd asked, Kalim, swallowed apprehensively. Real, live, dragons. Right here? It was too soon. Too soon. Could they really handle something like that? Could *he* handle that?

'Now, each grouping will be assigned to a pairing. Together they will be your teachers for today.'

On cue, five of the DRC's and the DragonCorps' active riders stepped forwards. Their footsteps beat as one, echoing on the polished stone. They took up position directly behind Tam.

Dressed in crisp working uniforms to a man, no one could detect any sign of rank or insignia on any of them. There was nothing to identify them as belonging to a particular wing or platoon either. Had they taken them off?

They did have a few things in common though – as different as they looked. They were all male. They were all looking equally imposing. And they all looked just as unimpressed with what they saw.

'Azure Group, front and centre,' Tam snapped.

Several of the students jumped; his voice so harsh and sudden.

Those remembering what their designation was either stayed put or managed to extradite themselves from the rest and moved down to stand before him. Others, who'd plainly forgotten, needed to be reminded, to general embarrassment, before they too joined the small stream of bodies moving closer and closer to the point indicated by Turing.

There was a certain amount of shoving and shuffling going on as they formed up before their teacher. None of them were too anxious to be one of those out in front and it showed.

'You'll be working closest to the opposing walls,' Turing told them coldly. 'So, in terms of the assigned zones, you will be the farthest away, therefore you will be the first to leave. Steele here will be your teacher and will take you there.'

He dismissed them with a nod in the direction of the closest man on his right.

Steele matched his name in that his hair, which surely had been raven black at one time, was distinctly greying out at the temples. He looked quite a bit older than the rest of them, but had a similar no-nonsense expression in his eyes as Turing.

A fluctuating, moaning clump, he squared them up and marched them off, careful to make sure he didn't "lose" any of them on the way.

'Amber, you're up next,' Tam called out like a whip.

This time he nodded towards his left where the shortest of the five riders stood. He had to be the stockiest of them all, the students thought; a bit square around the jaw and with heavyset brow ridges.

He too led away a small grumbling platoon, choosing not to hear any remarks they made along the way.

Mauve and Crimson (who'd quickly christened themselves "The Crimson Knights" – much to general amusement of those that thought that going for something that ostentatious from the start was just asking for it) followed their respective leaders; a spirited looking fellow answering to "Rimwald" and an intimidating figure that towered above the rest that had been introduced as Damon Van Velden.

There were plenty of those who were left who felt just a little bit sorry for the members of the Crimson grouping. Van Velden didn't look like someone you wanted to cross, even on a good day.

If Turing would have made it onto a wanted poster ... Van Velden hadn't, if for no other reason than that the printers would have been too busy shivering in a corner to print it.

It wasn't that he had any particularly scary features. In fact, if it hadn't been for his eyes, his cold eyes, he'd been quite handsome, in a rough kind of way. They weren't just cold either, they were calculating and had an immeasurable amount of power behind them.

Test me they said. Test me and you shall come up wanting.

He silenced any grumblings with a single "look" and took them away; much like a hawk might herd a flight of doves, had they been prone to such things.

A small number of stragglers that had finally managed to get out of bed were allowed to join the somewhat sorry looking number of people that made up today's crop of the Viridian team.

Unlike Azure, Viridian didn't have far to go. Their teacher, Kaimana, was a brown-haired fellow with broad shoulders and just a trace of stubble, as if he had forgotten to shave this morning. He indicated the area just beyond the amphitheatre itself.

As such, they didn't actually go anywhere per se. It was more like they moved from one side of a wall to another. Actually, it was very much like that, since the outer, slightly crumbled wall, of the theatre's centre piece was right at their backs.

It was more than one student who eyed its decrepit looks with suspicion. None of them were too keen on having rubble falling on them. It tended to hurt.

For the teachers it had an added benefit not to move the last, and smallest, group any further away. If there were any more latecomers, this would be where they'd end up, regardless of what group they'd normally have belonged to.

Being so close to the original location didn't give them any greater insight to what was about to happen than anyone else though. At the moment they were wondering just as much as what was really going to happen as almost everyone else who'd ever taken this first true practical had ever done.

In the backwater of Azure Group, Gaile was trundling along at her own pace. She wasn't entirely sure this whole thing was a good idea, not for her. She also didn't care much for all the sand and dust that the rest of those ahead of her were kicking up. It was, after all, landing straight in her face.

Were they *trying* to suffocate her before they'd even gotten started? When the dragons came, wouldn't they cause even more of this stupid stuff to float about? Wonder how close we'll be, came the unbidden thought. It was, regardless of anything else, something to wonder over.

Not that they were moving all that fast, keen on wherever they were going. Not the students anyway. You couldn't possibly even call it walking in some cases. But then, it wasn't exactly shuffling along either.

If the majority of her classmates weren't striding ahead, heads held high and confident that they'd be able to handle anything that might come their way, was it then strange that she felt even more worried about it than they did?

Not that she was really alone in that sentiment. In fact, it was a thought shared by more than one person. Maybe you could even go as far as to say that the majority of them shared that moment of inwards reflection, had you been able to take a peek into their heads and hearts.

Some did hide it better than others. Some, a very small some, didn't seem bothered at all, either showing excitement or, for an even smaller minority, an outright disinterest in what they were about to do. Which was, when you thought about it, rather peculiar.

This was something that wasn't exclusive to Azure Group either. They all had a mixture of people's anticipations, good and bad, within them, every single one.

Here and now though, each person certainly wouldn't have acknowledged that any other person could possibly be thinking or feeling the same about this whole thing. Each of them was far too wrapped up in their own worries, or for the more adventurous of the lot, their own excitement. They were going to be having direct contact with dragons after all. For many, it would be their very first time.

But as the students who made up Azure arrived in their designated zone, it was distinctly devoid of any dragons.

Actually, judging by a few of the comments drifting up from the small pack, Steele surmised that a lot of people would say it was distinctly devoid of anything – that anything just happened to be including dragons.

At this location the canyon floor consisted of sand, rock, bits of gravel and, clinging desperately to the shade of some of the larger boulders, some sparse tufts of hardy looking desert grass – yellow and brittle and ready to cut you if you tried to pick it, thanks to the minute spikes along the stems.

The lacking of the day's main attraction was causing a mix of relief and anxiety; sometimes in the same person. It did make you wonder…

He'd said they'd be working with dragons, right? Dragons were something you definitely wanted where you could see them. Maybe he'd meant really small ones? Like the itty bitty ones used for short range scouting maybe?

He hadn't said what they were going to do with them after all. They couldn't possibly intend for them to take on a fully grown one, did they? It had to be a young one … small and, err … cuddly … right?

Seeing nothing in the sky, many pairs of eyes turned to the ground, as if trying to will the creature into being by fixating on it.

It didn't look like there was anything there that wasn't supposed to be.

Vis-a-vis the sand, gravel and random bits of rock and lost looking shrubs there was most definitely a short supply of anything of draconic nature. There wasn't even a dragon shaped rock to be seen, not even a single lost scale.

'So, you think there'll actually be any dragons in this so called dragon course?' an annoyed member of the group whined.

Several of those around him, not having said anything themselves, nevertheless agreed and a noncommittal murmur of nods and muttering rippled through the group. Others gave Kay a less than favourable glare, silent but still speaking volumes, had he been in any state to notice.

As a result, the majority of the students completely missed watching the sky as, suddenly, a large shadow banked away from the sun at speed. A great screech echoed over the canyon, pitched high and low at the same time, as if made up by more than one voice. It bounced between the walls, rolling over them as if it had been a thick, hot syrup.

Below, chaos ensued as the students; young and old, ducked for cover. Some hit the ground flat out, hands over their heads, dust flying everywhere. Others scrambled for the nearest bit of rock they could find, getting it between them and whatever had made that noise as quickly as possible.

It had not been a friendly sound and it had ended in a guttural cry tearing into your very bones.

Just as they were about to hit the top of the canyon wall, the rapidly dropping shadow suddenly split into five dragons screaming out of the sky.

Four of them, at the last moment, braced themselves; wings stretched out, and landed hard. They were accompanied by a ground shaking rumble as the combined weight of the dragons hit all at once. A shower of small stones and sand thrown up by the impact rained down on the people.

Two of them shook themselves leisurely and began looking around. They had already scouted out which groups were where from way up high, but that didn't mean they couldn't make a show of it. They were here so that the students could learn about dragons after all. That meant they couldn't just be effective and aloof, as would have been expected on a real mission.

With that thought, they both squared their shoulders and stretched their necks into proud arches.

Their two smaller compatriots didn't quite make such a show of themselves.

Well, when you said "smaller" that might not have been the best word to describe them. It was just, well, that compared to those they were standing beside, as the dust from their landing settled, they were still distant enough that any student that hadn't already gotten good bearings on the size of certain landmarks in the canyon, only had the dragons themselves to compare with.

With that in mind, there were definitely four different sizes there, and, now that they could see a bit better, the students noticed something else.

'Hey, they're all different!' Dayu, standing almost immediately behind Van Velden himself in Crimson, cried out, in surprise.

'Well, of course, didn't you pay attention in class last week?' Robin asked.

'You don't need to be like that,' Dayu said, making a face.

'Quiet, both of you,' Van Velden ordered. 'Everyone will form two orderly lines and we will wait for our chosen dragon to approach us

He looked about. Some students were still covering behind what rocks they'd been able to find.

Some fine riders these ones will make, he thought - though he refrained from saying anything out loud and his expression didn't change from the permanent look of extreme officialness that it always wore.

He did admit one thing though. Dayu, was that the boy's name? He was right … the four dragons *were* all different. Not just in size, but in colour and overall shape as well.

Several pairs of eyes however were still following the *last* one, the only one that hadn't come down with the rest of them.

As they followed them, the fifth, who had long since climbed out of the dive, was circling above. When it was sure it had their attention, the pale looking dragon rolled over and fell from the heavens.

Just as everyone was sure it was going to hit the ground, it snapped open its wings. Using the speed of the fall it sailed further into the canyon, seemingly inches away from the canyon floor. It shot past the startled spectators before making a wide loop, flipping over and returning in the opposite direction.

It touched down at a sprint, running for several hundred meters before slowing down.

Turning around and approaching its assigned group at a leisurely, elegant trot, it was easily the most distinguishable among the dragons here today. It was just as easily the smallest one.

Where the dragon that had by now joined up with Mauve Group was, apart from the dust, a deep inky black and had a powerful chest and haunches which rippled with muscles as he walked, even under all those scales, and towered above them, this one was as far down the road of "opposite" as you could get and still being able to call the result a dragon. Or so plenty of those assembled thought.

Actually, *could* you call something like that a dragon?

Sure, it had the required amount of appendages; four legs, two wings and a tail. It even had a head with pointed fangs. It was … It was just … so … so … *small.*

This dragon was all thin legs and spindly body. Up close it was no wonder it hadn't landed with the others. One wrong sweep of their wings and it'd have been utterly crushed. It was barely larger than a big horse. A big, very pale, horse.

Even the wings looked as if spun from gossamer threads, they were almost translucent. If you could have ever called a dragon "frail" this one was it.

As order slowly restored itself, with a few of the more impressionable students who'd broken down into hysterics at the ordeal being gently led away, the rest of them gazed up, and up and up some more at the immense bodies that now shared this small bit of land with them.

'Wow!'

'I don't believe it, a real dragon. A *real* dragon. Right here!' Isolde exclaimed, her eyes sparkling.

'So bloody big,' some else said shading his eyes. 'I mean, there's no end to it.'

'Aye, Kalim,' Jens Andersson agreed with him. 'It sure is that.'

This was the closest either of them had ever been to a real dragon. It was a completely different experience than standing next to a scaled model or holo led you to believe.

Someone Jens knew had once compared a dragon to a house with wings.

It was silly to compare it to a house … this thing wasn't anything like a square block at all, Jens decided, even if it was big…

None of those things had come anywhere near close to capturing the sensation. For starters, they missed out on everything from the sheer "presence" of the creature to the warmth that radiated from their body, the heat of their breath, the scent of their forms.

This was something they were all experiencing by now but none more so than Amber. Amber was a group that their teacher, who'd finally gotten around to introducing himself as Dirk Geary, had taken for a walk at a slight angle to where the other groups had gone.

The reason for that was now clear. Theirs was easily the biggest dragon of the five. On top of that, they all agreed it was also the most dragony looking dragon of them all – though that black one they'd seen earlier came a close second. This one though, its colour was a deep sated red … like a sun setting in a very dark storm. No matter how far things had come from those old fairytales and the stories from when they were young, some people felt that there were just some colours that were, well, better suited for a dragon than others – at least if they wanted to be looking fierce and ready for battle.

'Look at those claws,' Akia breathed admiringly. 'So strong and elegant.'

'Never mind about the claws,' Jens objected. 'Just check out those teeth.'

They all looked at the teeth. It was kind of hard not to. They were very big teeth after all. There was probably more than one student who, despite everything they'd been taught, wondered if those teeth were going to come a little too close for comfort. They were busy saying 'I don't taste good' with their whole bodies.

It was hard to tell if the dragon noticed or not. It certainly didn't let it bother it. Its proud and stiff posture held its head, a head crowned with several curved spikes, high above.

Dirk spent a full minute staring up at the dragon before it, with a look that spoke volumes, settled down and became slightly, but not much, less intimidating. The expression of disdain remained. This one wasn't going to be relaxing any time soon.

'So,' Dirk wondered, 'who'd like to go first?'

Not all of the dragons were treating the students as if they were keeping them from something important, like proper work, far from it.

The one that had padded over to where Azure had gathered did so managing, despite its size, to look more like an eager puppy than the big scary predator he was supposed to pretend to be.

The tongue lolling out of his mouth and bouncing at every step and his tail arched and coiled over his back might have had something to do with that – to say nothing about the expression on his face, which, despite the amount of armoured face plating, managed to convey something both childlike and playful at the same time.

'All he needs is a bone,' Jim couldn't help but laugh. 'A big one.'

'I'd hate to see the animal he'd kill for it. That'd have to be frigging huge,' Drak shuddered. He was used to being the bigger, if not the biggest, person around. Somehow, the sensation of feeling small was a new experience for him. Here, if nowhere else, was someone he couldn't possibly bully (assuming the stupid creature even realised he was trying. It would probably just think he was trying to play with it). Drak wasn't sure he liked that.

'Now, who can tell me what we have here?' Steele asked.

The aged rider ducked under the dragon's neck as the sturdy brown head bent all the way down; after the body had unceremoniously slammed into the ground just beyond it that was. This dragon didn't have a very long neck. It did have plenty of body to make up for it though.

Now he surveyed those students still left. That made up the majority actually. Well, wasn't that a surprise. Maybe they had some guts after all?

'It's so … so …big,' one of them gasped.

'Yeah,' another one agreed.

'Are they all this huge?' Kay wanted to know.

'Actually, my friend here is quite *small* for a brown,' Steele slapped his hand against the dragon's strong body with a resounding smack. He then made a sweeping gesture encompassing the other groups as well.

'As you have no doubt noticed, all the dragons who are helping out with today's lesson are different. Rather than just bringing greens and blues, who tend to be among the smaller dragons, both in overall size and bulk, we've chosen to introduce you to a range of different ones, despite the difficulties that involve.

As you probably already know, the majority of the browns and bronzes occupy the opposite side of the scale in terms of size. What's small compared to a large dragon can look mighty big next to an even smaller human – and that's something that no drawing will ever be able to show you, not really. It can give you an idea of the scale, but you will never be able to appreciate the impact unless you're standing next to them yourself.'

Steele slapped his gloved hand against the dragon's hide again.

'As you can see, Ikki is much bulkier than the others, though less so than most other browns. Remember, the size distribution among dragons is *not* absolute and there is quite a bit of overlapping – especially among those occupying the middle ranges. Which are?' he gazed at them expectantly.

The students looked among themselves. Was that a question? Rhetorical? Were they supposed to answer it?

A few of them tentatively raised their hands.

'Yes, you in the middle, with the spiky hair.'

'Teran,' the boy answered. 'Sir? Umm ... that'd be reds and blacks, I think.'

'Yes, so it is,' Steele nodded at them. 'Now, today- yes? You had another question?'

'Umm, Sir?' the boy who'd answered the previous question looked a bit uncertain at this stage. 'Aren't that leaving out a whole lot?'

'Yeah, what about the others?' came the unmistakable whine from Kay.

'I've seen pictures of dragons in colours other than those,' someone else insisted.

'There *are* others, aren't there? Like yellow and white and ochre and gold and silver?' the last bit came out in an awestruck voice. 'I heard there's a silver here, attached to the DRC. Is that true?'

A quick buzz of excitement spread among the group at this. That was news to them. A silver? Could that be true? There hadn't been many silver dragons. In fact, they could be counted on a single hand and you wouldn't even need all your fingers, even if you counted every single dragon since the beginning of the corps.

They all turned their attention back to their teacher. Maybe he knew something more?

Steele silenced them with a frown. When *not* smiling, his features easily settled into a stern, no-nonsense expression. The touch of steel grey at his temples didn't do much to make him any friendlier looking. Not if he didn't want to be.

'There *are* a few other colours than those I mentioned, yes. But most of those mistaken for colours in their own right are merely hues or shades of those already mentioned. What's your name son?'

'Jim. Jim Walker, Sir.'

'Well then, Jim Walker, know this. There has only ever been one gold known ever since the race of dragons was brought back to us by the experiments at the Dragon Research Centre all those years ago and that was one of the originals. It is beyond possible assumption that we shall ever see another one like her.'

He narrowed his eyes for a moment. 'It is true however that there is a *silver* dragon in residence at *our* DRC. I strongly suggest that you do not go looking for him or try to find out who he is. If *I* find out that any of you have bothered him you will be most unhappy, is that clear?'

It was a much subdued voice that answered. 'Yes Sir…'

'Good. Now, to move on to today's actual lesson. This will undoubtedly be the first time that any of you have been dragonback I take it?'

A small, grim smile graced Steele's lips for a brief moment as he noted the rise of sheer panic that began to be emitted from his audience at this announcement. Being close to a dragon was one thing. Trying to ride one, that was something else entirely.

'As you can see, your dragon for today is already wearing what we like to refer to as a saddle. They are versatile and can be adapted to suit the situation. This one is suitable for carrying several riders at the same time. Today you will gain the feel of the experience. There will be no need for any of you to go airborne. You will all remain safely on the ground. Of course,' and here he couldn't help but slap his hand against the brown hide for emphasis again, 'you will still be many meters above it. There is a safety harness for you to attach to yourselves. I would recommend that you do not fall off.'

'Up … there … on … that?' someone shuddered at the very thought.

Their teacher chose to ignore them. This wasn't the first time he'd taken this class and some things he'd learnt along the way – like not hearing things at times. Giving those ones attention only encouraged them.

'Now, we'll take this in turns,' he announced. 'First few volunteers front and centre please!'

Some groups, like, for example the one that had greeted the arrival of the black dragon, had already begun their rides ages ago. The reason for this surely lay in their teacher – who, right from the start, hadn't seemed the patient type.

That dragon appeared to put up with being ordered around like a schoolboy, though those that caught sight of his eyes at a particularly stern harangue over how he moved with the students on his back, guessed that it wasn't out of sheer desire to be submissive. There was quite a bit of a grudge there. If it was just momentary or a more long lasting one, that they didn't know him well enough to tell.

He was quite the handsome fella, for a dragon, with smooth dark scales and an elegant cut to his brow and snout. Along with the unusual setting of his wings and the slight claw like appendage that they carried, it gave him quite the regal appearance.

He did appear to bounce around a whole lot more than Tam would have expected from his partner though. What was going on with that?

The black dragon was someone who could move practically soundlessly, both on the ground and in the air, which, when moving at night, made him just a shadow among many others. Hence the name he'd earned in draconic form; Nightwraith.

'So, how're they doing Cap … I mean … Carula … eh… I mean…?' Tam, sure he was getting into trouble already, leaned over as they watched another slow motion manoeuvre sending the "passengers" aboard the dark dragon reeling and gripping the safety-harness with white knuckled fingers.

'Rimwald. Remember? Today, I'm Rimwald. Don't misspeak, Turing. And, about as expected,' Hezan answered.

Studying the sight taking place before them, he wondered if he'd ever been that silly looking? Arms and legs all over the place…

'Sorry, Sir … but that bad eh?' Tam sighed. 'I suppose that's to be expected.

It was too much to hope for a natural somewhere in this bunch. It's their first time after all. It should help quite a few decide that being a dragonrider isn't for them.'

'It's useful for that,' Hezan agreed. 'Doesn't have as much impact as their first flight though.'

'True.'

'How's Wraithy holding up?' Tam asked about the black dragon.

'As he should be,' Hezan replied. 'He is a professional. Still have trouble following instructions I see.'

At that point, some noise up ahead distracted them from any further conversation.

'This isn't fun anymore,' came a high pitched wail, bouncing irregularly along with the dragon's gait.

'Mr Stibbins, kindly desist from strangling anyone,' Rimwald shouted in the direction of the black dragon as he quickly made to catch up with the lot of them.

Mauve group's dragon slowed down and came to a halt a few meters later. Hezan Carula sighed and strode off after the troublesome bunch to disentangle the remaining students and their limbs.

This was why it was such a hassle to have several of them in the saddle all at once, he thought.

The boy on the end was holding on to the person in front of him as if he thought the world would end if he let go. Presumably it would, for the student in question, who was turning distinctly blue from lack of oxygen.

With a firm grip Hezan pried loose the madly gripping fingers one by one.

'Just because you are afraid of something it does *not* allow you to go choking your fellow students,' he admonished the youngster.

Cole wasn't the only one who was unhappy about the recent turn of events. Judging from a number of voices that could be heard, going over and around each other until it was impossible to tell which group or dragon they originated from, there were plenty of trouble going around.

Shouts of 'let me off, let me OFF!' echoed around the walls of the canyon from various directions.

The only group that didn't have quite as much trouble was Viridian. They still had the odd person that wasn't too keen on being hoisted into the air by what in their mind equated to a huge ferocious beast, but mostly the novice riders enjoyed the experience.

It helped that Hwit was so small. Apart from the gait and the complications of trying to keep your legs away from the wings, she wasn't really all that different to ride from a horse – though, of course, you were somewhat lacking in terms of reins.

One thing that did *not* work in terms of steering an intelligent, sentient, dragon, was pulling at its mouth with something sharp. At best it would get you de-seated. At its worse … well, that was usually left to the imagination of anyone trying something that stupid.

Since they'd been instructed not to take things too easy on the newcomers, Hwit … or Hwit Tabernae as her full draconic name was (she was grateful she hadn't ended up with something like Tabula Rasa, oh the horror), didn't.

The lack of red eyes, Hwit having two lovely blue ones, suggested that the dragon wasn't an albino, but no one had still figured out what caused a very, very minute number of dragons to be born so small and pale enough to be mistaken for white. Their rarity usually meant they were named accordingly. As such, Hwit was thankful she'd just gotten named after a flower. It could have been much, much worse, she thought.

But, saying that, these youngsters were having far too much fun, even when she did "act up". After all, they didn't have very far to fall. To them it was a bit like visiting a fun-fair, or so it seemed.

Hwit didn't mind. She'd always been sociable and, since while in draconic form, tousling with the other dragons was generally a bad, bad idea for her, she sought out company more in her own size. Around here, that meant any humans available.

'Yay! This is great!' Pol shouted, waving his right hand at the rest of his group.

They laughed, thinking he looked right silly with all that enthusiasm radiating around him like a bouncing light ferret. Some of those who'd already finished their first rides looked a little jealous. They certainly hadn't felt up to such antics.

The dragon turned right, increasing its speed from a slow walk to an energetic and very bouncy trot.

'Woah, shit…' losing his balance Pol grabbed at the safety harness. 'Easy there.'

He could have sworn he heard a low chuckle from up ahead, where the dragon's head was. 'Hey, I'm sure you weren't all that great the first time either,' he grumbled.

Watching the smaller pair prance by, almost strutting like a proud peacock, the "teacher" assigned to Crimson Group didn't even allow a small chuckle to escape his lips at the sight.

Instead, he made a gesture at their own dragon, a blue with perforated wings, who, arching its neck into a long serpentine S, tucked in its legs beneath and lay down, allowing the students attached to its saddle to unbuckle and get off – however unsteadily. It looked not unlike a draconic version of a sphinx, haughty expression and all.

'Well, we do seem to have gotten some enthusiastic ones at least. That's better than nothing,' Tam, who'd made his way over to Kaimana, said.

The rider in charge of Viridian nodded. 'By the way, now that I've got you here,' Simeon lowered his voice. 'What's with these odd pairings? Wouldn't it have made more sense to use "actual" dragon and rider partners for this?'

Turing surveyed the immediate surroundings, and, finding no one within earshot, replied in hushed tones. 'I thought it would shake it up a little. Not to mention, some of these guys would know of some well-known pairings, but put everyone like this and they're less likely to feel comfortable in knowing who they're dealing with.'

'Yes … but … the way you've got it set up, you've got dragons impersonating riders, riders pretending to be dragons and the pairings you arranged are just plain odd. How in the world did you talk the Captain into helping out with this?'

Tam shrugged modestly. 'He thought it sounded interesting and wanted to see for himself, that's all,' Tam said. 'And I don't think any rider could ever impersonate a dragon … they just don't have the build for it … a lack the wings too.'

'You know what I mean, Tam!'

'Let's see if they're still enjoying it by the end of today,' Tam changed the subject and turned his eyes to the scene in front of them. 'I remember how sore I was the next day.'

'Yes. You got a ride with Aranai, didn't you? Captain Striker certainly wasn't holding back when he picked him for practical duty that day,' Kaimana agreed.

'Not in the slightest. But that was John Striker for you. He never did anything by half-measure, did he? These kids don't know how lucky they are. Just look at them. Not a worry in the world.'

Kaimana surveyed the situation throughout this bit of the canyon. 'That might be taking it a bit too far,' he said.

Of those that had already finished, a number of them were sitting very still and not wanting to move while others pranced about, having enjoyed the experience to the full (much to the detriment of the former, one might add).

Among those, Gaile had retreated to a dominant outcrop, nursing a couple of scraped arms and knees. She'd barely managed to stay on when it had been her turn. In fact, if it hadn't been for the safety-harness she would most certainly have taken a tumble.

Ikki might have been small for a brown – but he was still mightily big in comparison to anything else, and certainly in comparison to her.

The motion of the dragon was a case of an illicit mix between a rowboat in the rapids and a drunken camel if she was any judge; at least that was what her stomach kept telling her. It still made her queasy just thinking about it.

Her fellow passengers had *not* been impressed at the time.

Falling over and crashing onto the ground once the ride had finally come to a stop hadn't impressed anyone else either. In fact, it hadn't done much for her, come to think about it.

The young woman winced. She tried to turn off her nose. This uniform wasn't going to be good for anything for a while. It was going straight in the wash when she got back. She hoped that was real soon.

The great whoops from excited riders elsewhere made her cringe and seriously wish they'd stop. And the worst part? The worst part was that this was just the beginning of the day. They had the whole afternoon filled with classes on top of this.

Gaile buried her head. Today was just going from bad to worse…

…and so it did. Maybe not for everyone else, but Gaile certainly didn't think it was going to go down in the history books as one of her better ones. It certainly hadn't improved by the time the last class of the day was well under way.

It seemed to move into the minus range when she was called up by the teacher at the end of the class itself and had to, while everyone was making their way out, struggle past them to get to the centre of the old-fashioned lecture theatre, complete with rows of wooden benches. Who in their right mind had designed it like that? Were they crazy?

'Perhaps, Miss Ashworthey could explain "why" this is so?'

The teacher for this particular class, a hawk-nosed, very thin woman, regarded Gaile pointedly (a task for which her piercing eyes and nose were well suited) and waved an arm over the amassed works on her table.

She didn't elaborate further and there was an uncomfortable silence before Gaile felt compelled to answer a question she hadn't really heard.

'Umm … because it is?' the young woman ventured.

Clarissiia Bookman, was, as usual, not impressed. 'Miss Ashworthey. While I am not familiar with how they do things where you come from, I expect *all* my students to be able to not only explain their answers, but to provide a reasoned, structured argument to support their point. As such,' Clarissiia picked up the paper on top of the nearest pile, glanced at it to confirm that it did indeed say what she remembered it did and continued her oration.

'I quote; "Because it does" is neither reasoned nor structured. I believe that you could possibly consider it an argument, but this was not the type intended, I assure you.' Clarissiia ended the tirade by giving the student at the other end of the desk another stern look.

'Turn in another such "answer" on one of my tests and I shall be most disappointed, understand?'

'Yes, Sir,' Gaile answered miserably.

'Incidentally… You can't seriously have believed that we would accept such an opaque answer to such an important question did you? To be able to back up your point or to be able to justify your actions or concisely relay instructions require more verbal mastery than you have so far demonstrated. It is an important part of the word "teamwork". Think about that. You may leave.'

Clarissiia gave a curt nod towards the door, the matter having been handled swiftly and efficiently and, in the minds of the student in question, utterly without dignity from her end.

It wasn't until she was safely away from the lecture theatre that Gaile allowed the frown to appear, her jaw setting firmly and her lips little more than a thin line.

How dared she? The question had called for an answer and she'd given one – the right one even. And she'd failed because she couldn't explain "why" she thought it was the right answer or how she'd come to that conclusion?

Stupid people, Gaile fumed. What was their obsession with exact explanations anyway? She couldn't explain the scent of spring or the crispness of an imminent snowstorm either and that didn't change the fact that they were both very real.

Ok, maybe, when you got down to it you *could* explain those things – even if they were made up by a myriad of smaller things, all with their own reasons and scientific terminology – but by the time you had grasped the explanation and wrestled it down onto paper, the moment would have been long gone. Didn't that kind of miss the point?

Wasn't it enough that it was? She *knew* that it was the right answer – just like she *knew* when it was time for the flowers to blossom or the wind to change (more the latter than the former admittedly). She didn't have to consciously consider all those things that came before them; that they were made up of. Something deep down in her mind did all those minute calculations on their own, only presenting her with the answer (a bit like a highly efficient secretary who refused to divulge their sources).

Gaile could no more explain "how" she knew than a flower could "explain" why it turned to follow the sun or why you weren't falling over standing on only two legs when four made so much more sense. When you stopped to think about it, *that* was when you lost your balance. It was as much a part of her as her lungs or heart, and under about as much control. It was just the way something was.

'Apparently, being able to find the answers isn't good enough in this place,' she muttered mutinously. You had to explain them too. Bugger.

Give her a breeze in the face, the sun on her skin and she could give you the time of day. Give her a chart and a row of numbers depicting the same thing and she'd just stare at it blankly. The latter was definitely not conducive for academic studies ... or so she was finding out.

Lost in that private little world she ambled along the corridors. Mostly people got out of the way, realizing that she wasn't paying any attention to where she was going. Only most people though. Not everyone was as thoughtful and what inner turmoil there was, it was about to get a one on one introduction to the outside world as her inward reflection was shattered by an annoyed voice.

'Hey, watch where you're going,' someone called out.

'Yeah, this isn't some public roadway for the near-sighted,' someone else filled in.

'Look what you did! I nearly scraped my new jacket against the wall,' another one complained.

Well, wasn't that just swell? A gaggle of hangers on by the looks of it – one of those that would follow anyone popular enough to attract attention. And here she'd been thinking that her day couldn't possibly get any worse.

'Let us not waste any more time, ladies. There is much to be done on this new "project" of ours.'

The speaker was, judging from the way everyone was standing, the centre of attention for this little mobile gathering.

From a purely objective point of view, part of her could understand why. The guy "was" attractive enough, in a way. Just the type that the girls went ga-ga over.

And like so many before him, he seemed to have a personality that fit. That is to say, one that should be condemned, burned and, preferably, given a burial at sea where they weren't likely to ever bother anyone again, allowing for any complaints from the resident fish.

Part of Gaile desperately wanted to bare her teeth. There was something in the way he said it that suggested it wasn't work he was talking about, not to Gaile's ears anyway.

'Now, now, perhaps this lovely new lady would like to join us?' the silver haired god suggested, giving her a wholly artificial smile if she'd ever seen one.

'But Sera…' one of the girls complained noisily.

'You *know* how much trouble first years are,' another girl joined in.

'I'd rather chew my own arm off, thanks,' Gaile sneered.

'Then perhaps you'd care to move out of the way?' Sera suggested coldly.

Gaile, who at this point was looking like smoke was merely a second away from starting to pour out of her ears, stalked off in the opposite direction.

As if it wasn't enough that the teachers couldn't get to grips with the somewhat unconventional way she worked, she now had to get "propositioned" by *that* idiot on top of it?

Not that she believed he'd been sincere, she wasn't that stupid. It had just been another one of a hundred things to make the day worse than it already was.

Unlike her, *he* had plenty of friends, plenty of hangers on. And she didn't even have the advantage of that she was bright and he wasn't – maybe that was the worst bit. Acting like that, barely lifting a finger by the looks of things, and *still* being considered one of the top minds of the student body? No, that just wasn't right.

There were even rumours that he was allowed in the DRC itself, to be able to further his own work and experiments.

'Stupid, jumped up peacock,' Gaile gnashed her teeth at the very thought. He probably didn't have a single brain cell to his name, she was sure of it. Probably getting all that reputation for brilliance through entirely "other" means.

Well, *she* would never sink that low. She'd get where she was going through her own work – even if it meant that she had to take these stupid tests again and again until she understood what in the name of the seven stars that they were actually asking in the first place.

If it has wings...

After what felt like ages, Gaile finally managed to settle in. It felt good to have gotten the hang of how to get about in the Academy without getting herself turned around and having to double back on herself.

That just went for the normal locations though. There were plenty of places that they rarely visited, even inside the main complex. There were even more where they had never gone at all. Not until now that was.

Today, one such place was going to be giving up its mysteries to the assembled assortment of students who'd picked this particular timeslot to attend. As usual they'd been able to put their name down for a number of different times for the same class as there were still such a large number of them (much to the detriment of the teachers).

That was both an advantage and a disadvantage. On the upside, it meant you actually had a small amount of control over your own schedule. It also meant that you never knew exactly whom you'd be working alongside in these practicals.

For some things, you definitely wanted a person you knew you could trust at the table right beside you – and not necessarily just because they were handling sharp implements and should be able to be relied upon not to use them for anything than their official purpose.

Of course, it helped if you actually knew where you were going to do. Not much chance of anything like that happening if you weren't there, right?

In this instance, it was nothing short of a miracle that Gaile had been able to find the place at all. It wasn't exactly the grand central plaza. But then, they hadn't exactly been walking through the main thoroughfares to get here either

– wherever "here" was.

The corridors here were drab. You might even call them slightly abandoned in terms of appearance. That wasn't because they were – it was just that they weren't really seen by anyone other than maintenance personnel and therefore hadn't been designed to be architecturally pleasing – or regularly dusted.

It was like the plumbing, always there but not something you actively saw … except instead of funnelling water, it transported people instead.

In this case, Gaile caught up with the rest of those people only because they were standing about. The reason for this was fairly obvious. Their journey had been brought short by several tons of metal blocking their way.

This was a problem – as the locale they were supposed to attend was definitely showing as being on the other side of this hulking piece of steel.

'Is this supposed to be here?' someone asked.

Was there an answer to that? From here, it looked distinctly unimpressive. Actually, that wasn't quite the case. It was impressive – but only because of its sheer size, nothing else.

They looked about.

The corridor behind them was a lot larger than many others here at the Academy by far. It was low slung but massive in terms of breadth. Whatever they were bringing in (or out) of here, it wasn't small.

There hadn't been very many people passing through though, aside from themselves. At least, they hadn't *seen* anyone as they'd wandered on down here and they'd been walking for a good solid ten or twenty minutes.

The door (if you could call something that massive that) in front of them was the only thing that really stood out. That and the detailed analysis plate next to it.

To start with, it looked like it was metal, the "door" that was, and not just the door itself. The whole thing, even the frame, which was several feet wide, was solid, but very not polished, steel – or something akin to it.

There was a deep and resounding 'boing' as an older guy knocked on the big round centrepiece.

'Yup, definitely metal,' he said.

That was the second thing you noticed about it.

The first thing that you noticed was that it was just a wee bit bigger than most other doors that they'd had reason to go through up until now. It towered over them. In fact, it took up most of the end wall of the corridor, leaving only a few bits on the side because of its shape.

You could probably have gotten a whole airship through that hole if you really wanted to, and didn't mind some protrusions getting scraped off in the process.

The third thing you noticed was that it was round; the entire structure. It looked a bit like a safe would have done back in the day – except that this one had been built to accommodate full scale replicas of dinosaurs in gold … or something. It wasn't like the *dragons* needed locking up after all.

'What the heck do they keep in here?' Drak wondered.

'Eh, monsters?' someone in the back piped up, sounding distinctly unhappy with the idea.

None of them knew how to use the complex panel that they all guessed had to be the controls and most didn't feel up to experimenting.

There was always someone who'd push any button just for the sake of it though and a few people had gathered around it, touching it in places, seeing if they could get some sort of response out of it. The console however remained quiet.

That was, until, suddenly, there was a loud hiss … like steam being vented from a high pressure pocket, and the door came ajar.

'What did you do, Kalim? What the hell did you do?' Robin shouted as she jumped back.

'I didn't do anything,' Kalim protested, locking his hands behind his back.

Not that anyone believed him, but they had bigger worries right now.

As the door slowly opened the rest of the way, and, more importantly in the minds of several of those with more active imaginations, wasn't suddenly forced aside by something huge, mad and hungry, it revealed what lay beyond it.

A couple of them peered in. The rest of them had retreated some distance away – just in case.

Jim Walker waved encouragingly at them. 'Hey, it's ok … there's nothing in here.'

'Are you sure?'

'Yeah.'

None of them were too happy about following Jim as he wandered in, every footstep clanging against the metal grating that made up the "floor" – but the instructions for today's class clearly said to come here. Or, more accurately, it said to come to what was on the other side, as it appeared that the room beyond the door was a confined space. A very large confined space, but obviously not where they were meant to be.

However, that was about the only thing the instructions *did* say. This place did look a bit familiar though – even if none of them had expected to find something like this here. It was like a giant airlock ... complete with compressors.

'Are you sure we got the right place?' Isolde's eyes scanned the area confusedly.

'That's what it says here,' Kay Sternmasser rechecked his diom, just in case.

There was a minimum of chatter between them. That in itself was unusual enough. These weren't the quiet ones, especially not the younger students. Their faces showed a mix of anticipation and worry and many of them eyed the second set of heavy doors now in front of them with erratic eye-movements. Their many feet echoed against the metal grid flooring as they hesitantly shuffled forward.

This was their first visit here and none of them knew, not really *knew*, what lay beyond.

They *should* have known, but there was a peculiar thing about the maps and guides to the Academy. Some things they appeared to omit. Other things were there only sometimes – almost as if they were being tested not only on tests but on simple things like how they'd react when confronted by something new and unknown or how to overcome a strange problem where no problem should be or simply just remembering the path that they'd never actually walked.

Now that they were getting closer to the second set of doors on the other side, the one behind them swung shut. They jumped as it clanged into place.

What worried them at this stage was the possibility of having ended up in the wrong airlock. What if there really *were* monsters on the other side?

It became more obvious as to where they were only because those who'd been keeping an eye on the maps on their dioms, despite them having been of no use whatsoever so far, suddenly felt a wave of relief flood through them as the area behind those doors fell into place.

They'd all read about it. They'd all seen the pictures and short vids but that wasn't the same thing, not the same thing as being here, in person, about to step into it.

But it wasn't anything to be afraid of. If anything, it was either exciting to visit or just plain boring, depending on how you looked at it. For most, the excitement had obviously all been concentrated on "how" they got here.

Because what lay beyond was something that none of them considered all that special – except perhaps for its presence here … and even more so, its presence "indoors". After all, the normal place you'd expect a forest was "out-side" a building.

Not everyone was quite that awed. It wasn't as if what lay beyond the airlock was dangerous. It wasn't as if there would be dragons – and that's what they'd signed up for, to become dragonriders, not to become nursemaids to something with wings or to go all 'aaaaw' over how cute the little cretins were, was it? For it wasn't only trees that inhabited the world beyond the door.

Elon folded his arms. So far he wasn't impressed at all, not if this was going to be today's lesson. How dull.

Indeed, as the second set of doors hissed open and they stepped forwards, the interior of the Hive opened up before them.

And so, the class filed into the space beyond.

'Wow!'

'Would you look at that!'

'Can you see it?' Akia marvelled excitedly as something red flashed up in the greenery on the other side. She nudged the girl standing next to her. 'I saw it! Did you see it?"

'Look … are you *sure* we're still inside?' Drak wanted to know rather aggressively. He stared upwards.

'Positive,' Pol Breakmountain replied. Being on the older side among the students, he didn't let Drak's overbearing nature bother him, most of the time.

Drak continued to stare. It sure didn't look like they were inside anything to him – except perhaps a lush forest.

Despite appearances, far above them, very far above them in fact, the metal entwined glass dome that made up the top section of the Hive couldn't really be seen. Only in the smallest of patches and only closest to the wall could you, perhaps, catch a glimpse of it – if you knew what you were looking for.

Bits of light filtered through that "roof" and it was real sunlight, not the artificial stuff. Most of it was caught well before it reached the ground though so you still had a lot of old fashioned lampposts in places.

The reason for that was that the rest of the interior was absolutely filled with vegetation. From tiny grass and xemblents flowers to giant ferns and trees with trunks not even three full grown men would have been able to put their arms around and everything in between, the whole space before them teemed with life.

Something like bamboo fought for space alongside creepers inching their way across the branches, concealing them in a criss-cross pattern of mossy green, pale orange and the occasional dash of purple.

Everywhere you looked, all you could see was green and shades of green – with the odd bit of colour thrown in for variation. *Almost* everywhere any-way.

The outer wall behind them was a dull, uniform grey – parts of it still showing traces of yellow lettering. It curved ever so slightly. The Hive's basic design seemed to have been based on a circle; a very large circle.

In sharp contrast to all the vibrant green was the ground that lay immediately before them. It was a pale sort of ochre, most likely a mixture of sand, gravel and tiny wood chippings or something like that, Gaile figured once she'd managed to set eyes on it. Most of her attention was focused on the shadows lurking among the trees.

It made a soft, almost spongy, surface to walk on. Gaile tested it gingerly by bouncing up and down very discreetly. Yup, definitely spongy. And by the looks of it, the chippings covered this entire area up front, claiming a small part of the "forest" as their own.

'Will you look at that!' someone breathed suddenly.

Several students turned their heads to see what all the fuss was about. Others kept staring at the "woods". Some could have sworn they'd seen something moving in there.

Then they *all* saw it.

There, in the artificial pond that took up what open space there was left out here that the chippings hadn't already coveted, something sparkled. Just for an instant, a glitter among the reflections. Rings on the water spread out and a small wave soon lapped against the shore.

'Did you see?' Isolde asked.

'See what?' Kay tried to push his way forwards. It was hard – there were a bunch of much bigger people in the way.

Then the splash came again. It was quick, like a kingfisher and a tasty fish - there and gone in seconds. Now that they were looking right at it, this time it was accompanied by a flash of red.

'There,' someone pointed.

And there, on a rock out in the water there was a small red shape. It beat its wings, shaking the water from them and sending a small shower over the students closest to the "shore".

'Ah, man…' Teran complained loudly. 'Did it have to do that?' He shook his sleeves. There hadn't been enough water to get soaked, but he still felt wet. Not to mention annoyed.

The dragonling didn't let that bother it. It was quite happy ignoring them.

Now that it was sitting still, they could see that it didn't look exactly like a dragon in miniature – which was what they were often referred to as. Even at this distance they could see that it was skinnier and more stretched out. It also lacked distinctive horns.

It turned its small bright red head to regard them from its perch on the craggy looking stone. Its tail wrapped around the rock, the tip ended in a sort of arrowlike shape which waved back and forth. The long, thin neck, elongated snout and the delicate head with barely a trace of a brow ridge made the red dragonling distinctly different, not only in size but in shape, from a red dragon. The curved, perforated wings only made the difference more apparent.

'Can I see too? Can I? Can I?' Dayu, jumped up and down excitedly. He had trouble in crowds due to being, well, less tall than the average guy.

A commanding voice interrupted them before some of the more enterprising, or bored, students could wander off (not that some of them hadn't begun to drift away from the main group already).

'Everyone will have their chance, in time. Now, gentlemen, ladies, if you so kindly direct your attention away from the dragonling, adorable that he may be, and I'll have you sorted and all ready to start today's doings in a jiffy.'

The woman speaking, and it had to be a woman they agreed - it was impossible that she was a porcelain doll brought to life – though if she'd been sitting still you would have been forgiven for making the mistake, motioned for them to join her.

'Does that mean we get to work with dragonlings today, Sir?' Akia asked.

The lady smiled at them, an action for which her features were particularly well suited.

'Yes and no,' she replied. 'You won't do any actual work with them – but you will have the chance to study them up close. Now, if you can all divide into groups of seven or so and I'll have my assistants show you the first steps for today.'

Lady Amelina Gray nodded towards a small number of older students standing slightly away from the main group.

'Jasmine, if you could please take two groups and head over beyond the pond, I'd appreciate it. We're a bit too many to all work right here.'

'Of course, Sir,' the tall young woman Lady Gray had addressed replied, her flaming hair held back by a black headband disappearing behind her ears, and nodded in return. Then she turned to the assorted gatherers, picking people seemingly at random and marched off with them.

'As you can see,' Lady Gray continued as if the interruption had never taken place, '…all our assistants are third years. They are often referred to as Hive Helpers. They "help" with the running of the Hive, answering to myself and Master Gern. By the time you reach your third year some of you will also take on that responsibility. At the moment they're aided by a group of second years, but once you've progressed a bit further many first years will be asked to take up some of the smaller tasks as well.'

Lady Gray didn't wait for the grumbling to start. She knew what many of them thought of the idea. She'd been a grumbler herself – and look where she'd ended up. No, it was best to move on quietly and quickly. Keep them on their toes and they didn't have as much time to cause trouble.

And so she raised her arm. Holding it aloft for but a moment a hard swing brought it straight down then she immediately lifted it up again. As her clenched fist opened the small pellets she'd been concealing within made a high arc and scattered into the air.

The tiny seed-like foodstuff hadn't even begun to fall when it was suddenly raining dragonlings.

'What the...' Kay shouted as he ducked for cover.

Only a moment ago, they'd only seen one single dragonling. Now, a whole host had launched themselves from the trees.

Had they missed them? Had they been there the whole time? They couldn't turn invisible, could they?

Diving and swooping, the small creatures chased down the pellets with a vengeance. With a dash of wing and a snap, tiny jaws grabbed at the morsels as they fell towards the ground. The air filled with their tiny, eager, voices. If a single treat reached the ground it was soon lost in the melee that ensued.

The world around them was alive with flaps and screeches, eeps, critters and constant calls and warbling. Some students ducked and made a hasty retreat. Others remained frozen in place, too stunned to even move. A few of them were just enjoying the show, mostly those that had been far away enough not to get caught in the general ruckus.

One girl was running around screaming; a morsel has landed in her hair and several dragonlings had soon followed it.

'Aaah! Get it off. Get it off!' she cried.

Lady Gray continued as if nothing was happening and her "classroom" was having a perfectly ordinary day.

'As you can see – dragonlings come in much the same colours as their larger "cousins". We call them cousins but the relationship couldn't be further apart. While they might look like miniature dragons they are anything but. As I'm sure you know, they were originally a by-product of early, unsuccessful, attempts to recreate the lost draconic fauna of Casticia, the Empire's core world.'

While a couple of students were helping Akia, the girl with the dragonling in her hair – which was apparently loath to let go; maybe it smelled like food or something, Elon raised his hand in the classical pose.

'Ehrm, Sir?'

'Yes,' Lady Gray, losing her train of thought, trained grey eyes on him.

'Isn't this kind of dangerous?' he asked.

The change in the teacher's expression told its own story. Clearly, that had *not* been the right thing to ask. 'Nonsense,' she responded. 'If you want to work with dragons you can't expect to be coddled in cottonwad the whole time.'

'But dragons aren't animals...' Jim ducked as a red dragonling with a chunky looking face swooped uncomfortably near his ears. 'They're people. These are … are … things.'

Lady Gray gave him a stern glance, a small frown creasing her brow. Those in the firing line wished they hadn't been.

She wasn't the only one having been asked a version of *that* question. Most of her "assistants" seemed to be under similar scrutiny – many of them falling back on an equally similar response, including Jasmine.

Jasmine, on the other hand, didn't handle it *quite* as graciously.

'Since you're all such experts … why don't *you* tell *me* what the difference is between dragons and dragonlings?' she demanded disagreeably.

The head Hive Helper surveyed the small collection of students around her. They all looked useless. Where did they find these people? Some sort of dump? What was with that hair? It stood out all over the place. The guy couldn't possibly think that it looked natural? Such a waste...

'They're smaller,' Teran, the fellow with the offending hair offered hesitatingly. To tell the truth, he didn't like the look of this assistant. Sure, she was pretty enough, in a sort of artificial way, but the way her mouth kept catching her out, like it was trying to sneer without actually doing so, wasn't exactly appealing.

Obviously she didn't see it like that though, as she carried on.

'They don't have riders,' someone else stated.

'No Dayu, but they do have handlers, don't they?' the tall young man next to him countered.

'Don't they use them as some sort of scouts or couriers? I think I heard a couple of people talking about that.'

'They're not intelligent.'

'Dragons have a human form as well as a dragon … dragonig … draconic one.'

'Dragons are bigger.'

'Hey, I already said that.'

'No, you didn't. You said they were smaller.'

'Same thing!'

After a few minutes suffering through the non-creative hubbub and the suggestions dying down, Jasmine cleared her throat delicately.

'Yes, the two prominent differences are their size and their intelligence. Dragonlings are animals. As animals they can be trained to do simple tasks. Oh, and do get that thing off of your head,' Jasmine ordered one of the boys sharply.

This one had been annoying her from the start. The way he looked like everything was amusing him like if there was no tomorrow. Stupid guy.

Dayu grinned at her sheepishly. The red dragonling had taken up station on his head. Standing on his shoulders it was treating the rest of his head as a sort of extra curly divan, front legs stretched out and tail twitching mischievously.

Red dragonlings were more common than red dragons, far more common, but their number were still small compared to the rest of them. Many of them however were counted as among the brightest of their kind and were, as such, highly appreciated when it came to work.

This one seemed to have a much more playful nature than a lot of its fellows. A more squashed face too, now that they got a closer look at it.

'You look quite foolish,' Jasmine announced, then promptly turned her attention elsewhere.

'Everyone, pick one of these blue balls and some treats from the casket over there. That will encourage them to come to you,' she said, waving one hand in the vague direction they should go.

'As you can see, all the little ones here have been extensively trained,' Lady Gray stroked the pale blue creature perched on her arm, affectionately.

The dragonling crooned at her, rubbing its cheek against her fingers.

As they were all finding out, despite their similarities to the full dragons they had just as many differences. One of the most pleasant of those differences was that they didn't have scales. Instead they were covered in hair so fine that it was like if it wasn't there at all. It did however make them soft and velvety to snuggle.

Their talons did grip tightly though, so it was best not to let them make themselves at home wherever they wanted on you – or you'd be paying for it later. It didn't take long for that lesson to sink in, and they quickly donned the special padded bands which could be attached to almost any part of the uniform.

'Fully trained dragonlings can act as scouts or messengers and we have a range of surveillance units that they can carry. In places where a dragon or human can't reach or would be too noticeable in, they are ideal. The same goes for when there is interference for more technical equipment.

They're a great deal more sensible than artificial droids or remotely operated machines. But, they usually don't carry the units unless there is no other option. While these little guys are quite intelligent, one of the reasons why we have an airlock into the Hive and not just a door is that they can be mischievous in finding new games to play or to play with. They are *not* sentient so can not always fully comprehend the further results of their actions. Nor can they, as you've undoubtedly noticed, speak.'

Lady Gray was having to raise her voice against the background chatter, chitter and random squawks and squeaks – not all of them being emitted by the dragonlings.

'You should all now have a blue ball, some treats and, hopefully, a dragonling. The ball is stuffed with some aromatic herbs that these little guys are quite fond of. It tends to keep them around. Why don't you spend some time getting to know each other and we can discuss the basics tenants of dragonling behaviours once you're done. See if you can work out some of the every-day tricks that they've picked up while you're at it.'

Unlike the Lady, Jasmine wasn't the least bit interested in offering her charges tips and tricks. She stuck to the absolute basics and, once she'd gotten them started, let her mind wander elsewhere.

Jasmine, in other words, switched them off. She didn't like being on dragonling duty. In fact, she hated it. It messed up everything and it always got scheduled for the most inconvenient times. Every minute spent here was a minute *not* spent with her chosen one.

There were quite a few minutes not spent where she wanted. He had quite the habit of disappearing, he did. Where did he go? That's what she wanted to know.

Was there something else? Someone else? Someone more interesting? Wasn't she one of the best looking young women here? No, wasn't she *the* best looking female here? And the most popular on top of that. How hard could it be to get a guy … just *one* guy? One very special guy.

No, not someone ordinary for her. She deserved someone as extraordinary as she was. And he *was*. Most certainly he was. He was *divine*. That was the only word she could think of that captured enough of him. Absolutely divine. And even better, there wasn't another one like him anywhere in the DRC. All she had to do was to get him all to herself. That was the only real problem – he never seemed to be alone. There were always people around him. He was mighty popular, Sera, the silver haired god.

She became lost in those pleasant thoughts. Yes, it was such a cruel fate, keeping them apart like this. But soon, she was certain, soon she'd get him to pay more attention to her, proper attention, just to her.

As such, Jasmine was mightily displeased when the commotion among the students grew loud enough to finally grab her attention. 'No, no, no, you're doing it all wrong!' Jasmine snapped.

'I'm not doing anything at all,' Gaile objected.

Gaile was by now the only one in her group that didn't have a dragonling dancing attendance on her, blue ball or no blue ball.

'Maybe that's the problem,' Jasmine huffed. 'If you can't even attract one of these, how do you expect to gain the attention of a fully grown mature dragon?'

'Maybe this thing's defective?' Gaile held the soft ball up to her right ear and shook it.

There was no sound.

There wasn't supposed to be a sound. It wasn't like they were hollow with bells in there. They were stuffed to the brim with fresh leaves, like they were supposed to be. But it was worth a try. Maybe it was the wrong type of leaves?

'Oh give it here,' Jasmine snatched it from her impatiently.

'Hey … I …' Gaile protested.

'You have no talent for this,' Jasmine sneered, waving the blue ball around.

Gaile watched her apprehensively. Did she think that the ball was suddenly going to start working if she did that? She'd done that herself – lots and lots, in all different ways. It hadn't helped.

Taking a couple of steps backwards, then turning to leave, Jasmine raised the ball to her face, ready to toss it aside after a sniff. Whatever had she done to get stuck with this job?

It was at that point the few remaining dragonlings that were still in the trees, their eyes glued to the ball, decided to switch focus.

As one, they plummeted towards the ground and the free ball that none had claimed. They loved to play, and balls meant play. Lots and lots of play.

To a dragonling, a lot of work was play too. But this was special play … all fun and nothing they needed to do to get it. And now it was free.

Seeing them coming towards her, right in her face, Jasmine fumbled her step. Throwing her arms up to try and regain her balance, the ball still clutched in her hand, she stumbled.

The dragonlings followed.

Wings slapped into Jasmine's face, scratching her skin as they did so. A green dragonling tried to land on her hand. It was pushed aside by a bigger black tugging at the ball with just its jaws while two blues were having a small tussle right before her eyes.

'Shoo! Shoo!' Jasmine cried out. She waved frantically, her arms drawing weird squiggly pictures in the air as the dragonlings easily avoided them.

Losing what little balance she had left, she staggered backwards into the shallows of the pond.

'Aaaaaaah!' she screamed. Her body struck the water with a resounding splash as she toppled over, dragonlings still clutching the ball that had attracted them in the first place.

Spluttering and spitting out the mouthful of water, her hand finally unclenched. The little blue ball drifted off on a small wave and the dragonlings abandoned the young woman to follow it instead.

Jasmine struggled into a sitting position, eyes as hard as agates boring into Gaile who was still standing as transfixed on the shore.

Water dripping from her now flat and so very not luxurious hair, Jasmine tried hard not to look as furious as she felt. Seething, she gritted her teeth. How dared she? How dared she do something like this to her, Jasmine?

And, as if to add to the cruelty of the situation, the others were laughing *at her*!

'This is *all* your fault,' Jasmine hissed.

'Nice one, Gaile,' Jim said.

'Yeah, best one yet,' someone else agreed.

'What'll it be the next time? Drop a teacher into the maws of death? That'll certain to up the ante, won't it?'

'Certain to get you expelled.'

'Not much else around here that would,' Kay snorted.

'True,' Reena nodded. 'Really shoddy entrance criteria.'

'Yeah, even you got in, didn't you?' the other boy laughed.

Kay rounded on the student who'd fired off the last comment. The rest of them, figuring that the entertainment was over, went back to their dragonlings.

'But … I … I don't … I didn't … do anything,' Gaile protested, looking uncomfortable with all the attention.

Her objections won her little favour though, at least with the head Hive Helper.

Jasmine spent the rest of the lesson going through the motions with even less enthusiasm than usual. When she thought no one could see, she shot the troublesome first year dark, covert glances.

'This isn't over,' Jasmine muttered darkly at those times. 'This isn't over, not by a long shot.'

The rest of the time in the Hive turned out to be remarkably uneventful in comparison. As the students began to relax they started enjoying the tasks they were being asked to get their charges to perform.

Slowly they also began noticing the differences between them, even those that shared the same colour. Claws and talons, length of curves, the fuzziness of the ears, types of teeth and the most obvious, wings and faces, all differed, although, between some individuals the difference was barely noticeable.

The only one who didn't enjoy it was Gaile. To her, the day was anything but a success.

After that initial little "disaster" she spent the entire time standing off to one side, having been completely and utterly unsuccessful at attracting a dragonling. Even when a group would try and share theirs, all that would happen was that it would go unresponsive.

This day was turning out even worse than her first ride, she thought.

Even when Lady Gray herself tried to coax a dragonling to come to this new student, she failed. To her, that made no sense at all. The little ones never acted like this around people, certainly not someone they'd never met before. It was doubly perplexing.

In the end, while the rest of them cleared up at the end of the lesson, the lady called down one of her most reliable charges and waited until they were firmly settled on her arm.

'Go on, you can touch him,' Lady Gray encouraged the hesitant looking student, nodding to the brown on her arm.

Gaile wasn't so sure she shared her teacher's belief in this. Even so, she did reach out her hand, with herself being as far away as possible.

The dragonling remained as if cast in ice. Lady Gray could feel it quivering. Was if fear? Rage? It made little sense to her. There were no other signs that would give her a clue either.

Gaile quickly returned her hands behind her back, shaking her head.

The moment Lady Gray relaxed her grip, the dragonling took off for the branches of the forest.

'Strange,' she spoke softly. 'I've never known any of them to react like that. Usually when they don't like someone they'll make certain that everyone knows. The amount of threatening noises they can produce is really quite diverse. They'll even bite and claw you if you're not careful if you're someone they really feel they don't want to be near. I've seen unfortunate souls have the whole pack gang up on them, but I've never seen *any* act like this.'

The teacher offered the discouraged-looking student a small smile. 'Don't take it so hard. Not everyone is suited for this right from the beginning. I'm sure that it's just a matter of time.'

Gaile nodded glumly.

Lady Gray watched as the troupe began their trek out of the Hive. They didn't have to take the back-way this time, but using the front entrance meant they had quite a bit of a walk ahead of them before they got to the main doors.

It really was strange, she thought. It was almost as if the creature had actually been afraid of the girl.

'No,' Lady Gray pushed the thought from her mind. That was just foolish, overactive imagination at work. There was bound to be an absolutely ordinary explanation.

Gaile wasn't bothered about an explanation. To her it was just another thing that didn't work out like it was supposed to. There were plenty of those in her life. She'd hoped that there'd be less of them here, but it increasingly looked like things hadn't changed in that area at all. Had she really changed enough for that to go along with it? Probably not. Not yet anyway. There was some hope that things might soon be different.

Ok, it wasn't a very big hope, but it was there. She just wished she had even a single clue as to where to start this change of life, but, the universe was, as usual, refusing to divulge its secrets. Nothing new there then.

She looked down and realized that the rest of them had gotten ahead of her.

'Drat,' she called out, picking up speed to try and catch them up. There was still the afternoon to go.

* * *

Not that some habits weren't harder to break than others. Getting lost in daydreams when going from one class to another, or even from one end of the cafeteria to another, Gaile was soon known as someone whom it was best to get out of the way of, simply because you were probably going to see her long before she saw you.

To her classmates it was inconvenient, but, apart from a few, they'd come to the conclusion that it was easier that way.

Unfortunately for Gaile, her classmates weren't the only people she was likely to run into – often quite literally – and not everyone was very under-standing about it either.

'Well, don't do that again!'

'I said I was sorry. It was an accident.'

'That's what they *all* say.'

'Excuse me?' Gaile blinked, not sure she'd heard that right.

'Kindly watch were you're going in the future. I don't particularly enjoy having people barrelling into me. Also, you shouldn't run in the corridors.'

'I *already* told you. I'm late for class, so I wasn't paying attention!' Gaile snapped.

'Whatever,' Sera waved her argument away, looking down on her from his superior height and turned his eyes away.

Of all people she had to run into when she was in a hurry and it had to be him? That was just her luck. Gaile fumed. Could this day possibly get any worse?

No, wait, don't think that. Stupid. Stupid. Now it was probably going to be worse. She mentally tore at her hair. Oh, such a foolish, foolish thought.

Sera wasn't all that happier about it. Though, in his case, the reasons were entirely different. The people they let in today, he'd never understand it. Couldn't they at least have some sort of entry criteria other than the whole "we'll accept anyone who's on time" policy?

If nothing else, picking some with at least a trace of talent might help with the drop-out rate. And that wasn't the worst of it either. No, not by far.

'Don't bother me again,' he demanded coldly. Twirling on his heels he left, each foot set down firmly.

Still fuming, Gaile stalked off in the opposite direction. She seemed to be doing a lot of that lately.

Great, now she wasn't just going to be late – she was going to be *really* late. And all thanks to that … that … twat. The kind of people they let into this place. She couldn't imagine a dragon choosing that snotty airhead as a partner. They supposedly had more sense than that. And if one did do so, she'd eat her hat.

Mind you, she'd need to buy one first.

As it turned out, Gaile wasn't the only one who'd ended up arriving after the set starting time.

Part of that was probably because they weren't in a lecture theatre or lab. They weren't even in the normal part of the Academy. By the looks of it, the teacher of the day didn't accept that as an excuse.

 They'd assembled at one of the points where the Academy and the Dragon Research Centre proper connected. The staff might use the entryway a lot, but for the students it was the first time that they were being allowed into the DRC.

At first, it didn't look so much different. The biggest change was actually the people, who, when they saw them, moved with much more purpose than the students, even the third years, did themselves.

Wherever they were going, it was sure taking ages getting there, some of them complained.

The teacher ignored them. His stern features didn't mellow at their noises, which he silenced with a look. That was easy. You didn't want Damon Van Velden looking at you. You just didn't. There was something about him…

When they finally came to a stop in a small nondescript corridor that looked no different than a number that they'd already walked through, they'd worked up quite a sweat.

The door didn't look like much fun. It wasn't anything special, just a bit drab really. It had a small plate with "A4" written on it in raised letters just at the right level to meet your eyes.

Some sort of designation maybe?

'Step lively people, this isn't a place you want to wander off in or you could easily lose and arm or a leg or both,' Damon instructed sternly, his grey eyes boring in to the people before him.

'Beyond these doors lies danger if you're not careful! You will form ranks. You will follow orderly. And you will not, I repeat *not*, wander off. Azure group to the front.' Damon's voice snapped out his orders like a staccato machine-gun.

Several of the students fidgeted before him. No one moved. As a result, he gave the class what nearly passed for a glare. 'Everyone understand? Dayu, I'm looking at you.'

Dayu tried not to respond, while a mix of 'Yes Sir. Yes Teacher and yes Mr Van Velden,' promptly ensued from the other students as they shuffled into something resembling the right order. Some even sounded sincere. But it was only when Damon was happy that he'd heard at the very least a mumbled acknowledgement from everyone, that he gave a sharp, curt, nod.

'Ok. Listen up folks. Today you are going to visit the Armoury,' he said and silenced the excited whispers that erupted with a glare and a half.

It didn't stop all questions though.

'Sir? What is this? I mean, are there more of these things?' Kalim asked, giving the large lettering the eye.

Van Velden regarded him coldly for a moment. 'You are about to enter the Armoury. The door is marked A4. Is this in any way not self-explanatory?'

'Yes, sir,' Kalim sighed.

'Good. There are several entryways into the Armoury. The main doors are marked A1. I believe that you will find them somewhat larger. Now, if there are no more questions?'

The expression on his face this time around ensued that there really were none. There wasn't any sound from the small class other than their breathing. Most of them had endured through Damon's lectures and practicals before. They couldn't say that they enjoyed them, not in the sense that they were fun. They were, however, often more, well, explosive, than, say PMD – which held the record for the most boring subject on the whole planet. No, make that the Universe.

Then, once everyone was quiet, he released the locking mechanism on the door.

Stepping through that door was not unlike stepping into a whole different world. Well … maybe not one filled with trees and magically singing blue-birds.

The corridor behind them had been nondescript; a service corridor more than anything else. The ceiling had been barely above their heads for the taller members of today's little excursion party.

'What the hell?' echoed forth from more than one pair of lips.

What lay beyond was, if possible, even more cramped than the corridor behind them. It forced them into single file, with a certain amount of shoving involved.

As they moved forwards it wasn't the only thing that caused goosebumps.

'Where the rach did the floor go?' one of them exclaimed.

Dayu, looking down, saw little but a flimsy looking metal grating and a few wires beneath his feet, a foot or so above the floor, or what they assumed was a floor. It was so dark it was impossible to be sure.

'What's that noise?'

Several of them tensed up, alarmed by the thumping, grinding sounds that came from somewhere beyond what they could see.

'Move on up, you in front. You're blocking the way,' Damon's deep voice carried even among the din.

Reluctantly they moved on, one step at the time.

They didn't have far to walk actually. As they reached the other end of the very short "corridor" the space they had just transversed was changed from strange to being designated "just one of those places that got left behind when they last remodelled." It was a place that didn't have a purpose of its own, not anymore.

A few more steps forward and, for those that passed through the blocking on the other end, the poorly lit tunnel erupted into light and space. And noise. It was impossible to miss out on the noise.

'Holy crap!'

Cole hadn't taken more than two steps before he stopped, his mouth opening on its own. He leaned over the railing that was now blocking the way down, the very, *very* long way down.

'Can you see this guys?'

'How are we suppose to see it Cole, you're blocking the way, stupid,' Drak growled.

'Move on up there,' came the commanding drawl from Van Velden.

Cole did move, but he sidled sideways, his attention pinned on what was happening down below.

'What *is* this place? I thought you said we were going to the armoury? Like a stuffy old closet where you keep the armour, right?'

'The Armoury, duh,' Dayu rolled his eyes. 'See the difference?'

'Well, how was I to know there's a difference,' Jens objected. 'This place is huge.'

'Maybe because he told us, I don't know, a whole forty seconds ago or something?'

Jens' surprise was justified. He'd just forgotten who they were keeping the armour for. Instead of the narrow confines between the walkway and the floor there were now several stories worth of height below them and, at the bottom of that, the fact that you could see the floor was doing it no favours.

The metal path was swung from cables in which it was suspended from the ceiling. It wasn't actually just one path, but a whole section of them forming an intricate pattern along with dozen of its kind, close enough that the tallest of them could almost reach up and touch the panelling above them.

They crisscrossed the space up here and shuddered beneath their feet as the students followed the person in front of them, some orderly, some not so much. Realising where they were going, the excitement was beginning to show.

So was the vertigo, for some of them.

The first thing that struck you weren't the sights though; it was the sound, or sounds to be more accurate. They smacked right into you, like a deft right hook – and took half of your ear with it as it passed, or washed over you, enveloping you in its entirety.

There were calls and commands, questions and answers being thrown back and forth through the "room" and gabbled into communication devices of all sorts – and those were just the human sounds. They could barely be heard.

For human voices weren't the only thing in here making noise, far from it. Most of the irregular ones were played out against the background of hard heels on concrete and unyielding metal. Machinery, whirring and clicking, drove the accompaniment to the orchestra of swooshes and spinning, groans and the occasional screech where something didn't work out quite as planned.

Some of those came from several of the great robotic arms, themselves many stories tall and each disappearing into the floor below. They were capable of lifting several tons at once and went about their business with an effectiveness that bordered on the manic.

Each "arm" was designed to reach down into the vast storage beneath the Armoury and call upon the right combination of gear for any occasion. That was their main purpose in life. The reason they were so big was pretty self-explanatory, after all, what they had been made to serve weren't exactly on the miniscule side.

The Armoury itself was situated, very much so, on the ground floor. If you opened the vast bay doors you needed just to put one foot in front of another and you'd be standing on the ground outside.

At the moment, the doors themselves were closed, so it was impossible to see that the "ground" here didn't continue on forever. The Armoury was the section of the DRC that lay closest to the actual canyon nearby. Part of that was because it made it easier for the dragons to take off. The bigger reason however was that, when the place had been rebuilt after a rather large earthquake the whole thing had been relocated above ground.

Before then, the whole Dragon Research Centre had been, not just much, much smaller and more compact; it had also been almost completely subterranean. Today, only the vast storage space where the kit was placed remained below ground. The reason for that was that it had been the least affected by the quake and also that it would have been the most inconvenient to redesign above ground, needing to either sprawl out or to be built upwards. Much easier to keep it as it was.

Not that any of them were thinking about that at the moment. They were far too busy ogling what the arms were dancing attention on.

For, between those was something else, something far more impressive than any amount of machinery. And, judging from the complaints emanating from one of them, far noisier.

A dragon.

Actually, when you stopped blinking and backed up a bit in your mind's eye, you realized that there were in fact three of them. Each one was being fitted by a different set of arms. None of them were being fitted quietly. And none of them were anything like those that had taken the students for their

First Ride.

'Shit!' Kay exclaimed. Drak, moments later, followed with a 'Holy Crap!'

'I didn't realize they could be so *big*,' Isolde breathed, now leaning forwards to get a better look as well.

Gaile, in the meantime, was holding on so tightly to the walkway's sidebar, which she was very thankful for being there in the first place, that her knuckles were turning white. Why did they always have to do these things from the highest point possible? Was there something wrong with going in through a door on the floor?

Yet not even she could deny the impression of sheer extraordinariness of what they were seeing. It was just not her top priority at the moment.

'That one,' Jens pointed. 'That one's a *bronze*. Have to be. Just look at those metallic looking scales.'

'Look at that *size*,' Pol agreed. He joined Isolde in leaning forwards to see better.

'As you can all see,' Damon's voice rang out over the rest of the sounds, 'one of the Northern Patrols is being readied for their next run. It is a journey that will last several weeks and take them through some of the coldest regions on the planet, including the notorious Kiba Pass and the Last Turn Trench. These are treacherous conditions in which to travel even when not on duty. You will not be considered for this tour unless you show reliability, dependability and calm in even the most dangerous situation. The dragon and rider combinations that are chosen for this run are among the very best in the DragonCorps.'

Damon Van Velden, their teacher, was watching the dragons being fitted with an intense look in his eyes. The arms of the Armoury flew, each with a meticulous attention to detail, almost as intently as he was watching the students at other times.

The large bronze stretched out both head and neck, almost hitting the suspended walkway, causing several of them to jump back. He was so close they could even make out large individual scales as he brushed past. Yawning widely, he revealed the many canine teeth that adorned his jaws, each the size of a small arm.

'Wouldn't want one of those taking a dislike to me,' Elon shuddered as he eyed them.

A shiver ran through the dragon's body. He gave a violent shake as the arms, their job done, retracted into their casings and fell silent. Turning here and there, the bronze proceeded to inspect the saddle and the assorted equipment to see if any had come loose.

It hadn't. He huffed, satisfied that it was secure.

Of course, this wasn't your ordinary flying saddle. Actually, they weren't sure what it was, it was so, so, well, big. It stretched across a large part of the dragon's back, part of it even reaching down below the shoulders while leaving plenty of room for the wings. This allowed for both protection and plenty of hold for the equipment they carried, partly as a precaution, and distributed it as well as possible in terms of weight.

You didn't want it heavy in the wrong places. It made taking off a nightmare and flying like that, well, the word "drag" came to mind. You certainly didn't want it to come loose during flight either. At the same time, it had to be accessible - in case you needed it - so it was all about compromise.

Like most of his kind this bronze didn't sport an exuberance of decoration in the knob and bony protrusion department. He did have quite the robust features and a pair of heavy brow ridges that wouldn't have looked out of place on a brown though. The eyes, set deep in their protective sockets, rolled once in the direction of the visitors, the dragon then turning his great head downwards, content to consider them permitted in the area. Or, possibly, they just weren't interesting enough to pay attention to.

'What'you think Bahemon? Snug enough for you?' The man on the ledge running along one side opposite to the arms tightened his jacket with the last strap.

He just has to be the rider, Dayu thought. So did the rest of them. He did look the part, that was for certain. Strong, self-assured and dressed for somewhere that didn't look particularly warm. That made sense, if he was going along on the trip north.

The dragon shook himself again, more for emphasis than anything else, then raised a front leg and flicked it delicately in the direction of the enormous hangar doors that lead out of the cavern-like behemoth of a "room".

He yawned and shifted a bit closer to the ledge running parallel to his right hand side.

'At the very front end there you can see the central control room for this facility,' Damon interrupted their private reveries, nodding towards the protruding structure at the edge of the ledge.

It was almost entirely surrounded by windows. Rounded and bent it looked a bit like an upturned fishbowl with a clouded roof, especially since they were watching it from above – though not by much, it too was quite high up.

'That's our next stop. Let's see if you can find us a route across. Mind the dragon,' Damon said.

Several pairs of eyes tore themselves away from the scene below, where the rider had quite sedately stepped onto the saddle from the railless ledge. He was now inspecting the smaller features to make sure they too were secure, strolling up and down the dragon's broad back quite happily.

Was Van Velden serious? They all looked at each other. This place was a maze, up here anyway. Had they gone walking on the floor it would have been easier, but then, how would they get up into the control module? It didn't look to have any doors or stairs down below, only the entry from the ledge itself.

Also, some of those suspensions didn't look like they were entirely firmly anchored – as if they could be swung out of the way to accommodate unusually large specimens. Were they going to come unconnected when they walked on them?

They did manage to make their way across though, with a few precarious moments when the bronze and his rider moved out along with his companions, two fierce looking blacks. One of them had slight finger-claws on his wings, unusual enough among dragons and seen even less often on anyone of his size.

The other one was by far the most muscular looking black they'd ever seen (although, truth be told, they hadn't seen all that many, especially not this close) and even had a whole set of decorative bony fringes.

The entire structure shook violently, bouncing in response to the motions below as the three dragons passed beneath, the bronze up ahead. First the head, then the neck, body and tightly folded wings, followed by a long sinuous tail ending in a very stylish sort of frazzled sail that scraped against the walkway and sent it clanging ominously – the students on it holding on for dear life.

As they did so, the bay doors were opened, showering them all in blinding light.

They quickly shielded their eyes, though, for some, that meant letting go of what they were holding on to. Several students ended up pressed flat against the walkway, trying to keep themselves from falling off.

Thankfully, the sheer size of the "animals" meant that they passed by quickly and, after some had picked themselves up and pretended they'd never been down on all fours in the first place, no really, you must have imagined it, they managed to pick their way across to the command module.

Gaile was happy to be back on more solid ground, or what at least felt like solid ground. The "ledge" was actually partway down a partition wall, separating the right and left hand side of the Armoury, but it was wide enough for several people to walk side by side without any problems. The wall behind it reached all the way to the ceiling, giving at least the illusion of stability. The only problem was that it was a long, long way off the actual ground. Not to mention, it had no railings. She tried to stop shaking. If there was one thing Gaile had a problem with, it was heights.

Everyone has a weakness, she thought, but why does mine have to be heights? How could you be a dragonrider and be afraid of heights? She swallowed, wishing she was somewhere else instead.

The control room couldn't accommodate them all at the same time, not without them getting in the way of the on-duty staff anyway, so they took it in turns. In groups of three they were be allowed to enter and have a look around. Look around under the watchful eyes of the staff that was.

Gaile was more than grateful when her time came, because in here she didn't have to suffer from vertigo. Indeed, once inside, she forgot all about feeling dizzy. Turning her head this way then that, she tried to take it all in.

So, this was where they ran the Armoury from was it? This place wouldn't have looked out of place on the bridge of a starliner, Gaile decided, before realizing that she'd spoken out loud and clasped her hands to her mouth in horror.

But rather than telling her off for such an outrageous comment, the on-duty officer who'd happened to overhear her just laughed.

'It does have that kind of feel, doesn't it?' he agreed. 'Don't think we have much luck running a ship with what we've got here at the ACC though. You should see the command centre for the DRC, now there's some serious steering power.'

'Sorry … I didn't mean …' Gaile hesitated. What on earth were you supposed to say at a time like this?

'No worries,' he waved it away. 'You're not the first to say that and I highly doubt you'll be the last. All riders come through here at least twice in their life, if not more. Once on their first tour and a second time for the final exam. And they all get surprised the first time around.'

'That happens here?' Gaile's interest suddenly perked up.

And, as moths to a flame, both Kalim and Reena, who'd come in at the same time, soon joined her.

'Sure do,' Reena nodded, fingers in her shirt pockets before remembering where she was and quickly snatching them out again.

'We need to pack up a bit first though. See those?' the officer, whose name was Max, indicated the closest of the sets of arms.

'Yeah,' the three students nodded.

'Those arms in here get folded and retracted down into the storage area below us. That gives us a bit more space. Still crowded though. Dragons aren't exactly your average sized critters, I'm sure you've noticed. Thank heavens that only the unattached ones attend in dragon form.'

'It's true then?' Kalim asked, eyes alight. 'About the storage I mean?'

'I've heard there's miles and miles of shelves down there. Every kind of item you could even imagine and it has at least one of them,' Reena added.

'Well,' Maximilian stroked his chin thoughtfully. 'I don't know about miles and miles, but it's pretty big, I'll grant you that. Big robust shelves where all the equipment gets stored when not in use. We've got everything and I do mean everything that you could possibly need or want on a mission, from bandages for the first aid kits to the one piece chest armours for the first line dragons.'

'So the texts are right then? Everything is stored separately? Every single item?' Kalim wanted to know.

'Doesn't that make it a bit complicated to … well, pack?' Gaile frowned in the direction of the arms.

'If you had to do it all by hand, I'm sure it would be. But the system here is very effective. It can assemble a whole travelling kit, from the individual links in a modelled saddle down to the energy bars in your food packs in no time at all,' Max explained proudly.

'Those saddles are awfully big,' Reena peered at the screen detailing the fitting of a smaller blue. 'Don't they take up a lot of space?'

'Don't they store them in pieces or something?' Kalim asked, looking over her shoulder.

'Actually, I'm glad you asked,' Max said. He bent over and worked some of the controls. The screen flittered, now showing nothing but a blank, dark, liquidy surface.

'This is just a simulation of course, but it should give you kids a better idea of how the whole thing works.'

The small crowd gathered closer, peering at the screen below them.

'There're several different ways that can be used to get a saddle when a dragon or rider requests it,' Max explained. He pointed at the screen which was busy showing different types of saddles, going well with what he was talking about. It probably wasn't the first time he'd used this recording, even today.

'The fastest and often simplest way is to use one that's already constructed. We do keep a few around that can be manually adjusted with straps and buckles as well. Old-fashioned perhaps, but they have come in handy before.'

'Like those old leathers that they make us put together in class?' Kalim suggested.

'Exactly,' Max agreed. 'Now, we do have a few of the most common sizes and forms of the more modern version of those as well, of course. The second way is to construct a "saddle" from smaller, interlocking pieces. A bit like the blocks you'd have played with back in nursery. That's the most common way today. Our "pieces" are a lot more adaptable than square blocks of course and they are what most of our everyday normal equipment for the dragons is made from. The pieces are called up and assembled by the arms to fit perfectly to the specification requested. In fact, there are a lot of "favourite outfits" stored on the system so that they can be swiftly retrieved without a lengthy discussion and scans about what's and whatnots of the whole thing. Then, there's the third way...'

Max tapped the screen again and it switched from showing the fitting and creation of several saddles back to a black screen.

'Did it break, Sir,' Kalim asked hesitatingly.

Max smiled. 'Keep watching,' he suggested.

A heartbeat later and something swished into view, beginning to rapidly draw lines, then structures, then building blocks. Layer after layer, ever more complex, they grew with each one.

'The last and the more unusual method these days as we have so much in storage already, are the custom jobs. These are few and far between, you understand. These machines here can create just about anything in terms of armour or even just general items; plates, saddles, facemasks and the like. It doesn't do too well with sensitive electronics though, so we have to add anything like that in a second stage.'

'Cool, Sir.'

'Glad you like it.'

'So, what would they use this for then?' Kalim asked, 'I mean, if there's so much there already?'

'Hmm,' Max regarded the rest of the control room thoughtfully. 'I have actually never had a request for one of these myself. I did say they were rare. But say it needed to be in a specific material, or a dragon wanted a personal set from scratch, those would be it, I suppose.'

Maximilian, realizing that he'd never actually thought about that for years, laughed nervously. 'I'll tell you what. Next time we get a request like that, I'll let you know.'

'Really?' Kalim's eyes lit up. 'Thanks, Sir.'

'Don't mention it. Now, better get back and let the next batch have a look around.'

The three of them nodded, but Gaile hesitated and, as she was about to leave the room she turned around.

'Yes,' Max, who was still watching them, asked.

'Is it true? About the final exam being held here I mean?' she asked.

'You didn't believe me?'

Gaile cast her eyes downwards, examining the floor. The whole question made her uncomfortable and the obvious chagrin of being, almost, accused of lying made Max appear less than friendly.

She must have looked quite pathetic, because even with that in mind, after a few moments, he took pity on her and answered.

'Yes. If you think about it you'll understand why. This is one of the few indoor places around here that even a couple of dragons can gather at the same time without getting crowded. Everyone is made to wait along the ledge you came in on and, one by one, are allowed to approach the gap in the railing. If they are chosen by a dragon they go on to becoming part of the DragonCorps and if not, well, there's always next year for those unwilling to give up.'

'I see.'

'Now, scoot. Don't monopolize the place,' Max said. He grinned, just to show her not to take his last words too seriously. Gaile didn't really feel up to returning the favour though.

It still didn't answer the biggest question of them all, the real reason she'd asked. It was a question that was banded about a lot but no one she'd over-heard had been able to answer it.

How did the dragons know whom to choose?

Gaile hadn't talked to anyone who could understand the question. She hadn't read anything about it either. Maybe it was just too difficult to explain? Too different from person to person to define?

She did have a few ideas that *could* explain it.

For instance; they might be following the progress of *all* the students – getting constant up to date reports and analyses on them and deciding from that. Or maybe they were just walking among them? It wasn't as if you could tell after all.

Gaile threw a suspicious covert glance over her fellow students in today's class, those she could see anyway. It was hard, very hard, to imagine anyone of them being a dragon – and it wasn't the part of looking just like any other human that was the hard part, they did that all the time anyway.

Maybe there was a third way that she hadn't thought of yet?

Of course, it was possible that the entire thing was totally random. Or maybe it was just one big scam and some bespeckled bureaucrat somewhere made the decision, but that was just seriously depressing. Gaile shook off the thought as they descended down to the floor level at the end of the practical lesson.

She wished she could get the thought out of her mind the rest of the time as well, but it was always there, her constant companion.

'How the blast do they choose?' she mumbled to herself.

See, there it was, back already. Curses.

As expected it didn't go away in the next few days either, like if she'd really thought it would. That would be like thinking that her vertigo would be cured by the snap of a finger … or a couple of fingers even.

Friends and Foes

Sitting alone at a table in the open-spaced cafeteria/lounge, Gaile had shoved her study guides to one side and was busy staring longingly out the window. That wasn't hard. The windows in here reached almost from floor to ceiling and were displayed in a series of arches gently spanning across the southern end of the room.

They were also rather a bit more than just plain transparent glass. If they hadn't been, the cafeteria itself would have been almost as hot as it was outside because it got a lot of sun.

The special treatment worked wonders though. Even just a thin and, to the eye, transparent, layer was enough to be able to filter enough light to make it nice and bright but to keep out the associated heat.

Of course, they could have run with plain old repwis, but those were more for places that *couldn't* have an outside view. Putting in a replication window with a continuously updated visual display when you could just have ordinary ones? Yes, there were places that did, often for security reasons, but here they'd opted for the old tried and tested style.

In fact, the style of the windows themselves was old too – more eighteenth century France than anything else really. At least, that's what the guidebook said. Gaile didn't know any more about old Earth than anyone else did (considerably less actually, she hadn't found it that a fascinating subject of study at all) and would have been hard pressed to tell the difference between two countries even if her life depended on it.

Actually, the term country was a bit foreign to her. She understood the theory, but the way she thought of them was akin to liking them to separate planets but squashed flat and scrunched up against each other.

Her quarters didn't get to see the sights though, old-fashioned or not. Whoever had designed them hadn't even bothered to add a repwi. Even that artificial view would have been welcome – and with enough imagination it might have almost seemed like the real thing. At the very least it would have made the place brighter.

Maybe she should get a few posters or something? She did have the wall after all.

'Guess they can't be bothered since there was so many of us and most probably hadn't even been expected to last a month,' Gaile mused.

It had taken a little longer than that for the ranks to start to thin out. There had already been those that had dropped from the course. As expected, by the teachers, First Ride had been an eye-opener and it had taken its toll on the first-year numbers.

'Maybe they'll move us elsewhere as we move on in the course and there's fewer of us?' someone had suggested at the time.

That'd be nice, Gaile thought. She really wasn't cut out for this barrack style living. She liked her privacy too much.

Of course, it'd be typical if what they got next was some sort of shoe box, all uniform grey and narrow walls. Gaile wasn't usually the type that was claustrophobic, but that thought made her shudder. Maybe it was more the dullness of the image she now had in her mind than anything else.

She'd been so caught up in her thoughts for the last half an hour that her lunch, which was waiting patiently for her at its plate, was beyond slowly getting cold. Normally she liked ham and cheese for lunch, but today she just didn't seem to have any appetite.

Gaile poked unenthusiastically at some of the greenery on the side. It wasn't that she was bored. It was hard to be bored with so much new to learn and do. No, that wasn't it. Maybe it'd be more accurate to say she was frustrated. Frustrated over her own lack of progress, over the way she wasn't making any friends, over how little time she had and, not the least, being frustrated over being frustrated. How typical. She marvelled at the idiocy of it all.

The cafeteria was a public place though and her reverie was brought short by a loud burst from a nearby table.

'Can't you do something about it?' someone practically screamed. 'It was your bloody fault in the first place.'

Gaile curled up tighter in the cosy chair. It was hard to keep anything private if you decided to vent in the combined cafeteria and lounge. Its open-spaced design didn't really allow for it – even with the use of dividers here and there and plenty of pot plants. To say nothing about the amounts of people that frequented the place. But she wished people could at least try not to be so obnoxious. There was no need to shout.

Actually, calling what she was sitting in a chair wasn't doing it justice – she barely occupied a corner of it where she sat with her back pressed up against a comfortable fold, though her feet did dangle leisurely over the stuffed armrest on the opposite side. There just happened to be a whole lot of unoccupied area in between. Sometimes being of a smaller persuasion did have its advantages.

'…telling you. It's a *ghost*,' came the loud voice again.

'There's no such thing as ghosts you idiot!' someone shouted back.

The voices sounded familiar, and despite not wanting to get involved, or even seem interested in the shouting match, Gaile tried to see what was happening out of the corner of an eye. It made said eye feel all crinkly and dry, but she managed to get a decent view, enough to identify the speakers.

Gaile recognized one of the voices as belonging to Kay, who was usually voicing his opinions quite loudly anyway, but she'd never heard him screaming like this, unless it was at his sister, who seemed to be able to get him worked up into a furious state just by saying 'good morning.'

Listening in on other people's conversations wasn't something Gaile normally did – probably one reason for why she wasn't only the last person to hear the news, but by the time she'd heard them, they'd ceased to be news at all.

She wasn't the only one who'd stopped and was paying attention to what was happening either.

Her ears trained in on the voices. Among all the others in here at the word "ghost" caught her attention like a well-tuned radar station. Gaile tried to appear lost to the world while at the same time straining to make out what they were saying when, after a while, they stopped shouting at each other.

'… one of the … heard … Armoury …' Kay's voice drifted past.

'Rubbish,' came the much louder reply.

'… moves around … didn't touch … at night,' Kay insisted.

Gaile cursed silently. The bunch of people in the next sofa-group over had chosen the perfect time to erupt into an almost unanimous laughter. Kay was getting hard to hear as it was, mumbling over his words. There didn't need to be extra distractions.

'Sure … did … come … to be.'

'Forget it, I still don't believe you. You're just making excuses for losing it. I know you are, you know,' Derek said.

'… ain't … student body … everyone … officer said …. been happening … years,' Kay kept at it doggedly.

At that point, Gaile lost the rest of the conversation because the lounge erupted into an exited hubbub of nonsense over something else. Something apparently more exciting than watching Kay and Derek arguing.

Looking around, Gaile suddenly wished she was somewhere else. The cause was easily identifiable; having just stepped through one of the two main entryways.

A large number of students just seemed to surge forward, while a smaller number feigned disinterest or were satisfied with just watching from a distance. Those that tried to move in close had to battle for space with the small throng of people that were already there, having entered with him, orbiting him like small planetoids around a polar star.

In the centre of admirers; laughing hopefuls approaching and heart-struck girls making calf eyes at him, the small click of hangers on that followed him everywhere and the general population, along with the two girls he was having on each arm, was the uncrowned king of the student body. Gaile had run into him before. His name was Sera.

At least, that's how all the students referred to him. Well, *almost* all the students. Some had far less flattering names for the "guy". Their voices were, however, lost in the general excitement.

'Oh, show us again, please, pretty, pretty please?'

'Just love the way you've done your hair today Sera…'

'You got to tell me how you get your skin so glowy.'

'Yes, do tell us Sera…'

'Me, me, me…I want to be next.'

The noise coming from his intrepid fans were grating on Gaile's ears. She winced. Of all people who had to show up today, it had to be him. Or maybe she should say; them. Did they ever sleep? How about classes? Did they go to them or did they stand around waiting for their Prince Charming to finish his?

In any case, he'd been hard to miss even if he'd walked in all on his lonesome; a state in which few had ever seen him. If he ever was alone, he certainly kept that private.

And with his long, almost silvery-white hair, flashy, yet elegantly cut uniform and almost flawless features he would have stood out in practically any company even if he hadn't wanted to. Easily reaching a head higher than practically everyone around him didn't make him stand out any less either. He certainly seemed fond enough of that hair, the way he kept touching it all the time, she thought.

Probably bleached it something silly so that he'd get even more attention, Gaile grumbled.

No, he certainly wasn't wont for attention and it wouldn't surprise her at all if the idea of losing his status was more than he could bear. He reminded her of a male Jasmine, albeit one better at manipulating his fellow sophonts. And yes, true to form, *she* was in the midst of them all, as usual. You hardly ever saw Sera without also seeing Jasmine somewhere nearby, preferably as close as possible if she had anything to say about it.

No, he certainly didn't lack attention or company or companions of any kind, not that one. He was probably as popular as it was possible to be and not be worshipped as a god.

Sera flicked a strand of hair out of his eyes, smiling at everyone around him. He bent down and whispered something to one of the girls, who blushed and giggled coquettishly. Straightening up, he chuckled in turn.

'Why don't we find somewhere to sit my lovelies,' he murmured. 'We don't want all that precious lunch hour to go to waste, now do we?'

This caused another set of giggles from several girls nearby, each who fought for a spot in the spotlight as the group made its way across the lounge and into the cafeteria.

They were followed by an evil glare. If locks could kill, Sera would already have been melted into oblivion and beyond.

If only *he* hadn't shown up, she would have heard the rest of the story. Blast it all.

Her narrowed eyes followed her target as he swept through the lounge, gathering up a host of people on the way. Gaile imagined a large bull's eye stuck to his back, fiery arrows streaking towards it. But even while on fire, the imaginary Sera refused to cooperate and do something as coarse as writhing in agony and continued on as if not noticing the difference.

Typical, Gaile growled. Clearly mind over matter wasn't going to work here.

And speaking of matter, maybe this "ghost" was worth checking out? It'd be good if she could do so before everyone else got the same idea. If she caught "it" she'd be the talk of the centre, if lucky.

'Yes ... why not,' Gaile nodded to herself. She'd give it a try.

And so it was that she found herself, several hours later, *not* sleeping quietly in her bed. Somehow, Gaile had managed to get into the right part of the DRC. Ok, it had taken a few wrong turns and a couple of narrow escapes from being noticed, but she'd done it. She was here. Now all she needed to do was to find this so called "ghost", right?

The great cavern-like locale that made up the Armoury lay shrouded in darkness before her. You would have thought it'd be more of an around-the-clock operation, but no. From down here, entering from a corner, it was a lot of empty space. You might not be able to see it, but you sure knew it was there.

The metal walkways that hung suspended from the ceiling so high above could only be made out, barely, because of the emergency lights that never went out and which clung to the ceiling plates just above them.

Another set was strewn along what would have been only slightly above the height of any human standing on the floor. A few other sets, pale white rather than dim yellow, and much smaller, made up patterns on the floor, with some tiny green and red mingling with the others. Most of the floor was as dark as you'd expect though.

Why there would be tiny patterns of light on the floor was beyond Gaile. And from floor level it did indeed look chaotic, if you didn't know how to discern the patterns within. From above it looked akin to the guiding lights found on any shiport. Maybe that was what they were meant to do? Maybe the only difference was that they weren't meant to guide huge metallic hulks of different shapes and sizes to and from wherever they came from but hulking beasts. They still didn't make any sense to her though. Why would they need them if they didn't operate the Armoury at night anyway?

Here and now they weren't guiding anyone though and much of the Armoury was, unless you had some remarkable night vision, as dark as the night outside. Actually, it was probably darker – no moons in here. Since this was something that Gaile was sadly lacking (night-vision, not moons) there wasn't a whole lot for her to see in here.

The great robotic arms and machines that guided them hid in that darkness, looming somewhere just out of sight, their shapes lost against the general background of nothing.

Sensible people not on duty had long since returned to their beds or other sleeping arrangements of choice. The Armoury was abandoned by humans, present company excepted. It was however not totally and utterly abandoned by everyone, or maybe that should be *everything*. Not if people were right about the whole ghost thing.

Gaile felt her way forwards along the outer wall. Since the bay doors were in that wall it was the least obstructed space in the entire place. Even so, going anywhere was slow. The light from the diom, rolled up and put in torchmode was preventing her from walking around without seeing where she put her feet, but that was about all it did, maybe a little more.

It was too late to be able to be considered evening and way too early to be called morning even by the most hard-core early risers. It was, in other words, right in the middle of the night. That didn't mean much in a place like this. But she was still beginning to wish she'd stayed in bed and not bothered. She'd been here for ages now and nothing had happened. The place was deader than a graveyard.

Even so, she stayed still, hoping to hear *something*.

Ages seemed to pass and she was just about to give up, when a 'plink' came from one of the far end corners.

During the day it wouldn't even have registered. Now it echoed, making Gaile jump nervously. Not the best idea in the circumstances. If something *was* in here, it had probably heard *her* now. There went the surprise element, Gaile fumed.

For a moment there were no further sounds and the Armoury went back to appearing deserted. Gaile held her breath, slowly counting to ten.

There was another sound, much heavier this time. It was followed a moment later by the noise of metal scraping against metal. Something light, but heavy enough to fall if you dropped it, bounced against something else, equally metallic, before striking the concrete floor below with a resounding 'boing'.

Gaile edged closer.

Another *thing* clanked its way down from on high. It rolled a considerable way from the nuts and bolts that already lay strewn below the shelves stretching far up the back wall.

Now that she was looking up, Gaile realized that the shelving units didn't just stretch up high; they reached all the way up to the windows high above.

The small but noisy thing was soon followed by another one. It seemed to be coming from the top shelves by the looks of things. Gaile peered upwards. If it hadn't been for the moonlight up there the emergency lighting wouldn't have been enough to make them out by. Even now they were a bit dim. Nothing moved. Was there really something up there?

For a precious moment the entire contents of a shelf tethered on the edge. All it would take was one final nudge. Whatever was up there soon obliged.

This time it wasn't just something tiny either. The whole thing crashed into the shelves below, taking a bunch of content with it, before they all hit the ground in a cacophony of sound.

This time it was accompanied by a great deal of muttering interspersed with some swearing. Not from the midnight ghost, but from Gaile, who'd had to dodge out of the way of a few of the smaller flying missiles as they ricochet off without care or concern for what was in the way. The floor and walls weren't likely to complain about getting hit. Gaile was … a lot.

It was obvious that the Armoury wasn't quite as deserted as you would have expected. It was also obvious that she wasn't going to catch whatever it was from down here. It was even more obvious that whatever it was causing all the ruckus, it probably wasn't a ghost.

'Rats!' Gaile took a deep breath and grabbed on to one of the supports and shook it. Nope, it was bolted to the wall. That one wasn't going to come loose in a hurry.

'Great ... you just *had* to be all the way up there,' she complained, mumbling to herself as, step by hesitant step, she climbed upwards.

It was a good thing the shelves weren't set very far apart or she would have had trouble. Forget that, she was still having trouble. And when, a few minutes later (it was slow going when you had to stop every few seconds and gather enough courage to keep going) she hadn't made a whole lot of progress, Gaile looked down.

'Oh gods ... shouldn't have done that. Deer sweet lonely heavens, I shouldn't have done that.' She pressed her body against the shelves and tried to swallow her own heartbeat.

'Ouch!' Something hit her. For a moment, the lone shadowy shape scrabbled for purchase, hooking an arm around one of the supports for the shelf-units. An errant foot found somewhere to stand on that wasn't already occupied by some sort of machinery or pieces thereof.

'You little sod!'

Gaile aimed an unpleasant look in the direction of the top shelf which was not all that many above her now. She tried hard not to think about just how few shelves there were between her and the top, because the fewer there were there, the more there were between her and the ground. She swallowed, trying to repress a shiver. Her hands were already shaking – she really *hated* heights.

'You did that on purpose, didn't you?' she growled at her mysterious assailant.

The creature above her merely gave her one of those looks before calmly selecting another bolt. Gripping it firmly in its jaws it stretched out its neck and let go, right above her.

It hit her again.

'Stop that you hear!' Gaile yelled at it. 'Now, be a good boy and come here, won't you?'

It wasn't as if she was expecting an answer but the infernal little thing merely blinked large, soulful eyes at her. It then flexed a wing experimentally, looking around for something else to drop on her.

Gaile seethed while clinging on to her precarious position. The upside was that she'd discovered what was causing all the trouble. The downside was that as a dragonling, even if she managed to get to the top shelf where it was reigning supreme, it had wings and would, probably, just fly away.

Damnit. She could have sworn that it was actually grinning at her.

This has been a stupid idea from the beginning. A stupid, useless idea. Who did she think she was? Trying to do something like this on her own? Oh yes, that had been real smart, hadn't it? It'd be just like someone like Dayu. It'd be typical for someone like him. Typically reckless that was. Not her, seriously?

What was a sensible person like her doing here? And in the middle of the night too. Did she really think that they'd accept her if she accomplished this? Had she stopped to think about what would happen if anyone actually found out?

But it had seemed like such a good idea at the time. Ok, maybe not a *good* idea but at least one that had merit. A useful idea. Yes, that was it. An idea she could use to improve in both the eyes of her teachers *and* her fellow students.

It had seemed much simpler back then though, when she'd first planned for this. Much simpler. She hadn't counted on all this.

Gaile tightened her hold on the support beam, trying to pull herself up just a little more. Her other hand loosened the string and noose just a bit. This would be pointless if she lost hold of what she was using to catch the little menace.

'Nice dragonling...' Gaile tried to sound more confident than she felt.

Who'd have expected that the "ghost" of the Armoury was actually just an escapee from the Hive? How'd it get out anyway? From what she'd seen, all the times that she'd been there, they locked down that place pretty tightly.

'Now, just stay right there and we'll soon have you back home, ok?' Gaile said.

Her calming tones didn't seem to be working, or maybe they worked a bit too well. The creature chattered at her admonishingly.

Having apparently exhausted its immediate supply of missiles it looked around and focused on a bigger bucket towards the end of the shelf. Grabbing hold of the handle with its teeth, it pulled at it. When that didn't move it the dragonling gave of an annoyed squeak. It took a tighter grip and tugged at the handle again.

Almost there, Gaile thought. Just let me get up one more shelf and that's it. You keep focusing on that thing dragon and you won't even see me coming. That was the plan anyway.

The dragonling wasn't having any of it though. If there was a game being played here then the only rules it knew, were its own.

Rearing up, its tail wrapping itself around the top beam of the tower for support, the dragonling gave a mighty tug at the bucket. It rocked unsteadily. Then, tipping over on its side, rolling as it went, it went over the edge and regurgitated its content everywhere, including onto the one who'd released them.

The dragonling gave a surprised squeak and scampered out of the way. Unfolding its wings in a hurry it took flight.

Gaile raised her spare arm over her head trying to protect herself from the sudden rain of spare parts.

The falling parts clanked against the shelving units and their content, ricocheted against others and struck her with unpleasantly sharp pain. Several of them hit her knuckles and the back of the hand she was now desperately trying to hold on with.

It hurts. It hurts, part of her mind cried out. Gaile was quickly losing what little balance she had left. Along with a great many other things she lost her grip and slid and bumped downwards, clutching desperately at the external support beams as she did so.

'Aaaaaah…'

Her nails tried to dig in to the metal beneath them. But she was no dragon. She did not have their claws. The holes in the beams caught against her palms and fingers, tearing at skin and flesh alike.

Feet and legs knocked against the units on the way down. A moment later and Gaile landed with a resounding 'thud' on the concrete floor.

Mostly on the concrete floor anyway. Unfortunately for her, the floor was currently occupied by some of the things that had fallen down before her.

They weren't welcoming. They weren't nice to land on either. To Gaile they were a short, sharp flash of white and then everything went black.

As the sounds of the accompanying avalanche died out, now that no one was throwing things around anymore, the Armoury returned to silence.

Gaile eventually awoke to something hot and raspy being repeatedly applied to her cheeks and chin. She turned her head with a low groan. She didn't turn anything else. It was probably a good thing that she could feel it all but … was there anywhere that *didn't* hurt?

The licking, which had stopped when she first woke, quickly resumed. Now that she was making noises they were followed up with several buffs and butts, not all of them gentle. A small foot pressed against her chest. The claws were felt even through her jacket. They weren't sharp, just persistent.

Gaile forced herself into a sitting position, gently pushing the creature away, making it whine in protest.

'I'm up, I'm up,' she told it.

Well, nothing seemed broken. Now that was a minor miracle. She gazed up at the unit she'd fallen … err … slid … down from and then quickly averted her eyes when her stomach gave a lurch at the sight.

Insane, that's what she was. Completely and utterly bonkers.

Turning her attention downwards her eyes were immediately drawn to her prior assailant. Now that she could see him up close, he was actually kind of cute.

'And you're nothing but trouble, d'you hear? You could have killed me,' she told it.

The pale, practically silvery, dragonling sat up straight, its tail twitching. As it watched her with its jaws open, Gaile wondered for a moment if it was going to attack her.

A shiver rippled across its body, shaking it from nose to the tip of the tail. As it caught sight of its own tail, twitching, tantalized it began chasing it around and around for a couple of turns, then looked up at her expectantly.

'Oh no,' Gaile said, shaking her head. 'If you want someone to chase you, go find someone else. I've had quite enough for one night.'

The dragonling made some sort of crooning sound, then bounded forward and rubbed its head against her neck.

'Easy there,' Gaile admonished it, harshly.

It whined unhappily. Then it's long pink tongue gave the nearby chin another couple of licks.

'It's almost as if you could understand what I was saying,' Gaile stroked it gently on the head and was rewarded by a low purring. 'Well, there's my imagination going overboard again.'

She cradled the now docile creature in her arms as she got back on her feet. It seemed happy enough now for some reason. Well, it certainly was better than having it attacking her.

It was a lucky thing that it wasn't bigger or what it might have dropped would probably have been able to squash her. Yikes ... what a thought.

'Now, what say you that we get you back to the Hive *without* telling anyone, shall we?' Her voice had been growing steadily softer, to the point where Gaile even treated her new charge to a small, affectionate smile.

Sure, he *was* trouble on four legs - six if you counted the wings - but he *was* cute. Even more so now that he was content with keeping still and apparently happy to play "adorable puppy". Talk about mood-swings.

'How in the world did you get out in the first place,' she asked him. 'That place's supposed to be locked down pretty tight? Oh well...'

Gaile surveyed the scene around them. It looked not unlike as if the place had been struck by a small and extremely localised tornado. Guess more things had fallen down in that last avalanche than expected.

'Well bugger that. I'm not cleaning *that* up. I'd be here all night. Besides,' she added thoughtfully. 'It's really you who should be cleaning it up seeing as you dropped most of it.'

She scratched the dragonling under the chin. 'Let's this be our little secret, shall we?' Gaile whispered.

'Now, be a good boy and stay quiet until we get to the Hive, ok? The last thing I need is to get caught in the corridors in the middle of the night with you in my arms. They'd probably think I'd stolen you or something.'

'Eeep?'

The dragonling regarded her for a moment, then tucked its head under a wing and promptly seemed to go to sleep.

'Oh you're just the life of the party, aren't you?' Gaile observed. 'You have all the fun while I do all the work. Is that how this is going to work out is it?'

The journey to the Hive proved remarkably uneventful. Somehow, prowling through deserted corridors at night proved much less of a challenge when there were two of you, even if one of you couldn't hold a decent conversation to save their life. Gaile somehow didn't feel that 'eeep' qualified in this matter.

For a moment there was the question of if the doors would open or not, but thankfully both the outer and inner doors of the airlock hissed open without any protest.

As the inner door shut behind her, there was a brief moment where Gaile felt her stomach turn into a pit. What if they couldn't be opened from the inside? She just had to put her mind at ease before the worry gnawed a hole and escaped into the outside world.

It took a little longer to find the opening mechanism on this side. Where it had been merely a large, obvious, button on the other side, here something had to be twisted and pressed down on to make it swing open, to give her access to the button itself.

Must be so that it doesn't get interfered with I suppose, Gaile thought. Some of these creatures were supposed to be quite bright for what essentially was a lizard with wings. But, what else was new?

She regarded the closest specimen of the species in question napping comfortably in her arms. Yes, that'd be suspect number one if she was any judge.

Not wanting to walk into the plant-filled bottom level of the area ahead, Gaile hesitated. In here the only lights were those on either side of the door. There was a touch of moonlight, but it wasn't much. It had trouble getting through the vegetation that resided between the floor and the glass dome on top. The lights beside the door though, were a comfortable dull yellow. They glowed in their protective wire cocoons.

She carefully sat down tonight's capture on the ground in front of her.

The change in motion must have woken it up, for the dragonling yawned and swivelled its head to take in the new surroundings. It looked up at her, an almost quizzical look on its small, delicate face.

Gaile knelt in front of the little thing and stroked it on its tiny head with a couple of fingers.

'You know, I almost wish I could keep you,' she confessed in a murmured whisper. 'When I'm here with the class none of the other dragonlings even as much as look my way. It's kind of nice to know that you don't *all* hate my guts,' she smiled.

The dragonling gave off another 'eeep' and took a couple of steps towards her, rubbing up against her leg.

'You're quite the pretty one, aren't you?' Gaile chuckled. 'All pale silver moon, all over. Hmm … silver … yes … no … not quite right … Silber? How about that? I'll call you Silber. That means silver in … err … yet other language I don't actually remember. Sorry. Silber. Do you like that?'

'Eeeop?' the dragonling "said" and begged for attention.

'Guess you're harder to train than that eh? Alright, now, be a good boy and stay put, ok?' Gaile said. She backed away slowly holding her hands out, indicating for him to stay put.

For a moment the creature looked uncertain, then it got up as if it meant to follow her.

'No, stay!' Gaile repeated more forcefully this time. She didn't really want to raise her voice in here. Goodness knew what might happen if she woke up the resident population. If nothing else, someone would be bound to notice. She'd been lucky so far. She wasn't going to count on staying that way.

The dragonling stopped, hesitantly. Then, as if having considered its option it flexed its wings a couple of times before flapping up among the leaves and branches of the big trees nearby.

Gaile breathed a sigh of relief only when she'd gotten through both doors and Silber hadn't sneaked out along with her.

Well, that was that idea down the drain then. Everyone else seemed to do all sorts of things to impress or to prove they were serious about this whole affair. Why did she have to find it so hard, what everyone else found so easy?

Even so, and here Gaile managed to smile despite the disappointing outcome of tonight's little adventure. It looked like she'd actually made her first friend here. Ok, so he was small, four legged and went 'eeep' at her, but it could be worse. She chuckled. If nothing else, he *was* cute…

With that in mind she headed back to her own bed and a few hours of sleep before the day started in earnest. Hopefully no one would have noticed she hadn't been there.

Back in the Hive, on one of the lower branches, the small dragonling watched the door to the airlock with startlingly intelligent eyes, glittering like liquid silver in the night.

First Flight

Time just flew when you were having fun, or so the saying went. It did pretty much the same thing when you were too busy to notice it was passing. Days followed upon days, turned into weeks and metamorphosed into something akin to months.

Things didn't change all that much though.

At least, they didn't change on the surface. Under the surface, now, that was a whole different story. It was incredible what having just one sole friend could do for you.

That was, unfortunately, not going to help her today. No matter how small or skilled at hiding he was, Silber would have been hard pressed to sneak aboard one of the Academy's shuttles and not be noticed, not when they were filled nose to tail with chatting students of all ages.

As such, there was no way he could be here, at the destination of those shuttles, either. Of course, Gaile realized while she was doing everything she could not to think about where she was, he should, technically, not be any-where other than the hive. That little fact did not seem to stop him from being so. Therefore this was one situation where plain logic was obviously not go-ing to be the winner.

Was that a touch of wind she felt? No, wrong thought. Let's not be think-ing about that. Let's not think about that at all.

Gaile trailed behind the rest of them, deeply unhappy. This was, right now, the last place she wanted to be.

'It's an awfully long way down,' Pol commented, leaning against the railing, trying to make out what was below them.

He was one of the few feeling quite so brave (or not bothered by what he was seeing, or not seeing, as well might be the case) but then he'd always had a head for heights. The rest of the hopscotch group for today were standing at what they deemed a safe distance from the edge of the platform. None were too keen on getting any closer.

There might be a railing they figured, but if a powerful gust caught you that wouldn't help one little bit. They were thousands of meters above sea level after all – and there was absolutely nothing between them and the ground below aside from the platform itself. Nothing at all. If there had been a moun-tain there that meant that there were only a few feet to the ground, then it was an invisible one.

Besides ... there was only a railing at *this* part of the platform. The flat bit, almost devoid of structures altogether, that was right to the left of them wasn't so well equipped. Not strange, since it had served as a landing and general use area for dragons for a long time. It had been in service since well before the DRC itself, that is, the first, subterranean one, had even been constructed. That in itself wasn't strange. Tendril Station was a combined floating plat-form and monitoring station – these days. It hadn't always been so.

Even today, it sailed across the skies of New Retmia, locked in the very same pattern as it had been back in the days when the original settlers had first arrived. It wasn't that they couldn't choose to set it to another one, but no one had ever been able to come up with a more encompassing pattern. Any that had been suggested had catered only to a small section of where the cur-rent "road" took it.

In that way Tendril Station was a "relic" if you were fond of that word, harking back to when the Casticians had first colonized the planet a couple of generations ago. They'd first set it up to monitor the world from a safe dis-tance while living as a part of it before finally deciding that the world was both safe (always a relative term when it came to space exploration) and suit-able (which was a nice optional – and they could afford to be fussy).

Back in those days, it had been able to travel in space (albeit not under its own power) but those days were long gone. Anyone trying that today would soon find themselves with a serious lack of air ... to say nothing about lack of heat. Space was cold and the station hadn't exactly been maintained at an air-seal level – there were plenty of cracks and openings where it could escape. It had been old, already back then.

The platform had long since given up the last of its residents from those days – but the DRC still used it both as a "refuelling" station, rest stop for patrols, general testing area and, of course, for First Flight.

There were few things more intimidating for new students, fresh from the "safe" and accommodating life they were used to leading, than first climbing on-board an intimidating looking dragon and then having to push off from the relative secureness of a "solid" ground beneath their feet, dropping straight down (not that the dragons usually employed such simplistic tactics) and leaving only the screams behind them.

In fact, there was no other, single or multiple, test that the Academy set that resulted in a greater reduction of its student population. At the end of the day, it left behind the foolish, brave, foolhardy or just plain stubborn, to continue with the course.

That was what they were here for today. And for some, the day nearly ended there. Not all of them were happy about that little fact.

Some hours previously they'd all set out, every single one of the first years, without knowing just what lay in store for them. Had they known, it would have been a safe bet that some might actually have chosen not to come, to pretend to break a leg … *really* break a leg.

Maybe that was why no one had seen fit to tell them?

As it was, they'd been herded around like a flock of unruly sheep, sheep that needed divvying up and stored separately at that.

'Alright. Everybody aboard. You know the drill,' Damon Van Velden directed a group of students to one of the centre's shuttles.

Every single one of those students boarded under his scrutinising eyes and they did so quietly and in an orderly fashion.

You might be able to conceal something from Van Velden, but it usually came at a price … later. They'd learned quickly enough that he had little to spare for cheeky subordinates *or* cheeky students and treated them with the same contempt.

A little further away on the roof that also served as a convenient landing platform for the smaller shuttles, Tam Turing was directing another, much rowdier, bunch. His expression, while stern, also hinted at a note of worry. It was a big day and the first chance of something going majorly wrong in the course … and by that he rhymed the word "majorly" with "fatally" – though he did so quietly and by trying not to think about it (outside of taking precautions).

It was a trying time for students and teachers alike, although for very different reasons.

The danger was enshrined by the very nature of what they were about to do. It wasn't the kind of thing that you approached with cotton wad and some sympathetic words for those who failed – you either shaped up and achieved the desired outcome or you didn't, simple as that.

It wasn't like they were asking the students to, magically, over-night, have become rocket-scientists after all. Not that that comparison made any sense to Tam. It wasn't like there were any rockets around, unless you counted fireworks, and you hardly had to be a scientist to understand those.

He wondered where the saying had come from.

Anyway, it was simple, with a capital S - in theory.

It was, literally, unheard of, for this day to come to an end without *something* happening. Tam just hoped that it wouldn't be anything beyond scrapes and bruises and ruffled egos.

The shuttles themselves weren't overly big – they only took about ten to twenty people depending on high tightly packed you wanted your passengers and cargo. *Most* of the students were going in two of the Academy's own transports. Those were equipped to take several hundred passengers each, easily and with room to spare.

The big ones had to land on the ground due to their weight rather than up here. The roof might hold them, you never knew, but so far no one had been willing to chance it. If it did break there were bound to be protests, not the least from the people the roof had just caved in on. Getting squashed by several tons of whatever probably wasn't very fun, he conceded.

It was unusual for the DRC's shuttles to be pressed into service for this, Tam mused. Normally, by this time, there'd be far fewer students around –

many having decided over the course of the last few weeks that being part of the DragonCorps was fine, but not as a rider, thank you very much.

'We'll just shuffle sideways into something encompassing a little less danger of becoming a small flattened speck on the ground,' they seemed to say. Add to that the even greater number who just decided to leave altogether and the amount of students had thinned considerably - or would have, in a normal year. This current batch seemed somewhat more resilient than usual, or why else were they still here?

A grim smile graced his already tense features. Well, after today, there'd be bound to have been reduced down to a manageable size; a lot more manageable.

Tam performed a last visual check, then stepped inside himself and took the seat next to the pilot, to whom he offered a recognizing nod.

'Ok, we're good to go,' he said.

As the engine's whine grew louder, the power levels rose and, as they reached into the green zone, the pilot eased the craft into the air with a practiced hand.

As it was rising up, they were treated to a stunning view of both landscape and the DRC complex itself.

Most of them had already seen it before, and, not bothered about seeing it again, were busy talking to each-other instead. The complex was big, they *knew* that. They'd never realized just *how* big until the first time they'd seen it from the air, but those days were behind them. Why bother staring at it now? It was an old hat to such as them.

Only the 'ooohs' and 'aaaahs' from the few who *had* had their noses glued to the viewports anyway aroused the interest of the majority enough to find out what all the fuss was about. It surely couldn't be that exciting, could it?

'Will you look at that!' one of the students in the back exclaimed.

'You should have seen 'em a second ago mate,' someone else replied with a chuckle.

For down below, the ground to the left of the Armoury was filled with dragons, the riders already almost too small to be made out at the shuttle's rapidly increasing height.

There were plenty of green dragons of various shades as well as a throng of blues and browns. What looked like an entire contingent of fiery reds were standing slightly off to one side while the bronzes, their metallic sheen easy to pick up in the bright sunlight, remained still, allowing the milling crowd around them to get organized.

Several black dragons were like shadowy holes against the ochre background, while any "white" ones were too few in number, and too small, to be made out clearly, assuming they were out at all.

It might not be *every* dragon in the DRC down there, far from it, but there sure were plenty and more than enough to be impressive. None of them had so far seen, up close and personal that was, any large gathering of dragons. Seeing just one or two just didn't compare. What would it be like to be down there with them? To have, everywhere you turned, these massive bodies and feet, not to mention talons, around you?

To the students it looked not unlike a battalion getting ready for war, albeit perhaps one that didn't need to worry if they were on time or if the other party were going to show up and run over them like a steamroller if they didn't bother to take it seriously.

'They must be getting ready for something really big,' Drak breathed out.

'That's more dragons than I've seen in my *entire* life man,' Cole agreed.

'They're a bit small from up here, kind of like toys,' someone else pondered out loud.

'You wouldn't say that if you were down there with them,' the girl to the speaker's left sniggered.

'No, probably not,' Cole grinned and a spout of laughter broke out among the students.

One of those sitting further up front leaned forwards and vied for the attention of their instructor.

'What's going on ... down there I mean,' Reena clarified, in case she'd be misunderstood.

'What?'

Tam, who'd been quietly humming along to his favourite tune, tried to tune his mind back to the here and now. He looked down just as the dragons disappeared from view.

'Oh, that... The new riders are going out for some field exercises that's all,' he said.

'That's *all*?' the girl wanted to know. She didn't sound like she believed him.

'It's rare for all the non-initiated riders and dragons to go out in force like this, together, but you'll find, if you get that far, that there are a few occasions where you'll take to the skies with your fellow companions, under the careful eyes of more seasoned riders of course. It's all part of the curriculum,' Tam assured her.

'So, there isn't something going on that we should know about then?' Reena pressed.

'Not at all. Now, stop worrying and relax. There's a bit of a flight until we reach our destination, you might as well enjoy the ride,' Tam said. And with that he turned back around.

Reena on the other hand leaned back, her normally gentle brow now creased; always a sure sign she was thinking hard. There was something fishy going on here, no matter what anyone said about it, she thought.

By the time they'd been cooped up for well over half an hour, the initial excitement of going somewhere new had faded. Whatever else, the journey itself was utterly boring. They were too high to see anything but clouds … and these didn't even make out any pretty shapes; it was just flat … like a land made solely of ice, far beneath them.

Plenty of students, devoid of their dioms (which had needed to be turned in before they left) or even just plain old pens and paper, were looking increasingly mutinous, Tam thought. They weren't used to going this long without some sort of stimulus. That was one thing they were going to have to work on if they planned on staying in this business. There was no such thing as being entertained twenty-four seven in this job.

If you were so busy, your eyes glued to a tiny screen watching something fun, you were far more likely to miss out on the things you were *supposed* to watch out for, either on another screen (like important changes in readings) or in the world around you (like that waterspout off to the left). All in all, you had to pay attention, or be ready to pay attention, or you weren't likely to come home, except in a long wooden box. You couldn't rely on your dragon to see *everything* for you.

Well, they wouldn't complain of having been bored by the time the day ended, he was willing to bet on that.

Some further twenty minutes of utter dullness ensued before something actually happened.

'Hey, look at that,' the shout erupted into the silence like a whip.

'What? Where?' came from several throats at once, though not necessarily at the same time.

'There,' Akia pointed. 'I see 'em, just a little to the left of us.'

'Aye.'

'Wow!'

Again, noses pressed firmly against the steelglass.

There, not a hundred yards from their left, were three dragons in an arrow-head formation. Clearly heading the same way they were, their wings were almost leisurely beating the air. Any dragon worth their name would use the wind to glide and conserve energy if not in a hurry. These ones had to be going somewhere important.

As the shuttle passed by – pulling ahead at a not that great a speed (clever minds suspecting that the pilot had slowed down as to not overshoot the trio. Whatever you could say, a dragon was not as fast as artificial transportation, not at higher speeds and going straight forward), two of the riders waved at its passengers – several of whom waved back. Others were too stunned to see dragons in flight in the actual air to do anything else but just sit there and stare at them.

In the lead was a red; a very sleek red with vast, almost angularly sharp wings and an elongated and slightly angular snout to go with them.

Behind that one came two blues. One, the more compact of the two, had what at this distance looked like a small second sail, fluttering behind their main wings, where the tail met their body and a further one at the tip of the tail itself. Their face was rounded, the scales smooth and small and, from this distance, impossible to see.

The other blue that flew beside it, while not as elongated as the red, was far more so than its partner. Its wings had gentle, curved joints and just as curved wing membranes as well as two small stripes, if you could call them that, at the end of its tail, a bit like an anglerfish. It kept its legs tucked up neatly against its body, allowing for minimum drag.

The wings were stretched out to the max, feeling the wind for the best and most advantageous position as it drifted gently from side to side, a bit like a slow motion fish out of water. Even at this distance you could make out the knobby faceplates and nostrils a small jet would have been proud of. It rolled a yellow eye at them, though that they could not see.

'Already making plans are you?' asked the rider of the last blue.

'Of course,' Allurion shifted position slightly, his wings vibrating gently. 'It will be a busy day. It pays to plan ahead.'

'For some,' Dianne agreed. 'I know Elsa and Ikki hope they won't have anything to do. Like everyone else on standby.'

'Always do, this day. And it is never so,' Allurion replied. 'All we can hope is that no one will be lost.'

'Hey,' Dianne slapped her thigh. 'When have we ever lost anyone at this?'

'I'm just saying,' the dragon replied cautiously. 'It pays to be careful and to plan ahead. But not too careful. We need to find out what they are made of,' he insisted. 'Anyone can ride a dragon if all it does is fly straight and true. If that's what they expect – there are fairground rides for that,' Allurion scoffed.

'Now, don't go scaring the new students,' Dianne admonished. '...too badly,' she added, after some thought.

It was a little while longer before the shuttles began their descent to their target.

Actually, to call it a descent was a bit of a mockery, if you were thinking of a satellite to ground kind of thing. It was more of a glide, slightly downwards but mostly horizontal. Their goal wasn't exactly down *on* the ground after all. Coming in head on, all four craft, in order, lined up their approach.

There, right in front of them, secure in the same patterns that had been holding it since first arriving to this planet on the very borders of the Castician influence, right next to the great nebulae walls, so many years ago, loomed the platform the people of those days had alternatingly called "Home" or "Tendril."

It didn't seem all that big at first; just another dark speck in the sky. Then, as you came closer, you realized that what had seemed like small bulges or the odd box on top of it, were in fact vast towers reaching into the sky and aerodromes that covered the surface.

Tam found himself wishing for more of a cloud cover on this side. That would have hidden the platform from view until the very last moment when the shuttle would have burst out of a cloudbank, right above the artificial floating island of steel, glass and metal. It was always an impressive sight, no matter how many times you'd seen it before.

He knew some of the pilots, if those conditions were present, would even increase their altitude, maybe even take a detour to get the right effect. They too knew that some added drama on this day only made for better riders and the rest of them didn't complain about the sight, that was for sure.

Sadly enough, this time they had to settle for the dark island to increase in size naturally. It sat nestled in a cloudless valley, the nearest front miles away. But he did notice that they were keeping it straight in front of them. That way the students wouldn't be able to see anything until they actually came in over the platform itself.

As they passed the outer edge, the world beneath them ceased to be one of blueness and white, with bits of landscape thrown in for good measure, and instead became an almost uniform grey. Very dull grey it was too as they got closer.

Tam reached out for the speaker system.

'If you'd all like to look out your nearest viewport,' he suggested, sounding officious, 'you'll note that we are now arriving at Tendril Station. We expect to be landing shortly. Please stand by to disembark in a prompt manner once we've come to a complete stop inside the hangar.'

'What?' someone asked sleepily.

'What did he say?' another one yawned.

'Is that..?'

'Yeah, must be…' Pol agreed.

'You know, I've read about this place but I've never expected to go here,' Akia kept staring at the dull grey beneath them. 'Sure doesn't look anything like I expected.'

'Nah … boring…' someone else shared their opinion.

As an opinion it matched that of a lot of their fellow students. It sure didn't look like much. Just grey and flat and … well … dull. Ok, and some partially faded painted lines that crisscrossed the flatness. All in all, *not* what they'd come to expect from the history books (which had a tendency to show off the station's more interesting features as history was wont to do).

As such, it was a sleepy and not terribly organised group that trouped out of the shuttle and into the hangar where they'd landed.

They looked about. It seemed that the others had already landed *and* disembarked. They didn't look much livelier though. It had been a dull ride for everyone. Even those with superfluous imaginations that could keep them occupied during such flights were stretching, trying to get some life back into them.

There wasn't much time for that. Typical. Van Velden was being bossy as usual. Tam wouldn't have minded a break himself.

'Everyone will form two lines, taller people to the back,' Damon instructed. He surveyed his charges with a practiced eye.

After their first few "encounters" with him, the students who still remained at the Academy had learned, some the hard way, that there were teachers you could get away with fooling around with and there were those that you couldn't. The twenty or so odd students under Damon's watch filed into ranks with a minimum amount of fuss.

They weren't happy about it, but they did it.

'Today you will face your biggest challenge since you arrived at this Academy,' Damon's dark, crisp voice carried easily, even as the engines of the shuttle behind them were winding down and despite the sounds from the rest of the hangar intruding.

They all looked at each other, if only for a brief moment, before they returned their attention to their teacher.

'Yes, Sir,' they chorused.

'Today will be as defining for your future in the DragonCorps as your Final Exam. If any of you have any doubts, at any time, do not hesitate to advise the nearest official,' Van Velden continued.

Unlikely, all things considered, Damon thought. Then he pushed those intruding and distracting thoughts away, took another deep breath and continued. 'Today is all about facing your fears. If you can not face your fears *and* overcome them then you can not be a rider, do you understand?'

He whirled on them like a snake pouncing on a mouse – the power behind it enough for them to draw back significantly in surprise.

'Yes, Sir,' they chorused again – some less enthusiastically than others.

This was stupid they thought. They didn't need this … it was like being back in pre-school and being treated like five year olds again. Typical waste of time.

'Good,' Damon Van Velden nodded. 'Today will be … your First Flight.'

He savoured the gasps that followed this announcement. They didn't look bored anymore. Some of the students certainly looked less confident than only a few minutes ago. Excellent – the sessions today might weed out quite a few even here. First Flight usually did in his experience.

He hadn't, of course, had any problems with his First Flight, but then it had been rather *different* for him compared to what most of the students before him now faced, Damon admitted. Though, perhaps not … no, he shouldn't think like that. There was as much difference between swimming and being dragged along helplessly behind as it was to be or not be in total control of your actions. It wouldn't be easy for anyone to just give that up. That was to be expected. Still, these ones … well, it'd be interesting to see how they reacted either way.

Pol nudged the person standing next to him in the ribs.

'Hey! No need for that.'

'Thought you needed a wakeup call. Don't look so gloomy.'

'Do you *realize* what we're supposed to do?'

'Quiet,' Van Velden snapped.

As he told himself, it was hard to face a fear of flying, or heights, or even to understand it, when you had none yourself. To him the air was as natural an element to move in as water was for a fish to swim in. That did not mean he expected any less than the best from *his* students. It just meant he wasn't totally unaware of that it could be an obstacle … for some.

Perhaps that was another reason why they'd chosen to split up the students into three groups, he thought. After all, they could have used another large cargo transporter if they'd really wanted to – so splitting them into several units must have some other significance. Though he could not yet tell what that reason might be.

'Dayu, stop eyeing that door. Don't think I don't see what you're doing!' Van Velden's deep voice echoed against the shuttle's hull.

'Ah, come one. I was only looking,' Dayu protested.

'Then stop looking!'

Dayu returned his eyes to the ground. 'I wasn't doing anything, honest,' he breathed to his companion.

'Sure sure, I believe you,' his friend said, looking all the world like he could barely contain his amusement.

Damon surveyed the twenty or so young, and not so young, men and women. Yes, he did seem to have an unusual large amount of what he termed "trouble-makers" on his hands – students that you needed to keep both one and two and perhaps even three eyes on (how unfortunate that he only had two to go around) as much for their own safety as for everyone else's.

That Kay Sternmasser was there, he noted – looking pleased with himself as usual. Probably expecting to become the hero of the day no doubt, Damon thought.

The far less loud, black haired kid next to him, what was his name again? They all looked alike after a while. Hadn't he used it just a moment ago? Ah, yes. Dayu Abe. How could he forget? Better keep an extra eye on that one as well. Dayu tended to develop bouts of "curiosity" – the contents of barrels with lids, boxes with locks and shut away at the deep end of a cupboard, whatever may be behind locked doors, and he could vanish at a moment's notice if you took your eyes off him.

He could be dealt with though, if you thought of him as a cat on two legs. There were others that were more difficult.

But Tendril Station wasn't a place you wanted to let anyone wander about in – especially not a young boy with no concept of the word "danger". Damon nodded to himself. Yes, for a teacher, Dayu spelled trouble even more than Kay did – who you usually had no trouble telling where he was, just a question of heading for the noisiest argument really.

Was there anyone else here that needed extra, extra attention? Maybe, but those two stood out, even in this group.

Best get going then, Damon thought. Lots to do today.

'Very well. Stay in your lines and you will follow me silently to today's training area. Failure to attend will mean failing the test.'

The last he added as a benefit for anyone that might think of sneaking off to investigate something more interesting instead. Not that he thought it'd actually deter them.

Further in, deeper in the hangar, Tam was organizing his lot in a similar, but slightly less militaristic fashion.

'Sir, Sir,' a young looking one waved his hand for his attention, almost jumping up and down on the spot.

'Yes, Jim, what is it?' Tam answered tiredly. You easily felt exhausted when you'd been around Jim Walker for even five minutes. Where did that boy get all that energy from?

'Is it true? Is it? Are we doing First Flight? Today? Right now? Here?'

'Yes, Jim. That's exactly what you're doing. Now, if you could all please calm down and I can explain a few of the main points here before we head on out.'

'Sweet,' Jim's eyes glowed.

'Your enthusiasm does you credit Jim, but please try to curb it at least a little. We don't want anyone falling over the edge today.'

'Sure, Sir,' Jim winked at his teacher.

'Now … what was I talking about again?' Tam had momentarily lost the little red thread and him reverting back to his private personality rather than his teacher persona made several of his students chuckle amusedly. They'd learnt that Tam Turing wasn't nearly as scary as he looked, even with that scar running down his cheek and constantly frowning expression.

'You were going to tell us about -' the boy looked over his left shoulder.

'- the main points,' Akia filled in for him.

'Ah, yes, the main points … *The* main point – Don't. Fall. Off. The. Edge. Don't wander up to the edge curious about how the "Down There" looks from the "Up Here"d. Don't wander too close to the edge and accidentally bump into someone you don't like. Don't think about the edge. The edge is beyond your world,' Tam stopped for breath. All that had come out as a single sentence.

He gulped for air a couple of times. 'Now, how this works is very simple. One by one you'll be taken on a short flight by one of our resident dragons. Ordinarily it is only the unattached dragons that help out with First Flight – as it allows them to observe the students in person – but as there's so many of you this year, quite a few of the fully fledged members of the corps have volunteered their services as well.'

'Sweet, Sir.'

'Yes, well... You'll find that the saddles we're using today are single-seaters only. Can anyone tell me what that means?' Tam asked; keen to get the students actually involved not to mention away from analysing *him*. 'Not you Jim, let someone else answer.'

'Aww ... man...' Jim sighed.

Laughter erupted at Jim's reaction. He always was the first to volunteer for anything – unless it involved cooking.

'Umm ... it's a saddle that doesn't really do anything except be there for you to sit on?' Isolde, the crew-cut brunette, offered. Gear wasn't really her field of expertise.

'Exactly right. Anyone else want to have a stab at what that answer means in turn?'

Teran, looking rather unhappy about it, raised his hand. 'That we're on our own,' he suggested.

'Yes. Today there will be only you and a dragon and the wind of course,' Tam added the last thoughtfully. 'It's perfectly normal to feel anxious. If you feel confident enough though, you might even want to suggest something specific to your dragon. Tours of the Tendril Station tend to be popular among those already having some flight experience as pilots. Do remember to ask them *before* you take off, as it's unlikely that they'll be able to hear you during flight and it's impossible for them to speak directly to you. And, please, don't try to get up to any antics out there. There are no bonus points for showing off.'

'Now if you could all follow me and we'll head off to our area right away. We're supposed to be working out at the third quadrant of FF.'

The students trooped off after him, several of them looking anticipatory rather than nervous, remarkably calm in fact considering what they were about to face. A couple of them threw glances back behind them where, in the shadow of the academy's largest personal transporter, the remaining several hundred strong group were receiving *their* pre-flight lecture.

Wonder why they've split us off, some of them asked themselves.

Indeed, the largest group by far today, standing several rows deep in attendance before the grey hulk (the transport in question pricing efficiency over prettiness – either that or someone had delivered it forgetting to have painted it and no one had bothered taking it back yet) of the personnel transporter, were doing so under the watchful eyes of Captain Hezan Carula himself.

His presence today, when he not only expected them to have found their feet at the Academy, but also to now be aware of whom it was who was addressing them, cut a far more imposing figure than he had when they'd first seen him helping out at First Ride. Perhaps it was the expression in his eyes.

Hezan's black gaze played across all of them, choosing not to notice the murmur that rose from the assembly.

Today he wore the official pips that had been missing before, which, along with the insignia on each arm, announced him as the Captain of the third Wing; a unit more commonly known as the Black Hawks.

That wasn't because every dragon in the unit was a black one, which was a common misconception. It wasn't because they were exceptionally bird of prey-like either. The name had a far simpler origin. It had been the designation of one of the units aboard the Orion, the ship that had become the unintentional settler of Casticia. As such, it carried a lot of weight and it tended to be quite popular, still, to give places, children and other things along those lines names associated with what and who had been present aboard that ship.

To their right, the short wall of the hangar had been retracted and showed an almost uninterrupted view of the platform, which, in the distance, rose in several layers of boxes and spirals and spires. *Almost* uninterrupted because it also contained a dragon. More specifically, it contained Astarot, Hezan's long term partner.

The bronze dragon, his dark, almost blood-coloured scales shimmered in the sunlight. He had taken up position along-side of the opening. Laying down, neck arched high and appearing to be gazing off into the distance, he looked not unlike a draconic version of a sphinx; the same old gleam, knowledge and power in his eyes.

While the dragon might look like he was staring off into the ether, none of the students chose to test this by trying to sneak past while everyone else's attention was somewhere else – no matter how eager some of them were for what promised to be an exciting day.

'Aww man…' Jens Andersen exclaimed, sounding almost as disappointed as Jim had earlier. 'Couldn't they just have had watchdogs instead? That's so unfair.'

'Probably worried they'd try to chase someone and fall off,' the girl next to him stated in a matter of fact kind of voice. 'Now, shush, I want to hear what he says.'

Returning his own attention to their "teacher", Jens sneaked a last look at the impressively spikey dragon by the door. Someday…

'As you can see, several of your teachers are on hand today to help you with today's lesson, as are a number of second and third year students – who you will appreciate have already undergone the very same trial as you yourself now face. Much more recently so than any of us, and who I hope you will feel comfortable to turn to, should you yourself have any hesitation about what is about to take place.'

Hezan clasped his hands behind his back and gave a nod to the small gathering of people standing just off to his left before continuing. 'In a few moments we'll begin assigning you to the groups that you'll be working in today. Your flight, should you choose to accept it, will take you from Tendril Station down to the surface, where you will assemble and wait to be picked up when the trials are over. Food and drink will be provided as it is likely to be a long waiting period, especially for early fliers, until everyone has returned.'

He gave them another stern glance at this point. 'Tendril Station has a very long and proud history. Many of us are the descendants of those who lived here while determining the status of this planet and many dragon expeditions have set out from here. First Flight continues in this tradition – conducted much the same as it was back in the days of our grandfathers and our great grandfathers. Today you will step into their shoes and should the future choose to smile upon you, today as well shall become etched in history as the beginning for a new generation of riders. Good luck to you all and may the Stars of Solon guide you.'

Hezan turned, gave another nod to the assembled student helpers and teachers and strode off the small platform and out into the sunlight. He disappeared from view only as long as it took him to mount his dragon.

Astarot, with his rider secure, turned his back on the hangar and with a mighty blast of wings and muscles leaped into the air. The downdraft knocked into several of the students, sending those who had not had the foresight to brace themselves into a confused tumble along the floor.

He *could* have just walked over to the closest edge of the platform, which was very close indeed at this point – but what was so impressive about just jumping off somewhere?

Watching it all from within that large group, Gaile felt anything but anticipatory of today's little events. Or perhaps you could say she *was* anticipating it, in the worst possible sense of the word. The young woman swallowed nervously. Heights…

Picking up the students, in some cases quite literally, off the grey floor, the assembled teachers and helpers started organizing them into smaller groups.

Well, that's the only good thing that's happened so far today, Gaile thought, as she searched the crowd for familiar faces. No Jasmine. That was good. The last thing she needed was that … that … *person* making things more difficult than they already were.

Sera too was notable by his absence. Another good point. Geeze, they were just piling up, weren't they? Guess they were worried he'd be a distraction, she figured. They'd probably be right too.

She swallowed again. Why couldn't they have started off from the ground? She'd been much happier about that, or less unhappy, anyway. Silber wasn't here either. That was probably yet another good thing. She loved the little darling, but he always ended up getting her into trouble. Much like Sera distracted a large portion of the female population, Silber did the same to her, though for *very* different reasons.

Actually, on second thought, maybe it was a *bad* thing he wasn't here. Trying to sort through his latest antics would, if nothing else, have kept her mind occupied on something other than the miles and miles between her and the actual ground. Odd, in a way, since she wouldn't have been bothered if the whole thing had been hanging in space instead.

Despite her misgivings, Gaile accepted the coloured lot she was given and went to stand with the others in her group for today.

When they'd first started out this whole thing at the Academy, they'd thought that the group names were a bit lame and that they'd stay with them for the entire duration of their training. That had caused quite the bit of fuming from some of the students, to say nothing about a certain amount of rivalry, teasing and, sometimes, more.

As it turned out, they'd been nothing more than convenient markers, labels in fact, to identify parts of the whole. Once the student numbers had dwindled somewhat, they'd been split into other groups, often seemingly at random. Guess colours were pretty basic when it came to names, like that. Useful too.

Gaile hoped that there were more thoughts going into it than that. But, even so... The DragonCorps was *supposed* to be an organized organisation, if that was at all possible.

'Who organises the organisers?' Good question. Not one she really had an answer to but a good question even so. Not something that she should be worrying about right now either, she decided, as they were effectively herded off to their spot for the day.

Approaching the area they'd been assigned, the first thing that greeted Tam's little team were two dragons circling each other, snarling and hissing.

One, a cerulean blue with its wings partially unfolded, snapped angrily at its opposite in this powerful dance. That one, a clear, charismatic red, scales flexing as they moved, swung their head back and forth. Neither ever took their eyes off the other. Their tails whipped uncomfortably close as the team hesitated at getting anywhere near either of them.

A calm dragon that knew where it was and what it was doing was one thing. An annoyed, or angry dragon, seldom thought further than whatever the cause of said emotion was. Much like their fellow humans. That was why the corps didn't allow dragons into their ranks until they were certain that they could remain calm under pressure, *any* pressure.

But even with that it wasn't fool-proof. Dragons weren't robots. Besides, even robots and machines had a tendency to throw a fit at times. It was safe to say though that the younger and more inexperienced the dragon, the more likely such outbursts were.

The difference between a teenager throwing a tantrum and a dragon, was that there was likely to be a great deal more collateral damage than a slammed door.

'Stay here,' Tam ordered his charges and strode forwards.

'Ladies, this is not the time or place!' Tam had to shout at the top of his lungs to make himself heard over the racket.

The red dragon turned her head away and huffed importantly. She took a couple of steps to the left and let herself tumble off the edge of the platform.

A loud screech erupted from the remaining blue's throat. Having bounded over to where the artificial ground ended, it squared its shoulders and roared after the departing dragon. Then, satisfied that the other had truly gone, it sat back on its haunches, wrapped its tail closely around itself and turned their brilliant, green, cat eyes, on the small group of students.

'So, who wants to go first?' Tam asked, secretly glad nothing had happened.

None of those present looked terribly excited at the thought. Apparently that little display had shown them that it wasn't all violins and roses in this business. If you got caught out by a dragon you weren't likely to come anything but second – and considering the size difference, it would be a very permanent second at that.

The fact that the dragon in question might not even have known you were there and would be terribly apologetic and embarrassed afterwards somehow didn't make it any better.

Shaking his head at it all, Tam instead proceeded in telling the dragon off in a series of not very shy sentences coupled with some rather dramatic looking hand gestures, demonstrating exactly what he'd do if it happened again.

The dragon didn't look terribly impressed. It merely turned up its nose and lay down.

If it was ignoring him because he had no power over it or because it was being contrary just for the sake of it, was impossible to tell.

But, now that the immediate display of bad temper was over, several students noticed the small mounting block that had been bolted into the metal nearby. It was sitting right next to where the dragon had laid down, allowing for an easier time getting aboard than if they'd had to clamber all over the body of the creature to get into the saddle – which looked small and forlorn on such a formidable beast.

'Alright, alright. Let's try to ignore what we just saw, shall we?' Tam waved at them all.

In his eyes, the students didn't exactly look like they'd been terribly encouraged by the little "incident". Guess he couldn't blame them. On the other hand, they weren't cowering behind the nearest wall either. Although, now that he looked closer, some of them were hiding behind the less bothered members of the group.

It wasn't like they were used to what had just happened. Dragons usually saved their arguments for when in human form; it was less destructive that way. Few things, short of an avalanche or an earthquake, could cause quite as much mess, in as short a time, as two, or worse, several dragons, involved in a tussle … especially if they were some of the really big ones.

But sometimes tempers ran high and into the fray they went and when they did, there was usually no stopping them. He'd have to remember to report it – very unprofessional on such an important day as First Flight, even if both of them *were* still trainees themselves.

'Youngsters,' he mumbled under his breath, 'never change…'

Tam changed mental gears. 'Ok, Giselle here will take the first of today's flights. She's still a trainee, so she'll be one of the dragons that will be present for the Final Exam. Any volunteers?'

The small group of students shifted around uncomfortably. Did they really want to go on that thing? It seemed unreliable.

Not that Giselle was any less a dragon than they'd come to expect, quite the contrary. She matched the old fantasy stories better than most, being one of the few newly fledged dragons to sport a *full* set of horns. The two main ones were curved inwards and several others, smaller, protruded from the back of the faceplate at an angle.

This was one dragon you wouldn't want for it to get to affectionate with you. One head rub in the wrong place and you'd get speared through the stomach. Still … she did seem a little … unreliable. *Very* unreliable.

The blue dragon gave them an eyeful and snorted impatiently. She gave a small shake of her body, as if to say 'come on, I haven't got all day.'

At that point a sturdy blonde stepped forwards. He gave his teacher a comfortable nod and walked over to the dragon, proceeding to climb aboard, seemingly without watching what he was doing.

He casually checked over the gear to make sure it was all in order, gave the rest of them a thumbs up, and, to general laughter among them, shouted something along the lines of 'giddy up' to his mount – flexing his legs back and forth.

While it was doubtful that the dragon could feel his movements, there was no doubt that it had heard him. Giselle rumbled disgustedly, turned around and, without as much as a warning, fell from sight.

A cry came drifting up in their wake. 'Woaaaaah!'

Tam made a small annotation in his diom. One down, twenty or so to go. Not that he was expecting many to fail this test, not in this group. No, not this lot. There *were* one or two who didn't look all that happy about trusting someone *else* to do the flying around though.

Despite the differences in personalities, in abilities (not the least the ability to being able to stay focused) or even just general attitude to the world at large, over half of them did have *one* thing in common and it wasn't that they'd all signed up to the Academy either. The rest of them had, according to his notes, previous experience from the right perspective, for one reason or another.

No, Tam didn't doubt for a moment that they'd pass. *His* job wasn't dealing with the worried and the anxious, the nervous or frightened-out-of-their-minds or even those deciding at the last moment that they'd pass this up after all.

What *he* had to worry about was keeping in check the very real possibility that these young rascals might get a little *too* enthusiastic. Despite all that, a few of them weren't looking terribly keen at the moment. Maybe that stern talking to earlier had actually made a difference?

As Giselle, who was now seen climbing up above the platform's main level and, by the looks of things, was giving her rider a guided, albeit silent, tour of the place's main features, the rest of them started looking around for the next dragon.

There weren't that many of them, students that was. Of course, if you counted the general student number against the general dragon number it was easy to see which came out on top. Maybe it wasn't strange that they'd have to wait a bit after all. Of course, when comparing dragons and humans, it wasn't numbers that counted...

So far so good, Tam thought. Whatever sigh of relief he had been about to breathe stuck in his throat though as, at speed, something shot over them, catching them all in the downdraft.

Looked like they might not have to wait so long after all.

Tam shaded his eyes and narrowed them as the dragon turned out of the sun. Oh drat, he thought. Not him. Anyone but him...

The dragon executed a complex stalled roll and landed heavily a bit further away, still moving. It slowed down into a brisk trot while coming towards them.

A trotting dragon covered an awful lot of ground ... and fast.

'Guys ... I don't think he's gonna stop...' someone called out, sending the group scattering, eager to get out of the way.

'My turn,' Jim cried out, already running towards the rapidly approaching red. Compared to the blue that had just departed, this one was several classes above her, both in size and weight and, judging from the way they moved, experience.

Without either of them slowing down, Jim grabbed on to the rope being trailed from the saddle and, using their opposing momentum, half swung, half climbed into the saddle far above.

With the ease of a trick rider performing their favourite stunt, there was only the briefest of heartbeats before a loud 'Yeaaaah!' echoed over them. The paler wings of the large dragon flexed and, having never actually come to a stop, it launched itself back into the air – following up with a barrel-roll the moment they were clear of the platform.

'Yahoooo!' the new rider cried out, exhilaration in his voice.

'Jim! I said *no* antics,' Tam shouted after the rapidly disappearing pair.

This was exactly what he was supposed to be here to prevent. Typical. Trust Bloodbringer to throw a spanner in the wheels. They should have named him "Fool" instead ... or "Bloody Stupid", yes, that'd suit him, Tam fumed. Those two must have been planning *that* little stunt for ages.

He turned stern eyes on the rest of them, who were clearly awed judging by their expressions.

'Did you see that?'

'Yeah ... awesome.'

'Think I could try that too?'

'Now, you all listen to me,' Tam growled at them from between gritted teeth. 'Anyone else try a stunt like that and I'll have you all on X-duty for the next full month. Do you hear?'

'Yes, Sir,' came the somewhat unsynchronised answer from several throats. Scowling like that and even Tam looked fearsome.

'I'll deal with young Jim when we get back to the Academy.' Tam muttered something more, which was, thankfully, not picked up by any of those around him. He tapped his comm.

'Max, can you get someone up to keep an eye on Bloodbringer and Jim Walker?' he queried of the man normally in charge of the ACC.

Maximilian had drawn the short straw today and was, again, stuck inside the command-module they'd set up here to coordinate today's event and what-ever responses might need to be taken, up to and including, a full blown rescue.

'Bloodbringer and Jim Walker you say?' came Max's voice in his ear-piece. 'Wow. I don't envy you buddy. Ok, I'll see if I can get someone airborne to keep them out of any major trouble. Try not to monopolize all our resources today, Tam.'

'Thanks. I'll keep you updated on any further developments,' Tam assured the other man, at which point he gave his charges another withering glare.

'Ok. Have fun. I've got some trouble in group A brewing, so better go,' Max signed off.

Trouble? Tam frowned. Not the best news today. But then it wasn't exactly unexpected either. Group A was Damon's for today. Tam knew those students. He doubted that even Damon would be able to keep them all in line if they got all excited – and that was a lot more worrisome than what he had to deal with, with this lot.

Maybe he shouldn't complain so much over it after all?

Max had been right. There *was* trouble on the horizon. It wasn't coming in on the clouds as you might have expected. However, it wasn't coming from an entirely unexpected or unseen source either.

This was because over in quadrant A, Kay was having a loud, and increasingly threatening, argument with the green dragon that had been his choice. Not his choice per se – they'd been assigned different dragons by the drawing of lots. He'd just not had much luck drawing them.

That was the view of his fellow students. In Kay's eyes, the appearance of the green was nothing short of an insult, and he'd wasted no time in telling everyone just what he thought about it.

The previous one to come by had been an impressive looking bronze and Kay was less than pleased when finding, as his turn came, a green dragon with perforated wing-membranes and a tuft at the end of its tail.

It looked like an oversized housecat with its fur shaved off and a dye job, he complained, loudly.

Now his face was only inches from that of the dragon's and he was bellowing at the top of his lungs. The dragon in turn was making hissing sounds, its teeth beginning to show under its curled lip.

While personality didn't exactly match the colour of a dragon's hide, it was true that, in general terms, bronzes tended to be reliable and slow to anger. Greens on the other hand, usually being the smallest ones around, were often much more volatile, possibly because their size allowed it.

Neither of them cared much for insults.

The rest of the students had retreated, not wishing to get involved. Their teacher would have put a stop to it in an instant, they were sure of it. But their teacher wasn't there. He'd had to attend to *another* little emergency and, for the time being, they'd been left on their own until the next dragon arrived or Damon returned.

They weren't nearly as excited as they'd been only twenty minutes ago. Those were an awful lot of teeth. Dragons weren't allowed to eat people, were they?

Even if Damon wasn't there, the "argument" was attracting quite a bit of attention though.

The sky above them was slowly filling with dragons and their makeshift riders. Some were more equipped than others for today's little test. Several made a dip in towards them to find out what all the noise was about. That was more likely to be curiosity on behalf of the dragons than the student riders though, who probably wouldn't be able to hear it up there.

One or two of the shapes hovered much closer. Those were the real riders. They didn't look like they were intending to interfere, for the moment. Maybe they were happy to let whatever might happen, well … happen?

In the end, it only stopped as Van Velden, having come back at a run, physically manhandled the still swearing Kay away, back towards where he'd come from. Telling the rest of them, his voice like ice – that if there were any more like that they'd end up regretting it. He didn't need to say *how* they'd end up regretting it. His eyes alone carried enough suggestions.

The green dragon, disgruntled by the turn of events, made a few vicious remarks (at least that's what they all guessed the sounds were anyway, it wasn't as if they spoke dragon) and, after having taken a few minutes to settle down, reluctantly allowed the next student with their number to climb aboard. Shaking themselves unexpectedly, the student yelped in surprise.

The nerve of some…

They pair took off, making an elegant glide and soon settling into a wide spiral pattern, moving ever downwards.

Damon soon returned after that. There was no sign of Kay and under Van Velden's watchful eyes, the rest of them resolved not to draw his ire.

They were content with getting on with what the day held for them. There were far bigger things to worry about other than a dragon or two it seemed.

And worry they did.

They weren't the only ones. If anything, they were worrying very little, in comparison.

In what had been designated as C quadrant for today, being by far the largest area assigned, there had been a further division into smaller sections. Each of those sections was watched over by an attending teacher and a helper.

Among them, a number of dragons were coming and going, creating a much busier environment than that enjoyed by either A or B group.

It also meant that there was a lot more that could go wrong. One thing the teachers couldn't do; they couldn't grow eyes in the back of their heads.

There was a great deal more variety in how people were reacting to what was happening and what was being asked of them here. That was to be expected, seeing how C group contained the greatest variety of people and the ones least likely to be intimidated in any way by today had already been separated out into the two different, smaller, groupings.

As a result, it also meant that C quadrant was currently playing home to quite a bit of drama.

Everything from distraught tears and fainting spells wobbled their way through the masses. There were outright refusals to let go of the nearest support beam, in places replaced by screams of terror as a student's hold on a saddle had to be pried loose, them being too frightened to move. Everywhere tantrums were running wild.

They were about the only things that were. Because of all that both teachers and helpers were far busier than either Tam or Damon. It also meant they couldn't have eyes everywhere.

That was going to be a drawback.

* * *

It was a much more relaxed atmosphere down on the ground.

Well, ok, for *some* people it was relaxed – for others, maybe not so much. Dayu was firmly in the first set. In fact, you would have had to be either a rock (in which case you probably hadn't noticed you were flying on a dragon in the first place) or possibly Jim Walker (in which case you had probably not bothered landing yet) to be less affected.

While some of his friends were busy being patched up, Dayu was busy putting as large a dent in the field kitchen's supplies as possible.

'Ah, this is great,' Dayu said and tore off another piece of grilled fowl covered in some sticky kind of sauce with his teeth and brandished the short wooden stick they were skewered on.

'You guys *got* to try this!' he insisted. 'It's *really* good.'

'Ugh … don't mention … food …'

'Even the thought makes me sick…' Elon complained, hands clasped over his stomach.

'This whole place smells like a kitchen,' another one griped.

'I don't feel so good…'

'Are you kidding me,' Teran countered weakly. 'I just want to die. Can someone kill me … pleaaaase,' he whimpered.

As can probably be surmised, none of them were standing up. Of course, they weren't exactly sitting down either. It was more like a general lounging with none of the positive things attached.

There was a whole group of them in various poses, none of them comfortable, close to the entrance of the medic's tent, where they'd managed to stagger once they'd gotten off their respective dragons in the landing area.

The ones who didn't even manage that were carried here. Those were the ones taking priority inside, hence why the small group was still here, outside.

'Where's that pretty nurse? I need some medicine…'

'If you can still chase girls, you must be feeling better,' Reena chuckled, then immediately wished she hadn't, the bile rising in her throat. That had been some ride.

'Comff ouff ueys…' Dayu swallowed hurriedly, his speech once more understandable. 'Look on the bright side – did you all pass the test?' he asked innocently.

'We're down here, aren't we?' several of them growled, but not too loudly. That took too much effort.

'Just go away, Dayu. Just. Go. Away. Have some sympathy for those who *don't* have your iron constitution.'

Dayu shrugged. It was all the same to him. 'Fine. Don't blame me if they run out before you get to taste some…'

'Get lost!'

Too exhausted to even move, none of them really felt safe enough on their feet to throw something at him, or to try and chase him away. Right now they'd probably miss anyway. Were arms supposed to feel like jello-on-a-stick? Maybe that was legs. How many did they have now? Several groans circled the small gathering.

So that was what it was like to ride a dragon was it, several of them thought (when they felt coherent enough to string two thoughts together). Seemed like a highly overrated activity now that they were safely back down on *Terra Firma*.

Maybe it got better once you got used to it?

What if it got *worse*?

Not everyone needed to visit the small tent complete with camp beds inside for those who'd *really* taken to the whole thing poorly (hence why it was a *small* tent). The one that was currently the outpost for the site's reining doctor and their staff was adequate for the numbers they were expecting.

While they *were* getting a steady stream of patients, with everything from swelling globes, loss of hearing, mild (and not so mild) anxiety and goodness knew how many cases of nausea (of varying strength) the majority could be treated easily enough and were soon up and sent to join their successful fellow landed students in the much larger tent that made up the mess-hall or in simply lounging about.

It was quite warm and the sun was very pleasant. A good time for relaxing in other words. And relaxing was being done; once they'd gotten the right number of feet and their eyes stopped dancing in front of their noses.

Some of the smells from the medical tent weren't altogether conducive for a healthy appetite. From the large tent on the other hand there drifted all sorts of things; snatches of laughter. Music. Broken bits of conversation (though that mostly came across as a deep background humm) and scents ... smells even, of different foodstuffs.

And such smells they were. Waterfowls and fish. Vegetables. Cuts of meat of different types and not just prepared in one single way either. Sauces that made you want to dive in and swim around in them. Cakes with frosting on them so fine that it was like a glittering silent night.

It was enough to make even the most sated person salivate in anticipation – and then cry because they couldn't eat any more.

For those experiencing a more nauseating time now that they were back on the ground, it was War, Pestilence and Famine all reversed and rolled into one, stalking between them. Not quite invisible, but nothing they could really touch either. Even the tiniest whiff of cooking was enough to send weaker tummies reeling.

Dayu had a point though, they had to concede that, even if they did so grudgingly. By managing to ride (or at least cling on desperately to) a dragon from the station to the ground they'd all passed First Flight. It wasn't exactly complicated. Difficult yes, but complicated, no.

Whoever had designed the test (not that it had needed much in that department either) had obviously not known what they were doing, the students felt.

It was a good thing that the test didn't say anything about the *manner* in which the ride was conducted. It certainly said nothing about the manner in which the rider parted company with said dragon at the end of the journey being of any relevance whatsoever; probably for a good reason. If it had, more than just a few would not have passed at all.

As it was however, the only way to fail was to reach the ground through any other means than dragonback.

No amount of fainting or crying, parachuting or even breaking open your skull and pleading leniency would help you. Not here. Not now. You moved from Tendril (in the air) to the temporary camp (on the ground) or you failed the test, end of story. No arguments permitted. No appeals.

There'd be plenty of those that did fail, the sorry looking group thought. But at least *they* wouldn't be among them. If quitting sounded like a good option right about now – well, at least they'd be able to do it with their heads held high.

As it was, any decision of that nature was better left for tomorrow, when they, hopefully, felt a bit better and the memory of the experience had dulled down somewhat.

In the meantime – did those people over there *have* to be so loud?

* * *

'Whaaaaah! I don't wanna! I don wanna!' wailed the boy from the saddle of the brown dragon. His face all screwed up, he was bawling at the top of his lungs. 'Make it stoooop. I wanna go hooome!'

The dragon, who'd just been about to leap over the edge, carefully back-tracked a few steps, slowly.

Safely away from the border of the station it lay down, as to make it easier for the teacher and helpers who converged on it. They needed to physically pry the young man's white knuckled fingers loose because no matter how hard he cried about wanting to go home, he wasn't letting go of the saddle in a hurry.

How many did that make already? Amelina wiped her eyes and tried again. Actually, now that she thought about it, she'd lost count – besides, she only had to keep an eye on this patch. She had no idea how the other parts of C group were doing. Probably about the same, Lady Gray figured. It sure was keeping them busy. What a day...

A little further away, Lady Gray could see Saranon Duchamp breaking up a fight that had started out between two other young men. One was already sporting a bloody lip.

Foolish child, she thought. Of course "child" was anyone today, no matter what their age. It wasn't the years she always said, it was the actions that mattered. And today those actions were, in part, a sorry sight to behold.

'He called me a...' one of the two complained loudly.

'That's enough!' Saranon's stern voice stopped any further protests. 'Both of you. Take yourselves off and report back to the shuttle!'

'What?' the second of the two's eyes widened in shock. 'But... But...'

'Now!' their teacher snapped, his tone allowing for no further objections.

As the two of them trudged off to the hangar where the shuttle had been parked, still bickering, Saranon took a deep breath and looked about. He seemed to be needing eyes in the back of his head with this lot. How many times today had that thought occurred to him? Too many.

Clarissiia didn't seem to have as many problems from the looks of things, he thought. He'd never quite figured out why, but a lot of the students, in fact a lot of people in general, seemed to worry more about crossing the stern looking woman far more than they did some of the more impressive looking teachers.

Apparently it wasn't a skill that could be taught – though not from lack of trying on his part. He could be intimidating easily enough, but to do what she did? No, he'd have to go back right to the start and become a whole different person for that. Too much hassle for something so simple really.

'Tight enough for you?' Clarissiia asked the student she was supervising, adjusting the safety straps on the harness.

Robin Sternmasser nodded. It was an affirmative. She was ready. Almost there. Only another minute or so to go.

She swallowed the lump in her throat. 'Thank you, Sir,' Robin squeaked, her voice pushed into a much higher register than usual.

'Don't worry about it,' Clarissiia advised curtly. 'You'll do fine. Try not to overthink it.'

'Right.' The girl nodded again, holding on tightly as the dragon beneath her walked sedately over to the launch area.

She'd never admit, never, ever, just how scared she was when they plummeted into the blue nothingness beyond.

Gaile watched everything happen around her in a kind of a daze. There were plenty of hysterics out there, but she'd long since passed through the lands of hysteria and was currently jogging along on paths in a world that consisted of either nothing at all or lots and lots of fogs. Occasionally shapes rose out of it, but almost as quickly, they disappeared again.

She couldn't say she was looking forward to this. It was as close to a "do or die" moment she'd come since leaving home and it was taking a fair amount of willpower to not just turn and run. A very tempting thought, except that wouldn't work. Not if she wanted to be a rider.

That was a thought though. Had anyone actually become a rider after failing something like First Flight? Gaile couldn't say for sure. Somehow she doubted it, the way everyone went on about how you had to pass it, but dragons sometimes had the strangest reasons for choosing someone as their partner. Passing a stupid test … that somehow didn't seem to qualify.

But this day had been looming ever closer, as she'd known it would ever since before she'd entered the Academy.

Most DRC's held their First Flights in roughly similar manners; the style and location might vary, but the general approach to it never did.

It was pass or fail. Those were the only options. She knew that. The world might not be black and white, but some parts, like the one right here, were so just as much as they'd been back home.

How often hadn't she heard her older siblings talk about it? Brag about it?

Oh, how proud they were of being part of the "original" DRC – the very first. The Research Centre where the dragons of the bygone era of the planet's history had, in some part, been brought back.

What would they say if they knew she'd joined up here? On this far off "frontier" world? They'd probably laugh and think whomever told them were pulling their leg. *She*'d never join a DRC, they'd say. She always avoided it … always. Sister is such a baby, they'd say … such a scaredy-cat.

Why would she want to join the DragonCorps anyway? To become a rider? Don't be ridiculous…

Well, what did they expect? No one *likes* being pushed out of a nice and safe seat at several thousand feet without a parachute, to only be caught mere meters from the ground? And for what? To test a principle? To prove a point? Was it any wonder she hated … truly *hated*, heights?

By now, her younger brother and sister were probably wanting to join up as well, if they hadn't already. They weren't exactly children and they'd been getting the inside track all their lives.

No, Gaile might not know exactly "why" she'd chosen to enter the DragonCorps (or to try out for it anyway) after having come all this way to get away from them; dragons, riders, pretentious fools and stuffy old professors – but she was determined to manage, somehow.

Right now, that involved controlling her chattering teeth enough *not* to bite off her tongue and exercise enough control over her limbs to walk over and climb into the saddle of the waiting dragon, even when they were shaking and wanted to give out beneath her.

Even if she did need several tries and a bit of help to get aboard and strapped in, she finally did manage, all while staring straight ahead with unseeing eyes.

Gaile swallowed loudly, eyes widened in fear.

No more running, she told herself sternly. It was a good thing she didn't try to say it out loud. At the moment, croaking might have been too much for her.

The dragon did as dragons in this position were wont to do. It took off into the air, sending them into a dive with its wings extended.

By then, Gaile was already screaming at the top of her lungs.

But, no matter how much you scream – sooner or later you will run out of air. Or your vocal cords will cave in. It's also possible that you'll cease to have something to scream about. In Gaile's case, it lent more towards the first.

Eyes screwed shut as if they'd been painted with glue, she whimpered and tried to control her stomach. It told her that they were moving downwards – it was also mentioning that it would very much like to stop doing so, and threatened to move upwards on its own if its demands weren't met and by the way … did you remember what you had for breakfast this morning?

The dragon was descending in a lazy spiral. It was used to this and it wasn't necessarily going anywhere in a hurry. It was a pretty day and there wasn't a set schedule for any of this. They'd simply keep going until they'd run out of students, one way or another.

While it was obvious that this passenger was a less than happy flier, this wasn't supposed to just be a straight station to ground kind of thing. As they said, anyone could ride a dragon if all it was doing was "standing still" in the air.

The screams did grate on the ears though – and there were a lot of them in the air right now, some closer than others. They were just thinking about the best way forwards when another shadow appeared.

The green dragon's eyes snapped wide open, saw what was "approaching" and tried to veer out of the way.

For a moment, riders and dragons became but one tangled mess. Arms tried to fend off claws. Tails got entwined in legs and the four bodies joined together in a complaining orchestra of wails, gratings and roars.

For one fleeting moment Gaile stared straight into the eyes of the other terrified rider.

Some cold, detached part of her mind noted that they had a huge gash running across their ribs. The blood splattered into her wide open eyes, burning them.

Unable to see and not familiar enough with the equipment (to say nothing about not being in a state of having to been able to use it even if she had known how) all she could to was to hold on and make herself as small a target as possible and hope she didn't get crushed.

Both dragons struggled frantically to untangle themselves, and their equipment, as they fell.

A dragon without air support was even less aerodynamic than the proverbial rock. At least the rock was smoothed for minimum wind resistance.

But whereas the rock would have no knowledge of what would happen once it stopped falling, the dragons and their passengers had no such luxury.

A sound of leather creaking reached Gaile's ears. A second later and it became a snap. The dragon was tearing apart the harness, the stitched areas around the buckles the first to go.

Then, suddenly, the saddle came free, safety cables and all. Unfortunately, that meant that while Gaile was still safely fastened to the saddle, the saddle was no longer securely attached to the dragon.

It skidded, dragging her along with it. Somewhere there was another bump as something knocked into her.

The last thing she could remember was falling, her head a splitting pain. The sky surrounding them was so blue … so very, very blue…

* * *

The first thing Gaile became aware of as she drifting upwards involved people talking. It wasn't making much sense. Their voices sounded as if coming from far away. Very far away. They were more like whispers than voices, ghosts of voices and once she lapsed back into oblivion, she promptly forgot all about it.

Several hours later and the voices were back.

This time Gaile didn't notice them at all. She had drifted off into the ether of nothingness. If she had heard them, they probably wouldn't have inspired a great deal of confidence about placing her immediate future in their hands.

'Watch out!'

The abrupt shout was followed by the sound of lots of small things spilling out across a hard surface, scattering over a wide area right after the "going" of someone walking into something unstable.

'Now look at what you've done. They're all mixed up.'

'Sorry.'

'There's nothing else for it then. We'll have to test them one by one for frequency.'

'That's going to take ages…'

'You should have watched where you were going then. And pick up the other things you knocked off the shelf while you are at it.'

A bit of collecting and dusting off later, not to mention a lot of holding things up to the light and checking them against various charts, and the person that had dropped the things in the first place finally made their progress report – if you could call it that.

'This one – this one's got a perfect tonal match. And look, it's all shiny and clear. Beautiful crystal. I've never seen one in such good condition. Almost a shame to use it for something so mundane.'

'Hmm. You usually don't see this quality outside of D-comms. Hmm … it's a good match,' the second voice was back. 'Let's use this one. If it was good enough quality to be a D-comm then it wouldn't have been in that box.'

'True. It is pretty though. Just look at how it catches the light – almost like what a diamond would look like if lit from within…'

The recollections of those conversations conducted just beyond the brink of her consciousness would remain, though the words were jumbled up and the voices too – so that each time she managed to swim close enough to the surface, the old ones would fade away into something that could neither be called memory nor forgotteness. It was more like the recollection of a memory, or maybe of a dream, than actual memory. Just as confusing as well.

By the time Gaile was well enough, and conscious enough, to move around on her own again (her ears and balance having had trouble adjusting to whatever they'd needed to do to ensure they could function properly) several weeks had already passed by.

It hadn't been easy. Whatever else Gaile was, patient wasn't it, and for all that time she had no choice. Did anyone realize how difficult it was to do something as simple as walk down a straight line on the floor when your head was spinning and the world was trying to turn upside down the moment you did anything more exciting than sit up slowly?

Finally, however, she managed to adjust. Maybe not completely, but enough to do the rest of it on her own, back with everyone else. Whatever else happened during that time, she was now several weeks behind everyone else still participating in the course.

The passage of time had had another effect as well. This one not personal to her. When Gaile once more re-joined her classes, there were plenty of faces missing – or there would have been, had she actually gotten around to having memorized them in the first place.

There *were* however a lot more room in the lecture theatres and – much to her pleasure, while she'd been, effectively, out for count, the students that remained had been moved out of the barracks and into a more dorm like setting. They now had their own space, and, more importantly, their own door.

It was a very tiny space, but it was *her* tiny space and Gaile definitely preferred private to public.

Trouble in Paradise

"Can I borrow this?" Jim heard someone say.

Something went swooshing past his eyes as Drak waved something in Jim's face. Jim, in turn, batted it away, *his* eyes glued to the game on the table. He didn't appreciate the distraction. Now he'd lost count...

'Sure...' he said, 'but bring it back, you hear?'

'Sure, sure,' Drak was all affirmation.

That in itself should have tipped Jim off. Drak was definitely not the type to act like that, quite the opposite in fact.

As it turned out, he'd wish he *had* been paying a bit more attention to what his friend was asking and less to what he was going to do with his next game piece.

Drak hadn't expected quite such an easy victory. As a result, a big grin was plastered over his face as he headed out, his price grasped firmly. Looked like picking the middle of the game had been the right choice after all.

The game itself seemed to consist of moving small, intricately carved, figurines around a multileveled board with a small castle at the top one as far as he could tell. He certainly didn't have any interest in it. Such things were for losers.

Actually, he wasn't sure why Jim did? It wasn't like the guy was known to be able to sit still and concentrate for any longer periods of time, like, say, thirty seconds or so.

That had been a surprise, finding out that Jim liked to play these things. Usually he couldn't sit still long enough to pay attention, but for these, he could stare at them for hours while working out the best strategy. Apparently their movement in his mind was enough to keep him occupied.

Drak did feel a little bad about having so deviously waited until now to ask, but he figured nothing bad could come of it and he did want to go have some fun on his own. All this sitting around others was ok, but too much of it still bored him. He felt better when he had some elbow room. It would have been even better than that, if there had been someone around to pummel.

'What did anyone expect anyway?' he muttered to himself.

That was quite a change from when he'd first come here. Drak had, from an early age, easily fallen into the type that used their size to get what they wanted and weren't shy about it either.

Unlike Kay, he'd quickly realized that trying to out-argue a dragon was not the best idea if you wanted to continue being in the best of health. Besides … those teeth made him nervous.

"It's not the size," as Cole had said, "it's the bit they're attached to."

'And bloody right he is too,' Drak nodded to himself.

The thing they were attached to, in this case, happened to be dragons. Big, big dragons. It was one thing to bully someone who ran away from you. It was a whole different experience when the scrawny little runt whose nose you'd been trying to bash in suddenly outweighed you be several tons.

Now he clutched his price tightly to his chest (well, the central section of it anyway) and set off out of the lounge. What he had in mind couldn't be accomplished in here – not without causing a commotion (which could have been fun, if he'd been in the mood) the space being somewhat confined. He had to go somewhere else. But it was going to be a good day, he just knew it.

A few hours later and Drak wasn't quite as confident about that earlier elation he'd been feeling.

He wasn't sure *where* things had gone wrong, but they had. One moment he was fiddling with the controls and the next he was up to his ears in spare parts. Well, not really. But it felt like it.

It had been a good few hours though, he thought. Now it was time to pay the piper. Oh, how he'd always hated that saying. Stupid it was. He sat down heavily.

Once the game was over and the party was breaking up, Jim went looking for his friend. Well, *half* of him had gone looking for his friend. The other half had gone to check to make sure his treasure was being well cared for.

He found him … no, it, lurking around the back entrance way. Neither of them were looking particularly happy, but Dark at the very least still had all his limbs attached.

'You said "borrow" not "break"!' Jim shouted at Drak.

While not quite yelling at the top of his lungs, which had the habit of forcing his voice into a ridiculous (in his mind) squeak, he nevertheless had no trouble getting the point that he was not happy, across.

'I know, I know. I don't know what happened. Really, I don't,' Drak cowered (a rare sight if there ever was one). 'It just went from blue skies to cloudy in no time at all. And then it sort of just … fell down.'

'Clouds? What clouds?' Jim Walker growled suspiciously. 'We don't get clouds here at daytime – well known fact.'

The smaller of the two leant closer. It would have looked imposing if their roles had been reversed. As it was, he now had to crane his neck upwards to see Drak's face. Even so, he waved a finger under the larger boy's nose.

'You're just making that up,' Jim accused.

'No, seriously – there were clouds. Lots and lots of clouds. They just sort of bubbled up and then … well...' Drak shrugged, defeated. 'Then it sort of just fell down.'

'So where are they now?' Jim wanted to know.

There certainly weren't any around where the two of them were standing. The evening sun was just getting in its last bouts of sunshine and the sky was, if no longer entirely clear blue, definitely not containing any clouds, of any colour.

'My flier! My precious flier" Ruined!'

'Yes, Jim.'

Drak looked apologetic and not just a little bit embarrassed. He didn't like disappointing his friend, and boy did Jim look mad. He hadn't realized the guy was *that* attached to the model.

Breaking things on purpose was one thing. Breaking things when he hadn't meant too, at all, was another thing entirely. It looked like this one was going to get him in trouble. Maybe just a touch more trouble than he'd expected when the whole thing had fallen apart on him....

The higher ups he could deal with. Though, at this place, they did have a knack for choosing just the type of punishment that made you seriously think about doing something again … or at least getting caught doing it again. It was rarely the same and had only one thing in common – whatever it was, you did *not* want to experience it twice.

And so, at the Academy, even Drak had decided to not cause undue trouble – not unless he really thought it was worth it. Sometimes he ended up in trouble for just being him, but that was something else.

Getting into trouble with people he considered friends? Well, that was a whole different kettle of squid, or whatever the saying was. Maybe it was fish he was thinking of? Not that anyone in their right mind wanted to put fish in a kettle … did they? Anyway, he didn't like it. The troubling friends that was, not the fish in the kettle … actually, he didn't care for that either…

Most of the time that wasn't a problem. The reason was simple enough; he didn't *have* many friends. Right now however, it was looming…

He hung his head. 'Well … they went away again,' he said unhappily. It sounded stupid, even to his own ears.

'You know what? I think you owe me a new model glider, that's what I think,' Jim said.

'Yes, Jim. Sorry. I didn't mean to lose it, honest.'

Jim, in turn, shook his head and stuck his hands back into his pockets – which had the effect of making the smaller guy look a lot less menacing. It was amazing what predatory radiance could be discerned from someone so small … but maybe that was one area where size really didn't matter.

'Alright. Alright. Enough with the puppy eyes. Just get me a new one, ok? And pick up what's left of this one,' Jim told Drak.

'Right. Sure. Right away,' Drak nodded agreeably and scooped up the bits and pieces he'd been able to salvage. Then he hesitated. 'Would it be alright if it was at the end of the month? They're on back order…'

So, he'd checked already had he? Jim rolled his eyes at him, barely managing to resist the urge to bang his head against the outer wall of the DRC by which they stood.

Why? Why, of all people, did he get saddled with a best friend like this? Was there some sort of fatalistic divination involved? Would he look back at these years and laugh at them? Remember them with fondness? Or just plainly see them as the reason to why his hair had been torn out by the roots?

He sighed again as he ushered Drak back in from the quickly developing chill as night fell.

Maybe he was being punished? That'd be simple enough. Bloody vindictive universe if so though. He couldn't recall having done anything to deserve *that*. Unless, of course, the universe was getting into the business of pre-punishment? Smite today, cause tomorrow?

There were a lot of things you could say about Jim Walker – and by now a fair few of them were being said by his classmates as a regular occurrence. But it couldn't be denied that he *was* a bit of an oddball. There was no description that fitted him better really.

Quite small for his age, Jim had boundless energy and equal amount of trouble sitting still in class. He was always moving; if it wasn't a foot tapping or a finger (because he had to stay still) then the whole of him was bouncing around the place not unlike a mad ping-pong ball that had just won the jackpot. Maybe it was because of that, but he had a lot better hand to eye coordination than a lot of the others, whether they were in first year or part of the staff.

Despite that he'd never been much of a sports type, or so Drak figured. You sure couldn't get him to join up willingly when the more strenuous practices came about. The guy was quite the intellectual, when he actually could be guided onto a subject and convinced to offer his opinion.

Shaking his head at the whole thing, Jim dragged Drak back with him, hoping that a quiet game would keep his friend out of mischief.

'Raise you two,' Jim offered back in the comfort of his armchair.

'Two for me too,' Dayu nodded, one eye on the game and another one on his own pieces.

'No! You can't do that!' came the wail from the player to his right. Akia looked disappointed, giving Jim a small glare. She hadn't seen that one coming.

Jim, well, he seemed quite happy about it. He was also, Drak mused, equally happy to unite his fondness of reading together with his inability to sit still … usually without seeming to pay too much attention to either.

Drak wasn't exactly the slow and stoic type himself – though when standing next to the super-energised Jim that was certainly how he came across, along with much of the student body.

Drak wasn't sure he cared for the comparison even so. But the two of them had been friends for some time now, as unlikely as the association might seem at first glance. They'd struck up a casual conversation during the third week after enrolment. If pressed, he could no longer remember what they'd talked about or why'd they'd been talking in the first place. It wasn't like they actually had anything in common, not back then. But that hardly mattered.

Well actually, maybe "having a small row" would better describe it, as long as you left out the more physical aspects, after a disagreement over the bunk assignments at the first student shift.

In hindsight, Dark thought it to have been quite the foolish thing to have argued over in the first place, but he'd wanted the top bunk and he'd been used to people not arguing with him.

In this place he'd discovered that, no matter what, there was always someone bigger than you. Dragons didn't care much for you trying to bully them and, when out in the open, you did not want to find yourself suddenly running like mad for the nearest doorway with a snarling beast tearing after you.

The rules said that they weren't allowed to hurt you. As Drak had discovered, "hurt" could be a very subjective term … especially after finding himself on the opposite end of it.

Having Jim around had changed that – in more ways than one. He buzzed around his larger companion not unlike an overprotective tugboat around a starliner coming into berth – defusing a situation here, soothing ruffled feathers there and generally getting the two of them into a whole different set of troubles than the ones Drak had been used to; ones that, mostly, didn't involve the risk of getting their flesh stripped from their bones, except by accident.

He might not look it, but it was becoming more and more evident that Jim was a welcome guide through the reefs of socialness for his more hot-tempered companion.

And Drak had begun to change as well – not that he would, ever, admit to doing so.

Long after nightfall had … well … fallen, some students still weren't asleep. That wasn't all that unusual, but some of them weren't even in their rooms.

In Gaile's case she'd made a little side trip on her way back from the kitchens. Of course, going to the kitchens in the middle of the night was a side trip all on its own…

'I don't suppose you intend to show yourself?' Gaile asked, shaking the small bucket she was holding on to.

The bucket's contents rustled invitingly. It was the kind of noise that was fine to hear up close when the lights were on, but you definitely didn't want to catch it somewhere dark and damp and forbidding.

Even in the semi darkness, the gloom of the night, she stared up among the branches above her, wondering if it was even possible to catch a glimpse of something in this light, or lack thereof. A sign of movement perhaps?

Not that she really expected there to be any. She'd already been in here three times during equally many days as her little friend had chosen to disappear – *again*! Goodness alone knew what the Hive folk thought of her by now.

While the Hive was a pleasant enough escape from the harsh environment outside the walls, most people contended themselves with the few paths there were, mostly staying close to the large pond just beyond the entryway. If you were looking for something that couldn't be found there, you automatically ended up wandering around in places where *they* didn't.

Coming in at night once before hadn't helped either. At least, it hadn't helped then. Gaile was hoping that tonight she'd have better luck.

Where *was* that infernal little beast?

Some rustling in the leaves above and Gaile glanced up, holding her breath. After several minutes and still nothing, the young woman shook her head. Her shoulders sagged defeatedly.

Clenching her teeth, she figured she'd give this whole idea one more try then she might as well admit defeat and figure herself for being back on the list for "persona non grata" among the dragonlings.

'Here boy…' she called. 'Heeeere Siilber…'

Her voice was muffled and low. That was less so for not wanting to raise it at this hour than for worrying about drawing the attention of something out there, in the darkness. Who knew what might be hiding in the shadows?

While still on a path, this one had wound far into the "forest" and here it was distinctly spooky – especially in her current frame of mind. Even so, her voice still managed to carry quite the long way among the trees in the stillness of the otherwise so quiet night. Not strange perhaps. There wasn't really anything out here to impede it apart from the occasional tree.

Gaile peered up among the shadows one last time, sighed, turned around, and nearly jumped out of her skin.

'Don't do that!' she scolded him once her heart had stopped trying to pound its way out through her ears.

Sitting not two feet before her was the silvery dragonling that could be mistaken for no other; the dragonling she had "rescued" from the Armoury quite some time ago.

He looked distinctly smug. The tip of his tail twitched even as he sat perfectly still.

The stars alone knew how he'd gotten there so quietly. She hadn't heard a sound, not a single sound – not even as much as a twig or the flap of a wing or even the passing of the wind.

Ok, maybe that should be; not heard a single sound *out of place*. That wasn't quite the same thing. Although Gaile wasn't prepared to argue the different right at the moment.

'Ok, looks like I've got a ninja dragon on my hands,' she chuckled, albeit a bit nervously.

Gaile dipped a hand into the bucket and brought out a small handful of its content. 'See…' she held out the hand imploringly. 'Not nuts and bolts I'm afraid, just nuts. You'll have to crack them first.'

The dragonling remained stationary, showing no intention of wanting to move anytime soon.

It reminded her a little of a cat, the way he was sitting there almost haughtily; feet placed neatly in front and the long whip like tail circling the body on the ground.

When he finally deigned to move, and there could be no doubt about this in her mind, he did so in a manner that clearly stated, as if it had been chiselled into stone, "I'm moving because I choose to do so, not because I find you the least bit intriguing, human, and most certainly not because of *nuts*".

Indeed, the dragonling sniffed at the nuts in her hand almost disdainfully. He batted one experimentally with a paw and turned around, interest lost. Having finished exploring that avenue, he instead turned his attention to her pockets.

'Awwwrwoo?' he said.

There was a brief struggle between cloth, claws, heads and hands before Gaile managed to extract herself from the creature protesting at being shunted to the side.

'Enough … enough,' she told him.

Gaile pushed the inquisitive snout out of the way, trying to catch her breath between giggling too much. Her sides smarted. Those sides were ticklish; unfortunately in this case, they were the same sides where the pockets were located. Sitting down and having small dragonling feet trampling all over them had been quite the experience. Not one she cared to repeat though.

'Can't hide anything from you, can I?' Gaile shook her head, chuckling.

She felt inside one of the pockets that hadn't been torn open and, after some digging around through the general detritus that always seemed to accumulate at the bottom of the pockets of any garment that she wore (goodness knew where most of these things came from) she pulled out a small oblong wrapped in a rather garish orange paper. It rustled as she picked it apart.

By now the dragonling was making excited noises, giving every sign of just wanting to rush the thing and carry it off as his prize.

'Alright, alright, calm down,' Gaile chided him gently. 'You know Lady Gray said it's not good for you fellows to have too much of this stuff. They're not made for dragonlings you know.'

Gaile carefully peeled away the wrapping, having a feeling he'd devour it along with the sweet in his eagerness to get to the centre. Revealed below was a bright blue oblong, clashing horribly with the orange paper. It was kind of sticky to the touch and had been "liberated" from a bowl of sweets in the lounge.

Bending it sideways a couple of times it tore in two, very reluctantly on its part, and she offered a small piece to her winged friend. He snatched it eagerly and lay down with both front paws on it, tearing at it with sharp needle-like teeth. It created a long, drawn-out struggle, for the chew did not like to give up its cohesion, but, bit by bit, he munched at it vigorously.

Gaile had long since joined her friend on the ground, but avoided popping the remainder of the sweets in her own mouth. Its consistency was much like toffee, very stubborn toffee. In taste the two couldn't be further apart. It was a sweet that was much loved by children and dragonlings alike … and adults too.

Not that Gaile understood why. After she licked her now somewhat sticky fingers, she made a face. No. Definitely not one of her favourites. Yuck!

It was a while (not that you could really tell in here, with it not being daylight and all) that they sat there; one content, the other with their mind far away. It was at the moment a bit tricky to tell which was which.

The "toffee" must have excited the little thing, because, when no amount of begging made a second one materialize, he started bouncing around her happily.

When Gaile reached for the creature, it withdrew, just out of reach, before resuming his merry-go-round play.

'Alright – if that's the way you want it,' Gaile laughed. She pushed herself to her feet and made a quick dash for the dragonling.

The dragonling made an even quicker dash out of the way.

And so it went.

By and by, and without Gaile really realizing, though she was bound to have noticed on a subconscious level, the two of them went deeper and deeper into the Hive.

After a while, Gaile grew tired of walking in the dark. She stopped, slumping down against the trunk of a giant tree. Breathing hard, she leant backwards.

Blimey, if the little bugger wasn't fast. She should have named him "Lightning" instead of "Silber". Hmm … that had a nice ring to it actually. "Silber Lightning" … yes, she'd have to remember that one. There was bound to be something she could use it for.

When she'd eventually had gotten her breathing marginally back under control, Gaile looked around, wondering where she was. Judging from the sensation in her legs, they'd come quite a way from where they had been.

So, where were they now?

Not that she could see all that much. The open diom only offered so much light and here there was an awful lot of darkness, and no extra help, just large and very imposing, to say nothing about dark, trees.

'Silber?' Gaile called out somewhat hesitantly. 'Where did you go?'

Her only answer was the silence.

'Oh great,' Gaile muttered. 'Just bloody great. That's what I get for trying to be nice to you is it? You little cretin…'

Too annoyed at being, apparently, left here on her own to have gotten scared yet, Gaile removed the diom, switched it to flash mode and rolled it into a tube. It might not be quite as good as an ordinary flashlight, but it was plenty good as far as she was concerned, especially since the alternative was no light at all.

The narrow beam of light swept across the area. It showed what she already knew – she was surrounded by trees.

Wonderful, she thought. Why don't you tell me something I *don't* know?

Unfortunately there was no way of telling which were the trees she had already walked past and which were not. Gaile considered that quite the drawback.

The Hive might well be round, but it was also rather vast, and the trees had been placed as to mimic their natural setting as much as possible. It wasn't farfetched to believe that you could wander about in here for some time without finding the way, any of the ways, out.

This was a problem.

The second drawback was that while the diom worked excellently at telling you where you were in most of the DRC, in the Hive it was absolutely useless. Either they had excluded it from the system or they'd installed some sort of dampeners in here to block the signal.

That actually made sense, now that she thought about it. They did use the Hive for, among other things, testing people's sense of direction. That was another class that she'd failed. Of course, some people could get lost in a shoebox. Unfortunately for Gaile, she was one of them.

Ever since she'd taken that little tumble at First Flight it seemed she'd been having ever more difficulties with the practical classes. Gaile sighed. It wasn't that she wasn't trying, it was just … well … difficult, even more difficult than when she'd first come here. It was as if she felt tense about everything that involved trusting others.

Breathe in … deep … hold … hold … and release… She breathed out again. That was supposed to make you feel better, or at least more relaxed. Gaile couldn't say that it was working.

Thinking about what *had* happened, far more than about what had *almost* happened, never did make her feel anything other than concerned. Yes, concerned was a good word for it. See, no mention of anxiety at all.

Going back to the problem at hand, the final drawback was that they'd apparently left the path behind them some time ago. She'd been having too much fun to notice. Gaile cursed silently at herself. How unusually stupid, even for her.

As she swept the light across again it caught a flash. She quickly moved it back, slower this time. And sure, there he sat, looking more than pleased with himself. Though how she could tell, Gaile wasn't sure. Maybe it was just an impression that he'd be preening himself for a job well done.

'You're just having the game of "hide n' seek" of a lifetime, aren't you,' Gaile complained to him. 'Would you mind not having it with me?'

Silber stoically ignored her mutterings, his tail gently moving back and forth to the sound of her voice.

When he was certain that he had her full attention, at least, that's what it always looked like, Gaile would say afterwards, he turned around and walked, quite leisurely, away, turning his head to see if she was following.

Once they'd gotten going again, the silver dragonling took to the lowest branches, flittering from tree to tree, but still leading on. And this time, he kept within sight.

'Why have I got a feeling this *isn't* the way out?' Gaile mumbled quietly as she followed. Still, he did seem to know where he was going, so what could she do but to follow? It wasn't as if she had a better direction to go in.

It was some time after that that her ears started telling her they could hear things. More specifically, what they insisted was that they were hearing running water.

Not just any running water either. It wasn't like a tap or faucet that had been left on. This sounded more ... natural. Bubbly even.

Strange, Gaile thought. I wouldn't have thought we'd be anywhere near the pool, either of them. There were two; one near each of the two main entryways into the Hive.

Careful not to stumble, too much, on the forest floor, she pushed past the last of the ferns. A moment later the trees drew back and her sole beam of light illuminated a clearing. Well, part of a clearing. By now the sound was much closer, so she had obviously arrived at its source. So where was it?

Gaile let the beam play over the nearby features, happy to see anything but tree trunks for a change.

The clearing wasn't huge, relatively speaking, and, if you trained the light upwards, before it disappeared, you could just make out branches interlocking above. That explained why there wasn't any light coming down here, much, from the double skylight that made up the top of the dome and the glass ceiling above that belonging to the DRC itself. Whatever else, this place wasn't visible from above.

While not huge, the open area was large enough to contain a sizable, and by the looks of it quite deep, forest pool and a small brook that bubbled its way around happily. It also had a waterfall at least as tall as she was and then some at the farther end of the pool.

That must have been what I was hearing, she thought.

Once again there was no sign of Silber. But this time Gaile didn't mind so much. She was getting used to his odd comings and goings. Besides, the sound of moving water was a pleasant one and very soothing. It was a welcome relief in this parched landscape where she had not seen, heard or felt any other aside from the showers and the fountains.

She was used to having lots of water around, not to mention grass and bushes and trees. The few growing things that you got out here, tended to be dry and sad, in her eyes anyway.

Gaile settled down on the banks of the pool, dipping her toes into it. It was pleasantly warmish, once she'd removed her boots.

Well, she wasn't going to get back like this, but, and it was a very big but, there was nothing out here that was going to eat her. No leeches were going to fall down from above. No strange things burrowing up from below. No matter what her imagination was trying to tell her.

Under the soothing influence of the brook, Gaile made herself comfortable, stretched out and laid down, doing nothing but listening to the clear song of the water and stones, slowly drifting off into a deep sleep.

* * *

In the morning, Gaile had to find her own way back; her silvery friend once more having chosen to disappear. It was easier, since she could now actually see the paths (once she had stumbled about a bit).

Despite the amounts of sleep she'd gotten, the ground hadn't exactly been soft and she kept yawning her way through all the morning classes. She'd stifle one and be ambushed from behind by the next while she wasn't looking.

There was a strong pop in her ears. They'd been bothering her lately. Nothing much, just itching. The kind that no amount of swivelling your finger around could take care of. It was set deeper … always just out of reach. It had been doing that off and on ever since that little incident at First Flight.

Gaile wondered if she should go see someone about it. It probably had something to do with pressures and all that. She couldn't recall exactly what, but apparently all sorts of things could happen to the human body when you were flying around on dragonback. Maybe popping ears was the least of her trouble?

Her head was spinning. Gaile held on to the wall for a moment. Some unstable walking later and she found an empty seminar room and sank down against the interior wall in there, narrowly avoiding missing hitting the chairs set around the oval table.

Guess her sense of balance was off too. Great … as if she needed any more trouble.

She wasn't sure how long she'd been there, but after a while she started picking up muffled voices from the other side of the wall. It took a while before she could actually make out what they were saying.

'That is a bit harsh, don't you think?' someone said.

Damon put down his plate forcefully on the table, bits of cake flying everywhere. 'They need to learn that this isn't a play school Amy. I will not tolerate such behaviour in my class.'

'Yes, yes Damon, I'm sure we all agree but –'

'It doesn't seem to have worked anyway,' Duchamp said. 'The boy is still quite disruptive and appear to show no remorse for the trouble that he causes others through his behaviour.'

'Perhaps one day that will be something that we will all be grateful for,' Master Gern said thoughtfully.

'And a ball colliding with an ocean and a thousand new moons will be born,' Duchamp said scornfully. 'I'll believe that when I see it.'

'I still think that putting him, on his own, out on X-duty was a bit much,' Lady Gray repeated.

That in itself was unusual. Normally Lady Gray was one of the harsher taskmasters for those who drew her ire – but even she thought that Damon's choice of punishment was more than what she'd chosen to allocate herself.

Still, she wasn't altogether surprised, not nearly as much as some others. She knew all too well that the bronze dragon had a low tolerance for disruptive behaviour among riders, students and dragons alike. It could, at the worst times, get you and those that you worked with, killed.

'It didn't hurt him though…'

'It was likely that Kay would attempt to argue or bully his way out and even in this case he did attempt to do so. I believe that he has learnt one valuable lesson from this,' Damon stated. 'Attempting to bully a dragon that does not wish to be bullied is not a wise move and behaviour of said people during supervised interactions with students in a relatively safe environment is very different from working situations.'

'Still –'

'It was necessary,' Damon cut Master Gern off curtly. 'Incidentally, did you hear that they have re-instated the Windrider?"

'I do think I heard something about that, yes,' Duchamp agreed, glad to have the topic move away from anything student related.

'Excellent. That should prove interesting.'

The voices faded away as she drifted off.

An Underworld Adventure

Time passed, as time was wont to do, and it did so fairly quickly as they never seemed to have a moment's rest. At least that's what it felt like. According to the schedules, it certainly wasn't true … about having no time to rest that was.

They'd all settled into a fairly standard routine, which the teachers then seemed determined to uproot by scheduling odd practices at the strangest of times or taking their classes on trips and walks (often a hazard for those less fortunately blessed with balance).

Some things never changed though. In fact, it could easily be said they'd gotten worse. Like Gaile's reluctance to work with the dragons any time they were assigned one. Not to mention the dragonlings still refusing to go anywhere near her. Somehow it didn't help that there was one that did as he only appeared when there was one else around, not when you stood alone in the middle of a swirling pattern of tiny dragonlings refusing to settle down.

Still, this might be one step worse than even that. Ok, several steps worse. It certainly wasn't like she'd planned it. If she had, she would probably have considered opting out from the pain in her head, because it was with a very sore head that Gaile finally woke up.

As her eyes blinked away the faded images from her pleasant dream she was slowly becoming aware of an overwhelming need to sneeze. So, it was with a sniffle that she gathered herself together and got back to being aware of where she was.

Except she wasn't.

She turned her head this way, then that. Nope, still not a clue. Where the hell was she? Gaile scanned the area ahead of her but it looked like nothing than more of the same. Lifting her head from where she sat huddled against the wall she looked properly at her surroundings for the first time, even if it was through bleary and puffy eyes.

Not that she could see very much of it. What little there was of the emergency lighting still clinging to the ceiling gave a cold and diminished glow. Most of the elongated rectangles were dark, others broken, and one in the distance was flickering uncertainly, as if it couldn't quite decide if it was going to hang in there and do its job or if it was just going to take an early retirement, like so many of its brethren already had.

In company, and in the right frame of mind, it would merely have been annoying, that flickering light. Now, annoyance was the last thing she was feeling, except somewhere down towards the bottom of the barrel overflowing with emotions, none of them pleasant.

Looking around; the corridor itself was narrow and dark but had the same basic idea to it as the corridors she had walked through ever since she joined the DRC. It had all the hallmarks of not being "central" to the complex's network of connecting walkways, quite the opposite in fact.

Those areas tended to be airy and often featured windows on one side letting in plenty of light and were filled with people; light and people. Didn't look like this place had seen either in a long time.

This place reminded her more of a service corridor that time forgot than anything else. The type that has to be there in case someone needs to use them but which they never do. At least you never *saw* anyone using them. There might be a difference there somewhere, Gaile was willing to concede – though at the moment it was doubtful that she was giving it much thought.

All of those things were distinctly lacking here, she decided. Service corridors might look abandoned, but they were maintained. Their lights were functioning. They were dusted regularly. They certainly didn't have heaps of rubble in places or large holes poking into whatever was on the other side of the walls.

She rubbed at her eyes with her sleeve. They still stung. Sore and red they were and not for the best of reasons either. And on top of that, the air in here was irritating them even further, prickling them with the tiniest specks of dust imaginable.

She sneezed again.

Gaile wasn't sure where she was. None of this looked even remotely familiar. But that was only half her problem. The other half, and by far the more important, was that she had absolutely no idea of how to get back to where she *wanted* to be. At the moment that included any area in which you could find another living person to ask for directions.

This place didn't give the impression that it was much frequented by the living. By the dead, now that was a different matter. She huddled closer to the wall. Who knew what might be out there in the shadows?

The young woman sighed. It wasn't exactly like she'd chosen to be here now was it? Gaile wrinkled her nose at the dry yet murky scent of the abandoned and lost sign of civilization. No, she distinctly hadn't chosen to be here. She couldn't imagine anyone that would.

That wasn't a happy thought.

'Bah, who needs them anyway,' she finally muttered savagely, then jumped at the sound of her own voice in this empty space.

She wasn't the only one that did. Something scuttled off into deeper darkness than the mere shadows here provided. It disappeared into one of the many holes that abounded here.

Gaile froze. Every limb locked up, refusing to budge no matter how much she screamed at them. Her heart raced, her breath still sitting in her lungs like a lump of coal.

What if there was something out there? What if there was something out there that wanted to *eat* her? Something bigger than that small sound had suggested?

Big monsters with lots of teeth might not make it into these cramped spaces. But that left hordes, masses of little monsters with lots of legs, crawling out of broken walls, swarming over her body and dragging her off to whatever horrible fate awaited.

Were they here? Behind her? Behind the wall, waiting?

Gaile held her breath, trying not to make a sound. Several moments went by.

There were no more sounds like that. Whatever it had been it was gone. She eventually breathed out a sigh of relief.

It wasn't time to relax though. Every nerve in her body was tingling. Who knew what waited around a corner in this place? Where the heck was it anyway? The DRC might not be pristine, but she'd never have expected it to allow something like this around.

By now there was only the erratic 'drip, drip, drop' coming from somewhere further up ahead – or further back the way she'd come, what did she know? She'd been unconscious when they'd dumped her here. Bastards.

The only other sound in this place was the occasional ping and clank coming from overhead. Or, to be more precise, coming from the *pipes* that were running overhead.

There were several of them, almost all different sizes and they were all bolted to the ceiling. Well, they had all once *been* bolted to the ceiling anyway. Time had taken its toll and some of them had broken free of their manacles, with various degrees of success. They were, however, all equally dusty and equally rusty – unless stained brown was the colour of the year for these things.

There were some that were running along the walls as well, now that she was paying attention. Several of them were sporting gaping, if irregular, holes where the plates that had decorated the ceiling had given way and fallen, smashing the pipes in the process.

That explained the rubble at least.

Guess they haven't used this place in a while, eh? Gaile thought to herself.

Her mouth was too dry, and besides, judging by how her heart kept trying to force itself up her throat, she wasn't trusting herself to say it out loud. Not down here … wherever *here* was.

Her mind might insist that everything was fine and all she needed to do was to stay calm and sooner or later someone would come and find her; that was assuming that anyone actually noticed she was missing in the first place. Somehow Gaile doubted that. She *had* packed her bags and gotten ready to leave the Academy after all.

But that just meant she had to make her own way back. Nothing to it. Done more dangerous things. Her mind knew that. Her stomach and heart and nerves still saw monsters lurking in the dark.

And even if there weren't monsters, what else was there? Ending up here, some expedition coming along in fifty years' time for some renovations finding her mummified remains among the rest of the dust? Or worse, finding some scattered bones, their previous owner having been eaten by rats? No thanks. Gaile shuddered.

Telling herself she was being silly, her hand brushed against the cloth of the bag.

So, they'd left her that, had they? Well, wasn't that nice. To say nothing about a bit surprising. For a moment a ray of hope kindled inside her chest. She reached in for her diom.

Her fingers closed on nothing.

It wasn't there.

A further rummage around proved *conclusively* that it wasn't there, not even hiding at the bottom, below the scattered bits of paper and fluff you really didn't want to know where it had come from, and it was no point wishing for it to not be so. It was gone.

A sigh escaped her, much like her diom had.

Well, that was the most expected of today's events really. Foolish of her to think otherwise. Would they have gone and dumped her here and then left the easiest way out right in her pocket? Of course not.

Who were *they* anyway?

Pulling herself up on her feet, Gaile slung the strap diagonally across her chest, leaving both her hands free. So, essentially there *were* things she could do. Ok, so there were a lot of different alternative endings to each choice but it mostly boiled down to three (especially if you discarded all the ones that would most definitely lead to that pile of bones in the end).

So, what *were* the options here then?

Well, she could stay where she was. That's what they always told you to do, wasn't it? When you'd gotten lost that was. Stay put and don't stray.

On the other hand, she could explore in the direction to her right or she could explore in the direction on her left. Would thinking about it differently change anything? No, turning around didn't increase the number of options, it merely switched the directions. How quaint.

Not being sure which way she'd come in from, there didn't seem like "they" had left any evident clues behind. So, it was all going to be a question of chance.

Gaile took a shallow, half-hearted breath, tried to steady her already tense nerves, and set off along the corridor to her left.

It soon became evident that there weren't any doors down here so far. And, after having walked in silence for nearly half an hour, Gaile was beginning to wish she'd gone the other way instead. They couldn't have gone this far in, could they?

When eventually a door *did* present itself, any initial excitement of seeing something different quickly faded.

This door was clearly not going to be leading anywhere. It might, at some point, have done so, but it definitely did so no longer. It was a sad door; a door so far past its prime that it had no reason to even be called a door any-more.

To start with it was halfway off its hinges. Its bulky metal frame was bent sideways, as if pushed aside by some powerful force, and one part had been severed completely.

The reason for its twisted shape wasn't a great mystery. This wasn't the case of a rampaging horde from the bottomless pits of the nether regions. The truth was much simpler than that. Behind it, and spilling out into the corridor to such an extent that it nearly managed to block the whole passage, was rub-ble, rubble and more rubble of the earth, stone and debris variety.

You wouldn't have thought that a bit of rock and dirt could do something like that to a powerful metal door but in this case the manmade object had clearly come out second best in this battle of power.

No, she wasn't getting out that way. 'Guess the floor above must have caved in,' Gaile mused.

Well, it didn't help her get out. It didn't exactly help her to determine where she was either. None of the floors of the Dragon Research Centre that she knew of had big gaping holes in the middle. She was sure she would have noticed; if only by absentmindedly falling into it.

Judging from the maps of the Academy that she remembered, it was un-likely that this was just some odd forgotten little corner somewhere. It didn't have that kind of feel. It was unlikely that they wouldn't have cleared out such a cave-in by now and there hadn't been any news of such an event for as long as she'd been here, however short a time that might have been.

That had been her first thought – for why else leave the lights on, what little light there was? It didn't make sense to run electricity to all these corridors, and she hadn't seen it branch out even once so far, if you weren't using them.

But they would have cleared up the cave-in, wouldn't they have?

The people who'd dumped her here … they couldn't have had time to bring her somewhere else, could they? How long had she been out for anyway? Without her diom, down here it was impossible to tell.

So, if that was the case, who did keep the light on down here? Was it disused but still kept around for training purposes? Possibly. They did seem to like putting their students in the oddest situations; the practicals she'd had to participate in so far were proof enough of that. Who in the world's name could possibly get something out of creeping around disused pipes or learning to jump between blocks and other stuff in low gravity or any of the other strange things they'd been made to do so far?

Was there someone who was using it for their own activities? Equally possible … and a whole lot creepier.

Gaile regarded the large pile of debris stoically. She was tired. She was sore. She was hurting all over. She was scared stiff and she wanted to go home NOW!

There had to be a way out of here somewhere. All she had to do was find it.

Still shaking, Gaile took a step towards it. Then another step. Then she was scrambling up and over it, dislodging bits of concrete and masonry as well as the odd circuit board along the way.

For a moment she balanced precariously on what had looked like a solid block of stone, waving her arms desperately. It tipped forward to deposit her unceremoniously on a heap on the ground beyond, her body sliding down across the uneven surface.

Gaile winced as one of the steel reinforcements scraped across her thigh on the way down. Tears stung her eyes as she fought down the wave of nausea at the sight of her own blood, much of which was *not* leaking out but instead rushing to her head, wanting to do nothing more than make her pass out.

'Just no good with pain, am I?' she growled. 'Still can't hack it. No wonder everyone in class thinks I'm a waste of space. Laughing behind my back. I shy away from *any* chance of getting hurt.'

Truth be told, even the chance of getting bruised left her all shaky and sweaty in their practical sessions.

'What a bloody joke,' she swore once she managed to get back on her feet.

The pile of rubble, while reduced in size on this end, continued for several more meters until it was nothing more than just stray bits of debris scattered on the floor.

The corridor before her opened up into a small chamber. It wasn't all that big, but the lighting was bad and it was hard to make out what lay hidden in the corners, if anything.

From here Gaile could make out three different passages branching out. Or there had been three different ones in addition to the one she'd just come through once upon a time. The one farthest to her left, on the short end of the room, wasn't much more than another pile of rubble. It had probably been destroyed in the same event that had wrecked the bit she'd just passed, she figured.

Gaile eyed the two remaining openings somewhat apprehensively. It would make more sense to turn around and go back. This obviously wasn't the way out, to say nothing about it not being the way she'd come in. But, what if there was another way out and it lay just a little further ahead?

If she turned around now it would be no different from when you're were searching through a pile of paper and, having decided that it's not in the top half, since you've already looked through that part, you turn it over and start from the bottom, in case it goes faster to find it from that end, only to discover, when you finally do find it, that it was just one paper away from the last bit of paper that you had looked at when you were going through it from the top.

It was the universe's way of saying "Hey, don't try and second-guess me, so there", or so she felt.

After a brief moment of indecision, Gaile picked one of the remaining doorways, even though they were lacking in doors, and set off down that corridor.

This place seemed to thrive on long, winding corridors. Didn't these people build rooms, like normal people? It wasn't any more inviting than the first one had been. But, at least, it was a choice.

Things went a lot slower now, even though the floor was a lot cleaner. That last bump-and-scrape had messed up her leg and its insistent throbbing in rhythm with her heartbeat was both painful and distracting.

Gaile tried to circumnavigate any debris but on some stretches that proved more than difficult and the young woman soon found herself slowing down even more.

The occasional 'ping' from the pipes above still made her jump. And, every time, for a few seconds afterwards, it would set her heart racing and she'd stop and listen. It was becoming a familiar sound in this increasingly soundless and unfamiliar world. At least it wasn't totally and eerily silent, that was something to be grateful for even if it nearly made her heart jump out of her throat every time she heard it.

It was getting a whole lot drier.

Either the leak she'd come across earlier didn't extend down here or all this walking around was making her thirsty. Her throat was feeling raspy. All the dust and concrete particles her every step stirred up were leaving an even drier, stickier, taste in her mouth. It would have been nice to have one bottle of water down here, she thought. One swallow ... even a small sip would do.

Sadly that was the one thing Gaile was absolutely certain that she was lacking; that and a way out.

It felt like she'd been wandering around down here for hours. It felt like the journey was slanting ever downwards this whole time. Then, finally, the corridor she was in came to an end. It opened up into a chamber beyond.

Gaile had but time to take in the space covering several stories and a domed shape hugging the centre in the dim light when something fell on her.

The world turned black.

* * *

'This is just plain stupid,' Kay threw the bundle of leather onto the desk.

It hit it with a resounding smack and subsequently bounced off and landed on the floor instead. He retrieved it with a snarl.

'I mean, you've seen the Armoury. Do they seriously expect us to have to know this stuff? Who's going to use it?' Kay complained loudly, again. He'd been doing so, off and on, ever since this class had gotten under way.

A lot of the time Kay's griping got on people's nerves. Today, he was just putting his vocal chords into expressing what a lot of them were thinking – saving them the trouble of having to say it themselves. And saving them any trouble the teachers might decide to send their way should they have heard them.

Guess he did have his uses…

'It's just something we have to learn, that's all,' the girl on his right said while she was trying to figure out which two straps to hook up to a semi-circular "ring". At least she assumed that it was supposed to be a ring. So far none that she'd tried were working.

Had she used the strap she needed somewhere else already? Maybe this wasn't a connector after all? It looked similar to those in the pictures though.

The girl peered at the three dimensional image that was hovering over her diom. It clearly showed a neatly constructed saddle (one of basic ones, just bits of leather cleverly snapped together really). That was what it was supposed to look like, right?

Her eyes glanced downwards to her own work. Nope, didn't look like that at all. So what was she missing?

'I don't think we're expected to ever use it, not really,' Dayu broke into the conversation.

'Maybe for emergencies?' someone else suggested while struggling with a particularly stubborn clasp.

They licked their lips, trying to work out what had gone wrong, as they were now trying to tie two straps together that both ended in metallic rings. That couldn't be right, could it?

'Come on. Not Really? Seriously? Can you see *anyone* trusting a bunch of old straps of artificial leather and a few buckles to keep them safe when flying? Duh.'

'It's rach hide actually,' Jim, who was sitting on the other end of the round table, and therefore at the other end of the pile, announced calmly.

'What did you say you little snit?' Kay snarled. 'I know it's bloody… I'll teach you to swear at me I will!'

Kay made as to get to his feet but was pulled down by the two people sitting next to him.

'Jim means it's *made* out of rach hide … you know, the *animal*. Don't you Jim?'

Jim Walker treated the speaker to a short but intense smile, happy that someone hadn't misunderstood him.

'Yes. You see … artificial leather isn't very safe when working with dragons. It reacts badly to contact with dragon hide and deteriorates much faster than it would normally. It makes it unreliable. So all the old, and the new, when they make these ones,' he nodded at the mass of spare parts that made up the centre of the table, 'they prefer using the real thing. My brother says that rach hide is about the best there is for making reliable dragon gear.'

'And your brother's some sort of expert I take it,' Kay snorted contemptuously.

The smaller boy just shrugged his shoulders. 'You don't need to believe me if you don't want to,' he said, returning his attention to his own project, which was, out of all of those at the table, at least having a form. So far no one was quite sure what the form was, since it didn't resemble what they were supposed to be working on, but it definitely looked interesting.

Jim narrowed his eyes in concentration. What part should he choose next? This would be so much easier if they had only the bits that they actually needed rather than a whole pile.

A casual glance around today's class, which was spread out among several such tables, and it was easy enough to tell that Kay wasn't the only one who thought this was a waste of time.

* * *

Far down below the Academy it was a different matter entirely.

It was dark.

That was the first thing she thought.

It was dark and she was lying down.

That was odd. Not the darkness – her room was always dark after you turned off the light, having no windows. But the last thing she remembered was darkness.

The second last thing she remembered was getting knocked sideways by something, something with a lot of sharp and blunt edges.

She blinked a couple of times. That didn't help. The only thing it did do was prove that her eyes were hurting.

After a while Gaile managed to push herself up onto her elbows.

What was beneath her was cold and hard and had uncomfortable bits sticking out of it. Most definitely not her bed then. And here she'd been hoping everything had all been just another bad dream.

'Wow…' Gaile took a deep breath as the sight of where she'd ended up met her.

As that made her lungs and throat fill with dust, it sent her into a spate of dry coughs. Bending over double she clutched at her stomach as her diaphragm clenched at each spasms that the dry rack tore through her, forcing tears to stream down her cheeks.

When the last errant speck of dust that had tried to invade her airways had been dislodged and expelled, Gaile remained curled up for a while longer. Only when the tight clenched fist around her heart had stopped squeezing did she try to move again.

Though some of the pain still fluttered in her midriff, once the worst of it was gone her leg made itself reminded again. It hadn't appreciated what had happened, being handled so roughly. This time its complaints were joined by a throbbing in her hands and in her head.

As Gaile turned her palms over, she saw that they'd been streaked with blood from where her fingernails had dug into the soft tissue, turning the pale skin into an irritated red around small puffy wounds.

'Great,' she mumbled. And long nails were supposed to be good for a girl. 'Guess I'll just have to chalk that up to another part of another really bad day. And where the hell am I anyway?'

The last was added as Gaile raised her attention away from herself and started taking an interest in her surroundings.

It wasn't really wow worthy in the sense that it was great, pristine and amazing. It was more of the "what in the world's name is this place and what the hell happened to it?" variety.

'Well, wherever this is, it sure is big,' Gaile said, turning her head first this way, then that. 'Scratch that, this place isn't big, it's frigging enormous.'

And so it was.

Shading her eyes, more out of habit than any real need, Gaile took another look at what lay before her.

Now that she'd gotten used to the dim and subdued lighting it was a lot brighter in here than she'd first thought (though that matter could be debated). Sure, she still couldn't see the far walls, and the ceiling was lost somewhere in the higher reaches of the dome that stretched out above.

In any case, most of it was obscured by a pattern of crisscrossing and interlocking steel beams. One or two of which appeared to balance precariously on its brethren and at least one which had already broken loose and which now rested at a sharp angle, its lower end disappearing into the floors below them in the centre of the "chamber".

Stepping up to the railing maybe some ten meters ahead, Gaile gazed downwards. There appeared to be several floors below her, all arranged around the circular central area. Each one was surrounded by a walkway, so that you could walk in a circle, on each floor, around and around, without anything in the way.

The snapped metal beams had come crashing down, cutting a swathe through the mezzanine floors on the way. One, a particularly large one, hadn't fallen all the way down with the rest. Instead, its point had come to rest against the bottom, along with a great deal of other bits and pieces.

That was the down end (not that Gaile could see it). The top of it was pointing upwards, leaning on the far railing. It'd make an excellent slide, for the suicidal.

Judging from what she could see, there wasn't much in terms of furniture up on this level. Some severe looking benches hugged the walls at sparse intervals and what looked like some broken down machinery, though what type she couldn't tell from the distance, could still be seen as well, but that was it.

It probably would have looked empty even when in use. Now it didn't just look empty but desolate as well. That wasn't really a step in the right direction as far as she was concerned.

Gaile figured they were all broken anyway, because even those that looked intact, if you didn't count the dust, refused to give off even as much as a beep when she ran her hands over them. There were no lights to indicate they were hooked up to the grid either.

They did sound like there were several things loose in there when she tried shaking one of them. That one sounded hollow too. Scavengers?

There were one or two on the main floor that did remind her of other things though.

'Shoddy workmanship if I ever saw it,' Gaile muttered as she bent over to inspect one of them closer.

That one, which had more than a slight resemblance to a data terminal, with its smooth rounded edges and tiled oval appearance, she spent some extra time on. Gaile was hoping, against all reason, that it might offer up some clues to what was going on or to where she was.

It, however, showed no more signs of life than anything else in this place.

Only the sparse lighting suggested that this place wasn't entirely abandoned. It was a low, dull light emanating from a source here and a source there, apparently distributed at random.

They were probably some that hadn't broken when whatever had hit this place had, well, hit. Though why they'd still be working after all this time was beyond her. It brought the term "long-life" to a whole new level.

'Guess I should have known better,' Gaile sighed.

She refrained from giving the thing a solid kick. More because she suspected that in her current state she'd do more damage to herself than to the machine, than anything else.

The only thing she did figure out, was that this place was old. Not old as in antique. Not even old as in mysterious remains from the ages prior to the settlement of the planet. Just old. The style, what could be made out, had to hark back at least half a century. Ages in fact.

'Bloody long lasting light bulbs in this place if that's the case,' Gaile muttered, edging her way forward cautiously. 'So, someone comes down here then? It can't be anything official or they'd have had the placed cleared up a bit more. Either that or they're a *really* messy housekeeper.'

She patted the metal railing with its dust and rust and mused on further. 'So, if they can get in, then, logically, I must be able to get out, right?' she said to no one in particular. 'That's the idea anyway.'

Since the only place she hadn't looked was downwards, that had to be where she should head? Right?

Trying to find a way down to the floors below didn't turn out to be an easy task though. Gaile ended up walking all around the top floor twice before finding one ramp leading down, just a little farther ahead from where she'd been standing at the beginning.

It opened up into the wall behind rather than straight down the open centre, and therefore resembled nothing as much as just an empty gap of extra dark if you didn't know it was there.

'Bloody typical,' Gaile grumped. 'Don't they have maps in this stupid place? What kind of place doesn't even come with a floor plan? I mean, would it be too much to ask for, just something that simple? Like, first floor – residential quarters or fourth floor – cafeteria? I don't suppose there'd still be something edible around here, would there?'

It turned out that most of the floor directly below was inaccessible, but after some careful navigation the one below that proved much more interesting.

There were several open corridors (again), large ones, leading away from the main oval and a number of doors. Several of those had glass plates in their upper halves, some of which were even intact. They were strewn among the smooth walls backing the oval itself.

Tugging carefully at a likely looking handle, Gaile picked one at random and poked her head into the room beyond.

Yup, there was no doubt about it, someone *was* using this place. At least, someone was using it on some sort of semi-regular basis. The room might not be big, and it could have done with a light dusting, unlike the areas she'd just come through, which needed something more akin to a large multitask clean-up operation, complete with cranes.

The shelves along the walls had even less dust on them and many of them were filled with a mixture of storage boxes, files, odd looking items she had no idea what they were and a great deal of what appeared to be tools of different sorts.

A cupboard in the corner yielded an army of poles, some with spikes, others with brushes and some which looked like what she'd imagined you'd use to check the teeth of a dragon, if she'd been in the mood for guessing games. Those were all big hooks and leather strappings.

They weren't very happy with her opening the door and setting them free. It took more than just two hands to get them back in and shut the door on them. One kept falling into the crack just as she was about to close it.

Finally she gave up on it. What did she care anyway?

There was also a small auxiliary squadron of buckets, several torn and weary looking, covered with nicks and scrapes and odd pinches of colour. They clanked when you touched them.

Not plastic then.

Gaile fingered a bit of the leather she'd found gingerly. It felt smooth and slightly oily under her fingertips.

'Some sort of storage room then. So, wonder what might be in the others?' Taking only a moment longer to look around the room she was in, in case she'd missed something important, Gaile dismissed it from her mind and hobbled on to the next door.

She really hoped that she'd find something useful soon; she was beginning to feel a bit dizzy. Never a good sign when you're lost, alone and far from, for lack of a better word, civilization.

Of course, she was right in the middle of civilization as it was, just not a very active part of it and a distinctly not very useful part as far as she was concerned.

Sticking her nose in the second door proved disappointing. There was nothing but tables along the walls and floor.

The third door, however, proved much more satisfactory.

Gaile's eyes lit up almost the moment *before* she pushed it open. It was one of those with an intact transparent plate in its upper half and though that could have done with a bit of cleaning it was transparent enough to allow her to get an idea what was on the other side.

'Jackpot!' Gaile exclaimed. She'd found a kitchen.

After a few trials and errors and a very sore thumb (on top of everything else that already ached) Gaile determined that the kitchen was devoid of a functioning cooker or cooler.

Sucking at her injured finger, she systematically opened the different cupboards one after another.

Several of those along the bottom appeared to be filled with utensils. One, for instance, was crammed full of pots and pans of different sizes. Others held more traditional tools and others again were stocked with crockery.

'Blimey, there's enough here for a whole platoon,' Gaile breathed.

What the cupboards that she'd seen so far did *not* contain was any dust or webs. In fact, for a kitchen that didn't have any functioning appliances, the utensils seemed awfully well cared for.

'Odd that,' Gaile mused to herself. 'But I can't eat this stuff. A steelrat might find them an appealing appetizer, but I certainly don't.'

Having gone through the bottom level of cupboards, Gaile straightened up and started on the top row. This took some effort. By now moving around this much was making her even dizzier.

'Ah, so that's where you were hiding you naughty, naughty thing,' she mumbled.

Peering into it, the shelves of the unit were, while not packed, so at the very least containing a reasonable supply of stock; the edible kind this time.

A quick scan through the other two top cupboards revealed that they too held food.

Rummaging through it, though it had obviously been organized at some point; cans to the left, jars on the shelf above and several packages of what on inspection turned out to be dried soup (just add water) stuffed into what looked like an old ice-cream box along with a whole stack of transparent bags with dried fruit and vegetables.

'How useful is that? Just add water? There isn't any bleeding water in this place?' Gaile sighed. 'Guess the cans could come in handy. Suppose there's something in here I can use to open them? Still, I kind of hoped for something hot. 'Something hot to eat and a nice cold drink.'

It turned out Gaile was in luck. Maybe not on the cold refreshment side of things, but, the next shelf she investigated, after having dragged over a nearby chair so that she'd be able to see it properly, turned out to have a few lonely looking silver packs.

Normally she would have brightened considerably at such a find. Their labels marked them as emergency rations; beef stew and croutons or curried rice with spring onions, economically squeezed into the thin foil and ready to self-heat at the removal of the safety sticker.

As it was, she was feeling increasingly sluggish and it was all Gaile could do to pour some of the steaming stew into a small bowl.

Leaving it to cool slightly, she didn't bother with a glass, but instead tilted her head back and took a long drink from the bottled water rations that had been hiding in the final cupboard.

She immediately wished she hadn't when it sent her heart racing.

Closing her eyes for a moment until her body was once again more under control, or at least not protesting wildly, Gaile ate slowly.

Every bite, every spoonful, sank into her stomach to sit there like as many crumbs of lead. Instead of filling her with warmth it just made her feel nauseous.

She put the spoon down. No more of that for her.

Both her legs protested as she made to stand up, and, clutching the water bottle in her left hand, she staggered out of the kitchen.

Shoving the door aside awkwardly, Gaile barely took note of the room beyond other than seeing that it had something large and soft on the floor.

Grateful to be able to lie down on something other than concrete, Gaile collapsed onto the mattress blanket, curling up protectively on her left side. Wishing that her body would stop shivering, the world slowly faded away.

* * *

'Shouldn't we … you know … tell someone? It's been ages,' the second year asked, looking a bit uncomfortable and apologetic for bringing up the subject in the first place.

'Don't be an idiot, Derek,' Jasmine snapped.

The undisputed leader of their little group twirled a honey blond curl of hair around her finger. 'That useless little rubberneck is getting just what she deserves,' she said, a vicious smile dancing at the corner of her mouth. 'Can you imagine they'd even let someone like *that* in? Honestly…'

'Umm…' Derek hesitated. 'There isn't really any entrance requirement. I mean…'

'Oh do shut up Derek. You're such a bore,' Jasmine said, surveying her troops. Only half of them where here today by the looks of it. Useless bunch. What an inconvenience. One was away on a fieldtrip being held today of all days. Who did they think they were? She'd had plans.

'Besides,' Jasmine added almost as an afterthought. 'It's not like we went very far. All the little twerp has to do is walk up to and through the door. If she isn't too scared that is. I bet that she won't even have been able to move until she couldn't stand it anymore.'

'Yes, but…'

'Unless…' Jasmine turned her one hundred megawatt accusing stare right at Derek. 'Why don't you go back and check if you're so worried? It's not like those broken down old corridors are anything to be scared of.

Of course, I'm sure you don't mind her running to the Director the moment you do. I'm sure even that ingrate would have removed the blindfold days ago now and you see, Derek, that means she would *see* you. I'm sure I don't have to explain what that means, do I? She's probably just hiding out in the shrubbery somewhere, too embarrassed to come to class. What else would you expect from someone who can't even stay on a dragon without making a spectacle of herself?'

'She did fall a long way Jas,' another of the girls interjected meekly.

'Bah,' Jasmine snorted.

The tousled-haired Derek shook his head miserably.

'No? Good. Just in case anyone else is feeling foolish, may I remind you that Ashworthey,' she snorted again, 'what a name, tells the Director or anyone else who was behind this little stunt, we all know only the people here could have passed on that information. She never saw us remember. She never heard us. She doesn't even know there *is* an *us*. And she can rot in those vermin infested rock passages until the second eclipse of the moon for all I care.'

Jasmine took a deep, long breath and settled her features into something much more pleasant. 'I'm feeling like dessert,' she said brightly. 'Someone was kind enough to tell me that Manchio's have a new passion cake on their menu and I have just been dying to try some.'

'Oh yes, and they've got a new dispenser too. You know, that adorable boy from third period Navigations,' one of the other girls piped up.

The rest of the girls broke out giggling.

Smiling, as a general having just delivered the news of their newest victory and announcing a four day weekend in the same breath, Jasmine marched off her little gathering to the confectionary on the level above, leaving the room practically deserted.

Well, *almost*, deserted.

Having remained absolutely still during the entire conversation, no, from the moment that the chattering flock of students had poured into the otherwise empty lounge, hoping that no one would notice, someone closed the book they'd been reading with a minute sigh.

And this day had started so well. Now it sounded like it was going to become one big bother altogether. As it wasn't enough to have Jasmine as the biggest pain in the neck in the *normal* way, now she was causing trouble for him even when she wasn't even there. Cursed woman.

For a moment he debated the idea of simply ignoring what he'd heard. Pretending that it had nothing to do with him and that it wasn't his concern even if it had been; just like the group of people who had just left were obviously experts at doing. It was a tempting thought.

He managed to do so himself for an entire twenty seconds.

At that point the young man put aside his notes and unfolded his limbs. It always took a while to get back circulation into his legs after sitting cross-legged for longer periods of time. He did so anyway because while he was still sitting down it was quite comfortable.

Taking out his diom he tapped out a quick message, well, it was more along the lines of an excuse really, in case he wouldn't make it back to the next class. His might be having a very different schedule than most of the other students, but he still took them seriously – these days. That hadn't always been the case…

Hoping that this whole thing would resolve itself quickly, maybe this Ashworthey person had already found their way back to the grounds of the Academy proper and he could go back to what he'd been doing without any fuss, he set out for the closest access point to the underground world he knew of.

'These tunnels, the whole area, aren't something, or somewhere, that you just play around in. It's not a playground for the high and mighty,' he muttered under his breath as he was walking.

A rising annoyance with anyone foolish enough to treat them as such was brewing in his chest. They were dangerous if you didn't know what you were doing. They were dangerous if you *did* know what you were doing. But, at the very least, he wouldn't be lost down there.

* * *

Noise was filling her entire world. It was filling it from brim to brim, incessantly repeating itself again and again in the same sequence. 'Badung' it went. 'Bam, badung, dink.' Again and again, never stopping. Like a big clock, an enormous grandfather clock towering above her, leaning over her, its huge hands striking three as its mouth shouted incomprehensive harangues at her.

It grew until the world was nothing but the clock. Then the sky was the face, a pale ivory. Its hands too large to comprehend until those two melted together in a circle, the sky now a vast emptiness of black.

There were several moments before Gaile realized that she could still hear those same sounds; only now they weren't quite so loud. In fact, they sounded more like a beaker or metal cup was being was being slowly stirred by a glass rod.

Wait … that didn't make any sense. Gaile stepped back, figuratively speaking, analysed that thought and slowly realized that she was still lying down. There was what felt like a pillow under her head. The warmth above her, smooth, stretched and just a touch heavy, indicated the presence of what was most likely a blanket. There was something soft, compared to the concrete floor, underneath her as well. A mattress of some sort then?

She'd collapsed hadn't she? Fallen over, like some sorry excuse for a heroine. Couldn't even sort herself out, much less anyone else.

So, that meant she must be in the infirmary, didn't it? Then, why was it so dark in here?

Gaile blinked a couple of times. In doing so she became aware of the pressure of something else, namely what was tied over her eyes.

Well, that was inconvenient. How was she supposed to see with this stupid thing in the way? She hadn't fallen over and pierced her eyes, she was sure she would have remembered. Besides, her eyes didn't hurt. They just couldn't do their normal job with this idiotic thing tied over her face.

She reached up to remove it. Suddenly a sharp pain pierced her left arm.

The most intense bit centred just below the inside of her elbow. It spread out like some small fluid ball of flame and about as fast. It didn't just sting, it stung with a vengeance, like she could feel every single one of her blood-vessels right there burning with fire.

She tried her right arm instead. Ah, that was a bit better. Gaile managed to get it, protesting as it may be, moving.

Fingers not entirely under their owner's control scrabbled ineffectually against the bandage. As they did so, something long and sinuous brushed against her left side.

Had she been able to, Gaile would have startled at the touch. As it was, the surprise made her forget to breathe, remaining perfectly still.

Ok. Whatever it was hadn't moved again.

Once more she made as to take the whole thing off.

Again something slapped against her. This time almost expecting it, the sensation was somewhat familiar. Gaile tried shifting her arm. Yes, the tubular thing shifted as well. Forcing her other hand across her chest, she ran shivering fingers across her arm. There *was* something attached to it. Gaile fought back against the sudden lurch in her stomach, the stinging fluid in her throat.

'I wouldn't touch that if I were you.'

The voice really did make her jump, sending her heart racing into overtime.

'Right now they're about the only thing keeping you alive. That type of poisoning isn't something that you just play around with,' the voice continued calmly, echoed by the same sounds as she'd heard before.

'What?' Gaile croaked hoarsely. 'I ... I was...'

'Down in the dungeon. Yes, I know. You still are.'

'... I ... I see...' Gaile fought hard to gain some clarity among her memories.

For some reason her entire mind seem to swirl in murk, tepid waters. She could sense the thought-fish out there, but she couldn't see them. Only occasionally would one drift past, a vast shadow barely out of range, before it disappeared once again into the darkness.

'So ... not ... in the infirmary ... then?'

'No, I'm afraid not. And I'm afraid that you will have to stay here for a while,' the voice said.

There was the sound of something metallic being put down on a wooden surface.

'You've caused me quite a bit of trouble, you know,' the voice added. 'Quite a bit of trouble indeed.'

Gaile didn't answer.

Apart from that it obviously wasn't a question to begin with, she was far too occupied trying to trace where the owner of the voice was, to bother. She turned her head to what her ears showed her; guided by the sounds as they were moving around the room.

At least she presumed it was a room. By the *sounds* of it, it wasn't the infirmary. But she wouldn't put it past "them" to convince one of the juniors in there to play another little trick on her. They'd like nothing better than to watch her make a fool of herself ... again. Like she needed any extra help with that.

That voice... It sounded male. But then, she'd always been a terrible bad judge of those kinds of things. Best not to make any assumptions, for the time being.

She stayed quiet, trying to get a feel for the situation.

There was a 'gluck, gluck, gluck' right next to her, maybe slightly above. Gaile was jerked out of her reverie. That showed her for not paying attention.

Her fear must have shown on her face somehow because even with what little of it that was visible, someone answered her unspoken question.

'It's a refill for the straining solution. It's necessary for it to be fresh, so one batch doesn't last long. As I said, you have no idea how much trouble you've caused. To say nothing about what you've done to my schedule.'

'Would be easier ... just to drop me off ... at the doctors,' Gaile suggested weakly, still struggling to keep that fluttering, frightened note out of her voice. It didn't help that she was feeling dizzy on top of everything else.

Besides, her ears were killing her.

'No, I don't think so,' the male voice said, crumpling up the spent bag in his hand. 'That would be quite inconvenient for me.'

'More inconvenient ... than staying here?'

'In a different way.'

'They'll miss me,' Gaile said, trying to sound braver than she felt.

'Will they now?' the voice sounded further away now. 'And here I was under the understanding that you were quitting ... leaving the Academy. I suppose that you at the very least managed to avoid making away under the cover of darkness – unseen by anyone.'

Gaile turned her head away. That stung. Not sure what hurt her most – the reminder that she'd failed, fled like some half-baked idea whose time had never come, or the suggestion that no one knew where she was and wouldn't have cared if they did.

Actually, the second wasn't entirely true. But none of those that would care knew that she was down here. How could they? They didn't even know she'd entered the Academy in the first place. Sure, she'd gone off for further education, but not here and certainly not of this type.

Gaile bit back the lump in her throat. Clenching her fist sent a new wave of fire up her arm.

'Relax princess. I'm not going to hurt you. And trust me, you're definitely not my type, even if I was into that sort of thing,' the voice snorted contemptuously.

'It's simply that there would be a lot of inconvenient questions asked if I took you back up and I'd rather not have anyone find out about my little place down here. It's nice. I don't want a pack of lunatics raving about. It's *my* place. A chance to get some work done when actually being able to concentrate. It's far too busy up there. I'm sure that once you're well enough you'll be happy enough to leave without sharing this little secret with anyone.'

Gaile didn't bother replying. She didn't exactly agree. Her features hardened as she continued to listen. Princess indeed. What an insult. So, apparently he planned to keep her confined here? Well, they'd see about that.

Of course, there was the little problem of that she had no idea *how* to get out, but that was beside the point. More important right now was that she seemed unable to move enough to go anywhere anyway.

Again she reached up to brush her fingertips against the cloth. Good, her nerve-control seemed to be improving. Gaile made as if to remove the bandages she could feel.

'I wouldn't bother if I were you. I put some surgical tape over your wounds. It won't come off without a special solvent, unless you're planning on taking half the skin on your face off alongside it,' the voice told her, watching the young woman lie there, seething in range, unable to do anything about it at all.

'Now what?'

'It's the middle of the night. Sleep tight.'

'Oh you...' Gaile snarled. 'Great. Bloody, bloody, great! Just you wait until I can get my hands on you. I don't *care* who you are. I'm going to wring your stupid fat neck!'

On the other side of the door, and in a much lighter world, her would-be rescuer let himself into the kitchen, where he carefully placed the bowl and stirrer in the sink and went about returning various bottles to their rightful places.

Why him? Of all people, why him? All he'd wanted was a quiet place all to himself, away from all those crazy, giggling, girls and worse. To have somewhere where he could relax, be himself for a little while and enjoy doing things he often didn't get the chance to do without having someone breathing down his neck.

No. Apparently that was too much to be asked. If that Jasmine was absolutely going to have to shove someone into a cold, dark, place, couldn't she have chosen somewhere else to do so?

And why couldn't that little band of misfits have been discussing their dark deeds somewhere else? Somewhere where he *wouldn't* have overheard them?

And why, oh why, did said person have to start off in the wrong direction and, instead of reaching the nearest exit, winding up in *his* cosy den.

He stabbed viciously at the raw piece of cabbage with a grilling fork. And for this he was going to miss "things"? And that was the least of the problems, the least of the problems indeed.

* * *

Tam had his own worries to worry about, and worry he did. At the moment he was gazing out over the area set aside as the casual lounge and cafeteria of the DRC proper, several floors above the one belonging to the Academy. Much of it was showered in sunlight and appeared very light and airy.

He liked it up here. Most of the people here were slightly older than the students below, though there were a few distinctly young looking ones using the tables or sitting in the chairs or comfortable sofas enjoying some quiet time.

This was a very green place that, at times, reminded him more of a miniature greenhouse than anything else. A greenhouse where someone had found the space to fit some furniture into. It didn't dampen out all sounds though, but then, that wasn't really its purpose.

A loud burst of laughter from a group several tables away, tucked behind some bamboo screens and a large number of pot plants reached his ears and broke his contemplative mind. He straightened up, flexing his fingers.

Tam enjoyed people watching, or dragon watching as it may be, since it was practically impossible to tell the difference between an average human and a dragon in human form from a casual glance.

In fact, even with a very long scrutinising study you'd be hard placed to guess right more than fifty percent of the time and that was more down to the laws of average than anything else. You had to *know* who was who ... or, in this case, who was what.

But watching things, especially living things, was something that he'd always done, always enjoyed. It wasn't that he was trying to be inquisitive. He found it restful and it paid to know the people you were working with.

The kinds of environments and situations that called for draconic backup tended to also call for the kind of people you could rely on in a pinch. A casual, almost lazy, eye around the cafeteria was more of a hobby, going almost unnoticed even to himself.

Most people in the DragonCorps tended to cultivate it as a talent for professional purposes, but for Tam it was really more of a hobby. He wasn't sure he could stop doing it even if he'd wanted to.

And the DRC wasn't averse to capitalizing on his interest. As such, he'd often found himself in situations where he needed to use all that accumulated knowledge or gather new ones, quickly.

In a way, Tam counted his blessings. At least he wasn't the inconspicuous type in terms of appearance as well. If he had been, he was sure he'd have ended up with a whole different set of duties.

It wasn't, perhaps, strange that he'd ended up where he had this year. A lot of people had thought it was just a matter of time really. Still, him, a teacher? What would they think of next?

They might think it was a natural progression from where he'd been but even so, he'd much rather be out there, doing something constructive with his time.

As such, Tam's attention wasn't entirely focused on himself and it took a moment, not to mention a rather pointed punch on his arm, before he realized that someone had slipped in opposite and was now trying to get his attention.

Tam gave them a slightly apologetic grin.

'So, how's the new job,' the newcomer asked, sounding almost insufferably cheerful.

Tiosh tossed his jacket over the padded back of the bench-seat beside him.

'Don't ask,' Tam replied ruefully. 'Don't think I was cut out for this thing … at all. They're so … so…' he didn't find the words to finish.

'I noticed that yesterday,' Tiosh chuckled. 'Don't let them scare you. They're probably more terrified of you than you are of them.'

This caused a snort of disbelief to be expelled by his partner.

'You make it sound so easy. Why don't you do it? You really helped me out yesterday you know.'

'I know,' Tiosh drained the ember-brown liquid in his glass, something which was immediately followed by a very sour face. 'I know this is supposed to be good for you, but why does it have to taste so bad?' he wanted to know. 'Yeeuch.'

'Come on, Wraithy.'

'No,' Tiosh shook his head. 'You landed this gig – you pull it home. I and the rest of the crew don't mind giving you a hand with the practical lessons or a few pointers when you need them, but it's your job to do. And don't call me that like this.'

Tam sank back against the headrest and sighed. That's what he'd figured his friend would say. Still, it hadn't hurt to ask, had it?

'Could you at least tell me if there's any that's worth keeping an eye on? I mean, I know I'm supposed to be good at reading people, but I don't even know what I'm supposed to be looking for here! You've seen some of them, and you've been doing this for longer than me, a lot longer.'

'Thanks for pointing out my age. You should consider yourself fortunate if at my age you can still do half the things you do now.'

'Tiosh, at half your age I'll be crumbled bits of bone,' Tam complained half-heartedly, amused by his partner's reaction.

It was an old game and they'd played it for a long time, but sometimes the old games were the best.

'Ah, yes,' Tiosh rubbed at the subtle stubble on his chin. 'That is true. Maybe … hmm … no, better not say. Which ones?' He mulled the thought over, while signalling for another drink – something more palatable this time.

'It's really too soon to tell. But there certainly aren't any that stand out to me. No,' Tiosh shook his head. 'I'm afraid you will have to do this the old-fashioned way.'

'I was afraid you were gonna say that,' Tam turned his glass over a couple of times, then bent over and pulled out his diom. 'Suppose I should get back to work then.'

'And stop hiding up here. You need to be out there, where the students can see you, and you can see them. Do come visit though. I'm sure we can always find a place at the table for you, somewhere,' Tiosh called after him as he stood up to leave.

'You're such an insufferable tosh, Wraith…' Tam called back, the rest of which was lost in the background as he turned a corner, vanishing from view.

'A shame really,' Tiosh mused to himself as he stirred the straw in what the waitress had brought him. 'It really doesn't look like we have got any outstanding candidates at all so far. Still, the year is young.'

He put the matter to one side and returned his attention to the lunch he'd brought with him.

* * *

He was true to his word, Gaile had to admit that. It was quite a few days later and yes, she was still stuck down here and yes, she still couldn't see a thing thanks to this stupid, freaking blindfold.

What did he think she was going to do? Run straight to the authorities and tell them he was hiding out down here? Did he think they'd believe her?

Why would she want to do that anyway? Just because she'd see who he was? Was that some sort secret code or something? What did she care?

Gaile had been in a grumbling mood for the last few days; more so than the days before that. Maybe it was because she was feeling a whole lot better and had plenty of energy to spare.

Being the only person around, her would-be rescuer was getting the brunt of it. Not that it seemed to bother him. He seemed quite content to ignore it completely until she stopped.

Also, it didn't pay to annoy the person that brought your food too much. That was something that Gaile had soon realized. Sometimes it still got on her nerves.

Right now what was making her growl more than usual was turning the idea of returning to the Academy backwards and forwards in her mind, trying to figure out just how to manage it. She had, after all … left.

Ok, so it hadn't been an especially sorted exit, but even so.

The only person she could talk to down here though, didn't understand why it was bothering her so much.

'You did not formally register your leave?' he asked.

Gaile shook her head. His voice sounded as cold and annoyed with her as usual. That hadn't changed, despite the days that had passed. It would probably never change, she figured.

Still, I suppose I can't really blame the guy. It's not like I was an expected houseguest in the first place and even those can overstay their welcome.

'Then I foresee no problem.'

'Huh?'

He made an annoyed noise (at least she had always assumed he was a he). He always did when she didn't immediately catch on to what he was talking about. He had a quick mind and not much patience for those who could not keep up with him.

You really should slow down a bit, Mister Perfect. The rest of us are running out of breath trying to match your speed, Gaile grumbled. It was a close call, but she did *think* it, not say it out loud.

'If you did not formally withdraw from the course then you will be able to return to it regardless of how much time has passed.'

'Oh.' Gaile tried to sound enthusiastic, but the effect was somewhat mitigated by the fact that she pulled up her knees and put her arms around them.

The cords in her arm were long gone now or she wouldn't have been inclined to move them at all.

'However, housing arrangements might have changed again while you were here, as I believe it is customary after the transition into the further months when so many have abandoned the course. So it would be best if you were to speak to someone in charge of these matters to see what needs to be done.

In your case they will probably give you a check-up as well. Try as I might, your injury is still visible, though mostly healed. I don't think you'll be able to talk your way out of that one. You will, of course,' and here his voice took on a stern note, as if to dare her to disobey, 'not mention me.'

Gaile scoffed. 'As if. D'you think they'd even believe me? Who'd possibly want to live down here?'

'Someone who values their privacy.' He spoke with a strange mixture of tension and softness in his voice, adding to the cold trace of menace within it.

They seemed to have these little "arguments" quite a lot. Not that they were really arguments at all, more like, well, he wasn't sure what he'd compare it with really.

Time had flown, hadn't it? Several weeks had already passed since he'd found her down here. Strange … it didn't feel like that long. He supposed he should be grateful that she'd been unconscious for most of the time. Small blessings and all that.

Gaile still wasn't sure what to believe. Not that she had any real cause for complaint, not really; aside from still being stuck down here that was.

Over the last few days, ever since she'd regained full function of all her thoughts and abilities, Gaile had decided to ignore the peculiar discrepancy between the obvious, or not so obvious at times, dislike in his voice and the feather-light and gentle touch when adjusting her eye-patches or replacing the bandages on her arm and leg, or the tubes, for the time being.

Besides, she felt incredibly foolish talking and ranting at thin air and it was more often than not hard to tell if he was there or not. If he was doing something that was making noise it was one thing but beyond that he hardly ever made a sound.

Sitting down, he could remain perfectly still, not moving as much as a muscle, for what seemed like hours on end.

It was, slowly, setting her teeth on edge. Sure, Gaile was used to being ignored. She was the first to admit it, but this guy was taking it to a whole new level, making it almost into an art form.

Still, he didn't seem to feel the need to fill up the empty time with conversation either, unless she asked a question. But when he answered, assuming she understood the answer, he was always knowledgeable and happy to share.

Even so, sure, *he* might not feel he needed to talk to *her*, but she felt, after having been cooped up here for several days, that she did. It wasn't as if this hermit-like existence was something *she'd* chosen after all.

'Are you sure about this?' she asked, hoping he was still there.

'Of course,' he responded calmly.

There he went again, being so infuriatingly agreeable that she wanted to reach out and swat him on the head.

'Tomorrow, I'll take you back to the Academy. And don't worry. I won't let you trip over anything on your way up there. I am sure you have no wish to return here anymore than I wish for you to do so.'

Gaile muttered something incomprehensible and rubbed at the new bandages. It still felt sore there. Then she pulled the blanket over her head. If he didn't want to be polite than neither did she.

In turn, he stared quietly at the bundle under the grey piece of cloth. He managed to stifle a yawn. It was most definitely a yawn, not a sigh. He needed some long and proper sleep.

In light of everything that had happened, he did wonder if he'd done the right thing. He rubbed as his own left forearm. No, he definitely wondered if he'd done the right thing. It might have caused even more trouble than it had saved.

There hadn't seemed like an option at the time though. He'd seen enough to be able to tell that even if he took only an hour to get to the DRC or the Academy clinic and back, it would not have been in time. So he'd done the only thing he could think of in the circumstances, for a given value of thought.

True, he could just have brought her there instead, and, who knows, it might even have been in time. But he hadn't liked the idea. If he'd done that everyone would have found out about his little hiding place. And he hadn't, still didn't, like *that* idea, at all. He hadn't liked the idea of being responsible for someone dying just because he refused to do something either.

In hindsight, he wondered if he'd actually thought at all that day. And after that, there had been no going back.

He'd decided not to tell her what he'd done. It was probably best that way. Besides, it wasn't as if it'd make the slightest bit of different for her anyway. No, best not to trouble her with such things.

For as a result of that first meeting, being driven by something he could not yet place his finger on, he'd not chosen to make his way for something else. And because of that, that first transfusion had come from a concoction that wasn't on anyone's list of medicinal herbs or medicinal anything for that matter. It had been blood. *His* blood.

That had been the trouble really.

These last few weeks she hadn't spent recovering from the poisoning. She'd spent it recovering from the transfusion. Had spent it fighting against the burning, like liquid fire, running through every vein, every portion of her body struggling to acclimatize to the sensation. For she had no hope of trying to fight it in battle and win, it was too strong, too strong by far. He had done something that it was never wise to do and the cure had almost ended up killing her. He suspected it was wisest not to tell her that part either.

He should have remembered why his blood wasn't good for these kinds of things. Guess he'd been a bit preoccupied to let something that important slip his mind. That wasn't at all like him.

By now though, every last trace of it *should* have vanished from her system, which was what he'd been waiting for.

No, he'd never figure out just *why* he'd done it.

All shapes...and sizes

It wasn't the screaming, not really. Not unless it woke you up. Most of the time it was waking everyone else up while you carried on, oblivious to all. The walls could only insulate so much sound after all.

Why wasn't it a big deal? Well, except for those that did lose their own sleep because of it, there wasn't really a whole lot of it going around. Not anymore.

What there was, was a large number of people being extremely skittish. Many of them had been so for weeks afterwards. Heck, some of them still were. They were the ones who woke up, all stiff and shivering. Sometimes the nightmares covered them in sweat, cold, fearful sweat. Sometimes it was just the idea that someone was there, that you were somewhere else, that it was somewhere you didn't want to be.

You can move, you told yourself. You can move. Only your body wasn't obeying you anymore. It didn't want to risk attracting the attention of those things out there in the scary darkness, lurking in the shadows – even when every single light in the room was on.

All sensible thoughts suggested that you were safely tucked up in bed (unless you'd fallen out of it while flailing around wildly with your arms and legs and sheets and whatnots entangled into something that made the Gordian Knot (whatever that was) look like a playground puzzle).

Unfortunately, when it happened, "sensible" was the last thing that you could be called.

Before the wave had subsided and people started to slowly forget (at least the worst parts) and telling themselves that it hadn't been so bad after all) the dorms hadn't been the best place to spend the night – not if your idea of night involved getting any sleep that was.

Now that they'd gotten more individual accommodation it was only your neighbours that your nightly run in with the darkest recesses of your mind disturbed, not everyone.

Some, like Jim, didn't seem to have been bothered by the experience at all – quite the contrary. *His* casual approach to the memories made him the envy of many and the enemy of a number of people who didn't care to have their own, not so precious memories of the event, jogged, by his exuberant reminiscences.

Most had dealt with it the old-fashioned way; giving it time. That strange little invention that healed many things and caused leaks in the most unexpected places, including whatever memory banks you might stash your past into while you weren't using it.

By now, that number had reduced drastically. Those worst effected had, in many cases, abandoned their quest to become a rider, had admitted defeat and decided to find something more worthwhile to do with their lives; preferably something that *didn't* involve falling rapidly from great heights very fast.

As a result, there had been quite the exodus after First Flight, just like the organisers had expected. That had been some time ago now.

Gaile wished, sometimes, when it was really bad, that she was one of them. She wished, every time she woke like that, that she was one of those that the whole experience hadn't tortured at all.

Instead she lay in the complete darkness staring up into what gravity suggested was the ceiling.

One day … maybe? She'd get to the point where she was either used to it or it had decided to plague other, more recent victims. Or that, by some unsung miracle, she'd managed to get over it completely.

It didn't help that her ears had been getting progressively worse ever since she'd come back from the Underworld. Now, it wasn't just that they hurt, they also made strange noises. Buzzing you could call it. It didn't happen all the time, just once in a while. To start with anyway…

Now it was happening more often.

It was making it really hard to concentrate. It also made it just as hard to sleep. Trying to squeeze your ears out through your headrest usually wasn't a good thing. Gaile hugged her pillow tight and wished the sensation of falling would go away.

It was after one such episode that Gaile, having already been shaken up pretty badly, decided to go exploring rather than attending classes.

Though, perhaps, it was as much a small rebellious means of escape; a chance to get some air and clear her head. She just wished the air out here wasn't so freakishly hot. Every breath felt like you were trying to roast your lungs.

Wandering about, mostly at random, it was a while before she realised just how far from the complex she'd gotten.

Gaile shaded her eyes. The Dragon Research Centre danced in the distance. She knew she shouldn't be out here for much longer. It was best she started thinking about returning. She certainly hadn't brought a kit for staying out here for anything longer than just a casual walk.

She had, however, stumbled across something curious. As such, she was, for the time being, loathe to leave. Curiosity could be a good thing. It could also get you into a whole lot of trouble – more trouble than you really wanted to get involved in.

Perhaps it was something in the human nature though, going unchanged through all the generations. It was what made you look out into the sunrise and wonder what was beyond it; if there was another sky somewhere. Another world. Another life.

It was what had driven people across whole oceans. It was what had driven them into the far reaches of space.

Of course, in the case of the original settlers on Casticia, the whole "far reaches of space" hadn't been somewhere they'd gone by choice. It was somewhere they'd ended up through circumstances so strange that they were, even today, practically unbelievable.

Now, they were reaching out there themselves, searching across the darkness and the light alike, for something else; though none was sure what it was.

That very same force was tickling the nerve-endings in Gaile's body right now, driving her forwards when everything else said she should go back.

It wasn't *entirely* unexpected. She just hadn't expected to stumble across it herself. After all, there had been plenty occasions that had proven that the map of the DRC held by the diom was only accurate when it wanted to be.

Was it then so strange to stumble across features that weren't shown on the map?

'Well, what d'you know… There *is* a way down other than the stairs after all,' Gaile murmured upon finding such a shadowed corner even this far from the actual site.

It wasn't that she'd been wandering around aimlessly – ok, maybe it was, but that wasn't the point. It was just that she hadn't meant to wander quite this far from the complex.

You could barely even see it, the DRC, the buildings, any more. Some of that might be the angle though, for the structures, especially the spire like tower which looked like as if someone had tried to spear a donut – were actually quite tall.

It could also possibly be the heat, which was not helping by making anything and everything even remotely distant waver and disappear, turning everything into just another patch of ochre … however unstable it might seem to the eye.

'Look at us,' it said. 'We're sand … just rock and sand. Nothing suspicious here so just more right on,' as if it was somehow trying to camouflage itself.

Foolish thoughts, Gaile decided. She'd learnt not to trust her eyes out here. Not that she was supposed to be out here.

But foolish or not, intentional or not, there was no doubt that her little "stroll" had taken her quite some distance away from what served as civilization in these parts. That's what you got for daydreaming when walking about. Gaile gave herself a small mental kick. Not too hard … she *liked* daydreaming. It just wasn't a good idea when you had no one that could point out to you that you really should have been paying more attention to where you were going.

Ok, enough of that. She didn't need her own subconscious berating her – everyone else was doing a fine job in that area already.

She really should head on back, she thought. It wasn't good to be out here all on your own. But she hadn't expected to stumble across such an interesting way down into the canyon.

Despite some initial misgivings Gaile felt a surge of anticipation – the eagerness to see what lay beyond the other side of the hill. It wasn't the first time she'd felt that feeling. She usually didn't act upon it though.

Of course, in this case, the hill was very much a figure of speech. Around here, the only real way, was down.

Also, it wasn't just that there was a way down, and a very broad way down it was. It was also not supposed to be there. That made it all the more intriguing. At least, Gaile corrected herself; it didn't appear on any of the maps of the area, which wasn't quite the same thing.

It was always possible that she'd suddenly stopped being able to accurately read a map but Gaile wasn't ready to admit she was *quite* that useless. Maybe it had been forgotten in an update or, maybe, it had been deliberately erased. A mystery then...

'So, a road where no road should be, eh,' Gaile mused, intrigued by the very thought. There seemed to be more than you'd have expected around here that came under the heading of "unexplained". The subterranean DRC of the past. The flickering on and off in the maps. Corridors that shouldn't have been there. Things not being what they appeared to be.

Ok, so calling this thing a road might be taking things a bit far, she admitted, gazing downwards. It was more like a dirt ramp; a very, very large dirt ramp.

'This must be at the very end of one of those side-branches to the canyon. Hmm ... how convenient,' Gaile said. And as she approached closer it became evident that the ramp consisted of more than just dirt.

A rockfall wouldn't have been enough to explain it. It looked like the whole end of the side-branch had collapsed, leaving a rough, boulder-enhanced slope down into the canyon as the rocks had kept on rolling.

Now, it was a semi-steep slope, helped along on the path to road-hood by some artificial intervention, because there was no way the dirt and sand had just moved itself on top of it to smooth things out all on its own. Gaile wasn't quite ready to believe in sentient planets ... even less in sentient sand grains. So someone must have come along after the natural event and "helped".

It looked oddly inviting.

It also looked gentle enough in its decent that Gaile didn't feel that familiar pit of dread in her stomach as all her nerves froze up and she could do nothing but pant heavily trying to force down a desire to turn and run on the spot, or, better yet, throw herself to the ground and cling to it with all her might. The DRC certainly wasn't the right place to suffer from vertigo.

Also, because the road … branch … thing twisted some hundred meters ahead or so, all she was really looking at when looking down was just another wall – not a single sheer drop in sight.

'Oh, what the heck…' Gaile huffed and took that first all important step. 'It looks solid enough to me. Hell, it looks solid enough for a couple of armoured transport crawlers. Wide enough for them too…'

That certainly was true enough. The road down was easily wide enough to accommodate several of those large machines running side by side – and they still wouldn't have been cramped for space.

'Wonder what they use this for?' Gaile asked as she strolled on down.

Her leisurely walk ended many minutes later with her body firmly pressed against the rock behind her and her staring out at the sight beyond or, more accurately, trying not to.

The descent didn't become steeper here, in fact it continued much the same. What had changed or, depending on how you looked at it, what was gone, was the rock-wall on the opposite side. Here, the wall of the side-branch had abruptly come to an end and the road continued down into the canyon by hugging the wall of the canyon itself.

Gaile swallowed. This had *not* been part of the plan.

No, this was not a good idea at all. All that ever came out of following these stupid impulses were trouble – she should have known that by now. Not that she was really capable of coherent reasoning at the moment.

First Flight had compounded her already bothersome problem with heights … and it wasn't like they'd been slight to begin with. Getting pushed out of a moving shuttle high, high in the sky when you were five without a parachute could have that effect on you.

Before that little "test" she'd been able to at least enjoy pictures of places she'd never dare to visit, even getting about and around some relatively minor heights (admittedly with butterflies in her stomach).

Now, even just the very thought of heights of any kind, of sheer drops with nothing below but the certainty of going splash, filled her with dread. No, it did more than that. It created nothing short of heart stopping terror.

And now her breath was coming out in rapid shallows. Her heart beat against its cage, pounding against her chest as if it was about to explode. Her fingers had turned to ice and her legs to a myriad million ants all shivering in place.

She couldn't move. She couldn't even tell if she was shaking or not.

It didn't matter that the road was so broad. She knew where it ended. She could see where it ended. She knew what was beyond that end ... that *edge*.

Gaile tried to burrow into the wall behind her.

On top of everything else, as if it was possible to make things worse, the buzzing was back. But this time that might actually be a good thing. Even on its own it was enough of a distraction to focus her mind on something else, if only for a moment.

Gaile shook her head harder as if trying to dislodge a particularly angry bee lost inside her brain somewhere.

The sudden motion brought a wave of queasiness to her middle region, upsetting her already frail balance. She dropped to her knees, to all fours and finally ended up flat on her stomach as her shivering limbs all gave out in turn.

Laying there, there was enough of herself left within that she fought back against the humiliation of it all. That was about all she was able to do.

'Stupid buzzing!' Gaile gasped.

It had to start up again *now*? It had been bothering her for several weeks already, that incessant buzzing and it was slowly driving her mad.

It hadn't started out that way; not *that* loud.

At first it had been faint and hadn't made itself known very often. Gaile hadn't even given it much thought originally, she'd thought it was the heater.

Then it had started appearing while she was in class. That was when she realized that it probably wasn't some random sound she was picking up. But even then it was nothing but a frail whisper just on the verge of sound.

Since then it had grown; not just in strength but in frequency as well, appearing more and more often.

Hours could go by – wonderful buzzfree hours (how she appreciated them now that she had something to compare with) then "bam" it'd hit her.

Sometimes it would only be there a moment – then it'd be gone. At other times it could go on for hours, growing louder and louder until it filled her entire mind.

For one thing, when it hit, she could no longer concentrate; she had to use all her willpower not to start clawing at her own scalp, trying to tear the noise out with her own bare hands. Studying was becoming more and more difficult with every day and she'd already fallen well behind everyone else – as if the time she'd spent in the infirmary or the underworld hadn't caused enough problems in that area.

Paying attention in class didn't go much better these days, not when it kicked in at full power. It was all she could do just to remain in her seat, wanting nothing more than to lay her head on the desk in front of her and just concentrate on the pain, for by now even her insides twisted themselves into a knot whenever it appeared.

That didn't have anything to do with the sounds though. They weren't that painful. It was how she was handling them that caused the real trouble … or maybe not.

Except there was no buzzing.

There was no noise either.

It was just a manifestation of stress and she should try to relax, maybe take a few days off. That's what they'd told her when Gaile had admitted defeat and had let the teacher send her to the infirmary for a check-up when she'd almost collapsed in class.

After a lot of tests they'd concluded that she was absolutely fine. There was nothing wrong with her.

But she didn't *feel* fine, no matter how many times they repeated, in different ways, that there were no abnormalities anywhere; but she could try to include more iron in her diet, as her readings were a bit low.

That wasn't, in Gaile's mind, really helping.

'What do they want me to do? Go out and start gnawing on an old anchor or something,' Gaile had muttered viciously afterwards. Like iron deficiency was going to make her hear things. Would it? They would have said if that'd been the case … she was sure of it.

She was just as sure that there *was* a noise. She kept on hearing it, didn't she? She might not know what caused it, but she sure knew what it was causing. Whatever it was, it was a damn bloody nuisance.

After having been seen by the doctors a second time, and with the attending physician very much indicating that he didn't like people who were just wasting his time, even though he never actually said so out loud, Gaile decided to keep it to herself.

And so, to avoid any more visits to the infirmary she'd grown to loathe, she fought the waves of nausea, of worry, that followed every appearance of the infernal noise.

Curled up in bed most days, Gaile tried to get it to go away or to at least get used to it. She'd stopped going to class ages ago now. Trying to follow through on the continued and increasingly more complex course and assignments with nothing but her trusty diom wasn't the easiest thing in the world and she had long suspected that it wasn't enough.

She wasn't going crazy. She wasn't. The buzzing *was* there. She could hear it – so of course it was there, wasn't it?

This time it wasn't so much a low buzzing coming from far off as a murmur coming from behind a wall; a very thick and insulated wall that distorted every sound from behind it. Mumbling, droning on, seemingly without end. It was also getting quite loud.

Gaile clutched at the dirt below. Her fingers dug into the surface of the road, her nails scraping into the dust and gravel.

'Go away. Go away. Go away! Go AWAY!' she moaned.

But it didn't. It never did.

Then, as she was trying to concentrate on anything else but the sound, her resting place fell into shadow.

Great, Gaile thought. I didn't know there were clouds in this place; at least *they* seem to like me. It *had* been getting a bit hot.

Whining, from the indignity of it all, Gaile only turned to lie on her right side because there was a painful stone in the wrong place.

The downside of that was that she'd be looking out over the canyon, but right now she didn't care, she turned anyway.

At least she *thought* she'd be looking out over that place of rock and dust. And true, the canyon was still there. It was however no longer occupying the number one spot in her mind or her instincts' priority list.

The view of the canyon was still there; all as spectacular as usual and just as deep. It was still there – on either side of the great head and neck that now leaned over her.

Momentarily forgetting to be afraid of where she was, Gaile managed to scrabble upright, backing up against the wall behind her without even realizing what she was doing.

Her heart thumping, having abandoned its chest cavity and lodged itself somewhere in her throat, Gaile stared at the dragon before her, eyes wide.

The dragon gazed down upon her in turn, its powerful neck craned above, a clawed hand resting on the edge of the road.

For several breaths' worth they remained like that, locked in place.

Then the buzzing returned, more powerful than ever. Gaile dropped down, pressing her hands against her ears, her face against her knees.

The point of a claw the size of a man's arm and then some came towards her and "nudged" her in the side, quite gently.

'… small … come … frail … looking …can't … becoming … sun … not well … not … ll … You are not well?'

That last bit was clear enough to make sense. But it wouldn't have mattered if it hadn't been. The rest was more than enough to get her attention as it was.

Rolling over, Gaile stared up at the dragon's head above her.

'You just *said* … something,' Gaile tried to find her voice in such an imposing presence. Everyone knew that dragons couldn't talk while in draconic form, didn't they?

The dragon drew back in alarm. It blinked at her a couple of times; looking not unlike a schoolteacher being caught out by a more knowledgeable pupil. Its features shifted through a stunned expression all the way to polite puzzlement to indifference and back again in a matter of a few seconds.

'You can hear me?' it queried.

'Yes,' Gaile nodded.

Actually, now that she thought about it "hear" might well be the wrong word. The dragon wasn't actually making any sounds. While a dragon's mouth was well equipped for a lot of things, human speech wasn't one of them.

It wasn't very clear either, that speech. It was kind of like trying to make out what someone was saying standing next to a small waterfall or through some heavy interstellar interference. But she could make it out – enough to make sense of the sentences anyway … now.

She shook her head again. It was still making her ears itch, like if they wanted to be in on the game as well.

'How very peculiar,' the dragon observed.

Having apparently satisfied itself that she wasn't about to expire on the spot, the dragon sat back on its haunches. Even sitting down, at the bottom of the canyon, below the road, the head still reached far above the level of the road itself.

Either I'm closer to the bottom than I thought or that dragon's big, Gaile thought. Really, *really* big. Actually, describing it as big would have been doing it an injustice. A red dragon was "big" but this one, if its head was anything to go by, this one was frigging huge. Huge and still elegantly proportioned, its scales more akin to hide, having an almost polished quality.

The sunlight glinted off the minute, almost metallic, silvery scales.

Silver?

Oh crap, Gaile thought. Oh, boy … am I in trouble now.

It wasn't so much a question as a prediction. She edged her way to the left – all thoughts of the drop beyond gone from her mind.

'Umm … sorry, sorry … I'll … err … I'll just … err … go … shall I?'

'Leaving?'

Rising up and, with one large front paw, the dragon touched the rock-wall just in front of her. Its fingers flexed the talon, biting into the earth and rock, showering the immediate area in a hail of small stones and dust. It had blocked her passage up.

'I think not!' the dragon intoned deeply.

'Err … right…'

Gaile grimaced, hoping that it didn't show just how the adrenalin was pumping through her veins at this moment. Could dragons smell fear? She couldn't remember. Had they covered that in one of the lessons she'd missed?

The dragon arched its neck, bending forward once more until its head was on the same level as her. A large eye, almost the size of a football, regarded her from less than half a foot away.

Gaile fought down a deep impulse to turn and run.

It wouldn't do any good, she told herself. It wouldn't really help. It wouldn't be sensible. And the dragon would surely be able to catch up with her either way. She didn't have any reason to be afraid – did she? Not really … right?

But far more primitive instincts were kicking in, overriding the calmer, more analytical side of her mind. What little part of that mind that still thought clearly – even in circumstances like these – suggested that she was being foolish. The rest of her was screaming at her legs, frozen as they were, to stop shaking and start moving. There's a god awful big lizard with huge teeth in front of you, it said. Run. Just run, it said, and we'll worry about the consequences later.

It was a very big eye – filled with swirling colours that faded and shifted, drifting in and out of focus – a veritable kaleidoscope of luminescence, it almost seemed to glow from within.

The dragon's breath ... she was so close she could hear it. She felt it as it struck the wall, the warmth panning out in all directions.

'Why do you hear me?' the deep voice demanded.

Gaile shook her head fiercely, as if trying to dislodge a particularly annoying thought. Her ears felt like they were being left out of the picture, whining in objection.

'How is it that you can hear me?' the dragon asked again.

'What?'

Gaile, who'd been staring vacantly at a point right in front of her, was brought back to reality by the sheer force behind the question. It held hints of a vast dam, of which she was actually coming into contact with but a few minor trickles.

'What?' she repeated. 'I … I don't know. How could I? It's not like this has happened before.'

Her fear was beginning to be replaced by annoyance now that it was apparent that she wasn't going to be eaten. 'And I'm NOT little!'

For a moment the dragon looked taken aback at her outburst. Then a draconic chuckle reverberated in its throat. 'No, I suppose it has not.'

The eye then watched her in silence, as if trying to come to a decision. The dragon drew back until all of his body was once again beyond the edge of the road.

'Look ... I'm sorry. I didn't know there was anyone here. I didn't mean to bother anyone – really,' Gaile tried to look suitably apologetic. 'I was just out walking. Just taking a stroll. Didn't mean anything by it – seriously ... nothing at all,' she said, speaking all too fast and stumbling over the words.

'Would you like to come down? This is not a suitable place for a conversation.'

'Umm...' The expression on her face clearly apprehensive, Gaile glanced first to her left, then to her right and back again. There was no longer anything blocking her passage back the way she'd come. But did that really matter? Whom was she trying to kid. It was a dragon. It had *wings*. It could overtake her in less time it took for its heart to beat even once.

'So ... I can go?' she asked hesitatingly.

'If that is what you wish,' the dragon agreed.

For a moment Gaile just stood there. Thoughts and sensations, questions and worries were all jumbled up. She sighed, her shoulders slumping forward. I'm going to get in *so* much trouble for this, I just know it, she thought.

'Down that way?' she asked, casting a nervous glance to her right.

'Of course.'

'Right...' Gaile sounded anything but happy with this. She took a hesitant step forward.

Now that the head of the dragon no longer dominated her immediate future ... nor its teeth, her vertigo had once more returned. She eyed the rest of the descent apprehensively. She was loathe to make a fool of herself in front of this person.

'You fear this height?'

'Yes,' Gaile responded from between clenched teeth. Ok, so much for *not* making a fool of herself.

'Do not fear it,' the dragon spoke calmly. 'I will not allow you to fall.'

'Easy for you to say,' Gaile muttered darkly as she picked her way down.

By the time she'd reached the bottom and made her way over to where the dragon had been she was already half expecting him to have switched to human form. That would have made holding a conversation easier, not to mention she wouldn't have to keep on craning her neck to see him properly.

How could she be so sure the dragon was a he anyway? Dragons didn't divide genders by colour. Somehow, it just *felt* right. But, while the dragon had laid down, his head now resting on his front feet and his great wings folded neatly against his sides, he remained very much a dragon.

It would have been impossible to mistake him for something else; say, a rather lost and sorry mountain goat for instance, regardless of distance.

Some dragons made excellent use of their hide's natural colour to blend into different environments, but Gaile had trouble imagining somewhere where this one *wouldn't* stand out, whether he wanted to or not.

Now that she'd gotten a good look at him he didn't feel quite as immense as before – that long neck was quite the distorter in terms of expected size.

He still *was* immense, only a fool would argue with that. He just didn't feel it, not quite, as much, anymore. Had she gotten used to the idea that quickly?

There was no doubt that he was impressive though. Even laying down he was easily the largest dragon she'd ever seen – even counting her textbooks.

It wasn't the bulk largeness of a brown either, who tended to be on the compact side. Nor was it like that of a bronze but simply scaled up and with a new paintjob added.

Of what she could see, the body was sleek, slender and elegant but without that frail looking built of the "greyhounds of the sky". Great muscles rippled under the surface of his "skin" suggesting enormous reserves of power. But they weren't the oversized muscles of a brown either.

It was hard to see with the wings folded up like this and Gaile squinted to see them better in the sunlight. It was even harder as there was basically no change in colour between the membrane stretched between the five fingers of the wings and those of the wingbones themselves or the dragon himself for that matter, something which you would have expected in almost any other dragon.

Even black dragons had slightly faded wings compared to their bodies, as the membranes were distinctly thinner than their hides, and there were many who had various degrees of translucence depending on that thickness. But here it was nearly opaque – about as see-through as a black hole, almost.

She couldn't see the tail, but the neck, long and slender, didn't share the slightly darkened pattern that many other dragons sported on the upper side of their neck compared to their belly nor did he display any kind of segregated throat. The crest was carved elegantly in a gentle curve coming to a point further back, kind of like the tip of a horn, and two smaller ones protruded beneath that central one, curving first up then downwards.

The head was built along the same lines as the body – an almost sharp angle to the snout which then sloped gently upwards to the forehead. A wide jaw at the back of the gently triangular head grew narrower the closer to the slightly rounded snout you got. He had remarkably understated brow-ridges for his size, his eyes set far up on his head.

There was a slightly elevated ridge that rose just a touch above the rest of the face, running from the level of the eyes and down in the middle. Topped off with a main skull crowned by two sets of sweeping appendages between which you could spot just a slight hint of blue.

Most of the body was smooth, the scales so minute that his outer layer was more akin to a highly durable skin than the distinctly shaped scales found on many dragons.

When watching him you got the impression that someone had taken all the best features of all other dragons, reds and bronzes, blues and greens, blacks, whites and even gold, added a few quirks and chosen a new colour scheme just as a final point.

How many had there been, now that she was thinking about it? Silver dragons that was... Only a handful, Gaile knew that much from her own experiences. She didn't need a lesson to learn that. Actually, practically anyone could have told you.

Less than a handful even ... and they were all different.

Sure, there were differences within the other types as well, but they, generally, had more in common than they did not. The only thing that silvers had in common, as far as she could remember, was the fact that their silvery, almost metallic, colour and sheen came alongside the fact that they were, easily, the biggest dragons around.

'If you are *quite* finished?' the dragon said.

'Ah, yes … sorry,' Gaile stumbled over the words, embarrassment burning her cheeks. She'd completely forgotten where she was, she'd been so engrossed.

The young woman picked a comfortable looking spot some distance from the dragon and settled down. Cross-legged, she now faced him directly.

Well, technically she faced his feet, but still…

There passed several minutes of silence, as of two opponents sizing each other up before an inevitable battle.

'Have you been having trouble with your hearing?' he asked.

The question completely throwing her off guard, Gaile struggled to change gears. She'd been braced for all kinds of things, but that? 'Well … yes,' she admitted reluctantly and not a little bit confused. 'I suppose.'

'And you have been *hearing* sounds that others can not?'

'Very much so,' Gaile agreed.

'Describe them to me,' he rumbled.

'Hmm…' Gaile drummed her fingers against her thigh, trying to think fast. 'I think, hmm … that at first it was just a sort of low pitched whine – like someone had a faulty heater you know. That's what I thought it was, at first. After that … well … I suppose it started buzzing, you know, like a cross between a bee and a radio station trying to get through a plasma field. It stayed like that for ages, coming and going. It's really inconvenient you know.'

'And then?' the dragon encouraged her before she could get distracted by complaining.

'And then? It's been murmuring at me for days and just now…' Gaile shrugged. 'Well, you know that part.'

'Indeed,' the voice agreed.

'I even went to the infirmary. Well, was sent to the infirmary. They did all sorts of tests. But they all say there's nothing wrong with me. There isn't anything wrong with me, is there?' I'm not losing my mind or anything, am I?' Gaile's voice rose sharply, pleading.

There was another burst of draconic chuckle that washed over her.

At least she presumed it was a chuckle. He didn't answer though, only pressed on with another question.

'How much do you know about riders and dragons ... and about how they communicate?' he queried.

'Err...' Gaile hesitated. This was perhaps another thing from those classes she'd missed.

'Telepathy maybe?' she suggested, feeling foolish.

The dragon snorted and a sound like a small cannon going off erupted from him, sending her several nerves short of a basket.

'There is no such thing as telepathy. That is merely a myth. It is easy to see why people would believe such a thing, but the answer is much more mundane – although I will not profess to fully understand the details of *how* it works.'

He shifted his weight slightly as he gathered his thoughts. He knew for certain that they didn't teach this. It was something that you were only supposed to know if you were a rider. Oh, how complicated things had become.

Try as he might, he could see no other way, aside from brushing off the incident completely, pretending it had never happened. It certainly would be easier than trying to explain.

He gazed down at the small creature before him. Hmm ... perhaps *some* explanation would suffice?

'Very well. Listen carefully. There are many and varied ways that the different members of the DragonCorps communicate with each other,' he said, settling into what sounded suspiciously like a lecturing mode.

'The most efficient are the same means by which you yourself communicate with others, speech. This is aided, of course, at suitable times, by directional implements such as communicators and their like. This works well between humans or dragons in human form. There is also body language and more subtle, subconscious ways that we all surround ourselves with and respond to, though it is rare that we ourselves are aware of them.'

He took a deep breath and continued. 'It is possible, as I mentioned already, to communicate from dragon to dragon while in draconic form, though I hesitate to refer to it as speech. It can convey simple meanings, but nothing overly complex. And then there is…'

He hesitated again before taking the final plunge, not failing to note the renewed interest of his audience. '…and then there is the communication that happens between dragons and humans … or perhaps I should say, between dragon and rider. I emphasize that while we are in draconic form and can no longer speak a sensible language, a dragon is simply not designed for such a task, that does not affect our ability to understand it, as you will have noticed, I am sure,' he regarded her questioningly.

'Yes,' Gaile agreed and then added. 'I'm speaking out loud, normally, but you're … ehem … not.'

'Precisely. And do you know why that is?'

Aside from what you already told me, no? That's why I wanted to know in the first place, smart-mouth, Gaile thought. Outwardly she merely shook her head. Perhaps it was a very good thing that he couldn't read her mind.

'While here … like this, I have no problem hearing you. It would be a very different matter if we were further apart or, indeed, rushing through the air at high speed. And, of course, we would have no means of communicating then, responding back to any words we would hear, since, when wearing an insulation suit and helmet, a rider would be unlikely to hear us with any degree of accuracy.'

Nodding, Gaile indicated that she was following this so far. Maybe it wasn't a hundred percent that she could say made sense, but she got the general idea.

'Before I explain further, could you tell me? Has anything happened recently, before you started hearing these sounds? I gather that you have not always done so?' the dragon appealed to her looking down his long snout to where she sat.

Gaile felt uncomfortable with the question. It brought back things she'd rather not remember. 'I fell down,' she offered eventually.

'That does not seem indicative of what I was thinking of,' the dragon sounded disappointed.

'…three flights,' Gaile continued, her teeth on edge. 'I'm sorry. I don't remember it really. No actually, I'm glad I don't remember it. But I can't help you.'

'Three flights?' he looked at her, a puzzled frown on his face.

'First Flight. It was a bit of a … err … disaster. I spent two weeks in the infirmary, unconscious, apparently. They told me I landed really badly and they needed to do a bit of work on my skull to fix it,' she grimaced. 'But that's all I know.'

'I see,' he said. 'Perhaps that is the reason.'

'What? Wait a minute. I hit my head and suddenly I hear dragons? Do you know how stupid that sounds?'

'Very stupid,' the silver dragon agreed. 'It was not hitting your head that would have made the difference, but what they did to fix it.'

'So they mess with my head and *then* I hear dragons? That doesn't seem much of an improvement,' Gaile growled.

'Not dragons. Dragon. Singular,' he stressed, looking affronted despite not changing his facial expression.

'Great,' Gaile winced. 'And that makes me feel so much better. Thank you.'

The dragon cleared his throat importantly, a single glance enough to convey what he thought of her sarcastic interruptions.

'When a rider is chosen there is something important given to them. This is a department that I am not an expert in, but you can think of it as a receiver, though it is nothing like that,' he paused for a moment, trying to think of an easy way of describing something that he wasn't entirely sure about himself.

It was only when he caught a subdued 'ahem' from his public that he seemed to gather himself together again and continued.

'Well … as I said… A clear crystal from The Valley that has been imbibed with the blood of the dragon in question is placed inside the skull of the rider. This will begin to release minute particles of dragon blood into the blood-stream of the human.

It must be such small amounts as humans do not react well to the dragon's blood in their bodies and the result does not work indiscriminately once the adjustment period is over. Upon implantation a new rider will almost *always* complain of just such symptoms as you described to me earlier. For some it is less – for others … others can not bear it and the implant has to be removed less they … go insane, trying to claw their own brains out.

You understand, this is something that is not known outside of the community and it must remain that way. Once this trial period is over a rider should be able to "hear" when their dragon actively chooses to "speak" with them or sometimes when they are talking to themselves if they do so in a powerful enough voice. If they constantly picked up random thoughts it would undoubtedly be unpleasant.'

'No kidding,' Gaile agreed.

She knew that last all too well. She had, after all, been doing exactly that for weeks now. Had he forgotten that already?

The dragon merely looked down his long snout, giving her an eye until she saw fit to stop interrupting.

'Unfortunately it only works in one direction. While in human form we are unable to utilize this feature, though we do not know why. It does not ... yes?'

'Wait a minute right there,' Gaile, who'd been sitting quietly, protested, throwing her arms out. 'I am *not* a rider.'

'That would be blindingly obvious,' the silver dragon replied curtly.

'Then how come I'm the one stuck with this stupid thing then?'

'That much I do not know. It is, for now, somewhat of a mystery,' he agreed sagely.

'Great,' Gaile muttered. 'I think I'm more confused now than *before* your explanation.'

She sighed. Putting her arms behind her she leant backwards, staring up at the sky. It had gotten darker. This whole thing must have taken much longer than she'd thought. It hadn't felt that long. The conversation ... she sighed again. And this was just supposed to have been a small excursion to steal some time for herself.

Now what was she supposed to do?

The instructors are absolutely going to kill me for this, Gaile thought. Typical – and I wasn't even *trying* to get into trouble. Nothing new there then.

Raising his head, the silver dragon followed her gaze. It was indeed getting darker.

That was one of the unfortunate side effects of being located in this spot; the DRC that was. Once nature felt like it was time to turn off the light she didn't mess about. It wasn't quite as fast as flicking a switch, though sometimes it certainly felt that way. If you weren't careful or if you were distracted, it would sneak up on you easily. How inconsiderate of it.

'I would offer to bring you back but I…'

'…don't think it's a very good idea,' Gaile finished for him. 'I agree. That's the last thing I need. If the teachers don't cause trouble over it, which they will, given that little lecture we got about not bothering people, then the rest of the students certainly will. Thanks, but no thanks. I have no wish to wake up one morning with six inches of steel between my shoulder blades.'

'If you had six inches of steel between your shoulder blades it is unlikely that you would be waking up,' the dragon advised.

Gaile got back to her feet, working out the kinks from sitting down for so long. 'I'll get back on my own,' she said, then waved at him irritably over that last little jibe. 'Ah, you know what I meant.'

'That would not be advisable.'

'I can't well stay out here, now can I?' Gaile challenged him. Muttering under her breath, she stomped away towards the ramp. It was already beginning to get hard to make out more distant features.

Who did he think he was? Ordering her around like that? Pfft. It was bad enough that she had to hear dragons … why did she have to hear *him* of all the ones that lived here? Typical. Just her luck.

Wasn't it enough that some of the students seemed to have stirred up some sort of vendetta against her? She did *not* need the dragons to start doing the same.

'You are being quite foolish,' he admonished her calmly.

'So sue me!' Gaile growled.

Hopefully he didn't catch that part – she wasn't sure how sensitive this dragon's hearing was, it wasn't exactly something they covered in the textbooks. It probably differed just as much as it did with straight humans.

A moment later and she felt herself sailing into the air as the dragon picked her up.

'Aaaaah! Put me down. Put me down right now!' she beat her tiny fist against the massive fingers that cradled her, having hoisted her aloft.

'Stop struggling, I might drop you,' was the dragon's only comment.

Trying to keep his grip as gentle as possible, he moved forwards, minus one forearm. It took only a couple of steps for him to decide that this hobbled gait was ill-fitting for a dragon, to say nothing about uncomfortable and slow.

'Hold on now,' he told the sulking human, as, after an initial false start, she was deposited onto his back. 'This should be much faster.'

'Umm...' Gaile looked around. 'Hold on to *what* exactly?'

Considering he was a dragon, there was very little in terms of handholds.

'I probably should mention, eh ... I completely failed First Ride and that was *with* a saddle,' Gaile's eyes were getting a bit wild at this point.

The dragon laughed at her; actually, properly, laughed. At least, that's what she assumed those noised were. It shook her about quite a bit.

'Those...' he scoffed. 'This isn't anything like that,' he smiled inwards.

Even so he made sure to walk very slowly for the first few steps. A terrified human on his back could end up in all sorts of trouble and the last thing he needed was for her to fall and break her neck out here.

Soon though, surprisingly soon, the silvery dragon picked up his pace. Moving at a brisk walk he headed out into the canyon.

Gaile clung on as tight as she could at first, eyes closed. Only slowly did it dawn on her that her stomach wasn't rebelling and that she hadn't fallen off.

Risking raising her head rather than laying down flat with her arms and legs spread to the side for maximum support, oh how silly she must look, the landscape, what little she could see, wasn't moving up and down either, not much.

She pulled herself up. Still apprehensive about the whole thing, she was expecting the same experience as last time to start at any moment, regardless of what he he'd said about it.

'Relax human. First Ride is meant to be a terrible experience. The dragons do it on purpose. Stop worrying about everything so much,' the dragon once more spoke to her in that calm yet slightly amused tone.

Gradually, very gradually, Gaile sat up. Or at least her pose came to re-sembling someone sitting up rather than something trying to do an impersonation of a fried egg. He was right. This wasn't *anything* like that ride at all.

She could feel muscles moving beneath her, supporting her dragon. She could see the wings folded so neatly on either side, acting like a barrier from being able to look straight down.

By the time they reached what must have been their destination, since they stopped moving, Gaile had actually, for the first time since she'd come to the DRC, started enjoying the time she spent with a dragon.

Of course, stopping that suddenly had a few drawbacks.

'Whoaaaaah…'

Gaile held on to where she'd slid outwards onto the dragon's neck. 'Ugh … warn me next time, ok,' she scolded him.

'Sorry,' he apologized. 'I forgot.'

She couldn't tell for certain if he was sincerely apologetic or not, to say nothing about if he'd done it on purpose in the first place.

Gaile took in their surroundings. There wasn't all that much to see really. It looked the same as the rest of the canyon to her. 'Where are we anyway?' she asked.

'Look up,' the dragon suggested.

As she did so, some of the last light of the setting sun gleamed off what looked like a broken set of windows – a whole row of, mostly, empty frames several stories high, far, far above them. They were set directly into the rock-wall itself.

'Oh, I'm looking up. I see windows. Well, what were windows at some point. Why am I looking at windows?'

'The original facility, what remains of it. It has been abandoned for quite some time.'

'I can see that. Can't get much in terms of visitors,' Gaile quipped.

She watched as he brought them clear and, once around a corner, the remains of the place were present even down here, on ground level.

This part didn't have windows but seemed to consist of large, slanting metallic structures reaching ever upwards. Here and there more rectangular protrusions ran vertically, a thick base at the bottom and growing thinner towards the top.

But that wasn't what caught her attention.

In the centre, and set quite a bit higher than the rest of the structure, was a portal-like opening; a vast circular door.

'The old launch shaft,' the dragon answered her unspoken question. 'We can not enter that way.'

Gaile, having now seen where they were going, was already having second thoughts about the whole thing, and breathed a sigh of relief upon those news. The place did *not* look very inviting. Also, it looked a bit high up to tell you the truth.

'We will need to enter through the service gate, to the far right. The gates appear to have retracted into the walls,' her new companion explained. 'Unfortunately they can no longer be closed. There is also no power down here, so please hurry and make any preparations you need and make yourself comfortable while you can still see.'

As the dragon spoke, he entered through the dark doorway, turned around and lay down in the centre of what looked like a loading dock of some kind. The place would have appeared cavern-like had he not been so large. As it was he took up almost all the central space.

Moving around as to face the dark night descending outside, he tucked his tail in close and closed his eyes, content to ignore the human half of the duo for the time being.

In the morning she would be able to go back to the rest of them. That was good. It was better if he didn't get involved. He didn't need that. There was no…

'What about, you know … predators?' Gaile peered nervously out into the darkness and into the night beyond.

'What would attack a dragon in its own lair?' he rumbled.

'That's what worries me,' Gaile mumbled in return.

Apparently he wasn't going to change, Gaile realized. Did that mean he couldn't? That he was one of those few dragons who – born a dragon – remained like that throughout their lives? Or was he just refusing to do so with her present to see it? She couldn't tell.

It was by the light of her diom that Gaile finally managed to make herself a makeshift little nest from what she could scavenge from the remaining content of the place.

At least I don't have to worry about freezing to death, she thought. In this enclosed space, even with the door open, the warmth of the dragon's body stood as diffuse, invisible armour against the cold that had fallen over the land as the last of the light had disappeared.

In a few hours the moon would rise over the horizon, but Gaile wasn't sure how much difference that would make in here. Not only didn't she keep track of where it rose normally, even if she had, she wasn't altogether certain what direction they were facing anyway.

'Typical,' she mumbled, curled up where she was. 'Why don't I get to have *exciting* adventures like everyone else? No, I get the lecturing kind.'

And on that note, she eventually drifted off to sleep.

Watching your step

'No! Silber! Bad Dragon!' Gaile shouted from the doorway to the laboratory.

Her voice rang out over the wide and open room; easy to hear for anyone that might have been paying attention. Not that anyone was; not to her anyway

Where were they? She'd been chasing the small dragonling all over the place for the last twenty or thirty minutes. Leaving a small trail of destruction in their wake, the pair had moved from area to area in the Academy.

Now they were ... somewhere else. What she did know for certain was that they were both somewhere they shouldn't be. Students weren't supposed to have access to the DRC itself. What it said about dragonlings she didn't know, but somehow Gaile doubted that they were welcome uninvited no matter how nice it might be to see them otherwise

There was just something about small creatures that could fly and were insatiably curious that just didn't mix well with places where people were trying to work or, worse, perform delicate and time-staking calculations.

Paper had a tendency to scatter.

So did a lot of other things...

Not that Silber had let that stop him.

After partially wrecking a whole section of leaves set out to dry in a display of colour, trying to scramble over the stand, the small dragonling had taken off through a door that two members of the corps were just coming through.

That had cut off most of the pursuit from the Academy, but Gaile had been close enough, as the shocked staff had dived out of the way of the silvery bullet, to slip through before it closed.

She'd sworn out loud as her friend, who'd stopping briefly to give her one of those "looks", dashed away down the corridor. What else could she do but follow?

Happening upon the open door to one of the laboratories, he'd sniffed the air and hovered in place for about two seconds before streaking through the oh-so-inviting open hole.

By now, the dragonling had already upturned several stationary beakers after landing on a long lab bench, caused a stack of paperwork to be dislodged from an upper shelf and scatter throughout the room, as paper was wont to do when fanned by even the smallest of winds, and made the two assistants dive for cover as he swooped over their heads, all the while chattering at them as if they'd personally offended him.

Now he was scrabbling over a number of old-fashioned volumes of books that someone had stacked, very carefully, at the edge of one of the benches. Subsequently the books soon went one way and the dragonling another.

Silber called out, a complaining alto reverberating through the room as he shook his head to clear it.

The lab staff were alternatively clutching their precious work protectively or looking around for something to catch the escaped creature with.

'Get him!' one of the white-smocked lab assistants cried out.

'Don't let him near the petri-dishes,' called another. Spreading his arms wide the man guarded the desktops below the cupboards at the far end with flapping arms.

'Shoo!' he cried. 'Shoo I say!'

Silber, clearly unhappy with so many hands grabbing for him, hissed as another drew close. His tiny jaws snapped shut only inches from the young man's hands. The hands were quickly retracted.

'Not like that you fool,' a woman's voice, exasperated, called out to him.

'Oh, for goodness sake,' another one of the occupants of the room, apart from Gaile, bent into one of the floor-side shelving units and peered into it. She came up holding a flat package which she tore open, revealing a white interior. It turned out to be a large and very new lab coat.

'Just box him in,' she instructed the two assistants, 'and I'll do the rest.'

'Please,' Gaile pleaded. 'If you'd just let me get him…' she tried to manoeuvre in somewhere more favourable but everyone in the room, the dragonling included, kept changing places so often and so quickly that she had trouble deciding where to go.

Regardless of what she chose, she kept ending up the furthest from the actual action.

The doctor shook out her improvised blanket and suddenly flung it forward. Silber let out an ear piercing shriek and launched himself into the air, knocking over several beakers and some test tubes in the process. They proceeded to drench the formerly white lab coat which had landed exactly where he'd been only moments before, creating an unseemly array of large coloured splotches.

'Quick little devil, aren't you,' the doctor purred icily.

The dragonling circled the laboratory once more and then aimed for the only other door available – a divider with the top half in some transparent material.

'Dr Pters,' a calm voice inserted itself into the chaos. 'If you would be so kind as to close that door. Quickly now.'

'…yes, Sir … right away,' Pters stuttered and retreated into the adjoining room, pulling the door firmly shut behind him.

Silber let out a disappointed screech, touched the door lightly and angled off in another direction before the doctor behind him had time to grab him.

'I'll get you,' the woman snarled, waving her weapon in the air. 'I'll teach you to ruin someone else's experiments!'

Having landed on a top cupboard and momentarily being safely out of reach, Silber merely bared his fangs at her, hissing.

'Alright! Get me some of the red stuff from the jar labelled $N2^3$,' she instructed one of her assistants without taking her eyes of her prey. She'd slipped badly on that last spillage. Her hip was hurting and already a bruise was starting to form.

'And some gloves … and a mask, there's a dear,' she added.

Careful to don the gloves first, the assistants might be able to handle the stuff without protection, but she couldn't, the doctor threw the now still dragonling an unpleasant glare.

$N2^3$ wasn't dangerous – just plain foul. It'd be weeks before her nasal faculties returned to normal if she breathed in any of that stuff.

Silber was watching her intently, twitching. He leaped into the air the same moment as the good doctor thrust a handful of the powder in his direction. The dragonling, despite turning at the last moment, caught it full in the face.

He lost control, crashing into a heap on the floor, clawing at his nostrils. Eyes crossed, the silvery dragonling made scuffing, whuffing sounds of utter disgust.

'Aha! Gotcha!' Dr Rokoskiev exclaimed, tossing the lab coat over him. At least, she tossed it over where the small creature had been only moments before.

That was the second time he'd outguessed her. Unusually clever little thing. It was almost as if he knew what she was going to do next.

Silber retreated to the only safe place in the vicinity and smacked into Gaile at force. Trying to burrow in under her coat, as Dr Rokoskiev approached, a stern line to her lips, he stuck out a head and hurled a torment of abuse at her, snarling; a snarl that ended in coughing.

'And serve you right too,' Dr Rokoskiev observed. 'As for you young lady. I'm sure that you know that this area if out of bounds for students?'

'Yes, but…' Gaile tried to explain.

'Give me that creature and I'll see to it that he gets back to where he belongs. Which, I might point out, is *not* with you.'

Gaile, her expression like a sun sinking into a nether realm made out of stubbornness, clutched her friend tighter. The dragonling gave a surprised squeak.

'Now, now, there's no need for that, either of you,' the fourth presence still in the room spoke again.

As the man got to his feet from where he'd been hunkered down under a bench, Gaile wondered how they could have missed noticing him. Recent events certainly hadn't missed doing the same.

Something yellow and viscous was dripping slowly onto his face and shoulders from where it clung in large dollops to his hair. There was what most definitely appeared to be a burn hole, or what was left of it, in his right sleeve, which in turn had been soaked with something that you could only hope was water.

He walked towards them with a noticeable limp.

'Dr Cosgrove, I didn't see you there,' Rokoskiev appeared startled, though if it was more because of his sudden appearance or his actual appearance was anyone's guess.

'Obviously,' Dr Cosgrove noted dryly. 'Or perhaps knocking that vial of serum over me was quite intentional.'

He sounded stern, but there was a certain movement in the corners of his eyes that suggested all what not what it seemed.

Even so, Dr Rokoskiev looked abashed. 'Sorry, Sir, I didn't mean...'

'I know, I know,' Dr Cosgrove interrupted her. 'Now, as to these two,' he paused to regard the couple of miscreants for several moments while trying to gather his thoughts.

How odd. How very, very peculiar. Still, he wasn't the one to look a gift horse in the mouth – or gift dragonling in this case. Such an opportunity should not be discarded lightly. Perhaps he should ... yes, that might actually work even if all he could do was to give it a small nudge and hope for the best.

'You two certainly seem to have caused quite some trouble,' he said out loud.

'Yes, Sir. Sorry about that, Sir,' Gaile tried to look apologetic. She might not recognize the man in question, but she did recognize the name.

Privately she felt that the only one who had been causing trouble was Silber; all *she'd* been doing was trying to stop him. He'd been doing more of that than usual lately. An uncanny ability to pop up in all sorts of strange places, that was him in a nutshell.

'Your friend here is quite the mischief maker, isn't he?' Dr Cosgrove inquired gently.

'Yes, Sir,' Gaile replied.

'Why don't you go bring him back to the Hive, young lady. I'm sure he will be much better off for a bath or several. That $N2^3$ can be quite the shock I understand.'

'Sir. If you don't mind ... what is it?' Gaile tried to keep the now struggling dragonling under control.

'N2^3?' Dr Cosgrove asked. 'Oh, nothing more than smelling salts. Very strong smelling salts,' he smiled, only a hint of disapproval seeping through. 'But then a dragonling's senses are so much more acute than ours, especially their olfactory receptors. Go on now. I dare say your friend will stay calm for a few days at least.'

Gaile nodded, retreating quickly. She was thankful for that she didn't seem to be in line for getting punished over this little escapade, a minor miracle in its own right. Now all she needed to do was to find her way back. It'd be just her luck to end up even further into the DRC … best to be careful.

Dr Cosgrove's eyes trailed them until the corner around which the two of them disappeared.

'Dr Cosgrove? You don't mean to let that student off without any sort of repercussion, at all?' Dr Rokoskiev blinked at him.

She looked much more pleasant to deal with now that her face wasn't contorted into a grimace akin to a ruche on the warpath. Even so, she still didn't look altogether happy.

'My dear Asura, *that* was what they call an opportunity. An opportunity just walking in here all on its own. Well, maybe not entirely on its own, I imagine it had a bit of help, but even so,' the good doctor twinkled at her.

'An opportunity?' Dr Rokoskiev regarded him with a questioning gaze while he cleaned up the mess on his head, clearly not sure what to believe.

'Yes, an opportunity and what an opportunity indeed.'

'I'm still not following you, Sir?'

'That's alright. All shall be revealed, in time. Assuming we get that far,' here Dr Cosgrove sighed. 'Still, it's worth trying for, don't you think?'

'Sir? I really have no idea what you're talking about.'

'No, you obviously do not,' Dr Cosgrove nodded amiably. 'Incidentally, would you have considered busting up a lab just to make a point? Just curious?'

'Of course not.'

'And why not?'

Dr Rokoskiev looked at him aghast. 'I am a dragon, *not* a *cretin*!' Dr Rokoskiev said empathically and turned to attend to her own dishevelled state before starting on the clean-up. What a mess, she thought.

Rokoskiev had quite the bit to clear up but it didn't take her very long. She was just grateful no one had chosen to bother her about helping setting up for the fieldtrip that was coming up in the next few days.

That wasn't as strange as it sounded … they'd known better.

* * *

'Ok everyone, listen up,' Tam cupped his hands before his mouth. 'Can everyone hear me?'

A more or less affirmative murmur rose from the assembled students crowded together in the shuttle. There was no need to shout they thought, nothing wrong with their ears.

'Excellent. I'm sure you're all eager to get started with today's navigation exercises, so just a few words before we get on with it…' Tam noticed the raised arm and stopped speaking. 'Yes, Miss Sternmasser?'

'Please, Sir, is today a practical session?'

'I would certainly hope so,' he replied. 'I don't imagine flying you all, *all* the way out here just so that you can stand around listening to a bunch of people in white coats giving a lecture would be worth anyone's time, do you? Listening you can do in the auditorium.'

'Yes, Sir,' Robin sat back down in her seat, looking nothing if not a bit dejected. He didn't need to be so blunt about it.

'As I was saying … just a few words and then off you'll go. You've all had the classes, so you should all understand the theory by now. Many of you even completed the last set of assignments for which, I assure you, there was no single right answer.

Today, we'll see how well you can translate what you've learnt into action. Perhaps, that'll also show you the difference between understanding something in the classroom and being able to perform it in the field. There's still quite a few of you so some of the second and third years will be assisting.'

Erina took that moment to wave an arm in the air, to make sure they could see her. Tam was right, there were quite a few of them in here, and, aside from being a bit on the crowded side, it also meant that it wasn't all that easy to stand up and make yourself noticed.

'If you look at your notes, you've all been assigned a number. Those with a one, if you could follow your leader please.'

The tall redheaded girl managed to extract herself from her seat, squeeze past the rest of the row and move over to the doorway. Her bag was slung over her shoulder, the strap tangled up among the long hair.

'Ok people. All the Ones after me. Hup. Hup.'

Since the shuttle was a bit crowded, well, perhaps more than a bit, there was a certain amount of pushing, stepping on other people's toes and placing your hands where you grabbed other people's hair by accident while trying to pull yourself out of your own seat, before a third of the students managed to get out of the place.

'Twos… You'll be starting with our second course for today. So Johnston will be taking you over to the opposite end,' Tam instructed.

Stewart Johnston turned out to be a smiling, relaxed looking man, a bit older than the majority of them and someone who clearly needed a shave in the eyes of his teacher.

He waved cheerfully at them and, with a great deal less difficulty, extracted his third – half of those that were left. They disappeared out onto green field beyond. This was evidently grass country, wherever they were.

It had been a bit disconcerting at first, not always knowing exactly where you were. They hadn't been used to that but by now they'd had so many lectures and practicals where their dioms were confiscated that they'd begun to acclimatize.

It was still a strange feeling though; looking out over a land and not knowing where it was. Several of the remaining students were trying to see what was going on outside.

'Hey … what are they doing?' Drak leaned over the person closest to the viewport to see better.

'I can't tell,' one of the girls replied. 'They just seem to be standing there really.'

'That will be quite enough chatter,' Tam indicated the door. 'If you will all be so kind as to vacate the premises,' he said coldly, 'the third group is already waiting for you.'

As the day progressed, as far as Gaile was concerned, she was getting bored really quickly.

Working together with others for a common goal had never been one of her strong suits and today wasn't going any better than the last hundred times when they'd asked it of her.

The result was easy enough to predict ... had anyone bothered.

Now, she was spending the rest of the time on the first station her group had been assigned to, watching the rest of them.

They'd been working with small, fixed winged models; much like the one Drak had wrecked the last time he'd been allowed anywhere near one.

In this case "small" might have been the wrong word to use; several of them had a wingspan that easily measured over a meter. Compared to the full scale works that were being used on the next station over however, they were definitely "smaller".

The problem was that you weren't the only one using them and not in sole control of it either. You were supposed to work with your partner to get them through the obstacle course...

Here, the word "supposed to" was about as accurate as you could get. Some were having more trouble than others, even she could tell that. Others were having way too much fun for such an assigned task.

'Left. Left! Up ... no, Right! UP!'

'Jens, make your bloody mind up.'

'Left again. Right. Right. Down a bit. Up. UP!'

'Give me a break', Cole snarled.

'Noooo! You're going the wrong way!'

'Will you shut up and let me fly?'

'I'm supposed to be the navigator here,' Jens complained.

'So start navigating then.'

'I AM!'

'Boys, boys...' Clarissiia, one of their sternest teachers, who'd strolled over at the sound of the agitated voices, admonished them. 'Less arguing and more synchronizing from the two of you. You have already lost your glider model,' she pointed out.

That was true. It had given up the ghost and wasn't accepting any more input, no matter how much Cole twiddled the dials.

'Aww man…' Jens ripped off the heads-up display and shot his assigned "partner" a dagger-like glare.

The model in question had gone into self-suspended hover-mode as they'd lost control and was now floating just a few inches above the grass. It looked no worse for wear but for all the intents and purposes of the practical field experience they were undergoing, it had crashed.

'Now, where do you think you went wrong?' Clarissiia asked, her hawk-like eyes narrowing.

Neither of the two students felt much like trying to decipher that, so they just mumbled something uncommitted. She, of course, wasn't impressed. And, in turn, their teacher, having received the controller for the model back from Cole, busied herself for a moment resetting the thing's instructions so that it'd return to the starting line.

'If Cole wasn't such a backseat driver there wouldn't be a problem,' Jens huffed.

Clarissiia silenced the upcoming argument with a *look*. 'What do you think this part of today's exercise is all about?' she asked and quickly continued without waiting for an answer. 'It is about trust. Trust *and* the ability to communicate effectively. That is why only one of you can control the model and the other being the only one who can see where you're going.

Effective communication and trust are essential between a dragon and rider. To place your lives in the hand of another without hesitation takes no small amount of either.'

'But…Sir… I can fly these just fine on my own. He's cramping my style.'

'Mr Stibbins, that's quite enough. I'll hear no more of this. You two can help gather up the course once this is over.'

Both boys made the same sour expression at this piece of news. 'Ahhhh…'

The course that had been created for the model gliders (though why they were called that when they were obviously powered no one knew) was *huge*.

Actually, most of the obstacles themselves weren't that large, because the models weren't *that* big. There were small hoops, large hoops, ribs that needed to be crossed over (and sometimes under) some you even had to go through the middle of two of them.

There were places requiring zigzag manoeuvres, entering hollow pylons and having to guide the craft to remote openings (the correct one at that, as there were several to choose from) and many more. None of them where, by and large, neither huge nor heavy. What they were, were spread out – over a wide area; a very wide area.

Gaile felt sorry for the clean-up crew. It'd take ages gathering up all the pieces and making sure no parts had fallen off only to get left behind as they went back home. What a pain.

They weren't the only ones in their group having trouble with the exercise either. Small comfort, they thought, each to themselves. Failing among many was still failing and it wasn't even *their* fault.

With another few slicing remarks the two split up, going somewhere where they could watch the rest of the mess in better company.

'Aww ... don't take it so hard,' Kalim said encouragingly when Cole complained over what had happened.

The smaller boy had fallen foul of one of the block canyons already. He'd meant to say 'left.' He had said 'right.' The model had actually crashed into a three corners section of the wall, the proximity sensors not having reacted quickly enough in relation to the change in the engine output.

'Easy for you to say. At least you actually did something wrong.'

Kalim shrugged. It was just a lesson. They'd get more lessons to work on their teamwork, he was sure about that.

Some were obviously needing them more than others by the looks of it though. And so far not a single team in their group had managed to cross the finish line. Kalim, having a somewhat suspicious nature, wondered if the teachers had deliberately set the teams as to provide the biggest challenge? If they had, it would explain a lot. Thinking about it, it did sound like something they'd do.

There were a few that hadn't made a complete cake out of the whole thing, in the eyes of the other students that was. Dayu and his partner had gotten closer to actually finishing the course than anyone else.

His nimble fingers and keen familiarity with any tech allowed him to "learn" a new one quicker than most. Kalim had the familiarity, but he admitted his fingers were better suited for taking things apart and putting them back together again than this.

That was something you didn't need to hurry around with but could take it one step at a time, figuring out your next more. This wasn't anything like that. His fingers might be able to keep up, but the rest of him was having trouble.

Dayu's quick reactions had proven to work even when his navigator was less than observant. It had saved them more than once on the course, earning their team a small commendation from their teacher; a rare thing indeed.

His complete opposite could be found in Teran, who'd effectively barrelled ahead at full speed and subsequently missed the first hoop only to make a wide arch, swinging back to it and hitting the support from behind.

That itself was nothing short of amazing, considering the amount of grass he could have ploughed into just as easily. It had just been the *wrong* kind of amazing.

Dayu had carefully inched his way across the course in places. In the end, he'd still been caught out though. Even he found it difficult to compensate for freak winds that he didn't see coming.

'Wonder if any of the other groups will do better?' Jens asked of no one in particular. 'And wonder if they're having similar problems where they are?'

'Probably,' someone else replied.

They weren't wrong. Of course, some things *were* easier than others… On top that, it seemed to take ages until they were finally allowed to move on from the first section they'd ended up with.

It turned out she needed to wait again for her turn. Gaile grumbled to herself. What was this obsession with hurrying up and then going nowhere?

She spent the time until her turn staring out into the distance rather than watching the rest of them. Besides, it wasn't like she could follow what they were doing all over the place. She'd have needed to have brought some special eyes if she'd wanted to do that.

The rest of them were making quite a lot of fuss over this one though. Excitement was running high among the students.

Several of them had gathered around the parked gliders; pointing and pushing and generally testing the things out on the ground. For some it wasn't the first time that they'd be going up in one of these or something similar at least, but for those that had never even as much as run with a hanger it was a thrill to be allowed to play with one of these.

Of course, the teachers kept insisting that this wasn't some sort of game but when you had to fly around in something that looked like an oversized toy painted in bright vibrant colours then if you couldn't take it as serious as you should, well, that might be expected.

Maybe that was part of the test, Gaile mused. In this place she wouldn't put anything past them.

Gaile had regarded the controls of the glider with suspicion when the teacher had first shown them off but once you were in the cockpit they seemed remarkably simple and intuitive. The only thing was to remember to use her feet to control the flaps and not just relying on the rudder to turn her from side to side. Hand to Eye coordination wasn't her best talent and Hand to Eye to Feet was even less so.

These full-scale replicas were no more true gliders than the small models were; not according to one of the teachers she'd overheard. There was no way that a first year student would be entrusted with something that didn't have the power to pull itself out of any sticky situation that the student at the controls might have gotten them both into.

That made sense, she supposed. There seemed to be a height regulator on these things as well ... must be to prevent them from going AWOL, if you could apply such a term to a machine. Wait a minute ... Gaile's eyes narrowed. Considering some of the machines she'd known in her life...

Even so, she wasn't altogether sure if the teachers' main worry was the machine or the pilot that was controlling it? Either way worked, she supposed.

The single seaters were cramped and for once Gaile was grateful for her small frame – at least *she* could move around a little bit. People like Drak must have a terrible time with something like this. It was almost enough to make you feel sorry for the guy. She doubted he'd appreciate the sentiment though. He seemed determined to tough everything out the hard way.

Well, this was it then, she thought.

It took a few tries and more than a bit of fiddling but thankfully she remembered enough of the theory to tell which control did what; mostly anyway. Despite that it took more than one try for her to get off the ground.

The first couple of movements were jerky and for a moment the left wing dipped seriously close to the ground before she managed to get it to stay upright and level.

Some ten minutes later and it was still going ok. Slow, but ok.

So far she'd avoided any major mishaps, as evident by her still being in the air. In fact, it'd be true to say she was actually having fun. This wasn't anything like being on a dragon after all. This was you in control all the way – as long as you kept your cool.

Bringing the glider around in a lazy arch, as to line it up with the next obstacle, Gaile pulled back on the throttle until they were merely inching forwards. You were penalised if you remained stationary so it was important to keep moving. There was, however, no stipulate on a minimum speed forwards.

This hoop was narrow and not entirely round. While she might not get the best time, Gaile was determined to actually crossing the finish line in one piece; if you collided a wingtip with a plastic ring that would certainly mean that wasn't possible, so that was out of the question. She was careful and, so far, it seemed to be working.

Even with that in mind, it was hard not to enjoy this, for it was, finally, a little bit of freedom.

Clearing the hoop with plenty of space to spare, Gaile brought the glider down under the next bar, rolled almost effortlessly through the tunnel and pulled up sharply to avoid the solid wall that loomed out of nowhere afterwards.

Whoops … she hadn't seen that one.

It wasn't the most elegant of dances and there were many who could have taken it at far greater speed (who knows, maybe she would have been one of them if she'd had enough practice) but it was a good run nonetheless.

A small elation of satisfaction filled her blood with a kind of fizzing, making her grin widely as she pulled off the gear, once back down on the ground.

'Satisfactory,' Duchamp announced almost crossly, making a few annotations in his diom as she climbed out of the cockpit. 'Try not to laze about so much next time, Miss Ashworthey. These are gliders you're riding, not snails,' he added without looking up.

Whatever feeling of success Gaile had felt evaporated like a mist on a sunny day. Typical, she thought. For once I do something well, close to perfect (she'd made it through hadn't she? That was more than a lot of others had done) and do I get as much as a word of praise? Of course not ... such things happened to other people, not to her.

They could be praised for achieving the most *minor* of things. But even when she managed something major, they barely even noticed, and if they did, it was only to point out what she'd done wrong.

Annoyed with the whole thing now, Gaile stalked off in search of something to eat. That meant having either to go back to the shuttle and look there or to head on up to where the last station was.

The third station was occupying the smallest space in this pristine looking location.

While both One and Two were down below, away from the hill, where the land was more flat and mostly consisting of grass and the occasional boulder, Station Three had set up shop right on top of the small hill overlooking the grassy expanse.

As such, the group working there were right in the middle of all the trees that covered the knoll, a veritable oasis of verticalness in a land of a more horizontal persuasion.

They didn't need artificial obstacles. Most of them were having enough of a hard time just avoiding the *trees*. If you started turning those into rollers and barrels there would have been trouble. If you managed to miss one, another would appear in your immediate future as sure as the sun set in the west.

'It's not working,' Reena grimaced, her tongue poking through her lips in concentration. 'It just won't listen.'

'It listens to you, Reena,' Stewart assured her. 'But perhaps *you're* not listening to *it.*'

Reena switched her model over to hover-mode and waited for the second-year to explain. He seemed to be relaxed enough about this whole thing, much more so than some of the teachers. Of course, he must have done this last year, she told herself.

'Maybe if you told me what I did wrong.' she suggested pointedly.

'I just did. But you're not listening to *me* either. Look... Take a look around you. What do you see?'

'Trees,' Reena answered promptly.

Stewart rolled his eyes. 'Yes, that too. *This* is nature. It's not some perfectly controlled lab experiment. You don't just move your model around as if there were nothing else affecting it but its own power-turnout. There's wind. The certain way it moves around a tree. How the back of another shifts it around. Where plants are a hindrance. Where they aid you. What you can work with, gain from and challenge.

All these things are important. Clues to tell you what to expect if you know what to look for. What to listen to,' Stewart waved a hand around, encompassing everything that was around them.

Reena breathed out, annoyed, and started up her model again. There had to be a better way than this, she thought.

Somewhere over to her right another model came into close contact with a tree. It fell into the undergrowth, making unhappy, whirring, sounds. It was followed a second later by a loud complaint erupting from its operator. Soon after, they showed up to retrieve their model.

'I just can't see the point of this,' Pol grumbled as he tried to free legs or wings (or should that be legs *and* wings?) from the tangled mass where his exercise for today had fallen.

'I mean – what use is this? Flying models? This stuff is for kids.'

He wasn't the only one who thought so. *Most* of the students hadn't done this kind of thing since they were small, and in his case that was quite a bit longer ago than the average student's.

There was one difference between these and the model-gliders that the other group was using though. A very big difference actually, which probably went some way towards explaining why they were having so much more problems with them.

These gliders were, essentially, not gliders at all. They were all singular in form and, outside of the engines maybe that was true. But they were still all different. Each and every one of these things were model *dragons* and very faithful ones at that.

There weren't very many parts on them that *couldn't* be moved and while the hidden power-source did provide the necessary lift; complex calculations in the small on-board computer were set so that it was necessary to move the wings and a great many other things, to be able to get the models even to move forwards, to say nothing about around a tree and back.

A few of the students were still having trouble working out how to get theirs off the ground... The models kept prowling around on the soil while their frantic operators shouted at them, at each other, at themselves and, failing everything else, at the world in large.

In addition to that, from somewhere near the wooden tables of the resting area came clangs of metal against metal, coupled with loud shouts.

At first no one except those close by (who cheered and whooped excitedly) paid any attention. That some of the students were still having difficulties with the controls and models kept crashing into each other was common enough.

After a particularly large cheer however, Pol frowned.

'What *are* they doing over there?' he asked of no one in particular and set out to investigate.

He arrived as one model, painted green with purple stripes, leaped down from where it had climbed onto the trunk of a tree and pinned another one, one with a red base, to the ground. A metallic clang sounded at the impact as the miniature fangs tried to grab at the other before rolling off.

'You lose!' Kay exhaled triumphantly.

'What's that make now? Eight losses and one win?' someone else chipped in.

'Yeah, you can't...'

'What in the name of the Five Dragons do you two think you're doing!' Suddenly Stewart was there. He towered over the two of them, a storm-cloud having replaced his normal facial features.

'That is precious equipment!' the second year roared at them, eyes like slits with a pale fire between them. 'NOT some playground toy!'

He shooed the two apart. 'Look at this! I can't believe you two. That's it, I'm assigning a helper to escort you back to the shuttle and you can stay there until we're all finished!' He added, when seeing that the two involved didn't seem very perturbed, 'that means until we're *all* ready to leave *after* the half-year celebrations have ended.'

'Ah, come one…' Elon pleaded.

'That is quite enough. March!'

Realizing that arguing with this one was a lost cause, the two of them set off for the parked shuttle down on the lowlands, trudging slowly.

'This is so your fault,' Kay snapped.

'It was *your* idea,' Elon countered. He glowered at Kay for a moment and then returned to walking.

What a day. This sucked. He'd been looking forward to that party for weeks. A celebration in honour (well, that's what he thought of it as anyway) of those students who'd lasted through the first six months of the course. Needless to say, there were distinctly fewer of them than there had been when they first started.

This meant they were going to miss out on the food too.

There had indeed been plenty of food provided at the small collection of wooden tables up on the knoll, which explained why so many of those that had completed the three challenges were finishing up there rather than taking shelter in the shuttles that had brought them.

While they were enjoying themselves, Gaile however, was not. She didn't know what it was, but there had been something in said eatables that certainly hadn't agreed with her. That was, in a way, an excellent way of losing track of time. It did come with a bit of a drawback though, as Gaile discovered to her horror, for by the time she felt well enough to risk a few steps away from the "camp's" sanitary facilities, her stomach had reduced its complaints to tinges coupled with the occasional gurgle.

Not that it really mattered. The mere memory of the last half-hour or so was plain agony all on its own. It was impossible to tell if the tension she felt was the leftovers of that pain or merely the result of her intestines having knotted themselves into figures hitherto unknown to man, to say nothing about unknown to intestines.

Those had been some *bad* cookies, that was for sure. Maybe she shouldn't have eaten them? But she'd been saving the things because she loved them so much and really didn't eat one at the first chance she got, every time, so it had felt like such a waste to throw them out and not get to enjoy them. Well, that certainly had shown her, hadn't it?

Breathing shallowly but now able to remain upright without her shaking legs buckling underneath her, Gaile tentatively, and slowly, returned to the open area where most of the others had been gathered before. Not that she was particularly interested in their company. No, it was her trusty satchel that she was after.

She'd left that one on the shuttle when she'd made that mad dash for the bathroom. It had lots of nice things in it – she'd taken care to pack suitably for the fieldtrip after all. Chief among those she wanted right now was her water bottle.

Unfortunately, the satchel was nowhere to be seen.

Even worse ... neither was the shuttle.

Gaile came to a slow stop as she took in the scene around her.

Wooden tables and logs – check. Sparse trees in which the wind was picking up – check. Green grass descending from the knoll in all directions and matching scenery – check. Small, squirrelly creatures and things that went 'chirp' – check.

Total human population of the immediate area – Zip! Zilch! Zero! Nada!

No matter how you looked at that number it still looked the same.

Blast.

'Well, isn't this swell,' Gaile complained to herself, but not too loudly. That would have taken too much energy and right now she had little enough to spare.

'So, now what do I do? Grow wings and fly south for the winter?' She gave the tables a cursory glance but she didn't really feel up to sitting down right now. What she really wanted to do was to lie down and be able to stretch out those cramped muscles ... carefully.

'Well, it isn't like there's much I can do here is there?' Gaile said to herself, more to hear something other than nature than out of any real need to speak. 'It's not like I can walk into the nearest town from here. What am I supposed to communicate with here – smoke signals?'

That was the drawback really. This facility, if you wanted to stretch the word to include a few roughly hewn tables, logs equally, if not more, rough to sit on and a primitive, but highly effective, latrine, it was, no matter how you looked at it, *far away* from *everything*.

That was one of the reasons why they'd come all the way out here after all. No, best thing to do was to relax and just wait until someone noticed she wasn't there, Gaile mused. She snorted disdainfully.

'Yeah, right. Like's that gonna happen. Just like it worked so well the last time I ended up goodness knows where all on my own…'

Soliciting a nice piece of grass, sloping gently so that she had a good view, this place being picturesque enough, Gaile made herself comfortable, trying to think of some sensible way of getting out of here. It might be pretty, but she sure didn't want to spend the night.

Sticking her hands, and arms, behind her head, she spent some time watching the clouds – there was even one that looked like an overgrown bunny – and trying to avoid the pit of worry that was gnawing itself through her insides, telling herself it was just the remnants of some bad indigestion.

It was still warm. That was to be expected. If it had been around the DRC it would probably have been roasting even at this hour. That was another reason why they'd come all this way for this little fieldtrip assignment thing.

Maybe it was a kind of celebration as well, showing that they'd come halfway through the year. That made it mark a very significant moment in time.

'Can't believe it's been half a year already,' Gaile sighed wistfully. 'How doesn't time fly?'

It had been a busy six months; very busy. Especially in the steady stream of students walking out the door, having decided that a career at the DRC was not for them after all, department.

Not that Gaile blamed them.

'Poor sods. They certainly threw us some curveballs right from the start. That flight test sure was a real kicker in terms of student drop-outs … and some of them almost literally too.'

Mulling things over, her eyelids grew heavier and heavier until she finally fell asleep.

By the time she woke up again, bits of her ached and not the same bits as earlier either … not that those had stopped.

She rolled over on her side for a little while. There was a knobby bit in the ground that kept digging into her lower back. Well, that explained the ache back there then.

'They sure are taking their sweet time. Can't they hurry up a bit?' she complained, scanning the horizon.

By now the sun was beginning to approach that horizon. Along with it came an elongating of the shadows, stretching and distorting them as well as a new knot of worry. Clouds were beginning to gather as well. Her nap had been longer than she'd thought.

Gaile *really* did not want to spend the night out here. She really, *really* did not want to spend the night out here.

It was nice enough during the day and even then it had been better with other people around. It was more fun to do things when there were others to share them with; even if they had been a tad too noisy for her taste and at times she'd wished they'd gone away.

Well, she'd gotten her wish; they had. And now she wished, even more fervently, that they hadn't. Not *without* her anyway.

'Just my luck really,' Gaile yawned and stretched. 'And falling asleep really didn't help either.'

Despite her growing unease, and it still being nice and warm, she, without thinking about it, once more drifted off into a deep semi-slumber, that elongated moment when you're awake enough to know you're sleeping.

Oh well, if she was going to get into trouble anyway…

What woke her from that pleasant slumber – pleasant, for it contained no worries – was a loud rumble. A steep drop in temperature had arrived while she wasn't paying attention.

It wasn't high summer – not here – and the weather front already sending its tendrils of chills towards her was approaching and approaching rapidly.

Gaile eyed the horizon warily.

Where it had been pleasantly azure blue it was now a seething mass of grey. The clouds were rolling over and over, dark and light mingled together. Pushing and shoving and shepherded by the winds they tumbled over the mountains in the distance and made for the lowlands with a vengeance.

The mountains were soon looking like they were vanishing behind a veil of mourning shrouds before they were lost from sight altogether and nothing than a mere memory behind the curtain of rain that was drifting in.

The wind was picking up as well.

'Great,' Gaile growled. 'And here I thought it couldn't get worse. Just goes to show…' she made a wry face.

Things just kept getting better and better, didn't they? It was one of those times when you felt like you knew, just *knew*, that the universe was playing crooked dice with you and you were going to come off as the losing party no matter where they landed - *if* they landed.

She took a deep breath and rubbed at her arms. Maybe she'd feel better after moving around a bit. With the sun locked away it wasn't nearly such a pleasant day, what little of it remained.

Arms wrapped closely around herself Gaile trudged back up the small hill. At least up there, there were trees that might provide shelter from the wind. She just had to hope that it didn't pick up too much. No one wanted a few tons of wood toppling over you unexpectedly after all.

Five minutes later and rain was pelting the ground in an all-out assault. It wasn't just water falling from the sky – it was more like an unusually dispersed waterfall. In thirty seconds small rivers of deluge dug into the soil, crisscrossing all around, seeking the easiest way down the hill.

Gaile wrapped her arms tighter around herself where she'd taken refuge under a large tree. Its expansive branches, which almost touched the ground, created a sort of wooden cave nearest the trunk. It would have protected her from a normal rain shower. With this one you might not even have known the tree was there. The higher branches waved about, shaking their fists at the heavens.

She pulled the jacket tighter. The uniform wasn't made for this type of things. It couldn't stand up to this level of beating in the long run – but for now, it was a little bit of dryness in a world of wet. That wouldn't last long.

Whenever a particularly fierce gust came along, the wind drove the raindrops into her face as if they were pine needles. Every single one stung, sharp and ice cold. Burying her face in her arms, Gaile tried to keep out the worst.

Her hands had already gone numb and the rest of her was shivering. The only thing that was still completely dry and relatively warm were her feet.

Thank goodness for decent boots.

She didn't bother looking up. All that would give her was a wetter and colder face. There'd be no way in the world that she'd hear an engine in this noise and it was noisy. The world that had so shortly before been so tranquil that she'd complained about the lack of sound was, now, nothing but sound; a cacophonic melody played out by the oceanic orchestra of the sky to the accompaniment of its more land-bound choir, the trees, voicing their protest at this sudden change in treatment and now roaring like a whole chorus of lions at the breaking dawn.

Treatment, now there was a word; a word that never changed. It stayed the same no matter where she went. No matter what she did.

Wasn't that why she'd escaped to New Retmia in the first place, to get away from it? Not that it had helped much, Gaile thought bitterly. It had merely exchanged the type of treatment for another and that was no improvement either.

Instead of constantly being compared to her brothers and sisters she was now feeling like everyone was watching her and comparing her to someone else, anyone really, and she still failed to meet their expectations. She'd tried, at home, she really had. But she just didn't have the right kind of personality for that kind of work.

You needed to be dignified; to be in control of yourself and your surroundings. To remember who was what and who was who. Sometimes relations were the worst. Of all people, why did it have to be *them* she was related to? Everyone kept expecting her to show the same qualities as the rest of the family ... but she just didn't have it in her.

And here, the people might have changed, but not much else had. She still felt terribly alone, even after six months. Silber was nice enough but she didn't feel like she could talk to him, not that way. Silber the dragonling she could tell anything and that was such an unbelievable stress-reliever it couldn't be expresses in words but he couldn't answer her or help her. He gave the impression he'd been born stoic, knowledgeable and without any doubts of his own place in the world; for a small lizard with wings.

Half a year? Had it really been that long since she first set foot in the DRC? It felt shorter. Right now it felt like no time at all.

And things still hadn't changed. Maybe because she hadn't been very good at changing them?

What did she have to show for it anyway? Hadn't they proved, again and again, that she didn't have what it took to be a part of the DragonCorps, *any* part of it. Being a rider seemed no more than a distant dream, one of those dreams that kept disappearing into the distance as you ran, so that the harder you ran, the faster they disappeared.

Silber remained the one truly positive thing about this place, she thought.

Sure, he drove her insane. He was never where you expected him to be. He never did what you expected him to do and he frequently popped up in places he should have had no right to being able to get to. And goodness alone knew how he kept getting out of the Hive.

By now she was sure she'd chased him all over the Academy at one time or another and parts of the DRC too. She wasn't getting lost anymore – her constant battles with the escaped little critter had seen to that.

Gaile was certain she'd seen, by now, bits of the place that her fellow students hadn't even heard of. Like the time he'd ended up leading her to one of the DRC's laboratories; a particularly harrowing memory, more out of the sheer embarrassment of the thing than anything else.

Thank the stars that the lab people had laughed it off rather than report the whole little event. Students, even those chasing mischievous creatures on the loose, weren't supposed to be anywhere near the labs.

Now that she thought about it, they'd been a lot more understanding about the whole thing than most of the Academy would have been in a similar situation. Especially that head researcher. What was his name again? Dr ... Cos ... something wasn't it? Maybe that sort of thing happened all the time up there, on the higher floors?

Gaile hadn't expected him to keep the promise of not mentioning the whole thing to anyone but as the days had passed afterwards and she hadn't heard anything about it, she'd had to conclude that he had, indeed, kept his word.

No, so far, regardless of the amount of trouble he got her into, the dragonling remained the closest thing she had to a friend in this place.

'Great, wonder what that says about me? The only friend I can make and he goes 'eeep' at me,' she sighed dramatically.

Not that that stopped him from arguing with her. She just had to face the fact that the small creature understood *her* a whole lot better than she understood *him*. But at least he was someone she could talk to.

Her thoughts were interrupted by a large 'crack.' Gaile started, looking up, and immediately wished she hadn't. In the distance a light lit up, if only for a moment. It was followed a few moments later by another roll of thunder. The thunderstorm was no longer lurking over the mountains.

'Bloody stupid,' Gaile spat, lips chilled and stiff. No way they'd even *think* about sending anyone out for her in weather like this even if they *had* noticed she hadn't returned. The wind was getting something fierce. All she could do now was to batten down the hatches and ride out the storm best she could. A shame she had a complete lack of hatches to batten down really.

Gaile didn't bother about much for a while and it was pure chance that made her glace up when she did and see, dimly through the rain, blue pinpoints of light. Buffered by the wind the shuttle struggled to remain stable in its decent. It landed heavily and with no small amount of skidding.

Not bothering to keep watching Gaile returned to her introspection. What relief had flooded her when she saw those lights was quickly being shoved aside by resentment. Now that she knew someone had come for her, knew that she no longer *had* to stay here, she wanted them to leave again.

What worry there had been now turned its attention to all that would happen when she returned. She'd probably get scolded, again. Why was it always her that got told off? Plenty of others caused trouble, some even intentionally, but Gaile felt like it was always her that got singled out. "They" got away with it.

She wasn't sure how long someone had been standing next to her under the fir tree before she actually noticed them. They had remained quiet, not doing anything to announce their arrival.

Gaile sneaked a peek under her arm and grimaced. Oh great … that was just what she needed.

'Go Away!' she told them pointedly.

'Thank you. I appreciate you coming out here, the weather is just so bad, don't you think,' the voice didn't sound the least bit happy. 'Do you even realize how much trouble you've caused?'

There was no mistaking the arrogance of that voice. The tone alone was as cold as the rain around them and about as friendly.

Gaile burrowed further into her arms, content to go on ignoring him. Of all people they could have sent to fetch her and she had to end up with *him*?

'I would have thought that you would at least have been grateful, but I see now that was too much to ask,' Sera sneered.

Reaching up and wringing out his long hair, the water landed with a squelch on the ground. Folding his arms, Sera leaned back against the trunk. That, at least, wasn't wet.

'I have come to fetch you, you know. Do you intend to sit there much longer? I would have thought you'd want to leave?' he said.

'No one asked you to!'

'Actually, they did,' Sera made a show of inspecting a nearby branch nonchalantly. 'None of the other pilots were willing to risk flying in this weather.'

Actually, to say that none of the others had wanted to undertake the journey was a bit of an understatement, he admitted. It wasn't even brought up as a proposition. The airspace in the area had been placed in lockdown in anticipation of what was following immediately *behind* the storm system itself.

To say that they'd asked him to go was also stretching the truth a bit. Stretching it rather a lot actually.

'Aren't you cold?' he asked. 'You look wet.'

'Look, can we get back already? This storm is only going to get worse.'

'So go then. I'm not stopping you!' Gaile snarled at him.

It would have been a much more impressive thing if her voice hadn't broken halfway through.

'Aaargh!' Sera clenched his fists. One of them slammed into the tree trunk beside him. It groaned, creaking in protest.

'You're being extremely unreasonable,' he told her. 'Extremely childish.'

'I'm not forcing you to stay around. I didn't force you to come. So go already. I don't want to go back.'

'Some determination. The slightest hint of a setback and you go running off home, is that it? Is that all the backbone you have? It takes more than that to be a rider,' Sera scoffed.

'I know that!' Gaile screamed at him. 'I know. I know I don't have what it takes. I know no one wants me here. I know I could never pass the exam. But I don't have anywhere else to go!'

'This was my chance,' she continued in a much smaller voice. 'My chance to change things, to change *me*. To stop being compared to the rest of the family *all* the time. To stop running away from everything *all* the time. But … but … I'm still running. It's the only thing I'm good at … running away. And I can't even seem to do that right.'

Gaile sank back down, huddled against her knees and the trunk behind her, half of what she continued to mumble being lost between the wind and the tears of humiliation. Not that anyone could see them, the rain saw to that.

'I'm the only one who didn't pass first flight, the only one who didn't pass, who's still here. Everyone else knew they had no chance. Me? I woke up in the infirmary, the test long since over. I don't even remember what happened.'

'This isn't really the time to…' Sera interrupted, not sure what to say.

Gaile ignored him. 'I don't know why I do this anymore. Why do I bother? Can you imagine what kind of dragon would choose me as a partner? Can you?'

'Why *do* you do this?' Sera pushed the question out there brusquely. 'It's not the same reason so many others come here, is it? So many who, like that Jasmine woman, look at it all as some kind of popularity contest. All "look at me; I'm fabulous, I'm all better than the rest of you maggots. Bow down and worship me."

The voice had grown smaller and much more scornful and Gaile's ears, for all her feigned indifference, were straining to pick out enough words to make sense of what he was saying. Not that it was making sense. Wasn't he just describing *himself*? And since when did he refer to Jasmine as "that woman" with such distaste?

'It's not like that,' she protested.

'Isn't it?' Sera averted his eyes. His fingernails bit into the bark of the tree. 'Isn't it? Though I would have thought you would have given up by now.'

'No! It's not. It's not!'

'Really? Then why? Why else would someone like you join the DRC? You're all alike.'

'Just leave me alone!' Gaile returned the clear animosity. 'You could never understand. Someone like you could never understand what it's like – being alone. I've seen you. You've always got people around you. Always got people fawning over you, telling you how great you are, how much they love you and everything you do. You're one to talk. You're doing all those things, every one of them, yourself,' she was yelling again by the end of the first sentence.

'What? Do you think *I* enjoy it?' Sera bent forward, actually shouting back. 'Do you think I like it? Always, no matter where I turn there's someone new, someone else who follows me around and just won't leave me alone. I can't even walk into a room without being assaulted by groups of mad giggling girls. The women we shouldn't even talk about. I don't like it. I *don't* like it!'

'And I *don't* like being alone!' Gaile shouted back at him.

'You're not the only one!' he shouted back at her.

For a while they just stood there, breathing hard, waiting for the next volley in a rapidly deteriorating volume match.

With a drawn-out sigh Sera sank down onto the ground again, his back sliding down the trunk. He wiped the rain off his face, his long silvery hair long since plastered to his skull.

'Guess I'm soaked already anyway,' he said philosophically, his voice having lost the arrogant tinge it always carried. Now it just sounded tired.

It took some time before either of them spoke again. The hostile tension in the air hadn't gone – not completely. It was like the air just after the roll of thunder, it cleared the air, but for what?

'Do … do they really bother you that much?' Gaile asked timidly.

'Yes.'

The reply was curt, more like having come from someone having long since given up on a long lost cause.

'I'm sorry. I never would have guessed.'

A rueful smile hovered around Sera's lips for a few seconds. 'No, I don't imagine anyone would. Ironic, isn't it?'

'I'd have thought it'd be nice having people about,' Gaile thought for a moment, then added '…the right people.'

'A blunt, but accurate summary,' Sera agreed. 'The *right* people. Unfortunately, I seem to attract the exact opposite.'

'Shouldn't you have it easy to make friends?' she wondered.

Sera couldn't help but laugh. 'You really shouldn't confuse the container with the contents you know. Come now, you've *seen* them. Do you honestly think that they'd let the other kind just waltz in? That they'd let those anywhere near me? Do you think that they'd want to be there? They see the same thing you do. They draw the same conclusions as you did.'

'Then why? You act like that kind of person on purpose?'

'Caught by my own cleverness. Well ... maybe a bit more than that. I really *was* like that ... once ... a long time ago. Ok, maybe not *quite* that bad. Me and my friend would get up to all sorts of ... never mind...'

Sera shrugged. 'Something happened and I've been away for a while. When coming back, I didn't know where I was going, so I just ended up resorting to what was familiar. Now I can't seem to find a way out of it. Not without ending up with more trouble than it's worth. Besides, as long as they're there, they do keep the *majority* of crazy females at bay.'

'Better the devil you know..?' Gaile asked.

'Something like that,' Sera agreed.

There was another long quiet pause. Well, it was quiet in terms of lack of conversation. It certainly didn't lack accompaniment, the weather confrontations were playing truant and the storm was taking full advantage.

'So, why *did* you decide to try out for the DragonCorps?' Sera asked, this time almost reluctantly. Either he was worried about the reply or about starting another argument, she couldn't tell which.

Gaile in turn stared out into nothing for some time, trying to find the right words to say something she'd never really defined for herself.

'I thought that having a partner, a friend, someone I could trust, someone who accepted me for all that I am, good and bad and everything in between and for whom I could do the same, would be nice. Not sure why I felt so drawn here, specifically. It just seemed more likely that I'd find that here than on my own. But now,' Gaile shrugged defeatedly. 'I... I guess it's no more likely here than anywhere else. After all, I'll always be me ... and that's the real trouble...'

'What makes you say that?'

'Come on. Can you seriously see a dragon choosing me as a partner?' Gaile huffed. 'Let's face it. Even if I *wasn't* terrified of heights, even if I do dream of soaring through the sky, I'm basically useless at this. I can't get the hang of it and I know I'm not stupid thank you, so don't need to hear anything about that. It's just … I don't know. But you're talking to the one person who managed to get a minus score on the "Trials and Tribulations" test.'

'How did you manage that?' Sera couldn't hide his surprise.

'It blew up.'

In spite of being stated in such a matter of fact voice, or perhaps because of it, but the image paraded in front of Sera's eyelids, repeating over and over. He fought the amusement and, failing, exploded laughing.

Wiping tears of laughter out of his eyes, he was glad he couldn't see her face.

'Gee, thanks,' Gaile commented dryly.

'I'm sorry,' Sera struggled to get himself back under control. His sides were splitting. 'I know it's not hilarious but…'

'It *is* hilarious. If I'd watched it I'd have been laughing myself silly,' Gaile admitted. 'It's the failing the test that's the pain.'

'The tests aren't the important part. In the ends it's….'

'…the dragon that chooses,' Gaile finished the sentence for him in a sing song voice. 'I know. But seriously. Do you think any dragon would choose someone who can't even manage some of the basics? Actually, some of the not so basic stuff is actually quite easy … but the first bits? Would *you* choose to team up with someone you couldn't rely on? Couldn't trust?'

'Touché,' Sera acknowledged.

'I'm not stupid. I can get my head around some pretty complex ideas and concepts. It's just that the way they expect you to do things here just isn't how I'm used to finding the answers … any answers.'

Sera regarded her critically for a few moments. She'd been honest enough about it – as things were, he certainly couldn't see *anyone* picking her for a partner if there was anyone else available, whether for the Final Exam or just a simple class assignment. There were certainly plenty of more promising raw materials. Still … no, one grain of sand on the beach did not turn the tide…

If you looked at the bigger picture it made no difference.

Screw the bigger picture, he suddenly decided.

'I could ... you know ... help,' he offered.

'Ha! You don't want to, trust me. No one sticks around. You'd go mad in a week.'

Despite it all, Sera couldn't help but smile, even if it was only a little. Even when offering to help she was still fighting him tooth and claw. Not literally, of course, thankfully. He couldn't quite explain why, but he had a feeling that it was a good thing indeed that that was one department she was seriously lacking in.

'I think you might find my tolerance level a bit higher than you'd expect, if you consider what I go through every day already. I mean it. Oh, I don't know how much *use* it'd be – but I'd be willing to give it a try. At the very least I could see to it that something doesn't explode on you again – it's not *that* hard.'

'Are you sure you think it's such a good idea?'

'No,' Sera shrugged expansively. 'But we won't find that out by sitting here. And we really do not want to be caught out by what's coming after the storm.'

'What *is* coming after the storm?'

'Trouble.'

Sera pushed himself onto his feet, then reached down and offered her a hand.

For the briefest moment Gaile regarded it coldly, almost as if she wasn't sure it wouldn't burn her. Then she grasped it and allowed him to pull her up.

'Just one thing...'

'Yes?'

'Promise me that you won't tell anyone,' he pleaded.

'Ha. As if,' Gaile waved the very idea away as insane. 'Contrary to appearances, I have no wish to end up as the prey of one of those little hunting packs of yours.' She shuddered. 'I don't know how they'd react, but I don't care to find out first hand. Human females can be vicious.'

'You're telling me!'

'Be nice.'

A rider in training?

While the wind lapped against the transparent plate that made up part of the window next to her, Gaile regarded the graphs in front of her solemnly, her feet waving in the air.

Her blue eyes were focused but she didn't appear to notice the writing stylus which was – as regular as clockwork – tapping against her teeth every few seconds.

The large windowsills here lent themselves excellently to these little moments, she thought. With a bit of help from some cushions, the white wooded board which was a bit too stiff to lie down on comfortably, especially if you were on your stomach, was transformed into a nice cosy couch, after a fashion.

The stylus made another triumvirate against the enamel of her teeth.

Maybe she was thinking about this the wrong way? The assignment *had* seemed straightforward enough to start with.

When Duchamp had just handed them a few set parameters, keys to the weather data and told the entire class, which was by now a whole lot smaller than when they'd originally enrolled, she'd thought it would be easy, to say the least.

Unfortunately she'd turned out to be wrong.

An added bonus of there now being fewer of them was that it was beginning to be possible to get to grips with who everyone was. Well, obviously not *everyone*, there were some outright weirdoes, that was for sure, but in general.

Gaile liked that. It made life easier.

This assignment on the other hand seemed determined to make it more complicated again. She bit her lip, thoughts straying away from what she was supposed to be doing. She really ought to know this, but somehow it all looked different, like this.

Their teacher had told them to do some current course plotting. Gaile wasn't the only one who'd wished that Duchamp hadn't been so fond of giving them "live" exercises – it was so much harder to do these when the info kept changing every hour, or even more often if you were unfortunate – weather data not being among the most stable of fields at the best of times.

The setting had *seemed* simple enough to start with. She'd already had the "who" (or their assigned parameters anyway) and the "where" wasn't going anywhere either (the location being a quite solid piece of mountainous terrain on the map).

The problem was that they were supposed to guide their fictional dragon and rider as safely as possible from point A to point B within the time constraints given. Point A was located in the mountains while point B was set somewhere in the lowlands.

By now, most of them had picked up enough about navigations to be able to look at a map like this and actually being able to figure out the most obvious routes that it was possible to take.

That was fine – except when she'd put down the whole project an hour ago to go get something to eat, one route had seemed the best option and now the very same one didn't look good at all; the winds having changed and the updrafts with them *and* it was later in the day too so the light would be different, to say nothing about it suddenly having started raining.

Gaile went back to chewing on her stylus.

If she couldn't predict the weather, then maybe the key to success lay in predicting her teacher instead?

Needless to say, Gaile wasn't the only one sweating and losing sleep over the assignment.

'Aaaargh, I need a break...' she muttered. 'There's got to be something better to do than this?'

* * *

From a distance, had anyone been watching and hopefully none were, it looked like a white speck was moving up the canyon at speed. A white speck trailed by a small cloud of dust.

Loping easily across the stony floor in a gentle rolling gait, here and there it'd dart to one side then the other, as if pursued by some yet unseen enemy.

It leapt across and over great boulders then paused for a moment on a rocky outcrop. Setting off again, the dust-cloud obscured any vision of what might have been pursuing it.

That dust and gravel kicked up by the clawed feet billowed upwards, completely vanishing the side-branch of the great canyon from view. Well, the dust and gravel went up – the gravel quickly came down again, rattling as it bounced around on the uneven surface called "floor" in this place. The walls were quite narrow by now, not allowing for more than a few hundred meters on either side.

Narrow they might be … but another thing they were, was high. Even in this branch, and with the dust having almost dissipated, having lost its ability to remain airborne before the cloud reached above the "other" ground level, they covered everything in a permanent semi shadow.

Elsewhere the sight might have been unusual, but in a place where, somewhere nearby, there were lots and lots of dragons, it wouldn't have raised many eyebrows. Unless you knew what you were looking at of course – and again there was the hoping of that no one was.

As such, it looked like an easy, typical morning run of someone just wanting to stretch their legs – from a distance; a safe, out of earshot, kind of distance.

Up close, it was a slightly different story.

'Aaaaaahaaaaahaaaah…'

Clinging on with all her might, and with nothing to hold on to but bare skin and scales that wasn't the easy job it sounded like, Gaile was perched precariously just above the shoulders of the silvery dragon beneath her.

She swayed at every leap and bound (to say the least). She was thrown sideways at every jump and she slipped back with every stride (and there were a lot of those, it being the dragon's principal way of moving down here on the ground). Hanging on more by sheer luck than any skill worth noting, Gaile had long since given up trying to see ahead.

It wasn't the only reason. Sand in her eyes, poor irritated and red eyes that they were, saw tears every so often, stinging as they did so. They were not for seeing at the moment.

Not that she could think clearly right now, but if she had she would have reflected over the wisdom of this latest move. Sure, getting some practical practice had *sounded* like a good idea and it had taken some very fast, to say nothing about convincing, talking before she'd managed to convince the dragon but now she couldn't even feel her fingers anymore – even her knuckles where white, drained from blood by gripping so tightly to nothing. And on top of that, this bouncing up and down was seriously getting to her stomach.

'Slow down. Slow Down! SLOW DOWN!" Gaile wailed.

The dragon, wings folded neatly and tucked in tight against the lithe body as to not crash into the walls now so close around them, appeared to pay no attention. Though, for the next few moments they did seem to travel mercifully straight forwards. That made a change to the last ten minutes. Ugh…

Bursting past the "gates" of the branch and out into the larger canyon beyond, into the light, they came to a sliding stop in a shower of sand, scattering dust and rocks everywhere.

The last one being one jolt too many. Gaile lost what little balance she had left. Inching sideways, tipping slowly, she scrabbled madly for a handhold – any handhold – before she ran out of dragon to hold on to.

Losing the battle with gravity, her body tumbled towards the ground. The ground that was oh so far below. This was no small creature she'd been sitting on top of.

'Splat!' That was the word the teacher in the first practical lesson had called it. That's what you sounded like if you lost yourself, parting company with one of the bigger dragons. And that was on the ground. Suppose that the size of dragon mattered less if you fell off up in the sky. There was an equal amount to fall, just as far down from whatever dragon you were … eh … had been … riding. And it was only the final half an inch or so that mattered anyway.

How undignified, she thought, even as she was falling.

But she didn't go splat. Long before she reached the ground a large hand, claws carefully parted as not to hurt her, caught her body and then gently lowered it to the ochre coloured canyon floor.

Once there Gaile didn't move. Not that it made much difference. Even with her eyes closed the entire landscape was moving for her. Up and down it went. Up and down. Ugh…

Fighting down the nausea it slowly, if reluctantly, receded as her current bedding remained safely and comfortably still. As it departed, it whispered all too loudly that it'd be more than happy to return if she made any sudden motions.

'Nice ground. No shaking. Nice and still,' Gaile mumbled, slightly incoherently.

The sand felt scratchy and hot against her cheek. Then, with a grunt of effort she slowly rolled over onto her back.

Shading her eyes with one hand, which didn't really want to be there, still being shaky and tense from the previous ordeal, she gazed up at the cobalt sky. Pretty, she thought. Those clouds look an awful lot softer than what's down here. Bet it'd be lot less unpleasant dodging those than rocks. Less dry too, added a stray thought, chortling at her.

Gaile averted her gaze from the panorama that today made up the heavens, out here it was always supposed to be blue during the day, turned her head sideways and squinted into the glare of the sun, which inconveniently choose that moment to peek out from behind the cotton-balled sheep it herded.

Odd actually. You never got clouds in this place. Not in the day.

'You're being careless.'

The voice wasn't admonishing, well, not much. It was just stating the facts, cold, emotionless facts. Oh joy, for having someone with actual feelings around. Gaile resisted poking her tongue out at him.

'I am, am I?' she retorted instead.

'How long are you going to lie there?' the dragon asked.

'It's nice and steady and doesn't talk back,' Gaile replied.

Despite her words, Gaile slowly struggled into something resembling sitting up or at least slouching into a non-standing position. 'My head hurts,' she complained morosely. 'Wait, scratch that. *Everything* hurts. Even my fingernails are throbbing.'

The great dragon gave her a cold eyeful, not impressed. He had never really intended to teach her something like this. Had never really intended to teach her anything at all – period.

He still wasn't altogether sure how he'd been talked into this. Maybe he thought it had been the only way to make her shut up? It wasn't like any of it seemed to be sinking in. The girl understood the theory well enough, as long as it didn't involve things like calculating flight angles and such, but in terms of actually being out there and doing it, to being able to put the theory into practical use?

Well … it left a lot to be desired, that was all you could say about it really. She seemed to have a real block about the whole "dragon" side of the business.

The large silver dragon sighed. And his life had seemed so easy and uncomplicated until this year had started.

Below, flopping onto her back once more, Gaile dug herself a more comfortable spot and stuck her arms under her head.

'You know,' she said. 'This would be a lot easier with a saddle. Do you have any idea what it's like up there? It's not like there's an awful lot to hang on to you know. You really could do with some shoulder spikes or something.'

'That would not be a problem if you could learn to keep your balance,' her friend disagreed.

Gaile rolled over onto her stomach. Propping her chin in her hands, she settled for watching him, tucking one leg slightly above her and stretching the cramped feeling out of it.

'I'm going to be black and blue all over from today's work,' she announced, making an unhappy face. 'As if I needed *more* bruises. Besides, even if I do manage to get the hang of, you know, *hanging on*, you can't seriously expect me to fly like that, can you? I mean, it's one thing down here on the ground but up there? You can't be serious?'

The corners of his mouth twitched at the very thought. 'As tempting as that might be, perhaps you should master the basics *before* you're trying for the advanced level. I think you could concentrate on *"hanging on"* as you call it. There's more to riding a dragon than strapping yourself in. You're not being a part of your dragon like that, merely a passenger. A very skilled passenger in some cases it has to be admitted, but still merely a passenger. To truly *ride* a dragon you need to feel what they feel, react when they react, know what they know – that way you will never be caught off guard, off balance. You will merely be another part of the whole.'

'You know, there's just something creepy about the way you say that,' Gaile quipped.

The dragon rolled his large, colourful eyes at her and heaved a deep draconic sigh.

Maybe his irritation showed through, though he tried to conceal it, for a moment later Gaile pushed herself upright, brushing herself off. 'Stop being such a bore. I was only teasing. Isn't there any way to get our hands on a saddle though?' she inquired.

'Several,' he admitted. 'All involving us both getting into trouble. Also, perhaps you would like to inform me of what you would do with it once you had it? May I also point out to you that to use a saddle you first need to know how to operate the Armoury – and that is presuming that it would magically operate entirely silently and that no-one would notice. Or perhaps you were intending to use one of the old leather and strap versions … in which case I'm eager to hear how you would fasten it on your own? No. You are just going to have to learn the old-fashioned way I'm afraid.'

Gaile made a wry face. It was true … about the Armoury. She hadn't figured out how to get past that stumbling block either – even if it did lead to a less dangerous way of riding. At the moment it instead lead to a more dangerous way of losing these extracurricular lessons altogether. It wasn't exactly like they could just unhook one and walk out of the building with it.

Fitted into a large, no, gigantic, mostly open-spaced hall, or machine-shop floor if you liked that description better, with its metal walkways, robotic arms and watchful staff, the Armoury was a dragon's dressing room. That's how she'd come to think of it anyway.

Deep inside its belly were stored the vast amount of gear in different sizes, components and materials of all kinds that could, with the help of the built in interlocking system, be combined into almost anything; from simple saddles with straps to calling up full battle-armour and everything in between. Heck, she'd never even seen a battle-armour … just a few concept sketches. Had anyone actually ever used one?

For small dragons, keeping a saddle, albeit a large one if you compared it with a horse's, somewhere in their quarters, something that their partner would be able to both lift, carry and adjust themselves, was simplicity itself, if anyone had bothered.

Admittedly, and Gaile admitted it only grudgingly, for a large dragon that wasn't really an option. Only another dragon would have been able to lift such a thing and it was doubtful that they'd be able to adjust them. Nimble as a dragon's "hands" might be they just weren't up to that kind of delicate manoeuvres. And that was without even considering how they'd fit into the human sized quarters in the first place.

For a dragon the size of her new found friend, the whole matter was beyond laughable. Lifting it? Heck, if something like that fell on her it'd squash her flat.

Unwilling to admit it out loud, Gaile just grumbled a bit and dropped the conversation. She still thought it was a ridiculously hard thing that he was asking of her. It wasn't as if she'd be riding her future partner around without any gear, now was it? Assuming she found one – or they found her.

This was going to take a lot of practice to get used to, Gaile was certain of that. And, as it turned out, she was quite right.

* * *

And if practicing to stay on a dragon while it was moving was taking up every single bit of spare time that Gaile had during the day (and admittedly some not so spare time) she wasn't getting much of a break during the evenings either.

Some evenings even turned out to last far into the night … or should that be "early morning"?

It wasn't easy trying to catch up with where everyone else was. The amount of things they'd done and learnt during the times she'd been down or not paying attention was staggering.

It didn't help that she suspected her impromptu tutor to be throwing in a bit more than just the regular curriculum either. Some of the things she was being asked to do or explain certainly couldn't have cropped up during normal first year lessons, surely?

'I don't get this,' Gaile flopped over, the paper chart she'd been looking at falling to the side. 'I really don't get this at all.'

She rolled over again down on the floor between the low table and one of the chairs belonging to it. The carpet was one of those nice ones, all dark swirly patterns and long pale fringes. It was also comfortably fluffy and thick.

The chairs were nice too ... as was the table. And the sofa. And the ... and the... There were even curtains on the *windows*. Real windows with *real* sunlight. Although, at the moment, it was so dark outside that you couldn't tell.

It was very different from the small room that she stayed in. *Very* different.

Guess there were bonuses for being one of the top students in this place. The higher ups must really think highly of them to give them a place like this to live, Gaile thought, though she managed to refrain from saying so out loud. She was still stuck with the normal arrangements for a student of her year and time on the program. This was like a whole different world, literally.

Despite the ample space available, she still managed to get tangled up in a delicate and black bit of an odd weave and both she, the decorative piece of knitting and the two figurines that had been standing on it ended up on the floor; almost ended up on the floor.

There was no doubt as to where Gaile ended up, but the two pieces of china were snatched out of the air as they fell.

'I would appreciate if you did not break my house while you were here.'

Sera carefully moved a foot out of the way and placed both figurines firmly out of reach. Satisfied that things were safe for the moment, he returned his attention to his diom and his body to the sofa.

Gaile quickly gathered up the rest that had fallen to the floor, including herself, feeling very sheepish. Lucky her that they hadn't been glasses filled with liquids. She didn't think that would have gone down well. If nothing else, she probably would have gotten soaked. Well, maybe not, but who was counting.

She still wasn't sure *why* Sera had thought this place was best for this.

Wouldn't it be more likely that someone would find out? Admittedly, the corridor outside had had somewhat of a disused look to it. Not abandoned, just placed on hold for a while – maybe a long while, Gaile thought, remembering the stale smell.

Guess he liked his privacy. He was such a show-off in public, she had wondered, despite of what he'd told her earlier.

Ok, so *he* was the one who'd invited *her*, but there were surely better places to do this in? Less out of the way would have been good.

Now that she thought about it, she wondered why he'd agreed to help her in the first place. And what was he doing living in this place? Shouldn't his quarters be in the same place as the other third years?

Heck, that wasn't even the biggest mystery around here. The biggest mystery was still why in the world she had accepted the offer of help at all? Aside from sheer desperation that was...

'I thought you said you were going to help me,' Gaile complained through the corner of her mouth.

'I *am* helping you,' Sera countered without glancing up.

'It doesn't look like that from where I'm sitting.'

'Then perhaps you are trying to learn the wrong lesson.'

Gaile sighed. There he went again. There was no arguing with him when he got like that; going all "mystical" on her. That wasn't helping. It couldn't possibly be called helping. Unless it was supposed to aid her in coping with annoyances that was. Thanks, but she was pretty good at that already. Hence why a few people around the Academy still had their heads attached to their shoulders. Somehow she doubted that was it.

She straightened out the chart again. This time she carefully put something on each corner so that the silly thing wouldn't try to roll itself up.

What had persuaded them to use these old-fashioned style things? It was huge! She couldn't even hold it straight all at once on her own, not even with her arms spread wide.

Gaile peered down on it, frowning again.

This thing was filled with flowing lines in different colours. Some were straight, a little like arrows, some squiggly, some seemed to disappear if you looked at them straight on, but maybe that was her eyes.

The black ones at least made sense. Those ones denoted the landscape and she could read an ordinary map easily enough. Why did this thing have to have squiggly numbers all over the place as well?

Aaaaargh ... Gaile felt like pummelling something. What had she done to deserve this? It didn't make any more sense now than it had for the past ten minutes.

'If I asked you something, would you tell me?' Gaile queried, her voice casual and detached though her thoughts were anything but.

'Possibly,' Sera conceded. He was still engrossed in his own work, whatever that was. Now he seemed to be moving it around with a couple of fingers.

'Do you really think this was such a good meeting place? I mean, it's ... well ... a bit ... you know ... obvious.'

'It was *meant* for just one person. It has all the essentials and hardly anyone ever uses the rooms nearby, so there is only a small likelihood that anyone will notice you coming here. Especially as I took the liberty of setting up a few precautions of my own,' he added the last almost in passing.

'What kind of precautions?' Gaile's eyes narrowed suspiciously.

'Don't worry. It's not anything you need to worry about.'

'You could try being a bit more ... well ... involved you know.'

Sera tapped the screen, freezing whatever he was doing and put it down on the small round wooden coffee table beside where he was sitting. 'And you could try being a bit more...' he pinched his nose. 'Oh, never mind. Do you have to move about all the time? If you could take this seriously then so might I,' he said regarding her coldly.

Gaile resisted the urge to stick out her tongue at him ... or alternatively drop one of those heavy looking bronze figurines standing so conveniently close at hand now that she was sitting up, one of those with the armoured warrior and spear, on his head.

'I *am* taking it seriously. I'm just not very good with sitting still.'

'Hmm ... it would be my fate would it not ... there is already *one* in your year that can not remain still. I try to avoid him.'

'Why are you looking at me like that?' Gaile frowned.

'Hmm...' Sera thought out loud. A ghost of a smile flickered across his features. 'I think you might just have given me an idea,' he said. 'Give me a moment. I need to double-check something first.'

In one motion he swept up his diom and tapped it into life, skimming through a whole series of connections before starting to work industriously.

Good, it looked like it was closed down for the time being. Excellent, he thought. That would suit today's, no, tonight's, work nicely.

Quite a bit of time and an even greater amount of shooing motions later and the scenery for them both had changed quite a bit. Gaile couldn't say that she approved much. The room hadn't been such a bad place to be after all, in comparison.

Guess she should have kept her mouth shut ... she'd have to remember that. It looked like Sera had a rather different approach to matters than the rest of the school.

She wasn't sure she approved of *that* either.

'This was *not* what I had in mind,' Gaile shouted into the receiver built into the helmet now situated over her head.

She was balancing precariously on the airflow dancing around her, trying not to dip too far in any direction knowing all too well what would happen if she did. Needless to say she wasn't very happy about it.

Grating could be seen below, where the "wind" was coming from. It was quite far below by now. In fact, the only reason she could call it a grating was because she'd been standing on it not long before.

It was a good thing her hair had been carefully tied up and shoved under the helmet and the suit, for the stream of air was fierce – it had to be, to carry her so effortlessly. The one having to make any effort was her. The suit helped; even if it made her think she looked terribly much like a spacemonster ready to invade the planet with deathrays or something.

The wind might be artificial, but these wind simulators weren't known for their gentle and caring nature – or their gentle touch – any more than the real thing. Doing this without a suit ... that would have been a bad idea.

Gaile had had second thoughts about stepping into this in the first place. Actually, the second thoughts had appeared well before she'd been left alone in the dressing room to change. The suit had looked even less appealing hanging on a hook in a locker.

It appeared, when there wasn't a person in it, if anything, like skin peeled from a body and all wrinkled up, made into a suit of midnight black. It would give even the most stable person misgivings about what might possibly come next.

A calm and analysing mind realized, of course, that it was no such thing. But that little voice in the back of your mind, the one that you couldn't shut up no matter what, wasn't listening to reason. It wanted nothing more than to provoke. It wanted to stir things up, to make you run. Not thinking about where. Not thinking about why.

By now she'd had time for both third and fourth thoughts on the matter. None of them were particularly positive *or* reassuring.

There was also the little thing about *where* she was … and not just the bit about her floating around in the air either.

Having managed to stay "afloat" had been rewarded by steadily climbing higher and higher. How was she supposed to move downwards without ending up going down a whole lot faster than she wanted to? Gaile hadn't quite worked out that bit yet.

As a consequence, it was now a very long way down. And the only thing that needed to happen for the bottom grating to greet her all too quickly was losing control. As far as Gaile was concerned, that was not a comforting thought.

Instead, she concentrated with all her might on what she was doing. If she was too busy trying to stay where she was she wouldn't have time to be terrified. At least, that was the idea.

At the moment, it was more a question of just having moved past terror into that calm territory beyond where everything was surveyed by that cold, heartless, mind deep inside that sometimes shoved her less sensible feelings aside when sensing a threat.

'What is this place anyway?' Gaile shouted. Even with the helmet on, the sounds around her were roaring.

'You haven't come across it?' Sera asked calmly, his return question coming through clearly from the speakers in the helmet. 'And there's no need to shout, I can hear you perfectly well.'

'Well I can't and no, I haven't come across it. If I had known what this place was, do you really thing I would have agreed to this?' Gaile snapped back.

While she might find him intimidating under normal circumstances, she was far too occupied fighting a small battle with her panic glands to be bothered about that right now.

'It's called a windrider,' Sera answered her. 'It's largely used in teaching young dragons the basic ways of wind and air currents – allowing simulations of more mundane patterns and quite a few severe ones, so that they can learn in a safe environment.'

Sera adjusted a few small levers with his right fingers while keeping one eye on several others, especially the ones monitoring the heart and stress-levels of the "subject", and the other one on Gaile herself.

They were a bit erratic, he thought. Maybe more than a bit, but then that was no real surprise. The surprise was how quickly she'd started adjusting and tuning into it each time he changed the settings slightly.

At first, he'd watched the young woman paddle about with about as much grace as a wallowing cargo freighter with a bad engine but, when he'd pulled the settings up higher, much higher, all in one go, there'd been a change – especially in her heart rate.

Hmm… So, maybe that meant that as long as the situation isn't actually serious then she can't play it as serious? Was that it? Some sort of subconscious block that kept its owner in a state of "bumbling" unless threatened for real? How very curious if that was the case. Maybe it was just coincidence though. He could be reading far too much into it.

Sera didn't dare to play with the settings too much now. He had to confess it, if only to himself; he'd never expected her to even manage to get off the ground for maybe more than a few seconds at the time.

'Great. If you hadn't noticed … despite the webbing in this sorry excuse for a suit … I'm not a dragon.'

The strained voice crackled in his ear, bringing him back to reality. 'That is blindingly obvious,' Sera mumbled.

'What was that?'

'What? Oh, sorry … nothing. I was … just thinking out loud. No, it's not unknown for a few of the riders to come here as well. Not many, but a few feel it gives them a better idea of what they're working with out there. Or you wouldn't be having a suit – the dragons obviously do not need them.'

That was something which explained why this place was so big. Even juvenile dragons would need a lot more space with these kinds of activities than your average human, Gaile thought.

'An experience I'm also somewhat lacking in. Apart from once,' she admonished him.

'Yes. You did say, did you not, that you did not "get this"? It would appear, in this case, that you're having far less trouble with the practical side of the matter than the theory.'

'How nice. My teachers will be overjoyed,' Gaile quipped, secretly purring at the praise, small as it might be.

'Maybe you need a better teacher?' Sera commented. 'I'm going to lower the pressure or you'll be hitting the ceiling soon. You should experience a lightening sensation and, all things going well, drift slowly towards the bottom of the shaft.'

'And if I don't?'

'Then you'll crash and probably break your neck. But I'd suggest that you keep your balance instead.'

'Thanks,' Gaile responded dryly. 'I kind of figured out that bit for myself.'

The descent, such as it was, went surprisingly smoothly, though the last bit caused a bit of a problem, losing out to a tickle in her side and ending up on the floor grating with a huff … a gentle stream of air swirling around her.

She pulled of the helmet and breathing mask, along with her ponytail. 'How did you know about this place anyway,' she asked, trying to stay upright. It felt like she wasn't quite ready for bipedal locomotion at the moment.

And how in the name of the stars did you get access to it? I don't think they'd just leave this place open and powered up for anyone to just walk in here, would they?

'I have eyes and ears … and I know how to use them,' Sera responded calmly. 'So do you. I recommend that *you* learn how to use them.'

Grumbling something about problems of communication, Gaile refrained from saying anything that might get her into trouble and just stalked off into the small changing room attached to the chamber instead.

Actually, there was a good question there, she thought. But not nearly as good as the one about how he managed these things? It wasn't the first time either. Between Silber and Sera she was getting to see some highly unusual places in both the Academy and the DRC.

Ok, so with the dragonling she didn't get to spend much time in each. Instead she spent a lot of the time trying to lure him out of wherever he'd chosen to hide *or* running after him trying to catch him before he did something really crazy.

It seemed the dragonling only had two modes of existence; high speed or no speed at all.

He also had this astounding habit of taking advantage of when someone else opened doors to streak through them before they closed, often right over the head of the person walking through them. He didn't exactly have the fingerprints, access codes or anything else to get through them in any other way… He was quite the little opportunist, she had to admit.

But Sera? No, the place tonight hadn't just been locked. It had had a practically deserted look. Completely powered down and not expecting visitors until more reasonable hours could be arranged.

Admittedly that could well be because of the hour. Maybe dragons didn't like doing things in the middle of the night either? The majority of the people at the DRC and the Academy were asleep - or something akin to sleeping - and places always looked different in the loneliness of the night than they did during the day, she knew that. But even so?

Could anyone possibly tell her it *wasn't* odd?

Where were they anyway? They'd taken so many backdoors and service corridors, turned around by stairs and slopes, around corners and angles until she'd completely given up on even trying to determinate in which quarter of the buildings that they'd ended up in.

Gaile was certain of one thing though. Without his help, she would, without a doubt, get horribly lost trying to get back. She breathed out deeply. There was also the little fact that, once again, she was hurting all over.

Why was it that whenever she got together with any of her friends, she always ended up on the wrong side of something more powerful than she was?

'I feel like I'm just one big mobile bruise,' she complained as they were walking back, slowly, a bit later. 'They certainly don't put this in their adverts.'

Sera smiled quietly. 'The wind can be a harsh master, that is true. But better to learn here than by falling several miles and hoping you learn to fly before the ground hits you, don't you think?'

* * *

As it turned out, Sera wasn't the only one who thought that the windrider was a good example to use, even if he possibly *was* the only one who thought it was a good learning tool for someone that couldn't even stay up straight on a wooden training dummy.

Gaile was still nursing the bruises from that little escapade and that was several days ago. She wasn't the least bit pleased to have to encounter the thing again so soon. But at least this time she didn't have to play the main part.

Had he really expected her to manage? Maybe it had been some sort of test? She wouldn't put that past him at all.

It was therefore with half an ear only that she was paying attention to what their teacher was saying now that they were back.

Although, there was a difference... This time, she was up in the control room, not down on ground zero.

'As you can see,' Thomas Steele pointed towards the consoles and screens on which the data was being assimilated and recorded. 'We can here adjust for many different outputs, allowing for a simulation of many different weather conditions that you might encounter in the field up to, and including, small thunderstorms.'

Several of the students peered through the large transparent sheets that made up the visual view out of the command module.

What lay beyond the transparent view-pane was a circular chamber devoid of absolutely everything, by appearance, with smooth walls of large interlocking panels covering every visible surface. It was also empty of people.

Most of the students weren't impressed ... much. It was singularly uninspiring as far as they were concerned. Boring was another good word.

'One of the experienced riders has agreed to volunteer to show us how it all works. As you understand this is almost exclusively used in the teaching of young dragons these days, but we do have a few riders who like to come here as well. They say it helps them build a better bond with their partner.'

'So, what does all this *do* then?'

'Don't touch that!' Steele called out as Kalim was edging his fingers closer to a coloured panel blinking in swirling patches of light.

Kalim quickly put his hands behind his back. He still eyed it hungrily, like a cat with a particularly interesting mouse.

The rest of them were more interested in what was happening below.

In the chamber, far down below them, a figure wearing a very tight suit and helmet stepped out into view. Every inch of their body was covered with artificial material, black as the blackest night ... assuming that such a night gleamed where the light struck.

As the "door" swung shut behind them, they were busy checking over their equipment to ensure it was safe. Once the opening had shut it was impossible to tell there had even been an opening. It looked just like the rest of the place.

'Elsa, are you ready to go?' Thomas asked, first tapping the communicator experimentally.

'All good,' Elsa answered, giving the faces now pressed against the windows a wave and a thumbs up.

'Alright. I'm lowering the safety cable,' Thomas replied, twiddling with a couple of settings.

The controls up here contained a whole lot more than the few ones that he was using, far more of them.

When the dragons used this, it required someone of a more specialist persuasion than Steele to man the controls. Indeed, there was usually a full complement of staff up here.

For today though, there was nothing overall complicated to do and the students never did find out what all the rest of the machinery in this place actually did (assuming it did anything and wasn't just there for decoration).

At Steele's words, a thin cable came whirring down from above right in the middle of the chamber. Once it was within reach, Elsa grabbed it and hooked it to the corresponding arrangement on her back, despite not being able to see it, with a practiced hand. It was obvious she'd done this before.

'Originally this was only intended to teach dragons,' their teacher began. 'Dragons, being more robust than humans when in their draconic forms didn't bother with this safety device. It was only installed after the riders themselves started taking an interest.'

'Why not?' someone asked.

'There are many reasons,' Thomas answered, while at the same time not taking his eyes off the information that flowed before him.

'To begin with, it would interfere with the motion of their bodies and wings. While in human form dragons have the same vulnerabilities as any other human, as dragons it takes a great deal more for them to notice something. Mostly it was because the first rider who used this place broke both their legs, several ribs and cracked open his skull after losing control and crashing into the bottom.'

'Ouch.'

'Very much so,' their teacher agreed. 'After that they designed both the suits and the cable system. It's there as a backup in case something goes wrong, not as an aid.'

'Do you think I could have a go?' one of them asked.

'Are you out of your blooming mind?'

'Hey ... I can try, can't I?'

Gaile, who was watching the whole thing apprehensively, tried to keep her dismay from showing on her face. To her it looked like Sera had missed *that* little "detail" when they'd been up here.

Wonder how much else he might have accidentally "omitted"? She was beginning to wonder just how much she could trust anything he said.

This was the first she'd seen of the control room too. It was a lot more cramped than she'd expected. There weren't really all that many of them in here but almost no matter which way you turned you bumped into either something or someone. The people were preferential, they were a lot softer than the other option, though, as if to compensate, they disliked it a great deal more.

'Sorry, sorry,' she apologised, trying to move through the crowd towards the windows. She wanted a good view of this. Not that she cared. She just wanted to know what Sera had gotten her into.

Safety cables ... ha. She might have known... It was the story of her life, wasn't it? People making her do things one way when she didn't want to.

'Ok, everyone watching?' Thomas called out. 'I've got it at the most basic settings; just starting off ... can you see the wind?'

'No,' several off-put voices answered him.

Several students turned this way then that as if expecting it to materialise in the room they were in. What wind? They couldn't see anything. It was just them and a bunch of consoles and screens.

'Ok, how about if I do this?'

'No?'

'Still can't seem them? Alright then...' Thomas said. 'I'm going to release the chimes. Watch for it.' Steele carefully moved one of the selector switches.

Something was happening down below. They couldn't hear the small whirring with the sounds of the airflow overshadowing it every step of the way, but several small compartments opened up below the grating. They released some of their contents...

'Oooo, what's that?'

'Hey, I can see it ... I can see it,' Kalim exclaimed.

'Great!' Cole followed. 'Err ... what am I seeing exactly?'

Down below, from below the grating, small, tiny even, particles were being released. They spiralled upwards with the airflow. Dancing around lazily, outlining all the different currents in the room ... higher and higher they went.

'The wind you fool, *the wind.*'

'Thanks for that stirring thought Akia. Could you possibly be more obscure?'

'You mean obsequy.'

'No, I don't.'

Thomas chose to ignore the background chatter. 'Everyone got that? Yes? Good... Elsa, they're getting the idea up here. I'm going to up the strength now. Stand by, ok?'

'Roger that,' the rider replied over the comm. 'I'm ready whenever you are, handsome.'

With the airflow increasing, the woman down in the chamber didn't stay on the floor long. Arms wide, the artificial membrane between arm and rib-cage on the suit stretched tight, she moved around a bit like a seal playing in the shallows. The safety line remained slack, not needed.

'Whoo … look at that. I want to do that. I'm next!'

'Stop saying that, ok. You're not going!'

They watched entranced as the rider moved about, swooping through the room without a care in the world, diving and rolling.

'There are obstacles that can be released … some soft, some hard, that would need to be dodged or used as platforms. Of course, the soft ones will be kept in the air and tossed about so they're constantly getting back in the way,' Steele said.

'Wow, will we get to see that?'

There was a surge towards the window.

'Not today, no. Maybe another time…'

And with that promise, that wasn't even a promise, they continued watching Elsa's acrobatic display, wondering how long it would be until they too could do something like that.

That might be longer than any of them imagined…

For some, it might be even longer than that … if what their record was suggesting. Gaile wasn't the only one who was attracting less than positive attention. Some however, were doing so in a far less quiet way.

As they were sitting, days later, in the hangar, some having a break, others indulging in their hobbies, someone nudged Cole in the ribs.

'Did you hear?'

'Hear what?' Cole mumbled absentmindedly as he pulled out the wiring from underneath a small table.

'About Kay I mean?'

'What about him? If he did something again, I *don't* want to know. That guy is just too much'

Dayu chuckled. 'No, no, not that. I meant, what he had to do as punishment. You know, for the whole stand-up routine he pulled during First Flight?'

Intrigued, despite himself, Cole felt he just had to ask and simultaneously kicked himself as the words sped out of his mouth. 'So what was it then?' he wondered.

Maybe if he seemed interested, Dayu would say his piece and then go away and he, Cole, could get back to what he was doing.

'Having to retake every single fitness test, in *one* day,' Dayu said primly.

'You've got to be kidding me? That's like … no punishment at all.'

'I know,' Dayu winced. 'So unfair. D'you think he knows someone? You know what I mean?'

'*I* heard it was having every single point awarded deducted, twice, so that he's now on a minus,' another member of the impromptu crew threw in his piece as he slammed shut the lid of what she was working on.

Getting assigned to this was always a pain she thought, as it was always, always taking place after the rest of the official day was over and it always, always ended up taking longer than you thought it would. Akia made a face. Typical really.

'No, he got to help out Master Gern with the feeds in the Hive,' was the suggestion from Elon, who popped his head over the board where he was working.

'Shovelling dung out at the D-resort,' Kalim said, filled with glee. He did a little jig. 'Isn't it fitting? Isn't it?'

They'd gotten a whole interesting little argument going about the whole thing by the time Duchamp passed them by and told them, in no uncertain terms, what he would do if they didn't stop fooling around and started concentrating on their duties. And also that it was futile throwing around rumours of had or had not when no one of them actually knew for certain.

Maybe that was just as well, seeing how none of them could agree. Apparently they'd all heard a different story, each more farcical than the other.

In the disapproving words of Lady Gray, 'It'll be that boy flying out the window on a magic carpet off to pick the bejewelled eggs from the fabled caves of Ali-Baba next.'

* * *

Compared to some things, the windrider, despite scaring her stiff to start with was far preferential to some other things. It might have been less scary with the safety cable attached, but it was still a controlled environment (and in-doors too).

One of those other things was staring her in the face right now. She rather wished it wasn't.

This, no matter how you looked at it, was neither indoors *or* seeming very safe. The fact that it was in the middle of the night didn't exactly help either. She'd almost gotten lost trying to find her way to where she'd been told to be at this hour.

What was she doing here anyway? Had she completely lost her mind in coming here? It would have been nice if they'd have been able to do this during the day, Gaile thought. It would have been nice not to have to do this at all...

On the other hand, that would have also been a straight recipe for trouble, for more reasons than one.

'You know, I'm really not so sure about this idea,' Gaile said as she watched the clouds chasing across the moon. They passed swiftly and without a sound. The only reason they could be seen at all was because of the light from the moon itself, silvery and ominous, reflecting off them. It'd be even shinier if both of them had risen at the same time.

Other than that, there wasn't really much else to see … up there. There wasn't much to see down here either at that.

She peered into the sky above, a small frown creasing her brow. A helmet and mask were tucked under her arm. They were lighter than they appeared to be. That was about the only thing she was grateful about right now.

How had he managed to get her to do this?

'I mean, why at night? I can barely see the hand in front of my face,' Gaile said. 'Besides, it looks just a tiny little bit windy up there. And what's with this get-up anyway?' she tapped her fingers on the black helmet. 'With this on I'll look like a contender for the mud monster in a horror flick, don't you think? And why…'

A deep chuckle reverberated in her mind, bypassing her ears altogether, interrupting her flow of words.

'Would you prefer I answer those all together at once or separately?'

Escaped rays of moonlight reflected off some of the scales on her companion as he raised his head. Those were the only parts of the dragon that could be made out clearly. Other than that he was just a deeper shadow in the night.

That was another thing. She'd practically walked right into him when finally having found the right location. This place wasn't exactly on the main plaza after all. She just wished he hadn't hurried this on so much.

Ok, she did understand the importance of not letting anyone else find out but couldn't he at least have brought some sort of light, for *her* sake. *He* didn't need it, but she didn't have the excellent eyesight of a fully grown dragon.

Admittedly, it had been better bouncing off his hide than it would have been to have kept on walking and bouncing, much less pleasantly, all the way down the ravine beyond.

'One at a time, if you don't mind, thanks. I'm having enough trouble with this idea as it is,' Gaile tugged at a strap reaching crosswise across her shoulder and revolved on the spot. This thing was uncomfortable. Not strange really, seeing as it wasn't her size to begin with.

'You need to release the left buckle first before you put on the helmet. It will seal the gap between it and the uniform automatically, just like the protective suits you use for exercises. Strap on the breather last. You're not used to that one.'

'It's going to be mightily in the way you know, this thing?' Gaile gave the clinging tube a poke. Between it and the large dark glasses covering much of the upper half of the facemask it didn't leave a single part of her exposed to the elements. 'Couldn't you at least have found one that fit? Are you sure all this is really necessary? None of the riders I've seen use these.'

'You'll get used to it,' the dragon assured her. 'And to answer your questions in order while you finish putting it on – we are doing this at night for two reasons. Firstly, as you already commented on earlier, if we did this during the day you would, without doubt, be spotted. *We* would be spotted. Now, at night, we will be nothing more than a passing shadow in a dream long forgotten. Secondly, and perhaps more importantly, it has one huge advantage that I believe you have failed to identify. I'm surprised that you haven't spotted it yet.'

He waited, but when there was no reply forthcoming he continued, 'as you so frequently like to remind me, you are uncomfortable with heights. Obviously, tonight, there will be no height to be afraid of – nothing other than what is already around us. You can't see it.'

'Great,' Gaile rolled her eyes theatrically at him. 'And the outfit? I mean, I haven't even seen images of this stuff I'm wearing.'

'I'd have been surprised if you had. Mostly, when carrying riders, dragons fly low. It might appear high to you, but for a dragon, a real, strong, dragon that knows the winds and the ways of the air and the atmosphere, cruising around at several thousand feet is akin to scraping their bellies against the sand on the shore, playing in the shallows with the toddlers and dragging our feet in the water.'

'That sounds … painful.'

'No … merely boring,' he conceded. 'Alone, we can fly much higher. Heights at which there would be precious little for you to breathe as the oxygen thins out into nothing. The brisk chill of a cold shower for us would freeze you to the bone. As such, the suit, while not a standard issue, and you will kindly keep its existence out of public knowledge as you will the realization of the heights a dragon can operate at, will keep you from returning to the ground a statue of solid, very dead, ice – as long as it continues to function,' the last he added almost as an afterthought.

'Gee …thanks.'

Gaile, having finally managed to adjust the helmet and mask to something resembling comfort, shifted her weight around, trying to gain a sense of balance.

He might be standing still but with the wind picking up, she felt rather vulnerable in this, in her mind, rather precarious position between his wings, sitting just where the powerful neck merged with the body. Apprehensively, she swallowed.

She might have gotten used to staying on while on the ground, and by now only the most unexpected shifts unseated her, but that didn't mean she could do it while flying … up there.

'Actually, I have another question,' she asked, her voice having risen several octaves.

'Yes?'

'Why are we doing this *without* a saddle?'

'I thought we'd had this conversation already? Would *you* like to explain this to the ACC?'

'No, but that's not the point.'

There was a brief pause … more in keep with waiting to see who would speak first.

'And you'll catch me if I fall, won't you?' Gaile added when it was obvious he wasn't going to say anything.

'Having second thoughts already?' he asked.

'Hundreds,' she agreed. Her voice cracked and passed into a wail as the dragon spread his wings and leapt into the sky.

'Siiiiilbeeer!'

The cry echoed through the empty night, only the wane moon smiling at the curious looking pair.

The silver dragon quickly levelled out allowing his struggling passenger to gain a better handhold.

'Stay close and lean against me. You don't want the draft to knock you off,' he instructed. 'And remember, in flight it's difficult for me to see what you're doing, so if there is a problem you need to tell me about it. Don't keep it to yourself like you usually do.'

'Wouldn't dream of it,' Gaile assured him, her gloved fingers digging as deep into his scales as they could, i.e. not at all. Her feet did much the same. She wondered how he expected to hear her, up here.

Thankfully, the material on the suit reacted slightly adhesively with the dragon's skin, so she wasn't slipping and sliding anywhere … much. Lucky me, she thought ruefully.

I wonder if this'd be easier if I could reach around his neck? Like if he was forty times smaller or something.

Gaile pressed her body hard against that of the dragon. She might not be able to *see* the height, but she still knew it was there. It wasn't quite the same thing though.

Why, oh why, had she let him convince her to try and do this without a saddle? They could have snuck into the Armoury or maybe *acquired* one of the old assemblies from class. Ok, to reach around her friend they'd probably have needed several of them tied together but the point was that even a single leather strap would have made her feel better. Anything…

But no, he just had to go and insist on that they had to do this the old-fashioned way. Not even the full-fledged members of the DragonCorps did this kind of thing if they had another choice – not thousands of feet in the air. They weren't that insane.

And what did he know about "old-fashioned" anyway? The dragons of today had only been around for … what … a couple of centuries? It wasn't like there were tons and tons of paintings adorning long lost caves depicting brave dragons in sunset skies and their equally brave riders, as steadfast as if attached by instaglue, from the days of old.

Gaile's heart finally caught up with where she was despite her mind's insistent displacement tactics. It took some time before it stopped beating so hard against her chest that she couldn't think of anything else.

'Great skies of Retmia,' she breathed out.

It took even longer before her body, by now rigid, began to relax as she had not, by some unforeseen miracle, fallen off … yet.

But even with that, she didn't relax her grip even if that grip was little more than an illusion of safety. Maybe someday she'd be able to do this with her hands off, but not this day.

Her eyes slowly focused on seeing what was actually there rather than just whatever they'd been staring at, which at this point was dragonhide, which looked much the same up here as it did on the ground if your nose was only a few centimetres from it.

Not that it made much difference, she discovered. Face down and with her head pressed against the dragon's neck all she'd been able to see was black aside from the spots dancing in front of her eyes.

Even now, turning her head did little to improve the view. It still consisted of a great big nothing.

Gaile could feel the wind tugging at her but bent as low as she was, tugging was all that it did. She held no illusions of what would happen if she tried to sit up at this time.

'Why don't you try sitting up,' came the suggestion from the creature beneath her.

Damnit, was he reading her mind? No, that wasn't possible.

'I'm quite happy where I am,' Gaile replied, a slight trace of panic in her voice.

'As you wish.'

She risked a peek to the right. That didn't change anything. There wasn't even as much as a shadow speeding past out there.

There wasn't much motion from the dragon's flight muscles either and no sounds but those of their passing. If it hadn't been for that tug of the wind it would have been easy to believe they were stationary on the ground.

They were gliding; effortlessly sailing where the wind would take them. Well, it looked effortless enough anyway. Gaile had the strangest feeling the dragon was watching her, waiting for her next move despite the fact that his eyes, and that great head of his, couldn't possibly allow him to see what was happening on his own back without turning his head first.

'Now, what did you call me before?' he asked, derailing her train of thought … again.

'What?' Gaile tried desperately to recall the last few minutes. The last few words that she could remember were … goodness knew how long she'd stayed glued to his body with her eyes pressed shut. Oh dear…

'Oh … that…' she cleared her throat uncomfortably. 'Sorry about that. It's just…' Gaile hesitated again. The last thing she wanted to do right now was to offend him. It was a very long way down, promises or no promises. And could she really tell him she'd been thinking of him as a kind of large dragonling? She couldn't imagine the great silver dragon – master of the skies – would particularly like being thought of as a somewhat oversized pet.

'Umm…' she struggled finding the right words. 'I've got a friend … well … sort of friend … that I've gotten to know. He's the same colour as you. He's a dragonling. I suppose I just lost my head there for a moment and got you two confused somehow. You two are nothing alike – apart from the colour. He's mischievous, badly behaved, has a very lousy sense of humour and no idea of the concept of personal space. Nothing like you at all.'

It all came out in a rapid stream of words practically stumbling over each other to escape from the dam that had been holding them back. Now all she could do was to hold her breath.

There was silence for a while, as if he needed to mull things over before taking any rash action.

'You care for this creature?' he asked.

'Well, yes,' Gaile said, surprised and a little confused by the question. 'He's my friend. It won't happen again, I promise.'

'I see,' the dragon rolled his tongue over his teeth. 'Silber,' he tasted the word. 'Yes … I rather like it. Feels … right. You may call me that as well, if you wish. But please, don't confuse me with a creature the size of a bird.'

'No, of course not. Don't worry,' Gaile was laughing as a flood of relief passed through her. 'You two are nothing alike. Not at all confusable.'

'And yet you did so.'

'Oh shut up!' Gaile banged a gloved hand into his hide. He laughed at her in turn - a real, out loud, draconic laugh. At least she'd learned to think of that rumble as a laugh. It'd be a dreadful thought if it was merely him considering how to best roast her for a tasty treat.

'If you're feeling better, let us continue with this exercise,' he said.

And with that, the silver dragon, Silber, banked right, sharply and brought them right out of the cloudbank they'd been travelling in.

It had been pitch black for a reason.

Taking full advantage of the cloud's camouflaging abilities in the dark, knowing that the suit would keep his passenger from realizing or wondering over where the moonlight had gone, he'd stayed nothing more than a shadow among shadows until his rider had gained enough confidence – or at least until they'd stopped whimpering in terror.

The world, previously so dark, was now bathing in light; even the crescent moon was caressing the fluff below as it was singing it a lonely lullaby.

Gaile's hands clenched. She held on tighter.

The light of that moon, even if only a sliver, created hills and valleys below them. Soft as cotton, ghostly whispers of clouds and dreams of clouds drifted past. The same clouds that would be gone again in the early hours of the morning.

And he was still climbing higher. She realized this now that she had something to compare with. The relative positions of the clouds were changing and it was too much, and too constant, to be the clouds moving about on their own. Yet his ascent was gentle enough that it was barely even noticeable.

Slowly she began to sense the motion through his body, an almost imperceptible drift to the right and left, up and down, even as they climbed. Then, the vast wings, illuminated in the moonlight until they were nearly aglow from within, beat against the air, raising them further, more rapidly.

Now he began to move, turning, first gently, then sharper. First they'd go left … wings down, body angled, then to the right…

'Holding on back there?'

'I haven't fallen off yet it that's what you mean,' Gaile retorted loudly. 'I'd be much happier if there was something to hold on to you know.'

'You'll get used to it. You're doing fine.'

'You could do with a few lessons in inspiring confidence,' she muttered between clenched teeth.

'You'll learn,' Silber said.

He turned, far sharper than before, the fully expanded wings now beating steadily against the cold night air. The sudden movement nearly dislodged his passenger.

'One thing that you'll learn is to pay attention to the motions of your dragon. You can't be a good dragonrider and be blind to what your other half is doing. Feel the shift in the muscles, the dip of the tail, the rise and fall of the wings.

Learn to know what's going to happen next by the shift in that pattern, the small details that only you can tell who is so close by. Don't rely on your partner to keep you updated every time they're going to turn. Turn with them. Be a part of them. It's all part of your world and not all the textbooks in the world can prepare you for it. If you have it in you to learn it you will, if you do not, you will not,' he told her philosophically.

They stayed out there for several hours, each minute increasing Gaile's confidence; each mishap knocking it back down the same amount if not a bit more.

Eventually, the need for sleep drove them down. Well, drove Gaile, who could barely keep her eyes open, down.

By now she was holding on tightly without having to think about it anymore. Even so, she was so tired that they nonetheless turned homewards.

The less said about that first landing the better, Gaile always said afterwards.

She did walk away from it without any broken bones which counted as a plus point as far as her practical lessons were concerned. She'd developed a bit of a reputation by now for misjudging things and getting her movements wrong.

But that was in class. This was different. Here she'd learned to and continued to learn to trust the person she was working with.

It was amazing what kind of change that could bring in someone...

It would take more than just a few nightly flights to get over her fear of heights though. Her stomach still clenched up even at the thought alone but maybe it wasn't such an impossible thing as it had seemed only yesterday.

'Silber,' Gaile turned around.

Watching her friend, this massive shadow in the night, his silhouette illuminated by the ghostly light of the crescent moon, she, once more, wondered just why he was doing this.

'Yes?'

'Have any dragons ever chosen a partner who ended up not ... well... How do I put this? Were able to overcome their shortcomings? Not managing to become a full-fledged rider?'

There was a hefty pause before the dragon answered, as if reluctant to do so.

'There are those who, while chosen, never become full-fledged riders, just as there are dragons who choose to work in other fields. And yes, there are also those who, even after being chosen, are unable to adjust and leave the DragonCorps. It is not something that is spoken of often, you understand, but it happens. Dragons are not fortune-tellers ... we can not see the future. We are, in that way, merely adept at seeing beyond mere appearances.'

'I see...'

'Now. Go rest. Leave the suit somewhere safe where no one will stumble over it. I do not believe it would be wise to attempt to return it just yet and you will have further need of it. It would however be unfortunate were anyone to discover it in your possession.'

Gaile's only answer was a resounding yawn... 'S'cuse me,' Gaile stretched, trying to remain awake long enough to get back to her quarters.

'Once you progress to dayflights, it should no longer be needed and can be returned.'

'In two hundred years or so then,' Gaile huffed.

'Let *me* worry about that,' Silber chided her. 'You. Go. Sleep,' he stretched out a foreleg in her direction as if meaning to shove her along.

'Oh, I'm going, I'm going...'

'And make sure no one sees you,' he added as an after-thought as she disappeared from view.

Silber shook himself loose. This was going to be *a lot* of work. Why had he decided to do this? He *still* wasn't sure. Even if several things, a jumble of guilt, old memories, understanding, boredom and a strange kind of satisfaction from having someone around who wasn't the least bit impressed with him was all part of it. He could barely remember the last time anyone had scolded him, interrupted him or just plain ignored him, not since Riku was around. Not since Riku died.

Those thoughts weren't making his night any better. Amusement turned to sadness and, with a mighty leap, the silver dragon launched himself back into the sky – alone.

Expecting the Unexpected

She might have known it was too good to last ... those days when there was nothing but the two of them, learning, together.

By the looks of it, she wasn't going to be able to continue that. After all, why else would she have been called for such an official meeting?

'My dear, Miss Ashworthey,' Dr Cosgrove paced his office while speaking, towering over the lone student tucked away in the armchair in front of his desk.

The chair, made of green leather with hard pushed up puffs, was so large that Gaile looked even smaller than usual.

'I really don't know...' he mused on the idea, mulling it over in his mind as much as out loud.

'The case is quite clear Doctor,' Dr Pters, who was the only other occupant in the room, interrupted.

'So you have told me.'

The third party in the matter at hand pinched his nose, pretended to check his paperwork and continued speaking his mind. 'It would be unethical of us to continue to condone Miss Ashworthey's aspirations to becoming a rider,' Dr Pters stated quite calmly, as if nothing could have been more obvious.

'Are you suggesting that she be dismissed Endre?' Dr Cosgrove peered good-naturedly at his colleague. 'That would not be in keeping with our teachings *or* our traditions.'

Dr Pters looked a little taken aback at this, as if he hadn't expected any other possible outcome than the one he had already devised before coming up here. He'd even had all the necessary forms and such filled out and ready to be signed.

'Of course…' he tried to recover the momentum. 'I am merely suggesting that it would be in Miss Ashworthey's own best interest to *not* remain, considering the apparent risk to her life.'

'And yet she appears to be quite comfortable with that level of risk,' Dr Cosgrove let his eyes pass from student to colleague and back again.

His office seemed to have shrunk considerably by having them both in here or maybe he was just imagining things? Had he seen a dash of light outside the window a moment ago, reflecting off an old mirror on the inside wall?

He tried to think clearly. This was an increasingly difficult feat as the matter was going to need careful handling if things were to continue smoothly. Too much was at stake here to trust the whole thing to those such as Dr Pters.

'No, you just leave this little problem with me and I'm sure we can find an amiable solution to this.'

Dr Cosgrove made several shooing motions at the other man. 'Now, don't you worry yourself about this. Just leave it with me. I'm sure you're eager to get back to your work.'

'Yes … yes … of course,' Dr Pters hesitated but had to find himself content with being quietly, but firmly, bowed out of the office.

Dr Cosgrove closed the door behind him, corrected his steel rimmed spectacles that sat on his nose (the glasses were more for show than any real need) looking all the more the absentminded professor than what he was; the head of a fighting and training unit of dragons and riders and thereby the de-facto head of this planet's DragonCorps.

He only played that "absentminded professor" card when he needed to. He found it saved a great deal of arguing and being shouted at by people who were not going to be convinced with words anyway.

Depending on the situation, it could also put some people at ease. Despite that, for all his rotund little body, he was quite the nimble man on his feet. Nimble feet, nimble mind, he always said.

In another time he might have made an excellent thief - in his younger days that was - as it was now, he had to contend himself with being an excellent administrator. Elsewhere administration might be seen as a boring day to day task but for him it was a constant challenge. How many people had to, effectively, keep tabs on a whole planet? Not many, that was who…

Anyway, Dr Cosgrove thought it was a small blessing that it was an undeveloped planet that, mostly, looked after itself.

The people on the other hand required a more hands on approach – especially when the people were dragons. There was nothing like a dragon with a grudge to make you worry about small breakable things that might be nearby like, say; your arm, the house over there, the town you could barely see in the distance … things like that.

'Never liked that man,' Dr Cosgrove muttered to no one in particular as the door shut behind the retreating Dr Pters. 'Brilliant mind, absolutely brilliant, but he wouldn't recognize a catmonkey if it landed on him.'

He began pacing again, got a few steps ahead of himself, seemed to realize that the heavy satin curtains were practically fully drawn and proceeded to pull them aside.

'Ah, now that's better,' he said, much more jovially.

Light flooded into the office. Almost immediately the place, which had appeared dark and foreboding in its shadows with its heavy emphasis on dark wood and green leather, seemed to turn more friendly.

'Now, isn't that better, my dear?' he asked of his sole surviving visitor, not really expecting a response. 'I just wish they'd do something about the view. Sand, sand, sand, that's all I get these days. What I wouldn't give for a bit of ocean.'

The Doctor settled down into his own chair, his clear grey eyes gazing upon the young student before him. Dr Cosgrove straightened out the folders on his desk, finally finding the one he was looking for, the last one, of course, and opened it.

'Well, what *shall* we do with you?' he asked, sounding more like some bachelor uncle having found himself landed with a troublesome niece than a senior officer of the DragonCorps.

'I do dare say that Dr Pters does have one point, no matter how badly he comes at expressing it. If going by these,' he nodded at the information sitting in front of him, 'you do appear to attract your fair share of trouble.'

He made a point of studying those texts even though he'd read them all before the meeting. His other trained eye was studying the student much more circumspectly.

'Yes, Sir,' Gaile agreed feebly.

'Broken bones among students we are no strangers to, Miss Ashworthey. But I do believe I have seldom seen a student tack up such an extensive collection of injuries and happened occasions and still wish to remain with us.'

'Yes, Sir.'

'You *do* still wish to become a dragonrider, Miss Ashworthey? It is a dangerous profession at the best of times and you do not appear, going by these, to be particularly suited for this calling, attracting your share of...' he hesitated '...trouble.'

'Yes, Sir.'

Dr Cosgrove sighed. This conversation was not working out as he had hoped. In fact, it was difficult to think of it as a conversation at all. The word "conversation" implied by its very nature a certain give and take.

It appeared the reports had gotten one thing right; the girl seemed to react to authority, disliked authority, in either of two ways; complete submission or hostile aggression. Still, he doubted that things were quite as simple as they appeared. Things rarely were. In this case, he *knew* that they were not.

'Dr Pters appears to consider you ill-fitted for becoming a rider. And I am afraid to say that several other teachers do agree with him on this.'

'Yes, Sir.'

'You know the rules of course. We cannot make you leave. That privilege is yours and yours alone. Yet,' he sighed heavily before continuing, 'it might be prudent of you to take a small step to the side, for the time being only, I assure you. Make you disappear from the lime-light, so to speak. It might do you a world of good, allowing all the involved parties to forget *and* give yourself some time to reflect over what it is that is most important to you.'

'I understand, Sir,' Gaile fidgeted slightly.

She wasn't the least bit happy with being here for any reason. Today had been bad enough as it was. She didn't quite understand what the good doctor was getting at, nor could she work out if it was a good or a bad thing. Gaile hated feeling confused.

'I do wonder if you do? Hmm?' Dr Cosgrove stroked the stylus absentmindedly as he tried to gather his thoughts.

He was loathed to see the girl leave; a bit more than loathed in fact. He had his own reasons for wanting her to stay on. Yet it could not be denied that she had more than her fair share of trouble since she got here. He might not go as far as some of the others and refer to her as a trouble-magnet, for surely the girl did not do any of it on purpose, but she ended up suffering from the consequences just the same.

In fact, by looking at her file, listening to the judgement of others, even just believing the evidence of his own two eyes, he would have been hard-pressed to consider the girl as anything than less optimal material for the DragonCorps.

And yet…

Dr Cosgrove shook his head. No. Stranger things *had* happened. Appearances could be very deceiving indeed, he should know. And he had reasons of his own for believing that there was far more to this sad young woman that was sitting in front of him than mere appearances let you believe.

No. For the time being it was imperative that the girl remained at the Academy. It was also obvious that for her to continue with the normal curriculum, would lead only to one thing – seclusion – or possibly even an early death.

A rider depended not just on his dragon but on the other riders around him, or her. This was something that could be seen developing early in the relationship between the students, especially in the practical classes; many of which had the underlying purpose of just that.

To go at it alone, as they said, wasn't encouraged. It was necessary that a pair should be able to operate on their own but that wasn't the same as shunning others.

So, since losing this opportunity was the last thing Dr Cosgrove wanted, something had to be done. He had been given a gift, that's how he saw it. Now, it was up to him to find the best way to use that gift.

So, other arrangements clearly had to be made – somehow. Until such could be arranged, in the meantime, he would see to it that she was placed somewhere safe.

It did seem she had slight trouble with things that involved her parting ways with *Terra Firma*, but the rest appeared to be in hand. All that remained was to think of that "something". Maybe he should try and sort that out later?

Dr Cosgrove shook his head again, this time at the folly of it all. 'I'm going to reassign you for the time being, Miss Ashworthey ... until I can figure out how to best help you utilize your strengths and overcome your weaknesses. Until such time I will ask you to report to lab three every morning. Do you understand?'

'Yes, Sir.'

Ah, we are back to single line answers ... how well they were getting along... Dr Cosgrove thought.

'Very well. I'll see to it that you get a more detailed briefing sent to your idiom, but for now we will just have to wait and see.'

'Yes, Sir,' Gaile said, feeling, despite everything, that she should make *some* contribution to the conversation at this point.

'Off with you then. You can take the rest of the day as your own. No need to move out of your quarters, not until we decide how to proceed with this.'

'I understand, Sir,' Gaile rose to her feet, reading that last sentence as a dismissal. 'Good Day, Sir.'

'And a good day to you, Miss Ashworthey,' Dr Cosgrove gave her a friendly nod.

Watching the slight young woman leave through the same door that had so recently seen the passing of Dr Pters, he wondered if he had made the right decision. Still, an opportunity like this shouldn't be missed. What was it they said? Something about gift cows and horses ... or was that mouths?

There had been someone else, well, many actually, but one in particular that he remembered, who'd walked out of that door and away into the "sideways hop" and never come back from it. At least ... *not yet*. Dr Cosgrove had his own ideas about what he could do to change that too.

How long had it been? Ten years? Twenty? Thirty? He wasn't sure. It felt longer. He was however sure that it had been far too long to allow things to continue on as they were. Time for things to be shaken up a little. Maybe, just maybe, change was in the wind; if luck held true.

* * *

The optimism felt by Dr Cosgrove for the future wasn't exactly shared by the person to whom he was considering entrusting it, far from it.

Her heavy bag was thrust unceremoniously on the floor the moment she passed through the door to her room. It landed with a resounding thud. Following its example, the bag's owner allowed themselves to collapse over the narrow bed with a more muffled result.

Gaile burrowed into the soft covers, not really wanting to move. They enveloped her ... protected her from the world. The fluff from them got in her mouth as she tried to breathe so, with a grunt, she managed to roll over on her back.

She stared up at the ceiling. Not that she could see it, as she hadn't bothered turning on the lights when she came in, but it gave her something to do.

It was amazing that she'd actually managed to land on the bed in the dark and not somewhere else. What little other furniture there was in here, which consisted of a small wardrobe with some drawers, an even smaller desk and a chair along with a study light, were all pointy edges and sharp corners.

As such, none of them were at all desirable to fall on. Gaile should know that by now, she'd walked into those corners enough times to have a practically consistent bruise in the same place ever since her quarters had been shifted to this place. Not that she minded too much; it gave her a chance for some privacy. She just wished that the reason had been a happier one.

They didn't show at the moment; the bruises. That could either be because they were covered with clothes or because it was absolutely pitch black in here ... either one worked. The furniture wasn't the only thing causing them; not just odd corners at hip height.

Laying there, staring into nothing, Gaile couldn't understand why they bothered with the tests. It wasn't like anyone could fail them, now was it? Of course, she didn't have to worry about them anymore. She wondered if that was good or bad?

She'd been asking herself similar questions for weeks and she still hadn't decided. Say what you wanted about the Academy, but one thing you couldn't say was that they had very stringent entrance exams or criteria to meet. If you were upright and breathing and on time you got in; it really was dead easy.

Unfortunately it was just as easy getting out again. Hadn't she already proved that? So had many others, though, perhaps not quite in the same way. At least she was still here ... after a fashion. That had to be a good thing, right? Maybe not... No, she still didn't know what to think about that one.

And if that wasn't bad enough, if you weren't careful you might leave feet first or scooped up in a jar, the Academy being hot on these "practical lessons". She'd avoid that at least ... now.

No, the hard part ... the *really* hard part, was staying with it till the end, to the Final Exam. Not that much was known about what the Final Exam really *was*. Rumour told that it changed every year. That's what one of her teachers had said. But someone else, Max, in the ACC, he'd said they were held there, every year, hadn't he? So which was it? One of them had to be wrong, didn't they?

If there was one thing that this place was full of, apart from dragons, it was contradictions. Some days she felt like if she hadn't run into at least one before lunchtime there was something wrong with that day. Oh dear ... it really was getting to her wasn't it?

Gaile tried to shake it off but despite her best effort it kept drifting back again and again. It was just like when you had a really stubborn something lodged between your teeth and your tongue kept going there again and again but it wasn't actually anything there, it just felt like there was.

The exams ... they said that when you went, you went alone. Well, supposedly your classmates were there if they were choosing to take it, the exam that was, but since they were doing the same thing, they didn't count; they were just sort of generally there. When you left ... hopefully still in one piece, you had a new partner and had become a fully-fledged member of the corps.

Well, a very junior member of the corps with lots of training ahead of you but even so. Still, it meant you were one of them. It meant, and here Gaile breathed out sadly, that you had a partner to work with.

That was probably the thing she had looked forward to the most. She had very much wanted a partner. Someone she could share things with, laugh with, cry with, scold and be scolded by. And since this was the DragonCorps that meant her partner would be a dragon.

Wrong tense there, Gaile corrected herself. *Would* have been a dragon.

Oh, why did she bother thinking about *that*? It wasn't as if it mattered anymore anyway. For years Gaile had dreamt of soaring through the sky on the back of a dragon (something she'd kept very secret ... if nothing else, her family would have laughed their eyes out at the idea, she was sure of that). Finally, after some soul searching, a bit of travelling and a somewhat unexpected encounter along the way, she'd ended up here. But instead of flying high, all she'd done was crash and burn...

Just like everything else, she thought.

Again...

* * *

And so it was, a week or so later, that Dr Cosgrove, having been true to his word, had seen to that Gaile was kept occupied elsewhere, away from the rest of her classmates; away from the rest of the students...

So far, she wasn't impressed. Whatever else she'd thought that working behind the scenes was like, this wasn't it.

It was so ... so ... boring. Yes, that was the word. It described it superbly. The fact that it was accurate, if somewhat unflattering, didn't help matters much either.

For the time being, the bane of her life was rectangular; rectangular and boring. There it went again ... invading her life with its *dullness*.

The tank sitting on a desk in lab five didn't do much today. That wasn't exactly news. It never did. Occasionally there would be a bubble. It was, to one word, uniquely dull. No ... wait ... maybe those were two words.

Did that make it doubly dull? Probably...

Approximately the size of a large fish-tank – one with a transparent lid safely secured on top (what did they think the contents would do? Escape and gnaw someone's face off?). It sat there ... taunting her. It contained ... nothing or as close to it as it made no difference, Gaile thought.

The liquid itself was a cloudy pale blue that hadn't been able to decide if it was going to be opaque or transparent and had settled for being neither. It wasn't even sloshing about, stupid thing. And this was what they'd set her to do?

It wasn't bad enough that she was doing this, but she'd been doing it for several days now. There just had to be something more than this. There had to be.

The lack of decoration; underwater vegetation, algae and to say nothing about the lack of fish, suggested that while it might *look* like a fish-tank, it probably wasn't one. That was something she'd figured out long ago.

Of course, that might have been deduced solely from its presence in lab five to begin with, but that would have been too obvious. Gaile shook her head, slowly, as she stared at it without really seeing anything.

Nothing but blue dullness ... all day long. That's all she had to do these days. That was what she had to watch. That was what she *had* been watching – for several days now. Ever since she'd reported to the lab after getting what Gaile still thought of as "the boot", it had been her sole occupation; nothing but watching, watching, watching.

She'd even take getting lectured by Sera over *this*. Not that she had time for that anymore...

The days were remarkably similar. Was it any strange that they all just seemed to blur together? They all began and ended the same: a) arrive in the early morning. b) take out her note book. c) sit down. d) watch the stupid tank. How useful was that?

There were a bunch of instruments hooked up to the thing that were doing exactly the same thing; measuring everything from temperature fluctuations in different parts of the tank to light levels and goodness knew what else. The machines probably had a device there for measuring the happiness of the content for all she knew. It probably did so infinitely more accurate that she ever could, aided by nothing more than her eyes.

And yet here she was *observing* the dratted thing. What was so exciting about goodness knew how many gallons of odd-looking water anyway? Because that was *all* that was in there.

Ok, *almost* all. There was also the limpet. But that couldn't possibly count. The limpet was even more boring than the water surrounding it.

It wasn't *really* a limpet, but Gaile couldn't come up with a better explanation for it. It was small, limpet-like, and "sat" at the bottom of the tank. It never moved. It never did anything.

In fact, it was just as dull as the water. Which was probably why you forgot it was there after a while. It just sort of faded into the background.

They hadn't even told her what to watch out for, how unfair was that? Her instructions had effectively been summed up in "observe it and make a note of anything unusual".

Unusual how? That's what *she* wanted to know. Was it likely that the limpet would suddenly sprout arms and legs and try to climb out? Was that why the lid on this thing was sealed tight? You couldn't budge it. Gaile ought to know, she'd tried.

The young woman shuddered. That was not a happy thought – no matter how ridiculous it sounded. You heard things…

To make matters even better (or worse if you hadn't taken anything for your sarcasm), behind where she sat, the *entire* wall was covered in large shelves. And on those shelves were other tanks. Some were smaller. Some were bigger. There was the odd triangular one. A few were filled with dense redness that moved only sluggishly - almost like a bad batch of jello. Others bubbled away happily, their residents occasionally coming to the front to take a look at the world outside, or so you felt. It was like the interstellar aquarium from down under.

Still, it could be worse.

She'd thought that she'd had enough excitement in these last few months to last a lifetime. Now she was equally certain that she'd had enough dullness to last several.

Wasn't science supposed to be full of things "happening"? People making interesting new discoveries for instance. Revolutionising life and carving themselves into the history books? If it was always this boring then why did anyone bother with it? How many gave up at the first turn, never even making it to the homestretch?

Technically Gaile hadn't been assigned to lab five per se. She'd been assigned to Dr Asura Rokoskiev, who just happened to be working out of lab five at the moment, and who had greeted the arrival of her new "assistant" with the same amount of enthusiasm normally reserved for the mortally wounded unable to move watching the circling predators as they came closer and closer with every breath.

Dr Rokoskiev *had* been polite, but it was the politeness of someone who knew that they needed to be polite or there would be trouble. It was obvious that she'd rather not have had someone inexperienced underfoot. Her greeting had been accompanied by a smile that was disturbingly lacking in enthusiasm but was making up for it all the way by being more than a little creepy instead.

Maybe it was the way that the doctor smiled by retracting her lips from her teeth. It bore more resemblance to a gesture of hostility than anything else – albeit one without any growling attached.

Gaile rapped her knuckles against the glass wall. No reaction. Not that she'd expected there to be one, not by now.

'Doesn't this thing do *anything*?' Gaile complained loudly.

'It's doing something all the time.'

Rokoskiev's voice gave Gaile quite the start. Whoops, she thought. I didn't even notice her coming in.

'Is it?' she asked.

'Indeed,' Rokoskiev intoned coldly. 'You are merely not seeing it.'

'So, what is it exactly that I'm supposed to be seeing then?' Gaile asked boldly. It wasn't as if she could get into *more* trouble than she already was, was there? 'I can't see how this thing has *anything* to do with dragons.'

'That is a common misconception,' Rokoskiev corrected her. 'The DRC does not limit its scientific pursuits merely to dragons. By the time the dragons arrived on the scene the DRC was already a hub of cross-science research and development, involved in everything from studying the ever changing weather patterns to the creatures of the ocean, the distant stars to where we one day might travel, the earth beneath our feet and all that it holds. It went by another name in those days. We have merely continued in that tradition.'

'Oh…'

'This,' Dr Rokoskiev indicated the sad looking tank, 'could well be the discovery of the century. Perhaps even coming to rival the QDE-M, or Q-dem, whichever you feel is easier on the tongue, itself, if,' and she stressed the word, '*if* we can identify the correct circumstances in which it works.'

Gaile peered closer at the blue liquid. It didn't look like it was about to reveal its secrets any time soon. Could this thing really be almost as important as the Q-dem, which had allowed Casticia to expand out among the stars? Not that she understood *how* it worked – just that it did.

'So…' she began hesitatingly, she didn't want to make an enemy of the older woman, who some of the other assistants had mentioned in passing was part of the DRC's resident draconic population. 'Did someone invent this?

Wouldn't they already know what it does?'

At this Asura smiled, almost casually.

'If only that was the case. Science is rarely that simple and a lot of what we consider "great" inventions are actually either a side-effect to what the researcher was *really* working on if not an outright accident.'

Rokoskiev shook her head. 'This is a wholly natural substance. Very rare. By studying it and understanding how it works, we hope to be able to reproduce it artificially. Under the right circumstances it has remarkable healing properties and, if we're successful, it should allow for complete re-growth of lost extremities, even internal organs if the subject is fully immersed into it. As you can see,' she nodded at the tank holding the limpet, 'we still have quite some way to go before fully understanding it.'

'That sounds…'

'A little far-fetched?' Rokoskiev interrupted. 'Yes, I know. Many discoveries do before they become household words.' She smiled benignly and then dropped the bombshell. 'We're also testing *your* powers of observation by comparing your notes with the readings from the machines.'

Crap, Gaile thought. Well, that was her day ruined. They could have said something but that was supposedly the point. She would have taken the whole thing more seriously if she knew she was getting graded.

She still didn't think she'd have noticed much going on though. There was only so much of 'bubble, bubble, bubble' that a person could take before going blind to everything else.

Suppose there was the start of a bright new universe in there, she'd probably end up missing that too.

'I see,' she finally said, more to fill in the expectant silence than anything else.

Rokoskiev refrained from cuffing the insolent girl at that point, no matter how much she wanted to. It was bad form, but her palms itched. Dragons generally didn't raise their young with silk gloves.

What good an assistant who couldn't really assist was, she wasn't sure. This hadn't been *her* choice. It wasn't like the girl had any formal scientific training either, not at this level.

Dr Cosgrove better have a good reason for stitching her with them, Asura thought. There were plenty of other researchers around so there must be a reason or so she hoped.

The good Doctor rarely did anything without there being at least one solid reason behind it – more often several – and they didn't all necessarily occupy the same plane of thought either. He was one of the few people she'd ever met who could consider, truly consider, all alternatives, all possible outcomes of any given present or what might have led to the present, or find a fixed point in the future and see all the different roads leading there, from the small paths and streams feeding into the larger river, a highway system that was constantly moving and evolving.

The reasoning, when he tried to explain it, never made any sense or at least they couldn't understand it. But he would, almost unfailingly, be proven right, given enough time. Dr Rokoskiev had known him all his life. When he'd been a boy those traits had caused great difficulties with teachers at his old school, old classmates, even work colleagues. It had done the same when he'd come to the DRC.

Even as an adult they'd been very inclined to put him at odds with whoever was running things. His inability of actually presenting a reasoned and structured argument to support his cause had left more than its share of confrontations and misunderstandings behind it.

Now, as the head of Research & Development and de facto head of the Academy, he no longer had to present these structured arguments - not *that* way - and time had long since vindicated his ability and his keen insights.

Asura Rokoskiev trusted him beyond all else. She just didn't always understand him.

So, for now, she pushed the gnawing question of "why" into the back of her mind. Instead she concentrated on the "how". That, at least, was something she could do something about herself.

By the time Rokoskiev had had to wake Gaile up for the third time, the last time with a none too gently performed poke, she ended up just sending the girl to bed with orders to come back in the morning when she was "awake". What on earth was the girl up to at night if she could barely even keep her eyes open? Maybe she was better off not knowing.

Then the doctor herself proceeded to work for many more hours, far into the night (well, the early hours of the next day really) as was her custom. She herself didn't need much sleep and had a bit of trouble getting her head around that others were not quite so "lucky".

* * *

There was one upside to not having to go to class anymore, Gaile thought as she snuggled up in bed, trying to fall asleep. It meant she didn't have to endure *that* subject.

Others weren't as lucky…

'Philosophy & Methodology of Dracology has *got* to be the most boring subject *ever*,' Jens Anderssen slammed his diom down on the tabletop.

He felt the urge to throw it across the room, but, while hardwearing, the things *did* break if you were too rough on them. Fancy explaining to his mother why he needed a new one. No thanks.

It was still a loathsome subject though and the set readings and research for it weren't any better.

'Duh, what d'you expect?' Cole Stibbins joined in, eager to have his share if there was to be a general griping going on.

'True,' Elon agreed. 'Even the teachers hate it.'

'Right. I mean, have we had a single teacher for more than one lecture each since we started?' Robin Sternmasser rolled her eyes.

'It's like … I don't know … the abyss, or something. You walk in and your brain just turns to sludge after five minutes, two if you're having a bad day.'

'What's with this assignment anyway?' Kalim complained. "Analyse the origin of dragons as we know them?" Well, duh – *everyone* knows that story.'

'Right. It's not like it's a big secret or something.'

'I think perhaps that they want us to look at it in more depth,' Pol Breakmountain suggested.

'I mean, some guy finds some bones or something in a cave and goes home and experiments on them and poof, you have dragons. It's not like it's difficult,' Jens huffed.

'I think it might have been a bit more complicated than that Jens,' Pol said.

'Yeah, well … there isn't a whole lot known about it you know,' Cole complained.

'True,' Akia agreed. She leaned forwards, out of the easy-chair she was occupying in the cafeteria.

'Make it up and claim you misunderstood the question,' Elon suggested slyly.

'Elon – honestly!'

'What? At least you'd have something to turn in that way, right?'

'He's got a point,' Robin conceded grudgingly. 'At this rate neither of us are getting anywhere.'

Putting down his own diom and rubbing at, by now, tired eyes, Cole stretched out on the lounger and tucked his arms behind his head. 'It'd be easier if the whole thing wasn't so hush hush,' he said.

'True.'

'Come on, Jens! I wouldn't call the head researcher burning all his notes and disappearing hush, hush. Not exactly anyway.'

A loud slurp rolled over them as Kalim tried to suck up the last of his drink through a straw. He finished, only to be met by a round of frowns. 'Sorry,' he apologized sheepishly.

'It wasn't the head researcher anyway,' Reena chimed in. 'It was some crackpot's pet project – literally.'

'He *was* the head of that particular research, wasn't he?'

'Idiot. He was the only one in it!'

'He was still a nutcase,' Teran stated firmly.

'Brilliant though.'

'Ok – brilliant, but still a nut.'

'Mhm,' a round of agreements came from the rest of the small group including several from other people who'd just happened to overhear them.

'Give it a rest you guys,' Robin rolled her eyes at them.

'They do say he was inspired by ghosts of the past age,' a third year leaned over the back of a divider, lowering his voice conspiratorially.

'Ah man, not *that* old story,' one of his friends complained.

'Just ignore him people…' another one of them suggested.

'Well, what would you call it then?' Derek challenged.

His friend shrugged. To be honest, he wasn't sure what he thought about it either. But he was pretty sure it wasn't ghosts.

'Anyway,' Stewart Johnston continued in the same low voice. 'Someone, back when Casticia was the only settled planet of the Seven Stars, someone stumbled across these strange remains deep, deep underground in a cavern that had been sealed from daylight since the great cataclysm. Not that they knew what they were back then. Apparently the people that found it weren't interested in such things and the whole lot was donated to a run of the mill research centre, who in turn dumped it in storage because they had too much on their hands already. And there it stayed, until Jeran Crichter came upon in and decided to find out more about it.'

'That's what they say anyway,' another third year interrupted again.

'Derek? Who's telling this? You or me?'

'Alright. Alright – no need to go all snotty on me.'

They were, by now, holding the rapt attention of not only the small group actually working on the assignment but quite a few people nearby. People were even drifting over at random, wondering what was happening and if it was something exciting.

A lot of that might have been down to the voice and demeanour of Stewart, who looked more like someone telling creepy ghost stories or divulging state secrets than someone dispensing factual information, complete with gestures. He probably would have been including the spooky sounds too, if he thought he'd been able to get away with it.

'So, here we have this lone Crichter slaving away in the very bowels of the institute back on Casticia. He does all sorts of interesting things with the material he's found. Then he gets an idea and suddenly he's had it, a break-through. He's isolated the very thing he didn't know he was looking for...'

'Probably not on purpose...' someone else interjected to much general laughter. It earned them a none too friendly swat.

The group settled back down.

'So, now he thinks he knows what these things were. Things that he knew well, but only from ancient stories from way, way back before Orion was even built, in the really, *really* olden days … Dragons. He decides to take things a step further just to see if it can reveal some more information on what kind of fauna that roamed the planet before the cataclysm changed it and, possibly, if it was likely to happen again, what could be likely to survive it. No one likes living on a planet likely to go "boom" at any time.'

'He tried, and failed, tried and failed. Failure after failure. Then, through a sheer stroke of luck, he decides that, rather than working with the material he's isolated alone, he should try and incorporate it with something else, much like how the nightmares were created and, voila!' Stewart exclaimed loudly, making them all jump.

The loud noise woke them from the trance. They all knew what the result had been, after all. The very end result anyway. Not that it made the whole thing any less astounding.

'Somehow, against all possible reasons, whatever Crichter got from those samples, however improbable, something in there reacted to the presence of the human elements he used for clarification, used it as a base and launched itself back from extinction. And there you have it folks. The origin of dragons as we know it,' Stewart finished with a flourish.

'But...' Kalim said. 'That doesn't really tell us much you know.'

'And you can't possibly say it's more than guesswork anyway,' someone else added.

Pol held up a finger and waggled it at them. 'Educated guesswork my good people. Educated guesswork. Good enough for academics surely.'

'Anyway, considering the ratio of differentiation among the small groups of early dracona, it is unlikely that Dr Crichter succeeded in creating such a refined result from just a single batch. It's far more probable that he created several, each building on what he had learned from the previous. That would be sound scientific progress,' Pol announced.

'So, he made several. Neither quite human. Neither entirely dragon. It's probable after all that some of the draconic characteristics were watered down by the inclusion of the human element. In fact, we can see a re-emergence of what can be considered more draconic traits already, in the newer genera-tions,' Pol mused thoughtfully.

'Pol, you don't need to sound like a visiting professor to tell us that,' Kalim sighed. 'And that goes doubly for you, Reena.'

Neither of the two speakers took much note of being admonished like that or, if they did, they didn't show it. 'You did ask,' Pol told them.

'What d'you mean anyway? Re-emerging traits?'

'Well…' Pol rubbed at his chin. 'Look at it like this. You all know the story book dragons, right?'

A murmur of agreement and nods followed in the wake of the question. They did all know. Was there a single one of them who hadn't seen or read at least one story like that when they were little? Dragons crept up in the most surprising places. Sometimes as the hero. More often as the villain, a treacherous beast guarding their ill-gotten and bloodstained treasure, dining on young maidens until a brave hero rescued the kingdom and the princess with a single stroke.

'So, what you do. You take this fairy-tale dragon. Everyone knows what a dragon is supposed to look like, right? Let's agree to ignore the depictions of wingless ones for this. So, you take that and then you compare it with what we've actually got. Compare them to each generation and see what characteristics match and which don't. Doing that, you can clearly see that our dragons are becoming more and more draconic. Only somewhat so in personality but the traits are especially strong in terms of physique, in other words, in appearance and adornments.'

'You mean, you actually sat down and did all this?' Derek exclaimed.

'Of course. It's rudimentary for the course that we understand dragons on their terms, both as they are and as they are not.'

'English Pol, English,' Akia despaired.

She wasn't the only one. It wasn't that they didn't understand what he was saying but he didn't *need* to sound like an ancient six decades his senior, did he?

'So, what kind of things were you looking at then?' someone asked.

'Oh, things like; age, rate of maturity, deployment of wings, colours, shapes and forms, the beginning appearance of actual horns where the originals had none and other markings and, not the least, stories about abilities that exceed the physiological capabilities of the dragon in question.'

'So, were the original ones born or hatched then? I mean, it's not like they had parents, did they?'

Pol ransacked his memory for that one. 'I think they used some sort of artificial eggs so they'd have hatched, as dragons.'

'Actually,' Stewart lowered his voice again. 'There is one story that tells of one of the eggs hatching a human. The first heredrome; a dragon unable to shift forms. Trapped forever in the body of a dragon, or a human.'

'That's just ridiculous Stewart.'

'It's not impossible,' Pol admitted. 'There's a few of them around today too. Not many of course. But from time to time the dragon side overrides the human. I've heard there's been a very small number of those trapped in human form as well – unable to shift back after that first time.'

'Must be inconvenient, to be stuck as something the size of a house all the time.'

'Most likely,' Elon agreed and many others with him.

'You know,' someone piped up. 'Dragons are supposed to be magical creatures, aren't they? Don't see ours doing much magic, d'you know?'

'Of course not,' Reena huffed. 'That's just old fairy stories. This is the real world we're talking about.'

'Actually,' Pol mused, 'as Akia so kindly pointed out at an earlier time, there have been reports of strange occurrences among some dragons. But so far nothing conclusive has been decided on the matter. I believe they are keeping it very low key at the moment.'

'There you are then,' Stewart stated with a finality to it, challenging anyone to keep going.

'That doesn't mean anything,' Cole countered.

'Anyway! It's getting close to release time. What do you all say? Want to go play some fetch instead?'

This idea was met with general approval from the amount of nods it created. And soon a large part of the group had headed off to the outside. Now that evening was approaching it was cool enough to be out there without extra precautions if you wanted to stay long. There were also plenty of those who'd drifted in when the story had begun who were now drifting back to whatever they'd been doing before.

Pol remained in his seat.

As far as he was concerned, just because something hadn't been proven conclusively didn't mean the opposite; that it had been disproven conclusively.

In truth, in relation to the matter regarding the possible resurgence on extraordinary capabilities in the species known as "dragons" he considered the whole issue to still be very much open to debate.

Among those shadows drifting away, Gaile had to agree; it was a bit of an oddity. But then, there were plenty of oddities around when you started looking at things in more detail rather than just accepting them at face value. Many oddities indeed.

* * *

By the time another month had passed by and Gaile was showing no sign of pulling out of her self-inflicted slump, some people were losing their patience. Not all of them were being terribly polite about it either.

Actually, the dragonling had begun complaining after only a few days. He was used to getting more attention and now Gaile was having almost no time for him at all.

Not even getting into trouble made any difference; she wasn't there to get him out of it, which made it a bit pointless in the first place.

By the time she got any time off, she was so tired that she was no fun to be around; not like she used to be. Now he had to contend himself with just curling up and having a snooze in company. At least she hadn't given up on petting him; that had to be good, right?

Some of her other friends were more vocal about what they thought about it all…

It was when she'd finally had gotten around to visiting the most conspicuous, and secretive, of them, that they eventually lost their patience with her.

'You can't be serious?' Gaile stared at him, his face only inches from her own.

'Of course I am,' he gave her his best affronted expression.

'Silber! That's two night flights out there at least, and another two days … I mean nights, back. That means being away for almost a week. I can't take that kind of time off right now. I'm supposed to be working in the lab. Not that I actually do anything important, but that's not the point. They're not going to just let me wander off just like that, with no explanation.'

The dragon arched his neck backwards until it resembled nothing as much as a large, proud S. His eyes stared down upon her from that height, a statue of immobility. Its strength was absolute.

'Do you want to learn or don't you? I believed that you were serious about this?'

'I *was* serious, Silber,' Gaile threw out her arms in agitation. 'It just doesn't matter anymore. It's not a good time.'

Sitting back on his haunches, placing his forepaws squarely in front of him, wings extending, his head was even further up than usual. Winding his long, elegant tail around his body until the tip brushed him under his chin, he continued, 'to progress further it is necessary to go elsewhere. It is too visible to go flying during the day here and you *need* the practice. It would be too conspicuous for you to borrow a shuttle and I don't know if you can pilot one, which means we will need to fly there. I am certain however that you will be able to arrange for some time off.'

By the tone of his voice, he didn't doubt that either, that much was obvious, Gaile thought. He certainly seemed confident about the whole thing. Too bad that she didn't share his enthusiasm. Besides, she was out or practice.

'Why are you even doing this anymore,' Gaile confronted him angrily. 'I got thrown *out*, remember?'

'Merely moved along laterally,' the dragon corrected.

Gaile chose to ignore him. At the moment she was a bit too wrapped up in herself to have noticed if the sky fell down or so Silber felt. Why was it that she always managed to annoy him when he was already in a bad mood?

'I'll never be a rider. So all this practice is just a waste of time for you.'

'Foolish thought. You have as much a chance as anyone.'

'Oh sure. And that dragon will just materialize out of thin air will it? While I'm stuck in that stupid lab, doing stupid paperwork? The only one around here who thinks I'm worth the air I breathe is you, and you won't even be seen in public with me. That'll work, I'm sure. The new rider and her invisible dragon. A novelty if nothing else,' Gaile snarled, turned around and stomped off.

Silber heaved a great sigh, coming to rest his head on his forepaws, staring at the place she'd disappeared from view.

This was going to be more difficult than he had expected.

* * *

The one who took the longest before he started showing signs of being annoyed with her or disagreeing with her choices, was Sera. Despite that he was the most vocal of the three; he also seemed to be the one least inclined to do any talking.

Also, often when he did say something, she didn't understand what he was talking about. In contrast, the dragonling could chatter at her endlessly. They did have one thing in common though; she didn't understand what he was on about a lot of the time either.

The difference was that he was a whole lot easier to figure out. Body language could be a powerful thing…

At the moment, she'd rather have been back in the Hive getting scolded by those small teeth tugging at her hair and the occasional claw in her stomach than being here, even if *here* was in public.

There was something about having an annoyed Sera so close even if, on the outside, it was impossible to tell he was annoyed at all. She didn't need to see it though, she could *feel* it…

'I think you should reconsider your options.'

Those were the first words Gaile had heard him say since she'd told him that she wouldn't need any more help; the day … err … night, she'd told him that she was no longer part of the course, that she'd been dismissed.

That time she'd turned around and left before he'd even had a chance to respond. Since then there had been not a single word between them. Admittedly, this was mostly due to that Gaile had, and with quite a bit of effort at that, been avoiding him.

Now she was stoically staring down onto the screen in her hands trying to ignore him.

It wasn't working nearly as well as she wished it had been. Whether she wanted to or not, Gaile felt terribly bad about what she'd said and even worse about how she'd acted back then. That didn't make things any better, if anything it made them worse, lots and lots worse.

There could be no denying that he'd been a great help to her and her studies and having been a second pair of ears for an intelligent conversation had made him a lifesaver. Maybe that was why there was a pit of dread inside every time she thought about how she'd treated him on that day and every day since. He hadn't deserved that. It wasn't *his* fault she'd ended up getting demoted.

He'd never, ever, spoken to her in public like this though. Not that this could be called a casual conversation. Even from a distance, the frown on his face made it look like he was telling her off.

That probably said more about just how he felt about this than the tone of his voice – since that was nothing special, just as cold as usual.

Not looking up, the silence that followed her little outburst felt so long that she was sure he'd left. But not so…

'You are still part of this. Of everything this place is. If you want to turn your head away and refuse to see, that is your privilege. I think you would be greatly mistaken to do so.'

Sera remained standing, staring out the window by which she sat, a long forgotten lunch on the table before her. It wasn't like they were having a conversation at all. Anyone watching probably wouldn't even think he was talking to her, especially since his lips were barely moving as he did so.

He was the same cool, collected personage as he always was in public. Not a shirt button out of place, not even a single hair. His voice low, there was nothing in his behaviour or appearance to betray he was doing anything as untoward as speaking with someone like her, not even to pass a comment about the unusual weather they'd been having lately.

That he was actually telling her off, as a friend, was something that no one who was nearby could possibly even imagine.

She hated that side of him.

It would have taken someone who knew him beyond well to even guess that there might be something wrong and there was no such person within a million miles of the DRC. Gaile herself was a bit too busy wallowing in self-pity to pick up on the subtle signals that screamed "I'm very worried here".

'What options? No classes – no knowledge. No knowledge – no experience. No experience – no chance. I should count myself lucky that they didn't throw me out with the dishwater,' Gaile said. She didn't look up, instead addressing the air in front of her, her voice barely above a whisper, yet with a hard edge tinting it in crimson.

'And yet, here you are … reading, in your time off. There are other ways to grow. Other ways to learn. Knowledge is not the same as wisdom and neither need the presence of a classroom to be gained.'

'Even if I wanted to, I don't have the *time*. And if being honest, I never had the *ability* either. People like me never do. Black sheep *never* do. Not in the eyes of anyone else.'

Gaile swallowed painfully, her palms all sweaty.

'Maybe…' Sera hesitated. He didn't want to raise his voice here even if inside he felt like screaming at her to wake up. He didn't know what to say if anything he said would just end up being misunderstood. Whatever he *did* say seemed to come out wrong.

'Maybe … the eyes which *really* matter … are your own. And, incidentally, even if it probably doesn't matter to you anymore, I still think more of you than that.'

Sera flicked a wrist at the window, as if it had caused him some sort of offence, and walked on past.

Gaile remained in her seat, staring at the same screen she hadn't actually been seeing for some time. The rest of the cafeteria didn't go back to normal, it had never stopped being normal.

The world she was in however, it was anything but normal. Somehow things felt more and more confused. This wasn't how things were supposed to go. This wasn't the future she'd envisioned for herself.

Not sure how long afterwards it had been since Sera left that she was brought back to reality by a rough hand on her shoulder.

'Hey, what was that all about?' Derek demanded fiercely. 'What could Sera possibly have to say to someone like *you*?'

'Nothing, absolutely nothing,' Gaile shook his hand off brusquely.

Getting to her feet, she shoved the diom, without folding it, into her bag and made to leave.

'Excuse me,' she tried to push past him.

Derek grabbed her arm. 'Have you been bothering him? Jasmine won't like that.'

'Why would I do that? Mr High and Mighty has enough fans already, don't you think? Now let go!'

'Listen, you better show some respect,' Derek shook her violently. 'Sera isn't like you. He's the best there is. People like you don't even deserve to breathe the same air as him,' he growled.

'Oh yeah? Do I look like I care?' Gaile snarled back, not much caring for the treatment she was at the receiving end of. 'Let go of me!'

'I don't know what you think you are but when Jasmine's through with you, you're gonna wish you'd never even walked in through those doors,' he snapped at her viciously.

'I said … Let! Go!'

Gaile, tired of being at the losing end of the tug of war, whirled around. Her left knee caught him in the stomach with enough force that he bent double, releasing her and clutching his midriff with both hands in one single motion.

Her hands suddenly free, a moment later her right fist connected with his chin. Not only did it knock him back but it literally sent him flying, even if he didn't go very far.

Derek collapsed against the nearest divider which broke under his weight.

How odd, thought that calm detached part of her mind that wasn't panicking or preparing to run away. Hitting someone had never done *that* before. Maybe all that training had paid off after all?

Still, should it really have done *that* much damage? Gaile held up her hand, staring at it in surprise.

Her heart was still racing, pounding even. The very veins in her toes were throbbing. Every blood vessel, every nerve … for a brief instant it felt like they were about to burst out of their seams.

It was *still* strange. She hadn't meant to hit him *that* hard. It wasn't like she'd pulled back her arm for maximum effect either. But by the feel of it she could have sworn his jaw had not just cracked but practically shattered on impact. Were they supposed to do that?

Gaile hadn't exactly been in a lot of fights, none at all outside the early playground experiences, so she didn't have much to compare with. But wasn't she a bit small to do that? Sure, if she'd been twelve feet tall and built like a barrel it might have been expected, but her? She was small and he was a pretty big bloke.

Maybe it was a good thing he seemed to have been knocked unconscious by the fall...

She risked a glance in Derek's direction. He was already being surrounded. No need to worry about the infirmary getting hold of him then. That was good.

Unfortunately, one of Jasmine's other friends stepped forward, though Gaile noticed that the girl kept quite a bit of distance between them. Anxious not to get too close it seemed. How quickly things changed.

'You'll pay for that,' the girl hissed.

'Oh? I have no doubt about that,' Gaile replied agreeably. 'But not right now, don't you think? I'm late for an appointment.' Gaile turned and promptly left the cafeteria behind.

What the hell had just happened?

Her ears were still ringing or rustling maybe. What was it called when there were noises that you didn't even know could exist? And on top of everything, she could swear she was hearing the sounds of waves upon the shore.

Her fingers tingled and her feet too.

Maybe Silber was right *and* Sera. Maybe she'd better make those arrangements after all. She needed some answers and there were only two "people" she knew that had any hope of providing them. She'd visit with Silber tonight. She could only hope that the great silver dragon would be where she usually found him.

After how they'd parted company she wouldn't blame him for having found a new place to hide. Despite the fact that he was large and obvious, it was a big world out there even if you only counted the nearest areas.

Besides, he was a dragon... If he wanted to, he could go hide anywhere he could fly to. Why would he stick around here?

It was really inconvenient, not being able to speak to him unless he was right there in front of her. But first, there was something else that needed to be done.

Picking up her diom on the move, Gaile quickly sent off a message to the person she'd just been so cross with, hoping that Sera would understand what she meant even if she didn't leave a sender...

Trust and Tribulation

'Keep … going … you're almost … there,' came from between laboured breaths on his right.

It was falling on deaf ears.

Actually, it *wasn't* falling on deaf ears. His ears were working just fine. It was the rest of him that felt like dying wouldn't be such a bad option after all.

'I … can't … do … this…' Kalim took a final faulting step forwards and collapsed at the side of the running machine, panting heavily.

The projected scene on the half-circle screen in front and around them faded away. Gone was the lush tropical forest. Now it just showed a blank, slowly reverting to a mirror-like status. That view wasn't nearly as inspiring.

'Ah, that's so unfair,' came from the third runner, who now slowed down and stepped off their own individual track.

'We were almost at the next level too,' Isolde said as she ran a towel over her face.

'You … re … a … demon,' Kalim announced, still not having gotten his breath back. His chest felt like it was trying to explode. What his legs were feeling like was something he didn't even want to think about. They were, however, throbbing.

'You *know* there have to be at least two active runners or it shuts down. The points are easier to gather if there's three of you.'

'What where you before you came here?' Cole asked, somewhat miffed by the whole thing, 'some sort of marathon freak?'

Isolde huffed, her eyes narrowing dangerously. 'Just because I know the meaning of the words "staying in shape" and you guys don't…'

She didn't elaborate further but picked up her water and promptly left them to themselves. They weren't entirely unhappy to see her go.

'Geeze, Cole, that was … a bit … harsh,' Kalim panted.

'Well, what's this … obsession with being fit? It's … the dragon that does … the flying … not me,' Cole complained, pushing himself off the floor.

'Because you cannot always rely solely on your dragon,' the instructor stated from behind them.

They hadn't seen her come up. Guess they'd been a bit too engrossed in self-pitying. That was never good. Complain like that and there was usually a lecture at the other end waiting for you. That way their ears would get as much exercise as the rest of them but at least they didn't have to run anywhere for it.

'The DC doesn't ask you to be supermen or even professional athletes. It merely asks that you maintain a minimum level of fitness so that the others that will rely on you will know that they can do so safely. It's also,' and here she actually smiled, even if a bit harshly, 'considered a nice gesture towards your partner, who needs to stay in shape to be able to fly, to say nothing about doing their job.'

'But we don't have partners,' someone further away complained.

'Not yet,' Akia, on their left, corrected.

The two of them were occupying a second set of the tri-set running machines. One of those that had spoken wasn't on it however, but rather standing behind it and keeping tabs on a timer on their diom that they'd wrapped around their wrist and which was counting downwards in big numbers.

As the thing beeped, he smoothly stepped back onto his own track and began running. A few seconds later the system registered his presence and relative speed. Once it had done so, now showing three active runners, one of the two others dropped back for a breather.

So far, they'd racked up the highest number of points that any of the first year students had scored so far today.

Smart move, Elsa thought. The system needed two runners, but it didn't say they needed to be the same two ones the entire time. As long as no one other than the three that registered for the session tried to take their place, they could keep switching back and forth as much as they wanted. While they might not gain as many points as three people at once to start with, by alternating runners and allowing them to rest, they extended the period they could collect them in.

Of course, it only worked if all three were reasonably able to keep it up for extended periods of time. Kalim and Cole, even with that system, wouldn't have gotten far. Further than they had the way they *had* tried to use it though.

'This sort of thing doesn't build itself. It takes time. Don't you think that it'd be nice if you were on even footing with your partner, once you've found one?' Elsa Seawall asked.

She didn't receive a reply. That is, she didn't receive a coherent reply. There were plenty of general grumblings coming from students in the near vicinity and a few more choice expletives from further away – far away enough that she couldn't make out exactly what had been said, which was most likely the point.

Kalim and Cole weren't the only ones in the fitness centre that were dead exhausted. At least the guys in the pool had a bit of buoyancy. And there were those in here with more than just a bit of that.

Along the far wall (one of the short, distant, ones) stood what, from a here, looked like five giant snowglobes or what might have been mistaken for fishbowls. Only, in this case, there was no snow. The presence of fish could be debated ... it depended entirely on your definition of "fish".

These transparent tanks didn't have the semi-circular screens placed in front of them. Instead, the images were projected directly onto the interior "wall" of the snowglobe itself. Only the front half showed anything other than transparency at the moment though, the other sides remained open.

It *could* be adjusted to entirely encircle the person "swimming" in there if you knew how, but the default setting only extended it to the front and side. The back remained clear and see-through, mostly to allow anyone in there to turn around and clear their head if they started to feel dizzy or uncomfortable.

A lot of the other "equipment" in here asked for you to remain stationary (well, relatively speaking that was). The main exceptions were the running machines, rowing machines and the odd looking runaways from a giant's holiday decorations. As such, those were also the only three types with augmented reality displays.

Glasses might have made for a more immersive experience but they did kind of make you blind to what else was going on around you.

There were plenty of people whom weren't very fond of exercise for exercise's own sake, Elsa included, and the experience that you were actually moving somewhere, exploring places, helped.

There were a lot of scenarios; from realistic landscapes and locations that you could visit for real as well, to purely fantastical creations, including one where you had to race through a human body to beat the virus to their heart, carefully timing different sections as to not be going too fast or too slow.

The "in-house points" that you could earn by completing various tasks as you moved along was something that spurred on quite a lot of people. You could redeem the points, but, according to their instructor, they wouldn't know exactly against what until they'd reached their second year – and the second years remained mum on the subject.

Incentive, now that was the key. It might be different for different people but the main point was that the results created a more reliable body (provided it wasn't carried to extremes, hence why the system had a cap, both total and per day). Not that everyone was measured with the same stick.

'No point in counting rachs if all you've got are pineapples,' as Dr Cosgrove would put it. Elsa had never seen a pineapple in her life … they still hadn't found a fruit that anyone had cared to nominate for the closest equivalent of the old pineapple from the images and description out of the Orion's databanks.

'Great! It feels a bit like floating,' Pol exclaimed, following up his comment by executing a barrel roll. He made a good impression of a seal, except for lacking somewhat in flippers and being completely the wrong colour.

'Sir? It's just water, isn't it? Shouldn't he be thrashing about on the surface,' someone asked.

It was a question that several of the spectators wouldn't mind having answered. They weren't even going to consider going into that … that … thing, until they knew exactly what it contained. The air they shared with everyone. This was different.

'It's *special* water,' Elsa, their teacher for today countered and patted the large transparent bowl affectionately.

'Can I have a go next?' Teran asked. 'It looks a lot easier than running,' he added somewhat sheepishly when those close by turned to look at him with odd eyes. Teran *never* volunteered for anything if he didn't absolutely have to.

'Why not...' Elsa nodded. 'As you can see we've only got five of these beauties, but you should all be able to have a turn.'

Someone further back held up a hand imploringly. 'Please, Sir, if you don't mind. What do these things do?'

'Aside from the obvious? You can think of these as a more interactive and a lot safer alternative to the windrider which wasn't built to cater to humans. I believe that you've already been to see that?'

There was an answering murmur and nods.

'As you can see,' Elsa indicated the five people who'd descended into the bowls, 'they're quite popular.'

Indeed, the five people inside them looked far more like they were having fun than merely exercising.

* * *

Gaile had a whole different set of exercises to get through.

She laughed and threw her arms around as much of the broad neck in front of her that she could reach. That wasn't difficult, there was rather a lot of it and it was right in front of her.

That wasn't the normal way. Usually she was perched somewhere between the shoulder blades which was a much more sensible place to be, as it didn't move around nearly as much.

The reason she was so far up and personal in relation to the wide neck was because of the rather sudden stop. No, actually, sudden stops no longer bothered her. It was more because she'd been busy admiring the scenery and had climbed further up on the back and had been standing up when the stop had occurred.

This time she didn't mind so much. Instead she planted an affectionate kiss on a nearby and shiny looking scale.

'I don't care that I can't be a real rider. I wouldn't trade this for *anything*. Did you *see* that?'

Gaile settled back, watching things from this new vantage point. It wasn't so bad, here. She shaded her eyes. Yes, the view was quite spectacular even if she'd seen this place before. They had arrived several days ago after all.

It wasn't very comfortable though, she thought. Every time Silber moved, so did she. No, probably better to get back to her usual position. There she could sit, if not comfortably so at least securely, and she didn't need to keep her arms spread to hold on either.

Once back up there, she swung her legs back and forth. This was more like it. No studying from boring old essays.

There was the one downside to all this, Gaile thought. If she did learn enough, become the kind of person that'd get chosen as a partner, then she'd lose all of this – . Gaile was under no illusion that her friend, while perfectly willing to be a friend, would not like to be anything more. It was unspoken, hanging in the air, but she could feel it.

No, the kind of partner that would be suitable for such a great person was not someone like her.

She did wonder what kind of person someone like Silber would *want* as a true partner. Would they be strong and handsome? Clever, a mind like no one else? Maybe he'd like someone delicate and fragile, the way of the dragons of old had?

It was all academic anyway; Gaile's position that was, not Silber's. Her transfer from the student body into the staff was proof of that if anything. Junior academic assistants didn't magically transform into riders, now did they?

But, she still had this.

She hadn't expected to still have this. To be perfectly honest with herself, when losing her position among the students she'd assumed that she'd lost the privilege of being Silber's friend along with it. That he, who had been teaching her about being a rider, would not be interested in "hanging out" with someone who wasn't going to become one.

Gaile wasn't happy about admitting that at all, for it meant she'd failed to have faith in her friends; all three of them.

Ok, so Silber the dragonling probably couldn't care less if she was a student, an astronaut or a three-eyed monster as long as he got a treat out of it.

But she hadn't expected either Silber or Sera to acknowledge her once she'd let them know.

Turned out that she'd underestimated him … them … greatly.

'I'm glad you approve,' Silber's deep voice said as he dipped his left wing, sending them into a tight spiral downwards around the central spire of the valley.

Gaile barely batted an eye, leaning forwards to get a better look. Those outcrops, jutting out into the valley itself, looked like they might play havoc with the shifting winds. Best to watch herself here if they were going near them. They looked like the kind of things that Silber liked to swoop past with nothing to spare. She thought he could be quite the show-off when he felt like it.

While her second flight in class had been almost as disastrous as the first, though for entirely different reasons, and was, she believed, what had earned her that dreadful transfer into the labs - more as a consolation prize than any-thing else - Gaile suspected, here, on her own, with Silber, what fears she still had did the same as the snow was doing below them; melting away under the bright spring sunlight, a few tufts of green grass poking out even at this height.

Soon it would be high summer here … and even this spire would be adorned in green, clad like a summer lady in climbing vines and flowers. A haven for small furry things going 'cheep' and twittering skylarks the same.

Despite that, embarrassingly enough, she still couldn't stand on a ladder without getting dizzy. At the edge of a cliff, her legs buckled, butterflies re-turned to her stomach and it felt like she was back in her childhood again. Not all the way back though, in her very early years she didn't have any problems with heights … or depths.

Today it was only here, on the back of the silver dragon, that heights no longer held a terror. Him, her friend, she trusted; trusted him to catch her, should she fall. Trusted him to protect her, should there be danger. Trusted him to guide her, should she not see.

It was strange how something so untouchable could make such a differ-ence, she thought. But it did.

Maybe it was all just an illusion, she didn't know. But if it was an illusion, it was one Gaile hoped would continue to deceive her until the very end of days.

Silber executed a barrel roll beneath her.

Yelping in surprise, Gaile suddenly found herself flailing in the air, caught off guard. Suddenly there was no longer a dragon to hold on to. There was nothing but air. Air and lots of sky … or maybe those were the same things here?

It brought her back to reality really sharpish. She straightened out and, a few heartbeats later, landed again on the dragon's back with a resounding 'oomph.'

'Don't do that,' she admonished him sternly.

'Then pay attention,' he replied.

'Yes, yes,' Gaile nodded and then remembered that he couldn't see her and felt rather foolish. That was a habit she hadn't been able to shake. It wasn't like anyone was able to tell her she was doing it...

'It's beautiful up here,' she said instead, looking down at what had constituted their entire world for the past few days.

This was a region of not very tall mountains … mountainettes you could say. Even lower foothills lay scattered about and lush, green valleys nestled in between what, for lack of a better word, had to be called peaks.

A thin blue line ran through them, occasionally turning into white in places. Other blue flecks were dotted around, much smaller and not inclined to be running anywhere, though the trees had a tendency to obscure the smallest from view, even from up here.

'We didn't come here for its beauty. We came here because no one else does,' Silber reminded her.

'Old grouch. Don't go and spoil the moment,' Gaile sighed. 'You don't have an ounce of romance in you.'

The dragon snorted, sending ripples through his whole body. 'I keep my mind on the job. We came here to train, not to stare wistfully into the sky, listening to the birds and thinking about poetry.'

'Alright, alright. Don't get your tail into a knot,' Gaile settled back and cracked her knuckles. 'Well, are you going to get started or what?' she asked pointedly.

'Oh, you are going to regret that,' Silber retorted.

He allowed himself to drop several hundred feet on the spot sending her stomach reeling.

The cry from his back could be heard for miles…

'Silber you LOOUUSEE!'

But aside from that little incident, today was a good day. No matter the twists and turns, whether they went rock hopping or barely scraped underneath the great stone arches that surrounded the central spire, she still managed to stay on. There were a few close calls, especially with one of the stone arches which would have scraped her off had it been just a few feet lower.

Soon it would be time to return "home" but for the time being, the two of them, dragon and rider, danced in the sky as if there was nothing even called "tomorrow".

It wasn't even close to the end of the day and already they'd accomplished so much. That's what it felt like. These few days, here … they'd been filled, even when she was relaxing she felt she was learning something new or even just getting more comfortable with what she already knew.

The light was still clear and warm against the skin down here on the ground. She knew that because she'd just pulled off her flight-jacket and was now stretching her arms for the refreshing sensation it brought.

Gaile proceeded to do the same thing with both boots and socks and soon her bare feet were instigating small splashy noises in the tiny creek beside where they'd set down.

It was a very quiet stretch of water here and it seemed content to move sedately rather than conforming to the ideals of a mountain brook. That too was refreshing but mostly it was just a relief to be standing still. Gaile felt that, when she closed her eyes, the entire world was still moving around her at breakneck pace.

Whatever else you might want to say about the silver dragon, he didn't believe in taking it easy, once he'd decided to actually do something in the first place.

Even so, she had to admit that she'd improved by leaps and bounds in the few days they'd been here. Flying during the day really *was* different.

'You will catch a cold,' Silber said from behind her.

The voice surprised her. She hadn't heard him coming. Considering his size, Silber could be remarkably silent when he moved. It wasn't the only thing about him that reminded her of a cat … he also enjoyed curling up and taking a snooze in the sun and he had a curious habit of finding odd ledges and rocks to perch on.

Then there was the way he moved … gracefully, fluidly. Too bad she couldn't scratch him behind the ears…

'Let it go,' Gaile suggested. 'It's pleasant.'

'I would rather prefer not making the return journey accompanied by sneezing.'

'Oh, Silber,' Gaile exclaimed, exasperatedly. 'Where's your sense of adventure?'

'Adventure is one thing. Illness is another.'

Grumpy old grouch, Gaile thought. Has he been ill even one day in his life? If he has, I'll eat my hat. Mind you, I'd have to buy one first.

'There are still many hours of the day left,' Silber said. "We should not waste them being idle.'

Wishing, for the hundredth time since they'd come here that she could thump him, preferably somewhere painful, Gaile grumbled something in return. Sadly, him being a dragon and all, she could hit him all she liked, it wasn't like he'd notice. The only result would be her hurting herself. That was such a drag…

But … it *was* a bit rude and generally frowned upon. Still, if she could keep her temper with him, she figured nothing else could possibly rile her – unlike her family, where she'd flown into a rage almost before anyone even opened their stupid mouths.

It did not help in the least that she knew all too well that he was, usually, right as well. Actually, that might well be a large part of the grudginess she felt towards it.

So, with a few more choice grumblings on the matter, Gaile extracted her feet from the cool water. She stretched again, trying to ease out some of the knots she would swear were forming in her muscles while she wasn't looking. A long soak in a hot tub would have been nice tonight. Too bad they didn't have one.

Was there a single muscle that you didn't use in this business? Ok, usually you didn't have to worry about having to hold on, not like this anyway. The special suit did help but... Heck, without it she'd probably have slightly larger survival chances than a snowflake in a sauna to stay on even for something as the take-off because whatever else you could say about the event, calling it abrupt and disorientating didn't even come close.

'*Are* you trying to kill me?' Gaile queried casually as she clambered up the low bank.

Silber didn't even dignify that with a huff, let alone a reply. Always an entertaining sight, an undignified looking dragon. No matter what their size, they weren't the least bit scary-looking.

Of course, actually giving in and laughing at them wasn't the wisest of ideas, especially not if they could make life difficult for you. Laughing at your superior officers wasn't generally thought of as a good way for advancement.

'Would it be possible for you to take this seriously?' Silber asked ... again.

'I *am* taking it seriously, Silber,' Gaile said and rolled her eyes at her friend. 'Never thought all this flying was such hard work,' she continued, mumbling as she bent over to pull her socks back on.

The low voice probably didn't stop him from hearing what she said but it usually did stop him from responding to it. If he wasn't meant to hear something, he was happy to pretend he hadn't.

It could be really inconvenient at times, when he really *hadn't* heard something he was *meant* to hear. You just never knew. Silber seemed to like to surround his life with uncertainties, at least when they related to other people and their perception of him.

Was it always like this, Gaile wondered. It wasn't that she had a great deal of experience of seeing this side of the story, so to speak. The other end, yes, she'd seen that but, to be honest, she didn't quite understand that either. Actually, if you thought about it, she had developed a little bit of understanding for the difficulties faced by a novice rider. That was saying something, all things considered. Still, the other "trainees" didn't have to face *this*. No one threw them in at the deep end and hoped they'd be able to cope.

Oh, so Silber hadn't done that either, not really. It just felt like it at times. To call it a steep learning curve was the understatement of the century. It had, admittedly, finally started to show some results. Now it was just a matter of practice.

The dragon behind her unfurled his wings, raising them and stretching his body, a bit like a cat after a nap. It cast a wide shadow all over.

It would have perhaps looked cute, if he hadn't been standing so close. As it was, the massive body towered above her. Gaile didn't as much as flinch.

When they'd first met she'd have jumped at something like that. She would certainly have stepped back and thought about getting out of the way as fast as possible.

Now, she leaned against one of the forelegs to support herself as she pulled the boots, which she had so carefully discarded not that many minutes before, back on. She wished he'd allowed her a longer break, but Silber seemed to have only one speed of operation, his own.

It wasn't that it was slow or fast. It was just that he ran everything according to what he felt like. As a result, you ended up running madly to keep up with him *or* jumping up and down wanting him to get a move on and stop snoozing.

Gaile was certain that it was a never ending battle.

'Today we will practice our manoeuvrability, again. Of course, when I say *ours*, I really mean *yours*. You are still stiff. Try leaning into the motions a bit more. I know you can do it because you do when you stop thinking about it. It's when you realize that you should be doing something that you become all flustered and loose concentration.'

'Hand to eye co-ordination isn't exactly my strong suite,' Gaile said, as he helped her up on his shoulders.

'That, I believe, was my point,' Silber explained calmly.

He ran one of his claws over the soft earth beneath, digging deep into the grass, then the others. It left behind deep gashes in the supple emerald grass.

'Stop digging up the place,' Gaile told him. 'What are you doing, training to be a mole?'

Silber snorted. He gave a half violent shake, as if he'd suddenly gotten flees he wanted to get rid of.

Did dragons get fleas? If they did, she didn't want to run into any of them. They had to be huge … eeep.

'Hey!' Gaile shouted. 'Watch it!'

'Hold on then. Something that small shouldn't faze you.'

'You're just being difficult on purpose,' she grumbled back at him. 'Now, are we going to do this or not?'

'Yes Oh, Impatient One,' Silber responded.

A moment and several leaps along the ground later, he forcefully fought his way into the air. Gravity struggled valiantly against him for a moment then gave it up as a bad job and the dragon rose majestically on the strong up currents. That was definitely easier than making your wings do *all* the work.

'Comfortable?' he asked casually.

'You'd know if I wasn't.'

'What were we supposed to do? Why don't you tell me this time?' the dragon said and banked slowly, putting the sun behind them. His tail streamed behind him. A ripple went through it.

Apart from the wind, which wasn't more than a gentle kiss at this point, their motion through the air was the only thing that made a sound.

There were a few birds around, but they were mostly staying closer to the trees and bushes. Not that the two of them were very high up, quite the contrary. But then, they didn't need to be.

The downside of that was that Gaile couldn't really communicate with him. She could shout but that only had a limited effect and only when they were barely moving.

Silber still hadn't managed to, surreptitiously, acquire one of the communicators used by the riders. Even if he had, it wouldn't have done either of them any good.

To be able to use it you needed not only the com-unit itself but the receiver that had been attuned to it that, when the partners were assigned, would be embedded in the dragon's skull. As Silber didn't have a partner, he didn't have a receiver either.

Thankfully it wasn't like they were practicing her giving *him* orders. And she could still hear him when he chose to speak, like now.

'Now,' he said. 'We're not too high, so we should be able to use the features of the land coming up before us. Try to lean into the motions a bit more, that will reduce the wind resistance *and* make it easier for you to hold on.'

'Yes Oh, Lord and Master,' Gaile replied, though she knew he probably couldn't hear her. Maybe just as well.

At that the silver dragon twitched his tail. A moment later he banked sharply to the left.

The dive, quick and short, took them straight in among the narrow confines of an outcropping, between the rocks of the mountains and the trees that populated it.

Silber swerved around a large pillar of stone.

On the other side, they were met by what elsewhere might have been a sparse and scattered woodland (if you could call such a motley collection of trees that) but for the large dragon it was dense enough.

The branches didn't have any leaves. The trees themselves, while towering high, like arrows towards the sky, looked pale and strangely dull. Their short branches stuck out almost diagonally from the main body, tilted slightly upwards.

Branches? No, they looked more like spikes. Not something you wanted to be impaled on, that was for sure.

If it hadn't been for their colour and sheer size, you'd have thought they were some form of giant cacti. Or perhaps some clever and nasty trap built by a previous resident?

The rush of the air against her face pinched her with every bite. She'd forgotten to pull the goggles down … again. She really should stop doing that.

Thankfully, they were neither high up or going very fast at the moment, so they weren't strictly necessary, but still…

With one hand on the dragon, the other reached up and felt around her head. Oh, good, at least she'd remembered to put them on. That was something.

'Whoah!' Gaile suddenly shouted as a sharp turn nearly made her loose her grip.

'Pay attention,' Silber ordered her sternly. 'This isn't like a ravine or some nice soft grass to fall on where all you have to worry about are a few broken bones if you land badly. Fall off here and you will likely never need to worry about falling off again. Those are dangerous. The spikes on the host are not only sharp with small serrated teeth, they are also poisonous.'

Great, Gaile thought. And this is where you bring me to practice?

They had slowed down momentarily but now he speeded up again. They moved quickly through the formations that they'd practiced yesterday. It was a whole different thing when one moment you were looking at the sky and the next a spike passed by. It felt like he missed them by inches.

It had to be more of course … but it still felt like you could reach out and touch them. Probably lose a hand if you tried.

Every time Silber switched movements he picked up a little bit of speed. Soon enough the landscape was a rapidly deteriorating blur as far as Gaile was concerned.

'Don't turn so tightly,' she screamed at him at the top of her lungs.

The dragon's last combination was making her lunch a very unhappy customer. It had been making threatening noises for a while but without the means of telling him to slow down for a while, all she could do was to hold on tightly.

Gaile was wishing feverently that he'd stop putting so much effort into this. It wasn't like him to get enthusiastic. It wasn't like there was someone out there awarding them marks.

They whipped by a stretch of knolls, only a hand's breadth between them and the highest point. Then, the sharp pull of the sudden climb forced her back as he threw himself sideways.

'Slow down! Slow Down!'

She shouted for deaf ears. If the dragon could hear her, he was ignoring anything she was saying or shouting.

It felt like a million small explosions were trying to force their way out through her body. Her vision was going grey … all fuzzy along the edges. Blood pumped into her head.

It felt like a million years too until Silber evened out and began gliding, almost effortlessly. He barely moved a muscle, letting the wind do the job for him.

The climb from then on was almost lazy. Slowly, barely noticeably, they gained height. The view of their little retreat grew and grew until it spread out below them, fading into the larger landscape around it.

The sun was warm on her neck. Too much and it would have been roasting but with their motion gently cooling it, it was just right; soft and soothing.

It smelled crisp up here. Crisp and clear. Fresh scents drifted in on the light breeze. The grass throwing in an extra growth spurt now that the seasons were coming around. The trees were crowned in emerald and flowers turning towards the sun, lapping it up.

It was very different from the scent of the dry plains. Very different and very nice.

How long had it been since she'd enjoyed this? Gaile wasn't good with keeping tabs on time in her memories; she wasn't sure. Too long certainly.

She stopped trying to melt and, as her body ceased protesting, straightened up as much as was feasible.

It was nice up here, she thought. They really should do this more often *without* the exercises. What was it with Silber that made him want to make an example out of everything? To try and squeeze as much effort out of as little time as possible? It wasn't like they were in a hurry.

Taking the time to slow down and just enjoy things was important too, she thought.

'And stop worrying so much,' Silber interrupted her thoughts. 'Don't you trust me?'

'I trust you Silber, I do … it's just a long way down, that's all,' Gaile replied.

By the time night fell on their last day, Gaile felt a whole lot more confident, though she still didn't care much for things like barrel-rolls and even less for inverted loops. Being upside down in any sense didn't appeal much to the young woman who, in other circumstances, preferred to have both her feet on the ground.

She looked about.

Not that her eyes could make out much, not with the campfire blazing so close by. But the place had grown familiar enough that she didn't feel like she needed to see it to know that it was there. Memory served well enough. It cut out on the distractions too.

Another reason for why so little of what surrounded her was visible was due to the bulk of the dragon blocking it out.

Gaile wrapped the blanket closer and bit down on the food-stick that was part of the last dinner here. She was snuggled up tightly against a left front paw. It wasn't naturally a very good pillow but with enough padding it was quite comfortable.

As long as Silber didn't move that was.

'You have done well,' he acknowledged.

The voice seemed to come from far away – like if he was only half concentrating on speaking, distracted by something else.

A compliment? From you? Well I never... Gaile almost said that aloud. It was what she wanted to say. It would probably cause more trouble than it was worth if she did. 'Thanks,' she said instead.

A few minutes drifted by without either of them speaking. Gaile chewed almost absentmindedly. She felt sleepy but not tired. She was warm, in a kind of sheltered, comfortable way that you are when, for a moment, worries were far too distant to bother you and all you could do was to feel warm and cosy.

'Silber,' she said thoughtfully.

'Hmm?'

'Could I ask you something?'

'Of course,' he replied. He wondered what she wanted. She never asked him things, not like that. Not unless something had been bothering her for quite a while.

'Something's been bothering me,' she said.

Silber refrained from responding with a scoffing, though it was a close call. 'Yes?'

'I've been meaning to ask you for a while. But I wanted to see what I should ask first.'

That didn't make much sense to Silber but he waited patiently for her language to catch up with her mind.

'Something happened a while back. Kind of by accident really. It happened again a while later, also unintentionally. Since we came here I've been trying to do it on purpose. That was harder than I thought, but I think I've got it working. Only, I realized that maybe I shouldn't be doing it at all. So, I thought I'd ask you about it before going and doing something else.'

'Yes?' Silber replied. Sooner or later he was certain she would get around to telling him what she was actually talking about. He hoped that it'd be sooner.

Sometimes, by the time Gaile got to the point, he'd forgotten what she'd been talking about it in the first place, it took such a winding road getting there.

'You know that old tree by the pond? I kind of broke it,' Gaile confessed.

'It was most likely rotten,' Silber replied.

'And the trunk that almost fell on me?'

'Merely a coincidence.'

'Then I took a shot at the old boulder up by the Look-Out, when we stopped there yesterday,' Gaile continued.

At this Silber's ears would have perked up, had they been capable of doing so.

'That does appear ... somewhat ... unusual,' the dragon conceded. 'Are you certain it wasn't a coincidence?'

'Silber,' Gaile sounded exasperated. 'It turned into rubble.'

'Yes, that is a good point,' he admitted. 'Has this been happening long?'

'Hmm...' Gaile knotted her eyebrows as she dredged through her memories. 'Not really,' she finally said.

'Can you do it consciously, perhaps without feeling angry or frustrated?'

'Not really.'

'You are a wonderful well of information,' Silber sounded annoyed. Well what else was new?

'Then, perhaps, tomorrow, you can demonstrate this for me?'

'Silber,' Gaile spoke slowly, as if to someone slow of understanding. 'We're going back tomorrow.'

'Why, so we are,' the dragon sounded a bit surprised, as if caught out by the revelation.

'There will still be time in the morning. That will have to suffice. Once we return to the Academy, I will research the matter further.'

Gaile, having slumped down, motioned sleepily from below the blankets. 'Don't' think that'll do much good,' she mumbled. 'Never heard of something like that.'

'I believe,' and Silber placed an emphasis on that first word, 'that I have access to a great deal more information than you.'

And with that, his tone alone suggested that the conversation was over. Gaile wasn't going to argue. She was half-asleep as it was.

The dragon continued to ponder the matter long after his frail friend had drifted off among whatever dreams she might have, gazing thoughtfully up towards the stars.

Silber had, admittedly, never heard of something like this either, he concluded after watching Gaile go through the motions a third time in a row the following morning. It was obvious that *something* was happening. It certainly produced results. The question was what?

Not that he felt much wiser by the time the morning had come and gone, several shattered old logs along with it.

He could feel something … even before the actual impact. He just couldn't decide exactly what it was he was experiencing. It did suggest one thing to him though. That it wasn't Gaile, solely, who was acting in this matter. There was something else. Some sort of connection. A channelled connection perhaps? That sounded ludicrous even to his ears but it was the only thing that came to mind after such a short experiment.

He told her this much, along with a re-iteration of his promise to look into the matter once they returned.

Gaile herself regarded the row of wooden stumps and boulders.

'If you say so,' she said. 'If you say so.'

* * *

As Gaile and Silber contemplated their return to the Academy, they weren't the only ones who were thinking about the future.

Mind you, not everyone had such a personal stake in the matter. Some were just having general thoughts and others were more interested in "other" people's futures rather than their own.

Some of those doing the thinking of the last type weren't even students…

'Do those two remind you of anyone?' Tiosh made an almost unperceivable nod towards the antics of two of the students in the cafeteria.

'How d'you mean?' Tam asked, taking a large slurp of his shake.

The sound from the straw made his friend wince. 'Will you please stop that, you *know* how I hate that,' Tiosh grumbled at him. 'If there's nothing left, just go get a new one.'

'Sorry.'

Tam tried looking apologetic, but, scar or no scar, the almost boyish grin he was wearing made it hard to take him seriously at the moment.

'Shape up will you. You're supposed to be a teacher for heaven's sake,' Tiosh said and shook his head. 'Anyway, it's been a long time since I saw a potential bond form so quickly.'

With his friend's words buzzing in his ears, Tam took to studying the two people under discussion more intently. Maybe there was a point in what he was saying, he thought.

It *was* rare to see a possible rider and dragon bonding, assuming that's what they were doing (they could just be goofing off) so early. Normally the dragons that had been intermingled with the other students took several years to carefully decide who they wanted to partner up with but he'd be darned if he was going to admit that to Tiosh.

'Suppose so,' he said non-commitially.

'Oh, you're hopeless,' Tiosh exclaimed.

'I hope so,' Tam grinned mischievously at his old friend and took another slurp. 'I try.'

'Anyway,' the second man snapped sharpishly, closing the door on *that* conversation.

Under the table he re-crossed his legs, usually a tell-tale sign he was getting pushed a little too far. Tam decided not to tempt fate today. Maybe his friend had been having an unusually bad day. It never paid to antagonise him needlessly – not beyond a certain point anyway.

'It's rare enough on its own. But seriously, have you seen such a pair of troublemakers?' He nodded towards the group of students that had staked out the tables and general area closest to the food dispensers as their own personal property, the two they were talking about among them.

At the moment Jim was busy pacing up and down quite naturally, his nose in a book and a tall glass, from which he occasionally would take a drink, in one hand.

The only thing was, he was pacing up and down the narrow divider between two tables … and that wasn't all that stable even in normal circumstances. It certainly wasn't designed for having someone wander around on it.

Jim wasn't bothered. The casual display of balance and agility that would have had a world famous acrobat crying his eyes out in jealousy for something that had taken them decades to learn and which certainly wasn't to be thrown about so casually, as if it didn't matter, was, to him, not something that was worth noting.

The only way he would have noticed something was off was if he'd suddenly *lost* it. Besides, he thought better when his feet were moving and here no one kept trying to walk into, or over, him all the time. There were distinct disadvantages to being short.

'True enough. But they don't cause trouble, not exactly.'

'You *know* what I mean. But they do remind you of them, don't they?' Tiosh kept on asking.

Tam put his cake down. It hadn't really been a question, but still… Riku and his to be partner "Streak" had been quite the handful – all those years ago. More than just a handful actually.

To this day no one had ever found out why they'd ended up using "Streak" as the dragon's nickname (the alias by which a dragon was known in draconic form) but both partners had always broken down in laughter any time anyone had asked and they'd still refused to tell. Eventually people stopped asking.

Those names weren't something that were *officially* recognized (and registered), not at that stage. They never were, not until a dragon and rider had made a formal and lasting bond. But they often related to personality traits or behaviours from their "student" years and for some people it was just what they'd been called for ages beforehand.

Of course, they just as often related to something distinct about the dragon and, to help make it less confusing, while the names were recyclable, only one living dragon in the DC (across all the worlds) could carry it at one time; double-ups weren't allowed.

Tam figured that, as long as the number of dragons remained relatively small, that wouldn't be a problem. If their numbers started growing exponentially though, it was one rule that would end up causing a lot of trouble, to say nothing about headaches.

They'd probably just change the rule then, he figured. It certainly seemed easier. It was a pretty stupid rule to begin with anyway.

Some names grew on you. Some of them were obvious and some took years before they'd actually crystallized into their final form.

Nightwraith was one of those who'd "earned" his name as something he was often referred to as during practice, especially night practices, back when they were both still just trainees, thanks to his ability to swoop down in darkness as soundless as a passing thought, as invisible as a shadow.

None of that, however, had stopped them from thinking it was highly unsuitable and not the least bit dignifying for such an imposing presence as the dragon had possessed to be referred to as "Streak". It just wasn't right.

Yes, Riku and Streak had been close from early on as well and they hadn't wasted time sitting around doing nothing when they were bored either … which was most of the time.

They hadn't been bad in a sense of the word that Tam was willing to sign up for (even if he hadn't actually been around back then) and he didn't think that it had ever occurred to any of them to play a prank on anyone directly. No, that wasn't their style.

What they had done was to do things their way, *when* they wanted them, *how* they wanted them. It didn't matter much if it was the latest info from a secure satellite transmission, a secret recipe for the latest of Manchio's creations (back when the grandfather of the current Manchio had still run the place) or a special seat in class.

If they'd wanted it, they hadn't bothered hanging about waiting for the official release or the official refusal, should they have bothered asking. Unauthorized outings, snack raids and a great deal of showing off had constantly been on the table, according to Tam's sources.

That hadn't been the only thing about them that had attracted attention either.

Perhaps, as a result of all that or perhaps because they'd both been extremely handsome fellows, their popularity had known few bounds, if any;

especially not with the ladies. And they hadn't been above capitalizing on that popularity either, apparently.

Somehow he just couldn't imagine this pair doing anything like that. From what he'd seen, half of their little team spent as much time trying to get his partner "out" of trouble as he himself spent trying to get "into" it.

'You know, Tiosh,' Tam said, after staring out into nothing for a while. 'I'd rather not have another pair like that.'

Tiosh nodded in turn. How could he not agree? For they *both* knew that the story hadn't had a very happy ending.

'Too exciting. Too fun. Too exhilarating an idea to have someone to share the skies with you. It can become too much if it develops too fast, too recklessly,' he said.

'You'll keep an eye on them then?'

'Yes. And ... so will you.'

'Agreed. Let's not have another ending like that. Once is enough.'

'I would have said that once was one time too many,' Tiosh said. He poked at his teeth with a fingernail. They always felt loose like this. An unpleasant feeling, especially after having eaten something. It sometimes felt like he'd end up with his teeth in his food because they'd fallen out, not because he was chewing it.

'How is he, these days? Streak?'

Tiosh offered a noncommittal shrug. 'I see him around sometimes. After having spent the last few decades or so on his own, I suppose he finally got lonely for some company. Rocks don't hold very good conversations after all.'

'True. Think he'll ever choose another partner?'

'Doubt it,' Tiosh chewed on his lips, lost in thought. 'I know that Riku was killed before the formal bonding, but to a pair like that, I doubt that would matter. Anyone he meets will probably get compared to Riku and be found wanting. Doubt there ever could be anyone who could top that.'

'Good point,' Tam acknowledged. 'I'll tell Dr Cosgrove. I'm sure he already knows but it pays to be careful. Might drop a note to a few others as well. I know that Jim Walker isn't the type to do things that are all out stupid, it's just that...'

'…he has a very limited range of things that he qualifies as stupid,' Tiosh finished for him. 'Yes, I know. Just like his brother really.'

With that, the tall man stood up, stretching out languid limbs to the max. He'd spent all day sitting down and he felt it. A hot bath and some relaxation for him tonight.

'Are we still on for tomorrow?' he asked.

'Sure. Just don't be late or the Captain will chew us out again. Remember, last time your tardiness got us a yellow posting for *two* weeks.'

Tiosh wrinkled his nose at the thought. How could he possibly have forgotten? 'Don't remind me. Try to punch up a speed combination that includes snacks this time. I'd like to get a chance to beat Astarot for a change.'

'Right. Sure. Will do.' Tam nodded.

Considering his partner's apparent enthusiasm, Tiosh sought to clarify something before it got out of hand, again. 'Just, this time – let's *land* before eating them. No more of this "toss and catch" stuff. You wouldn't believe how chilled they get at that height,' he said.

'You sure are an old housewife sometimes you know.'

'Thanks…' Tiosh rolled his eyes at his partner and went in search of a nice long steaming bath … maybe even a bit of sauna.

Sometimes he didn't know what was more work; the job or his partner.

Mad Science

It had taken a while to get used to being back at the Academy after her little outing. After all that freedom, having to stay indoors and just move papers around, which was what she felt like was all she did sometimes, just wasn't the same. But then, had it ever been?

Gaile tried to stifle a yawn. As soon as they'd gotten back, she'd ended up working late again. That wasn't strange, she had a fair bit of catching up to do, but it was making a mess of her sleeping pattern.

Her friends weren't the only ones who had high expectations of the time she spent with them either...

'Could you fetch me the two new vials?' Rokoskiev called out, not taking her eyes off what looked like a microscope to Gaile, which she was studying.

Gaile didn't need asking twice. She'd spent all morning so far sitting in a corner, out of the way, and reading some of the old reports and circulations. It was fascinating, even if she understood less than half of it. But she was beginning to feel somewhat chair-bound.

She wasn't sure what her new mentor was up to today but the whole lab was filled to capacity with different set-ups, contraptions, experiments and even the occasional person.

Obviously Rokoskiev had had some sort of revelation in relation to her work while she herself was gone, Gaile figured. How long did the woman actually stay here every day?

To Gaile's eyes there didn't seem to be any coherent theme to it all. But she supposed there had to be one somewhere. If nothing else, they were all experimental – sort of.

It had been several months since she'd been "reassigned" as Gaile liked to think of it as, and, though she was reluctant to admit it, she'd begun to settle down in her new role. It hadn't turned out to be nearly as bad as she'd first thought it would be.

Once Rokoskiev, whom seemed to be the person she was expected to report to, even when loaned out to others, had gotten a decent grip on the idea that, contrary to both general opinion and class records, her new assistant was no dummy, far from it, Gaile's introduction to the world of the DRC had taken on a bit of a whirlwind quality, until there were so many new things, places, people and concepts greeting her every day that she went to bed with her head spinning. It had gotten a whole lot more interesting too … and tiring.

Indeed, she missed spending time with her friends in a less exhausted capacity.

Ok, so Sera might or might not quite qualify as a friend. That is, she thought of *him* as a friend of sorts but she'd always had the impression that he considered *her* more of a passing acquaintance. He wasn't exactly an easy person to get close to though – not the real him anyway. Hopefully she was reading far too much into it all but there seemed to be, even now, quite the distance between them.

There had, of course, never been quite the close camaraderie that she'd been able to build up with Silber; the dragon was far too stuffy and stiff for that and the easy-going (and quite often trouble-causing) times with her dragonling friend didn't even come close to match but she still missed them.

The only one she got to see these days in a way that was relaxing *was* the dragonling and usually she was so tired after work that it was more a visit in passing than anything else. He seemed a bit hurt by the lack of attention which made Gaile feel even guiltier. She'd have to make sure to find the time somewhere…

'Gaile? Gaile?!' Rokoskiev called again.

'What? Where? Yes?' Gaile stumbled out of her reverie.

'Keep an eye on the two sets to the right, won't you. And when the first one turns purple, pour some of this in there,' the doctor shoved a nearly foot long vial into her hands. 'If anyone wants me, I'll be in the meeting room next door.'

'I understand,' Gaile nodded.

She didn't bother with questions. While she wasn't altogether certain what pouring the highly fluid liquid into the experiment would do, that was apparently the point. At least the other researchers assured her of that. If they knew what would happen they wouldn't need to do it.

Computer models were excellent at telling you about things where all the parameters were completely known but throw in even as much as a wiggle in there and they all went to pieces (how many pieces depended entirely on the amount of detail that you were asking for) but for the unexpected there was nothing quite like just going ahead and trying things out.

Gaile did know that what were in both those particular sets was liquid plastasteele. Once its different components had been mixed together it was important to keep it hot, almost boiling, for once it cooled it settled and nothing less than a blast from a laser would even come close to melting it again.

In such a case it would unfortunately lose all cohesion and would not harden in the same way once it cooled again. It was a given that it was *not* something you coated spaceships with.

It smelled, there was no doubt about that. So did several of the other tests that were being carried out in this lab. Most were happily ticking along without her or anyone else having to monitor them. The researchers responsible for their long term upkeep came in on occasion, prodded them (often only metaphorically) shook their heads and sighed and went away again.

Wonder what this stuff is supposed to do? Gaile mumbled to herself as she made her way across the table. She shook the vial to see if it made any difference. If she was supposed to worry, Rokoskiev would have said so. But apart from making the contents slosh about a bit, it did little else.

It was an awfully big vial, she thought. In addition to being well over a foot long, it was a bit thicker than her fist, if she didn't scrunch it up too tightly. It was also heavy. Thankfully, only the bottom third actually contained anything.

Most of the test tubes Gaile had seen so far had been the small ones, the "normal-sized" version in her mind. You didn't need to make this so big, did you? Or maybe Rokoskiev had just run out and had grabbed whatever else was at hand. That sounded like her. Gaile nodded.

Maybe it was just a test to see if they could make the whole process smell better? One small step for science it might be, but for noses everywhere... Because even when set and finished plastasteele products had a bit of a distinct scent about them. It wasn't enough to make your nose twitch but it was there ... and it took quite a while for new products to lose it.

Gaile was intent enough on the two sets and her own internal thoughts that she didn't really notice the door to the lab open. There were people coming and going enough that it doing so wasn't anything special. But she didn't even notice her name being used, not even when the person addressing her was standing almost right behind her.

It wasn't until that someone placed a hand on her shoulder and spoke, quite loudly, in her ear, that she reacted.

'Hey!'

The person tried again to get her attention. This time they didn't fail. It was just that, for some time afterwards, they wished that they had, because at the combination of voice and touch, Gaile jumped, quite literally. She lost the grip on the vial, which now sailed upwards.

'Watch out!'

'Don't let it touch the others,' Rokoskiev called out from the far door. 'Hit the deck!' she shouted a second later.

The liquid, having described a beautiful arc out of its vial as the heavier glass started to fall sideways, lost its battle with gravity. It sloshed over several of the nearby stations.

A second later and a very large 'poof' later and a small cloud erupted, dark and menacing.

It wasn't a very loud 'poof.' It wasn't, for that matter, a very large cloud. That is, it expanded a lot but it wasn't very thick and dispersed almost as quickly as it had formed. It left behind an overpowering smell of camphor along with several bouts of coughing.

Gaile, having reacted with surprising speed to the shout from the doctor, picked herself up off the floor. She'd avoided most of the 'bamf' but wrinkled her nose at the scent. It wasn't her favourite even when she did have a cold and could hardly smell it. It always gave her a headache. In fact, she could feel one coming on right now.

Rokoskiev, who'd been quite safe at the other end of the lab, had avoided the whole thing completely though she was ever less fond of the smell, her nose being even more sensitive than Gaile's.

Several others were busy trying to sort out what they'd been doing, the entire thing having given most of them quite the start.

However, that left the third party … who had, no matter how you looked at it … *not* managed to avoid the minor explosion, far from it. He'd had the misfortune to be right between the station that erupted and the closest other person. He'd also been, just, too late in hearing Rokoskiev's shout.

Now, Asura Rokoskiev, having come over quickly, determined even at a distance that nothing was broken; people *or* equipment (assuming you didn't count the large vial that had shattered, thankfully not into a million pieces). She was watching the different expressions play over the face of someone she'd not expected to see here. She had most certainly not expected them to have been caught up in something like *this*.

They didn't look very happy.

'Are you alright?' Rokoskiev asked, not sure what move to make as the person opposite didn't seem to have decided just how they were going to react themselves.

She took in the view, which was a bit bedraggled now that she saw them up close. The normally spotless uniform was now splotched. The jacket was a whole kaleidoscope of black and grey and goodness knew what else, though much of the arms had been spared.

That wasn't the cause of her concern though.

It was his face.

It was *covered* in soot. That, along with hair that now looked like if someone had taken an electric frizzle to it, standing out at all ends like that, made him look not unlike a cat, who'd, frightened, had burred up tail and fur trying to make itself look bigger.

Well … here it had worked and he wasn't even a feline. Of course, parts of that hair had been covered in soot as well, making him the number one contestant in a competition fielding the year's best crop of "mad scientists".

He didn't look happy about it, Rokoskiev thought again. In fact, she'd have expected to have heard something really scathing by now, at the very least.

'I am *so* sorry,' Gaile tried looking apologetic.

Deep inside she was trying hard not to collapse laughing. Did he have *any* idea how hilarious he looked? He also looked somewhat angry … to say nothing about indignant.

Sera didn't bother with a response. He merely pursed his lips and gathered up the folders that he'd been carrying before and which had now scattered on the floor.

'Lady Gray wanted you to have these,' he said, offering the slightly tarnished box folders to Rokoskiev, who accepted them without a word.

Turning around, on the way out, he bent forwards, towards Gaile (who wasn't sure if she was meant to cower back or not).

'*You* need to be more careful,' he stated coldly.

With that, he pushed the door out into the corridor and disappeared, muttering something under his breath that neither of those left behind in the lab could discern.

'Well … that was … unexpected,' Rokoskiev breathed out, not having realized she'd been holding her breath in the first place.

That could have been so not pretty, she thought. There were people that you could get away with those kinds of things happening to and there were those that you, well, couldn't. Until now, Asura had always placed Sera very firmly in the second category, along with certain other people, like, say, Damon Van Velden.

The bronze dragon was an intimidating figure no matter what form he was in and having four sets of claws and teeth to make a small army of tooth monsters jealous didn't make him any easier to work with. It only meant that when you got a scolding, it could well be literal.

Of course, unlike Damon, Sera *could* be gracious about it but that was, mostly, in public. This was most definitely *not* in public.

Still, you shouldn't count your rach if they were raining on you. Best to just be grateful and hope that it wasn't just a case of him saving up any trouble over this little "incident" until later.

'Are you ok?' Rokoskiev turned to her assistant, who, if anything, looked even more stunned than Asura herself felt. Though not nearly as stunned as the rest of the people in the lab.

Neither was probably difficult to explain. A lot of the students, particularly the females, reacted like that to him. It would have been more surprising if she hadn't. Even though Rokoskiev had to admit that she wouldn't have pegged Gaile to have been bothered. Of course, seeing that kind of expression up close coupled with that tone of voice would have been enough to unnerve most people, infatuated or not.

'Aha,' Gaile nodded affirmatively. 'No bones broken.' She turned her eyes and looked forlornly at the experimental stations. 'Can't say the same about those though,' she winced. 'Sorry about that.'

Rokoskiev shook her head. 'We can set those up again. All we've really lost is a bit of time. But you really should get more nimble. Some days I would swear you could trip over your own shadow.'

'Sorry about that. Sometimes I just can't seem to tell how many feet I have to say nothing about if they're left or right ones.'

'I know, I know,' Asura picked up the two pieces of the vial. 'Still, it'd help, in a lot of ways, I imagine. You can be unbelievably precise at times, usually when you're not thinking about it and then something like this happens. Consistence, Miss Ashworthey can be just as crucial as ability. Now, let's get this place sorted out and then we'll go have a break or something.'

Rokoskiev ran a hand through her hair. 'Goodness knows I could do with one after a day like today.'

Now, there was a sentiment that Gaile could agree with completely.

* * *

'Kay, hey Kay! Are you coming or not?' Robin, having heaved herself off the plunger, addressed her brother a few days later.

His answer was a grunt. He didn't seem to be inclined to offer her more. Well, maybe she shouldn't expect any different. He gave the appearance of being permanently furious these days.

She'd have thought that, having the end of term and a whole period of no classes, ahead of them, to say nothing about being able to go back home and sleep in a "real" bed for a while, would have appealed to him but apparently not as even the promise of that looked like it wasn't making any difference.

Sighing over the folly of it all, Robin left him to his own devices.

Perhaps it was all for the better anyway? He'd had a foul mood ever since that "incident" at First Flight when they first came here. Geeze, that was ages ago… Hadn't he gotten over that yet?

Indeed, it seemed like the outcome of that event had carved a permanent blow into her brother's idea that he was some sort of re-born dragonrider who could do anything he wanted because he was too good not to.

Not that it had put an end to his, in her mind, rather exuberant attempts to promote himself. Quite the contrary. Now, however, he wasn't only a pain, and a loud pain at that, but a bad one as well. He just kept most of it out of the eyes of any teacher or member of staff likely to disapprove.

She shook her head as she went to join the others as they relaxed for the evening. Robin couldn't help but wonder if her brother would even bother returning for his second year.

The next few days didn't do much to improve Gaile's outlook at it all either. In fact, by now it was the end of another long, very bad day. Actually, it wasn't so much the end of the day at all, that had long since come and gone. It was more like the middle of the night.

She'd sure gotten to see a lot of this place by now even if most of it looked a bit different than it did during the day. She'd gotten used to moving around at this hour, even started preferring it to the daytime, for it was only now that she could be herself. Ok, so it wasn't a hundred percent, but it was a little and that was better than none at all.

Gaile chuckled, remembering that, at some point in her childhood, some-one had told her that at the stroke of twelve all the ghosts and phantoms came out to play and they didn't play nice. So good little girls and boys should stay safely tucked up in bed where no ghostie dared go…

I wonder what that makes us? Something like midnight raiders? Hmm … that had a nice ring to it. Gaile tasted the words, rolling them off her tongue. Gaile and Silber, the Midnight Raiders. It made for quite the name.

Admittedly they were a little short on the actual "raiding" side of things unless you counted the times when the little dragonling got whiff of some tasty treat and someone had been careless and left the door ajar just enough that a small paw, and the body attached, could tease it open.

There had been berries all over the place the last time she'd caught him like that. Their squishy juice had coloured much of Silber's hide, staining him red as he crunched them and crushed them when rolling in them. She'd learnt long ago to try and keep a close eye on him but sometimes that was just impossible. These days, a lot of the time she was able to recognize the signs, catching him *before* things like that happened.

Speaking of the little blighter, where was he?

Gaile squinted into the darkness but beyond the light offered by the old fashioned lamp she'd found there wasn't really much to see. He could have been sitting just beyond the circle and she'd never know. She wouldn't put that past him either.

Well, it wasn't as if she was worried ... much. He'd proven often enough that he could look after himself.

She sank back down into the hot water in the pool until only her nose was visible.

Aaaaah. This was more like it. It was so good, not just for general relaxing but for all those sore and complaining muscles and tendons too.

It had been quite the surprise, discovering that the cool forest pool at the heart of the Hive wasn't just a replica from a woods somewhere (unless there were natural ones that could, by the flick of a switch, be turned from cold to hot, even if there were far too much water for it to happen immediately) but a veritable hot spring. A fake one but who was counting.

Closing her eyes Gaile let her mind drift away. Gently rising with the steam that circled and twisted just above the surface they set out into parts unknown, half there, half not there.

It leant a whole different atmosphere to the place just as the flickering light of the candle lamp did (though it was tricky getting hold of the candles, it wasn't as if she had a believable excuse for wanting them after all). The light from it was much warmer ... or at least felt much warmer and friendlier than the cold rays from more artificial lamps. But maybe that was just her imagination.

A hot spring all to herself. That's what it felt like. It wasn't deep enough to go swimming, like the regular pool at the centre and it wasn't as steamy as the sauna by several lengths but it beat them without even trying. In fact, they weren't even in the same race to begin with. This one, she got to herself.

As long as she didn't count the dragonlings.

The sudden sounds from the trees at the border of the clearing, unexpected as they were, made her straighten up and look about warily.

'What was that?'

Her eyes darted between the light and the darkness, trying to penetrate the latter with sheer willpower alone.

'Hello?' she called out apprehensively. 'Anyone there?'

Straining her ears, they failed to pick up anything else. The forest had returned to its slumber. 'Silber? If that's you, you're in *so* much trouble.'

At that, something chirped from the top of the miniature waterfall. A wing connecting with the water showered her in cold spray.

'You little...' Gaile tried to defend herself from the watery onslaught. 'Stop that you little menace,' she laughed, splashing upwards and almost drenching the dragonling in hot water.

He squeaked in indignant protest, shook himself off and took a flying leap into the pool below. The dragonling landed with all the grace of a rock boulder, a great fountain erupting around him.

'Bad dragon,' Gaile mumbled. 'You shouldn't do that. You nearly scared me half to death.'

Back among the trees, now shielded by the noise made by the unlikely pair, Tiosh drew further back. Careful not to make any more sounds, he quickly retreated into denser surroundings.

Tiosh sighed, quietly. And he'd really looked forward to getting some "proper" relaxation today. It looked like that was off the menu, he thought. How unfortunate.

Despite the natural setting most people preferred the more artificial pools that were shared between the Academy and the DRC. For one thing, they were a whole lot bigger, more accessible and had all sorts of facilities tied to them.

This place on the other hand was more than just a little out of the way but that was one thing that Tiosh liked about it. It meant that there weren't a lot of other people around. It was hard to relax if there were a bunch of rowdies nearby.

Secondly, and probably the more significant of the two reasons as to why so few people came here, was that the dragonlings didn't much care to have their inner sanctum invaded by anyone.

They usually didn't bother Tiosh though, and if it looked like they might mind his presence (usually easily distinguishable by their agitated chattering and swooping about) he generally retreated gracefully.

So he hadn't expected any trouble tonight. Now that he thought about it though, he hadn't seen or heard a single dragonling in the immediate area. At the time he'd just been grateful since it most likely meant he'd get some un-interrupted time to himself but now he thought it was a bit odd.

Tiosh frowned. He wasn't a regular teacher so it wasn't that each and every student was familiar to him. However, most of the staff at the DRC was, if only in passing. And he'd be willing to swear that the person back there hadn't been a member of staff.

Curioser and curioser … as the cat said. What would a student be doing out here in the middle of the night? Aside from the obvious that was, he asked himself quietly.

It didn't explain where all the dragonlings had gone. The brief flash into the water had been too sudden for him to have been able to identify but where there was one there must surely be others? There had been at least one drag-onling present, hadn't there? So where were all the others? Tiosh gave himself a small kick for not having paid more attention at the time.

So, the big question was … why weren't the other ones there as well?

While mulling over the idea as he picked his way back to the path, Tiosh abandoned the idea of a swim. Instead he decided to just head back to his quarters and get some sleep. Maybe a long hot shower would do the trick?

He also resolved to keep an eye on this strange person and not just because students weren't meant to wander around on their own in the middle of the night. She shouldn't have been able to get in to the Hive at this hour. Even during the day access was strictly monitored as not to strain the ecosystem or upset the resident population. After dark, only people registered with the sys-tem should be able to come and go as they pleased and the access log would still identify who, where and when. Surely the system would have flagged it if an unauthorized person was coming and going during times that they shouldn't?

Did that mean there was someone helping her? Waiting inside as to open the "doors"? But there hadn't been anyone else around, had there? Could it be that she herself had somehow hacked the information network database and set up her own privileges?

The whole setting intrigued Tiosh enough that he decided to look into it and the easiest way would be to check the access logs. That might provide some answers. If they didn't, they'd at least provide him with a starting point.

He wasn't keen on throwing around accusations without having something to back up his point of view. Misunderstandings were so easy … and usually ended up causing more trouble than they were worth.

No, the key was to look into this quietly and without anyone else finding out. And in the meantime he'd let her be. It didn't look like she was causing any trouble.

Gaile herself, remaining blissfully ignorant of any of this, continued to enjoy the soothing session in the steaming water for a while longer.

Challenge the storm

Times changed, as times were wont to do. Days came and went and before they knew it, the Final Exam was looming ahead of them.

Well, it loomed more closely for those who were actually taking it but generally looming anyway.

It wasn't every day that you got to enjoy this, Gaile thought. She was leaning against the stone bench, closing her eyes in the sunlight. Her ears were filled with the sounds of gurgling, sparkling water from one of the central courtyard's fountains standing only a couple of meters away from where she sat.

The other sounds that filled them were the ones you'd expect when a large number of people got the chance to enjoy the outdoors. It didn't happen nearly enough, not in the minds of the students anyway.

The climate in this place wasn't exactly good for that kind of thing, not most of the time. It was pleasant to sit here very early in the morning (when the students much preferred to be asleep) or very late in the evening, before it got dark (when many of them were slaving away with the assignments needing to be completed for next day's classes).

There usually was someone out here at those times though; staff whose shifts meant they could make full use of the opportunity, students who bothered completing their assignments ahead of time or didn't care or simply the occasional person with insomnia.

Today however there was quite the crowd.

It was a week until the Final Exam and classes were out for the year. The students, first, second and third years alike were making use of their suddenly free time to do all those things they hadn't quite gotten around to yet or, for the less restless, were just relaxing, trying not to think about that day a week hence.

It was difficult to escape the pent up excitement. It seemed everyone or so close to everyone that it made little difference, was talking incessantly, speculating about who would choose to take the exam. What chance they had of passing. What kind of partner they'd get and that all elusive question that had had Gaile's attention from day one "how did the dragons make their choice"?

Rumours over the last one flew, one as unbelievable as the next, flittering from lips to lips, almost without bothering to pass through the brains of the speakers first.

Gaile still didn't know the answer to that question. She'd even asked Silber – the dragon that was, not the dragonling – she seriously wished she hadn't used the same name for both of them, it got confusing, even in her own mind.

She doubted that the dragonling could have given her a coherent answer beyond cocking his head at her and say 'eeep' in that querying tone he used when he didn't understand (or pretended not to understand, he sure had no trouble with the word "cookie" even if it just came up casually in a conversation). But the dragon had refused to explain it, merely stating that it was "complicated".

Speaking of the dragonling, where *had* he gone? Gaile was sure she'd seen him nosing about a flower bush earlier but he seemed to have disappeared again.

Oh well, she thought. If he has disappeared, he'll reappear later. He always does. She shook off any concern for the "Big Day" too. It wasn't as if it mattered to her anyway. Instead she concentrated on drifting away into the realm of imagination where she could ride the winds to her heart's content, the world beneath her and the future ahead, glittering in the distance.

It was a reality she was brought out of very abruptly, much to her displeasure.

Frowning, Gaile's eyes snapped open.

'I said, what are you doing here?' the person opposite (and upwards) practically growled at her.

Gaile blinked a couple of times in surprise. Who was this person? Did she know them? It didn't sound like they were the kind of person she'd *want* to know to be honest but they did look vaguely familiar.

'Don't you know, Jasmine doesn't like anyone stealing her favourite spot!'

Ah, that was why they weren't a complete stranger. How unfortunate. Gaile didn't feel inclined to be gracious so she thought some very unladylike thoughts at that moment.

'Why not hop along, don't you,' the tall girl scowled. 'She'll be along shortly you know. And you don't wanna be here then.'

'What are you? Some sort of advance scout?' Gaile wanted to know and quite brusquely too.

Normally she tried to stay out of the way of that "irritable person". There were so many other, far more appropriate, words to use but "person" had to do in civilized company even if that company was only her own mind. But she'd be darned if she was going to run from them like some scared little mouse anymore.

It wasn't as if the bench had some sign on it declaring it as "the property of Jasmine, trespassers will be shot" now was it? But everything Jasmine wanted she staked as her own personal property, up to and including people.

While a lot of people tended to just let her get on with it, as long as she didn't bother them, Jasmine wasn't exactly the Miss Popular she imagined herself to be, not outside that little circle of astonishingly likeminded people.

In her own eyes though, Jasmine was the Queen of the Academy. A Queen in search of a King.

Unfortunately, Gaile hadn't exactly managed to stay under the radar of that girl, not since that little Hive incidence in the beginning of the year.

'Go on then, scram! Aren't you going to move?' sneered the other girl, whose name Gaile couldn't remember.

'No,' Gaile stated calmly.

'There'll be trouble,' the girl warned.

'What's she going to do? Shoot me?' Gaile asked disgustedly.

'I'm gonna tell on you,' the girl snarled.

'Tell me what?' another voice cut in. The two of them had been so preoccupied with each other that neither noticed either Jasmine or the small horde that hovered around her.

The voice alone was enough to make Gaile wince. That was one whose owner she had no trouble identifying.

'Oh, it's *you*!' Jasmine gasped in mock horror.

Her friend looked triumphant. 'Just you wait. Jasmine will set you straight.'

'I didn't know I was crooked,' Gaile narrowed her eyes. They were definitely not welcome company on their own *or* together.

'Now, you just hear me, Ashworthey. I'd call you a washed up has been if it wasn't for that you'd never amount to anything to begin with. Do you *seriously* think you have a chance? You, who washed out. I'm going to get my very own dragon this year, so there. Why don't you just disappear? People like you pollute the place.'

Gnashing her teeth together it was all Gaile could do not to punch the older, and much larger, girl right in the face. To break her nose. It was so tempting and it was so close by, there was no chance she'd miss from this distance. Petite, it was far too small for her features, Gaile thought. Cracking it might even improve the silly cow's appearance.

'Well?' Jasmine placed her hands provocatively on her hips and leaned forward threateningly.

'Well what?'

'Are you going to get lost? Or am I going to have to take steps?'

'That means us!' several of her followers chimed in like an unwanted chorus.

'We can do it here and now or we can make "arrangements", the girl with the dark curly hair tasted the last word by running her tongue over her teeth.

'Oh really?' Gaile didn't sound impressed. With all the things that had been happening over the last year, a mere human making threatening noises wasn't exactly very high up on her list of being afraid of. 'Like you did when you chucked me into the underground, you mean?'

'What?'

'Oh, don't look so shocked. Did you really think I was so stupid that I couldn't even figure out it was you who was behind all that?' Gaile snorted contemptuously. 'What do you think I am? Some sort of brainless twit? Like you?'

Admittedly she'd been told who it had been that had gotten her stranded in the subterranean remains of the old DRC but she wasn't going to tell these clowns that, now was she?

'You have no idea who you're dealing with,' Jasmine snarled, her face contorting from her usual vapid smiles.

'The school's biggest loudmouth, you mean?' Gaile snapped back, getting to her feet.

In her case, standing up wasn't nearly as an impressive feature as if she'd been someone else, the top of Jasmine's head was substantially distant from her own. Very substantially.

'You little tramp,' Jasmine shouted, lashing out with both foot and hand.

Unexpectedly they didn't connect with anything unless you counted the air. She hadn't expected that... Gaile had never proven to be very nimble in any of the trainings she'd seen ... or worse, had had to be a part of.

'Get her!' Jasmine barked.

Her friends surged forward.

'Hey, that's me,' one of them called out from the middle of the fray.

'Sorry,' came from another, quickly letting go of the arm he was twisting.

'Get off!' Gaile hissed at the one that had managed to grip on to one of her legs. She didn't want to hurt them (ok, she did, but that might lead to some very, very inconvenient questions if she was the one who beat *them* up). 'Ouff...' She landed on the earthen pathway, a knee lodged in her back.

Drat ... she hadn't seen that one coming. How unfortunate...

One of those holding her down dug around in her colour matched bag then handed something over to her friend which glinted as it caught the light of the setting sun.

'Let me go!' Gaile struggled, wishing someone would be foolish enough to get too close to her face – she still had her teeth. Those weren't being pinned down. Oh how they'd regret it if they did.

Jasmine allowed a sinister little smirk to play with her face while she tapped the scissors to her chin, all the world the thoughtful student considering a problem on a test.

'It's time you learnt that you *don't* want to challenge me. Now, hold on tight...' Jasmine told her friends as she reached down and grabbed a chunk of hair. She chuckled at the thought of what was going to happen next.

If she had actually *known* what was going to happen next, chuckling would have been the last thing that she'd done. For at that moment Jasmine was hit full in the face by a small enraged ball … along with the accompanying feet, claws and wings.

'Aaaaah!' she screamed. Jasmine dropped the scissors, trying to fend off the growling and snapping dragonling.

'Get it off! Get it off!' she screamed.

Silber in turn shrieked, taking the opportunity to sink his needle-sharp teeth into a stray finger.

His claws were already tearing holes in the shirt below the uniform jacket as he fought for purchase while continuing to snap and snarl in the young woman's face.

A few chaotic moments later, Jasmine's friends tried to help her only to discover that no matter how busy the small creature might seem, he was still in possession of plenty of sharp things that could come their way too.

Jasmine ended up on the ground, face down to protect it, while her friends flayed at the viciously hissing beastie. As they once more closed in, Silber took wing again with a disdainful shriek reverberating from his throat.

Her friends gathered around her, many sporting cuts and bruises and bite marks, none feeling the least bit fortunate that the claws had done far more damage to their precious outfits, this time of day being one of the few times they would wear anything other than their uniforms, than they had to their skins. While they might not exactly be in tatters both humans and clothes looked distinctly worse for wear.

The dragonling circled the scene a couple of times. Then, apparently satisfied that they weren't going to play anymore, he allowed himself to be picked up by Gaile as he landed on the backrest of the bench.

If she did so to protect herself, to protect him, or to protect those he'd just attacked, was hard to tell, even for Gaile, but she held on quite tightly, a scowl on her face.

'I'll ... I'll … I'll … get you,' Jasmine gasped though she didn't come any closer. 'I'll tell Dr Cosgrove himself that you're training some monster to assault innocent people. You don't even have access to the dragonlings. You obviously stole that brute.'

And with that, Jasmine gathered what little dignity she had left, stuck her nose up in the air and marched off. She was going straight to the top with this, see if she didn't. This sort of thing couldn't be allowed to happen.

Where had that horrible little monster come from? Whether she liked it or not, as the head Hive Helper Jasmine knew most of the little menaces by appearance but she couldn't recall having seen that one. She would have noticed. It wasn't exactly inconspicuous, being all silvery and shiny.

That settled it. It must obviously be a pet. Ashworthey must have smuggled it in here somehow. 'Well, we'll soon see about that,' Jasmine muttered darkly.

Not everyone was as bothered about what had just happened though.

'I told you it was just a matter of time before something like that happened,' Elon said from a safe distance.

'Looks like you were right,' Dayu agreed. 'Don't suppose that it'll help much … nothing gets through to that one.'

'Shame really…'

'Yeah.'

They shook their heads, then went about their way and didn't hear the rest. Even so, the wind carried faint traces of scolding … albeit not a very harsh one.

'Bad dragon,' Gaile chided the dragonling gently. 'I'm sure well behaved dragonlings don't go around biting people's noses off.'

Silber huffed, puffing out his chest, as if saying well, then he wasn't some well-behaved, pampered pet. And it had only been part of a nose.

'Still … I'm glad you showed up when you did,' she planted a gentle but affectionate kiss on top of his head for which she received an appreciative chirrup. Silber stopped making displeased noises and started purring.

'Where *have* you been anyway? Honestly. I don't know where you disappear off to half the time.'

The small dragonling rubbed his head against her cheek then climbed up on her shoulder and, somehow, managed to drape himself around her neck like a large and very non-feathery feather boa.

'Hey, you're heavy,' Gaile complained.

The critter didn't seem inclined to move and not wanting to pull him off by force, assuming that he'd part company with her neck voluntarily, she settled for sighing and taking a couple of deep breaths. Then she bent down to retrieve what she'd been reading earlier.

Oddly enough, while there was, as always when it came to her minute friend, a small knot of worry for him that was just it, it was a *small* knot. Gaile figured that if the powers to be hadn't curtailed the dragonling's "adventures" by now, they were *probably* not going to do so just because a student or two came complaining.

While Gaile had no idea why, he seemed important to them, important enough not to just grab and stuff into the Hive, or isolation, for his little antics. Well, if he hadn't been, they'd have put a stop to him long ago, surely?

Maybe he was some sort of modern experiment? She knew, roughly, how both dragonlings and dragons had come into being (the new ones that was, not the old ones from ages past). Were they tinkering with them again?

It wouldn't be a farfetched thought. Create some sort of extra smart dragonling who could follow instructions and follow them much better than any of the normal ones. That kind of made sense, Gaile thought. After all, he was way too clever for his own good sometimes. It couldn't *all* be down to coincidence, could it?

* * *

The fact that Gaile wasn't actively taking the Final Exam didn't, unfortunately, mean that she didn't have to get involved with it. That little fact had caused her to grumble more than just a little bit but Rokoskiev hadn't left her much of a choice and had dragged her along to this stupid, boring meeting.

Now she just sat quietly and listened. She was under no illusion that she was supposed to have a speaking part in all of this.

'Very well,' Mich Cartwright tapped his diom to signify the closing of the nominations. 'If there are no other matters on the agenda?' he asked, but seeing as he'd deliberately kept the most exciting of today's points for last, no one else was much interested in bringing up anything to digress from the course of the conversation as the finalized list of everyone that was taking the Final Exam this year had been announced.

'There's quite a few this year I see,' Ren Sundau said.

'True. Plenty of good candidates there from our third years.'

'Plenty of first years trying their luck as well.'

'Yes. We don't usually see this many first and second years but it'll be interesting, this way.'

'More crowded certainly,' another member of the board agreed.

'Thankfully, the amount of dragons attending remain the same regardless.'

'Even so, I suggest we use another location this year.'

Hezan Carula held up a hand to stave off the storm of protests. 'I know that using the Armoury for this is a longstanding tradition as well as being convenient but for this year, perhaps we should consider an outside location?'

The expressions of his fellow board members ranged from disbelief to pure outrage. Not that he'd expected anything else. Well, there was one more thing...

He coughed. 'Perhaps I should mention that this recommendation comes directly from Dr Cosgrove himself,' he said calmly.

It took a few moments for this news to sink in, at which point the discussion grew, if possible, more intense. It had, however, completely changed contents.

'Dr Cosgrove?'

'What is that old rascal up to?'

'I doubt he'd tell us, Ren.'

'I doubt I'd understand his explanation even if he did.'

'Very well then. If Cosgrove "suggests" this then I'm certain that he has his reasons. Did he perchance also suggest a location?' Master Gern gave the first speaker a querying glance.

Hezan nodded in turn. 'He did. This year's Final Exam will be held on Tendril Station.'

'Hmm,' Ren stapled his fingers in front of him, a thoughtful expression in his eyes. 'I do believe that the *old* exam facilities are still intact. There will be much to organize.'

'We all know our assigned areas,' Mich said. 'I suggest we make the adjustments needed and keep each other appraised of our progress. The exam is less than two weeks away. Gentlemen ... Ladies... We have much to do.'

There followed a rather longwinded discussion (in Gaile's ears) on the matter of who should be invited where but she was only listening with half an ear at that point.

The Final Exam was basically around the corner. Who'd have thought she'd be approaching it from *this* perspective? She had to admit it was interesting seeing how things worked behind the scenes ...

'So,' Rokoskiev addressed her briskly as they left the meeting. 'I expect a report on today's meeting, an analysis of the people and the possible outcomes on my table by tomorrow morning.'

'Tomorrow morning?' Gaile spluttered, aghast at the very thought.

'Yes,' Rokoskiev nodded. 'That should help keep the matter fresh and concise. I will be expecting a similar one from the exam day itself.'

'From here?'

'Of course not,' Rokoskiev snapped.

'I'm supposed to attend this as some sort of record keeper?' Gaile breathed out.

She didn't like that thought one bit. Still, now that the subject had been breached, it would allow her to be there to see her "friend" achieve this momentous occasion. She just couldn't decide if the lump in her throat was because she was excited for him or because she was feeling dreadful about it.

'After a fashion,' her mentor agreed, a bit cooler than usual.

'Oh.'

* * *

By the time the day itself had arrived, the lump of worry Gaile had felt back then had failed to disappear. Indeed, it had been joined by several other symptoms of nervousness.

Maybe it's a *good* thing I'm not taking the exam, Gaile mused. I'm a nervous wreck such as it is.

She'd arrived at the station with plenty of time to spare and had, since then, had plenty of time to grow bored. Gaile moved restlessly in her seat as the chamber began to fill up with people.

I don't suppose they could hurry up this part a bit? I mean, if you've heard one speech, you've heard them all. There's really only so many ways in which you can say "we hope you prove worthy of the time and effort invested in you. Thanks for all your hard work and best of luck" really.

Gaile snuck glances left and right when she thought no one would notice.

They'd come to a completely different area of the station this time. It had to be relatively close to the "surface" she figured or how else would the dragons be able to get in and out? They were notorious for not liking to change form on the run, one of the reasons possibly being that they weren't wearing very much, being, in every sense of the word, naked. While in draconic form that was apparently not bothering anyone but once in human form...

There didn't seem to be any dragons in attendance at the moment though. They would have been hard to miss even in a place as big as this.

No, Gaile corrected herself. There didn't appear to be any dragons in draconic form in attendance. You know, the type with fangs and wings. She did recognize a few from the DRC including her "mentor" among the official "guests". The woman looked different in a uniform somehow. Gaile didn't think she'd ever even seen her wear anything other than a lab coat, she practically lived in the thing. Here and now she looked even stricter and more forbidding than usual. She'd tied up her hair real tight as well; it was plastered against her skull as the ponytail pulled it back, away from her face.

That actually went well with their current location, Gaile decided. At first she'd thought that they'd use the external hangars, like they'd done when they'd come here for First Flight. That would have been a bit bare, but it would have been sizeable enough.

This place fitted much better.

The whole thing was shaped like a humongous dome on the inside. It had to be the structure that looked like an oversized golf ball from a distance when you watched the station from the outside, Gaile decided; a golf ball tucked in and almost hidden, among a whole lot of surrounding structures that didn't make any more structural sense than it did. Needless to say, Tendril had changed in a somewhat different direction than originally intended when it had left on its journey in a somewhat more streamlined shape.

Good luck hitting it with a mallet (assuming you could find one several miles tall, or someone even taller to swing it), she thought.

The insides, while severe in their cold efficiency bore a slight resemblance to the amphitheatre. It was the seats that did that. They were arranged in a semicircle, row upon row reaching upwards from the floor almost up to the ceiling. Mind you, the pillars did help.

They must have used this place for more than just the Final Exam in the old days, Gaile figured. She wouldn't have put it past them. Something so important deserved something special but on the other hand, leaving a place unused except for one day of the year really didn't fit the Castician mentality; they were sticklers for multifunctionality. And if you were living on what effectively was an artificial island with finite space, you were probably doubly so inclined.

Either that or there had been a lot more people attending back then; everything from examinees, staff and spectators, compared to what it was now. Maybe the whole station had gathered.

There were still many, many people in attendance, even now ... there just weren't quite *that* many. And, since none of the dragons were present, there was a great deal of extra, empty, space.

Actually, those taking the exam itself weren't here yet either. They would most likely be preparing in a separate chamber somewhere. None of them would know exactly what the Final Exam entailed until they arrived. There were probably a lot of nerves in whatever room they were in, Gaile thought.

In the meantime, the entire chamber was slowly filling with other sounds as the artificial lights dimmed. They were replaced by livelier and far older illumination.

Somewhere in the background there appeared a steady beat. Drumming, low and steady, like a heartbeat. Like the torches, it came from around the edges of the amphitheatre and ... somewhere else.

Then she spotted them; not speakers but two, huge, drums flanking the even bigger central portal leading directly onto the main stage.

At that point, all the lights flickered and went out.

It didn't stay bewilderingly pitch black for long because, half a heartbeat later (a very frantic heartbeat for anyone who might think there was suddenly something that had gone wrong) the torches flared up again.

And not just the small ones either.

In rapid succession, small fires erupted all along the edges of the first row.

Burning for an instant, the flames leapt forwards, engulfing and devouring whatever tiny amounts of fuel that sustained them.

The ring dashed onwards and upwards, circling the central arena and, after a steep incline, erupted into a roaring torrent of fire as they reached the two large braziers marking the beginning and the end of the "ledge" at the opposite end from the seats.

Without anything further to eat, the smaller flames died down into mere embers and then little more than a ghostly glow and then nothing. Now, the only light in the whole place came from those two large metallic structures far above the portal and those torches that orbited the very edge of the theatre.

That was convenient, if you were in the audience. Now you could see all the candidates entering from a small door above the portal itself but they couldn't see you. To them, there was nothing but an abyss of darkness beyond that bit of light that embraced them, stung them with its heat. Darkness and sound, sound and darkness.

Lined up by the ledge, although to call it a ledge was a bit of an understatement, it was more like a very thick and wide overhang, almost on par with being a walkway, except it didn't have a railing, they took their places. Inches before their feet there was nothing but meters and meters of down until you got to the floor.

The orange, red and yellow of the fire flickered on their skins, in their hair, on their uniforms. Around them danced the shadows, highlighting their expressions.

They didn't look nearly as cocky or eager as they'd done a few hours before when they'd all been leaving the Academy. Not that anyone in the audience was close enough to see.

Back then there had been quite a bit of commotion, to say nothing about quite a bit of noise, at the "send-off" for those that had chosen to come here today.

That in itself wasn't anything unusual. It had looked like practically every student and quite a few of the staff, both from the Academy and from the DRC, had turned up just to see the examinees as they departed.

'Best of luck,' many of them called out.

'Go get'em,' and 'hoping for you!' and countless other variations thereupon echoed back and forth from throat after throat as the group of students were ceremoniously escorted from the main building to where the shuttles had settled down.

Wearing special outfits for this one occasion, they looked splendidly, if a bit impractical for everyday use, dressed in black, knee-high boots, shined until you could use them as a mirror, while fitted trousers and a model cut frock stylized and swept back on the sides were decorated with either silver, bloodied bronze or burnt gold designs and the odd ancient lettering.

The borders of the high collars were touched with sky blue. Long, lush and silken scarves trailed from their necks in a number of colours, the same as those of the dragons whose meeting they were heading towards.

Some wore those scarves trailed around their necks. On others they were just hanging down, plain and simple, fluttering as they walked. Others yet again had draped them around their neck and shoulders not unlike the robes of an emperor and with about as much pride.

If it hadn't been for the lack of hats, they wouldn't have looked out of place at the admiralty's bi-annual dinner party.

Some of them had been smiling, grinning even, revelling in being the centre of attention. Others had looked grimmer. Nerves mingled with determination.

For all of them, it was the culmination of all their efforts, all their hopes and dreams. Today would (well, not many of them were at the moment courting the possibility that it was merely a "could" that was involved) be the stepping stone that would launch them into a whole new different world (metaphorically speaking); the gate between tomorrow and yesterday.

A few of them had done this at least once already. For several of them it was the last chance before they would need to return to more mundane lives, seeing as you got a maximum of five tries.

But it was the third years, those among them who were taking the exam for the first time properly, after the full three years of studying behind them, an optimal (in their point of view) position, who looked the most excited, some minds already lost beyond the clouds of exhilaration (and several stomachs who'd argued that maybe they shouldn't have had such a big breakfast after all).

Not that Gaile had seen them. Like the rest of the official contingency she'd already been aboard the shuttle by then but she had heard them, them *and* the crowds.

Now she *could* see them. There were a lot more of them than she'd expected. They didn't look nearly as confident as they'd sounded when she'd walked past the prep room earlier.

They were standing, a bit over a meter apart, in a long row facing outwards, towards the arena, towards the audience. Not that the audience was important. This was the one time in the course when the view of their instructors amounted to absolutely nothing. If anything they were more there as witnesses to what was about to happen than anything else.

There was something that was missing. Something that was seriously missing. Gaile kept scanning the row of candidates, but no matter how many times she did, it didn't appear. He didn't appear. He wouldn't miss this on purpose, would he? No way. He was probably just running late or wanting to make an entrance. Yes, that must be it. That'd be just like him, she thought. It didn't make any sense. Gaile hoped nothing had happened to him.

The drums were still at it. By now, the only way she'd have noticed them was if they'd stopped. In no time at all they'd become part of the rhythm of everything that was happening around them.

Now, they were superseded by something else. A very clear, if deep, voice resonated out among all those that had gathered here.

'Today, we will welcome our new riders and their partners,' Carula announced officiously.

Gaile realized that he must have come to the end of his speech. What had happened to the rest of it? Drat! Had she zoned out so much that she hadn't even noticed? She hoped that her report wouldn't suffer if she left that part out.

'May the Stars of Solon guide you on this journey,' the clear voice reverberated around them again.

Then the speaker bowed once in the direction of the assembled students, again in each remaining direction of the four winds, North, South and East, before withdrawing.

As the last remnants of his voice departed another sound came instead. The heavy (or, for the eternally suspicious of mind "heavy sounding") doors at the bottom of the ramp slowly creaked open.

Pushed aside by mere muscle power, the double doorway (if anything so big could possibly be covered under the term "door") swung inwards beneath the portal almost hesitatingly. From within the shadows, deeper shadows still emerged.

Suddenly you could hear them. It was the only thing you could hear. One second there were drums, whispers and the breathing of anticipation mixed with just a bit of fear. Then the next, you heard *them*.

A moment ago you hadn't. And it wasn't just because of the metal doors blocking out the sounds either.

Clawed feet, paws, clanked against the re-enforced metal floor. Scales scraped against solids, ripping at the paint as they did so, creating deep funnels in the bordering walls that lifted the ramp from beneath the portal and onto the stage itself. The deep thump of a heavy thread, one, two, three, four. Then repeating. Others followed behind until it was impossible to tell which belonged to what.

Almost invisible, save for a reflection of fire on a scale, a horn, an eye, the dragons emerged from beyond.

When you thought about how much nerves and anxiety and anticipation that went into these few moments, it was no wonder that the entire place was rife with tension, the smell of fear.

Now, into that, came the overpowering scent of dragons.

Despite the awe-inspiring presence they presented, fighting off the sensation of being dragged into the whole thing first hand, the sounds of their breathing, the distinct motions of their bodies, Gaile was fighting an urge to turn around and look over her shoulder in case more of them were coming in that way.

By now the whole building seemed to shiver, rocking at each powerful move they made.

The drums picked up the beat … and the sound level.

Body after body took to the floor of the arena. All were moving and it was like watching a dark sea of colour and shadow ripple back and forth. It was hard to tell how many dragons there were out there. More than you'd have expected given the number of unattached dragons or the eye might be greatly overestimating how many there were, which would have been easy. In the dark, even one dragon could appear as a lot if they knew what they were doing.

Their voices had begun to add to the background as well; had *become* the background.

Here, a back foot stomped down, causing everything to shake. There, the tip of a tail waved perilously close. The tip of a wing brushed against another.

Milling and turning like a giant sea snake with more heads than body, twisting under the waves of light, one sinuous form undulating until your eyes couldn't tell what was dragon, what was shadow and where a shadow was merely another dragon.

Their voices called back and forth, rising and falling not so much in rhythm as in constant opposition, yet never growing into a crescendo. It was calculated, for all its elements of apparent randomness.

Not that any of the candidates were really going to have been thinking that clearly at this stage. Where they stood they could not see anything beyond the light that enveloped them. All their existence outside of that sphere was sound … and sounds that appeared wired directly into the more primitive parts of their brains at that.

Uniting, the dragons called out. They rose and rose until there was nothing but a deafening great roar shaking everyone in large chamber. Like a storm in the ocean it was not coming towards you, it was already everywhere, everywhere around you, filling you up until there were no more thoughts left. The sounds were not even trying to enter through your ears any more, they were going straight into the very marrow of your bones.

Then, abruptly, it all stopped.

Silence reigned.

Somewhere, a head rose out of the milling sea. Neck arched proudly, now above the shifting form below it caught the off bits of light, the red of the fire glancing over what could have been a dark blue hide if the shadows ever stopped twitching.

The other dragons moved out of its way as it slowly made its way towards the ledge. It didn't seem to be in a hurry but somewhere in there it must have come close enough into the field of vision of the candidates, because quite a few sounds erupted from the human throats.

The silence remained. The dragon barely made any sounds at all as it approached the far wall. Now it unfurled its wings, extending them until they blocked out almost all light, a pale glow passing through the thinner membranes of the wings themselves turning the warm orange of the fire into a cold pale blue. The light wasn't all it blocked. It also removed quite a section of the ledge and the candidates thereupon from view.

Carefully, the dragon placed its head at the level of the ledge, just before one of the students, effectively extending the room they had to move on.

The young man swayed on his feet, almost as if in a trance. He reached out and touched the creature before him. The hot breath from its lungs enveloped him, the fangs clearly visible as the jaw parted slightly.

Then, somehow, he swung down, along the neck, and slid downwards until he managed to reach, with a bit of climbing at the other end, the area right above the shoulder blades.

The dragon wasn't wearing a saddle. For the time being, the new rider would need to hold on best he could as the two new partners left the stage together.

As they disappeared from view, the orchestra took up its calling once again. This time, it was far less intimidating. The first step into the unknown had already been taken.

By now all thoughts of reports and tests had long since gone from Gaile's mind. In her head, no, in her very bones, she felt the rhythm of the choosing. It pulled at her on some subconscious level she wasn't entirely aware of. Like the tiny voice that calls out to you when you're standing at the edge of a great big void, urging you to jump.

In such a state of mind it wasn't strange that she couldn't really remember anything coherently after that.

There were bound to have been other dragons, other choosings, but if you'd told her there had been none, she could not have argued with you.

This sensation remained long after the lights had come back on and the dragons had all gone. As such, it was in a state of grogginess that Gaile made her way back along with the other representatives.

Or thought she did.

Eventually … it took a while … Gaile slowly started becoming aware of that she should have reached the shuttle by now. Swimming upwards, out of the cognitive maelstrom, she looked around and found, instead of the shuttle and everyone else, that she was surrounded by metallic and plastasteele walls, floors and ceilings. All too cramped for her taste, it that made up the inner workings of Tendril Station itself. None of it was anything which she recognized.

Great. Absolutely Fantastic! Lost … again! Gaile growled gutturally.

'I'm really making a really bad habit of this,' she muttered darkly as her eyes scanned the immediate area. 'I'm sure that getting lost *isn't* a skill much in demand in this place.'

Turning around, she started to head back the way she'd come which worked fine until she reached the first "crossroad".

Great, she thought again. Now what? Could today possibly get any worse?

* * *

Down on the ground, several hours later, things were picking up … and not in a good way.

'No.'

'But Sera…'

'No!' he said. It shouldn't have been possible but somehow that second 'no' managed to be even more vehement, even more empathic, than the first.

'No. No and No!' Sera repeated again for emphasis, in case he wasn't getting the message across.

It didn't seem to be deterring the other person, so far. They were looking as eager as always. Possibly you could have called it pouting if you really wanted to. If you didn't, she was managing it anyway.

By now, Sera, who none here had ever, *ever* even heard raise his voice, was attracting quite a bit of attention and not the usual kind either. The lounge had plenty of occupants at this time in the evening, especially now that the Final Exam was over. Many of them were now staring at the arguing pair with a look of genuine shock on their faces.

If none here had ever heard Sera's tones reach above a gentle caress, they had certainly never seen more than a faint puzzled frown touch his features.

Now, his brow was furrowed. His lips were slightly parted, as in mid snarl and those oh so gentle eyes were lined and glittering beyond recognition. It was like, before their very eyes, a silkhound was transforming into a dribbling beast; by the time you stopped being so stunned it already had its teeth around your throat.

'We could...' Jasmine tried again. She'd tried to reason with him (what she thought of as reason anyway, those with less well-mannered tongues might well call it wining or simpering or something of an even less flattering nature).

This new side to him had taken her a bit aback but she was determined to plough on, eyes firmly on her prize.

'Have you such difficulties understanding such a simple concept?' her silver haired god snarled contemptuously at her. 'Then I shall spell it out for you in a language even you could not fail to comprehend.'

'I was only...' Jasmine began.

She only stopped trying to reach for his hand, any of his hands, when hers was painfully slapped away. That stung. Literally.

'No! I *don't* like you. No! I will *never* like you. No! I will most certainly *not* want to spend any time alone with you. Understand? Not in a million years. Not if the stars themselves fell from the sky, pleading on your behalf. Read my lips. I. Do. Not. Like. YOU! End of story. Period!'

Sera wheeled about, already walking away when the other third year lunged at him, grabbed his arm and clung on tight.

'But I'd do *anything* for you, Sera. *Anything.* Anything at all. Ask. Just ask,' Jasmine wailed.

Fingers like steel suddenly gripped her wrist, locking it in irons.

'Ouch,' Jasmine cried out.

'Let go,' Sera intoned menacingly.

The pain more than the words made her do so but he didn't release her. Instead he bent very close, so close that his face was only inches from hers. Close enough that she could feel his hot breath.

She'd dreamt of that. But in the dream it hadn't been like this. It hurt. It wasn't friendly. It certainly wasn't romantic.

Sera's voice dropped so low it was barely audible. It was hardly more than a whisper yet so vicious that it sent chills down her spine. Salt water threatened at the corners of her eyes.

'You are cruel. Selfish. Heartless. And you're devoid of anything even resembling common sense. You thrive on belittling others. You have absolutely no sense of fair play and you couldn't even begin to imagine how much I loathe everything you are, everything you stand for. *Never* touch me again!'

'Let go,' Jasmine pleaded. 'Please, you're hurting me.'

'Really?'

'Please … I didn't mean … I thought…'

Sera bent further forwards until his lips were level with her ears. So close that no one could see his lips move or hear his words.

'Come near me again … and I will kill you,' he breathed softly into that ear.

Straightening up he forcefully released his grip on her, fear already spreading over Jasmine's face. She crumbled onto the floor, white, staring, wild-eyed and vacantly, into nothing.

He gave her a last contemptuous glare, one better suited for after having scraped some slime off your shoes and finding it trying to crawl back on. He felt better after that.

Then, a last sneer, and he was gone.

The lounge, which had gone deathly quiet, erupted into a cacophony of voices, everyone talking at once. What had just happened? Had they really seen that? Weren't those two supposed to be some sort of item or something?

Could he be an imposter? Sera would never act like that, surely?

* * *

Still in a bad mood, Sera stalked along the passages making his way back to his quarters. He hadn't started the day on a good note and it certainly looked like it wasn't going to end on one either. It was an exciting and exhilarating time at the Academy. While most students had been looking forward to the Final Exams, Sera had dreaded it.

Now the exams themselves were over and things were already changing.

It had already started. The strange looks. The whispers behind his back. People shuffling out of a room almost as soon as he'd entered it. The rumours.

Why hadn't he been there? That was the question on everyone's lips. Ok, so maybe not *everyone's* but close enough to make him uncomfortable. More than just uncomfortable.

The so called king of the student body had been a cinch for securing his very own dragon in passing that all important Final Exam; that was the opinion of practically every student who was prone to speculate on such matters. And he hadn't even bothered to show up? What was with that?

Ok, so *technically* every student who had been here for a year was permitted to put down their name for the exams. In theory they were all equal. In practice though, most of those who did were the third years and those who'd stayed on beyond that.

Another point that some people forgot was that, if, as a third year, you did *not* put your name down and attended the exam itself you automatically had to repeat the year. The same went if you took the exam and didn't pass. Most third years showed up on principle...

Of course, the Academy wasn't running some sort of perpetual motion machine with their introductory course into becoming a rider. You couldn't repeat the final "dragonless" year again and again. But you were entitled to five tries as a third year. Hence why some people took the exam already after just one year ... they felt it gave them an advantage; it being valuable experience. Some, of course, were just hoping they'd be chosen straight away...

But Sera... He couldn't possibly have *chosen* not to attend, could he?

As the tall, imposing figure charged through the hallways, eyes still narrowed dangerously, the rumours were already flying.

If it was because news travelled fast, exceedingly fast by electronic impulses or merely because he was wearing an expression that, if looks could kill, would have been brought in for questioning on the sinking of continents, but people were giving him a wide berth.

Even those that would normally have squealed with delight at his appearance were shrinking back. Some even took to hiding behind friends who hadn't been *quite* as ostentatious in their expressions of love.

Where was *their* Sera?

This wasn't him. This couldn't be him. This was some sort of monster in human skin. That thought was even more terrible. Their precious love, stolen in the night only to walk the grounds as a corpse … or worse.

The students noted his change of mood. In contrast, most of the staff did not or they appeared not to anyway. They could be seen, several of them, in pairs … forming small groups sometimes even just two or three, huddled together, talking in an animated manner in shushed, worried voices.

Sera didn't think anything of it. He wasn't curious about what they were talking about. What might have them all going around with such anxious faces, as if, departing, they had to own up and tell their scary aunt that they'd broken grandma's fine china playing house.

All *he* wanted to do was to get home, slam the door and pretend the whole bloody stupid world didn't even exist.

He'd thought that everyone pestering him, looking all concerned, about why he hadn't attended the Final Exam, was the worst thing that had happened today. Now he knew … his fellow students had reached a new low to which they could sink. Jasmine's little "act" was now the low point of the day … of *any* day. No, this stupid day couldn't possibly get any worse.

What did it matter if he'd been there or not? What business was it of theirs anyway? Couldn't they just keep their pointy noses out of other people's business?

Between them, their incessant questions, Jasmine and the general mood, the day was as bad is it could get, he was sure of that.

As it turned out … he was wrong.

But that possibility hadn't quite hit him quite yet. He'd had other things on his mind than keeping up to date. Henceforth, the possibility that things were about to take a drastic turn for the worse was the farthest thing from his mind. Sera was a lot of things but he wasn't psychic. The only way he could tell what the future would *really* be like was to live it.

It was at that point that Eggmonton ran right into him … quite literally.

The dark-haired youth bounced off, sending himself staggering backwards from the impact. That had been some speed he'd been running at.

'Oh gosh. Sorry. Sorry,' Eggmonton collected himself, took in whom he was looking at and gave an excited squeak.

Without any explanation he started dragging a very vehement Sera along behind him.

'What?' Sera tried getting his arm back without success.

'No time. Come on!' the other replied, urging him on.

'Egg...' Sera gave a mighty heave, wrenching himself free. 'I don't...'

'Stop arguing. Come on. Hurry!' Eggmonton insisted, grabbing on to him again. 'The Station's falling. And that's only the *beginning* of our problems.'

'What?!' Sera exclaimed, his eyes wide.

Ceasing to struggle, his long legs carried him easily beside Eggy's quick, but much shorter, stride.

'What happened?' he demanded. All thoughts of today's problems had suddenly been swept aside by a planet-sized crawler.

'Not sure. *Everyone's* getting called in. It looks like the weather's turning really bad.'

'A mere storm wouldn't trouble a place like Tendril *or* us. The platform shouldn't even notice it. It's been riding out storms since before you were born.'

Eggmonton shook his head. 'Not like this one,' he stated. 'It's not behaving at all like it should. There's something really strange going on. Don't know why but Tendril's changed orbital pathways. It's running straight for Lemar.'

'I thought you said it was falling?' Sera queried, wondering why Egg wasn't getting his facts straight.'

They hurried past a pair of card playing students as Eggmonton swiped his access codes to get into the DRC section of the complex. No reason to worry them, not yet, he thought. That was probably why nothing had been announced.

'It is falling ... just very slowly,' Egg said, knowing full well just how foolish that sounded. 'The stabilizers seem to be working flat out trying to compensate, but they're not up for this kind of strain. They're meant to keep the platform level, not keep it flying. It'll come down quickly enough once it reaches Lemar. It's amazing that they're working at all,' he added gloomily.

'Lemar sits high, but not that high. Tendril would have to practically skirt the ground before it'd hit them.'

'It'll hit the Cressolen Peaks first,' Egg said. 'They're trying desperately to recall the feelers but the platform isn't responding.'

'By the stars. If the tendrils hit those it'll destabilize the entire platform,' Sera gasped.

The other young man nodded miserably even as he was running. 'You haven't heard the worst of it…'

They passed quite a few people moving at a rushed pace as they made their way into the inner workings of the DragonCorps but as they entered through the main doors, no one in Command Central even as much as battened an eye in their direction. Almost no one.

'Egg, Carula needs you to go over the plans you brought with the team,' Ren Sundrau ordered, his face immobile. 'Sera … I'm putting you in Timms' team. They could use an extra hand.'

Sera nodded, his features now as expressionless as the other man's. 'Sir,' he acknowledged and headed to the indicated station.

Eggmonton had already disappeared into one of the adjoining rooms. In turn, Sera moved through the mass of people and machines until he reached Timms' assigned location.

They all looked worried, he thought. There was something about their eyes. Even something as serious as Tendril coming down out of the sky like the avenging angel of old shouldn't cause such concern … not unless it was likely to come crashing down through the roof of the DRC. And if it was heading for Lemar, that just wasn't possible. There had to be something else…

Maybe if it'd cross the lower peaks somehow and manage to pass over the Hilo research station it would definitely hit the higher peaks beyond that icy valley. The station itself might be located in the depths of the rock but if Tendril came crashing down around them they were bound to be inconvenienced.

But not even that would cause so much worry…

Getting a brief background of what they *thought* had happened, Sera sat down, working through the readings they gave him.

By the looks of it, the platform was already starting to disintegrate. It should have been sturdier than that. Maybe it wouldn't make it that far at all?

So far it had dropped several hundred feet from its cruise-altitude and was showering its path with debris. Chunks the size of a small house were being shaken loose and crashing to the ground far beneath it.

And that was just the station. He glanced over at the data on the weather. Crikey, that storm cell was big. They might need to invent another word to accurately describe it. It had already covered the entire peninsula and it was, by the looks of things, *still* growing.

It looked a bit odd too, now that he looked closer.

Even more worrisome was that it was also moving. The central eye wasn't going anywhere at high speed, but that wasn't the trouble. It was moving because it kept increasing in size, scoffing down any surrounding clouds and swallowing them whole and it wasn't bothering to stop and chew either.

If that keeps growing, Sera thought, we'll end up getting caught up in this thing as well as ending up *inside* the storm wall.

An hour passed quickly. They always did in some circumstances, especially on those occasions when you desperately wanted more time.

By now, reports were already coming in from Lemar, the mountain retreat, which had made contact with the supercell only a few minutes ago. Before then they'd seen nothing but increased winds as the storm's advance guard moved in.

Hilo wasn't noticing anything at all but then their instruments were mostly directed downwards and didn't pay much attention to the sky or the air around them. Not if it hadn't already been around for several thousand years at least.

Well, they were going to notice whether they wanted to or not, judging by Tendril's unsteady progression in their general direction.

They had already been warned, but Sera wasn't sure how much attention they'd pay to it. They'd probably close up anything they could and try and weather the thing out.

The messages from Lemar were broken and hard to make out. The storm must be effecting the communication somehow … but that didn't make any sense. The equipment they had would have made a small starship proud. It could penetrate even through the heart of an asteroid belt, anything short of an all-out plasma storm. It should not have *any* trouble with a mere planet-bound collection of clouds even if they *were* spinning in the wrong direction.

But still their communications were garbled.

From what little information they'd been able to gather before contact with the retreat was lost, their power had been cut. Even batteries, fully charged and full of juice, had fluttered to a standstill, ceasing to function as they were drawn further in and enveloped by the all-embracing dark clouds. The odd thing was, they still registered as full … they just weren't supplying any power. Was it going somewhere else?

'Crap,' Ren swore. He turned around 'That thing's getting bigger by the minute. It's *still* growing, exponentially at that. If *we* lose power like that we'll be sitting ducks out here. How long until it hits us too?'

'If the growth rate remains constant and it doesn't shift course, we'll come into contact with the storm-wall itself approximately thirty minutes from now.'

'I want every single D-unit outfitted and standing by that the Armoury can fit in that time. Use the old harnesses if you have to. How many do we have elsewhere?'

'Six teams, counting the Northern Patrol.'

'Notify them of the situation as well. Tell them not to rely on support from the DRC until this thing has passed. And make an announcement here, a separate one for the staff. There's no need for the students to start panicking. Find someone to inform Dr Cosgrove. He's in Illumi City. He probably knows already, but make this official.'

'Yes, Sir,' the officer saluted.

Ren glanced out of the bay repwi-windows. The horizon was already darkening.

He hoped the students would be sensible but he'd been in enough situations to know that a large group of panicking people were led by what was commonly referred to as "the mob rule". Well, if they ever had a chance of proving they had it in them to become riders, it would be today.

Why did this have to happen on the day of the Final Exam? Ren cursed silently. A lot of both dragons and riders had been celebrating their new comrades. The students and their new partners had done so excessively. Many would be of no use even if they could be outfitted in time. The last thing you wanted in the air was an intoxicated dragon.

Sera didn't get to see how the DRC met the onslaught of the storm though ... the next five minutes saw to that, even if, only five minutes after the announcement, the real windows of the Dragon Research Centre were already rattling.

At that time a message appeared on his diom, which he'd rolled up and wrapped around his wrist to keep it out of the way. He didn't bother looking at it. Right now anything important would be coming in directly on the official channels.

Another few minutes passed.

A screen to the left and several rows in front of him showed images of a large group of students trying to force their way into the Academy's shuttles, having, already, somehow gotten into the shuttle bay itself.

It was as his eyes diverted from the chaotic scene (what were they thinking? Trying to fly off in this kind of weather was crazy as it was but with a power eating storm behind them it was beyond insane) and back to his own work that they happened to pass over the diom. The message was still blinking.

Sera touched it. He meant to file it, to look at it later when he had more time. Instead he hit the wrong command and opened it.

Five seconds later and there was nothing left of Sera in the Command Central but a few lingering strands of silver hair.

'Sera! Hey ... Sera! Get back here!' someone shouted after him, but he didn't hear them.

Stupid! That bloody stupid... He was going to kill her. If, against all possible reasons, things worked out, he was really going to kill her. Sera swore as he tore through the now mostly empty hallways.

Please. Just please – don't let me be too late, he pleaded.

Dashing into the hangar, the bay doors thrown open in the high winds, he was just in time to catch sight of the last shuttle, wobbling badly as it rose into a sky that looked not unlike the boiling turmoil inside a QDE-M engine, had its contents been black and blue and grey.

Sera cursed loudly and violently.

Leap of Faith

It had started with the shivering. It shouldn't be possible for something so big to shiver … but that was the only word for it she had been able to come up with.

It wasn't the gentle shivering of some old engine either … the kind that was in the background that you could feel through the floor. This was the shiver, shiver, shake, that, when it started, made you wonder what was going on and, when it didn't stop, made you start worrying about what it was that was causing it.

By now it had moved way past that … way, *way* past that.

Everything shook violently before once more settling down. By now she knew it wasn't going to stay that way very long. It had been doing that for a while now. It made the entire floor and everything else lurch every so often.

The intervals were getting shorter between the quiet times too, she could swear it. Every time it seemed to go on for just a little bit longer before the stability returned or so it felt.

It wasn't like "stable" was a word that anyone around here was going to be using. The trouble was … there wasn't anyone here … except her. At least she hadn't seen anyone else and she'd been wandering and running through bits of this place until she couldn't move anymore.

The entire surface Gaile was on gave a mighty lurch as the final act in a cacophonic symphony. Odd bits, thankfully just smaller ones so far, occasionally fell around her. Avoiding being hit by those was a full time job and she didn't have a whole lot of space to manoeuvre in.

It had been doing that for a while. Plenty of nuts and bolts and rivets and the occasional plating … but nothing too serious, not where she'd been any-way. What it looked like outside the corridors she'd been stuck in she didn't know. There were a lot of Tendril after all. There had to be spaces where ladders, machines, even walls fell and crashed against the floor, shattering everything in their way as they did so.

She could have done with a ladder right now; an intact one at that. But there wasn't any … not where she was. That wasn't the only thing that it was lacking in…

It did have a good view though - had the situation been different - and the person doing the admiring not suffering from being Gaile.

Unfortunately, she thought, she wasn't anyone else. Even worse, she wasn't *somewhere* else either…

Gaile clung tightly to a short knob protruding from the wall beside her. They were thin and with no back to support her fingers and she hoped with all her might that she wouldn't slip or that the panels they were semi embed-ded in wouldn't come loose. She'd nearly lost her grip at that last lurch.

They were about the only thing in her immediate world that wasn't flat and polished or that had at least once been flat and polished. It was still mostly flat, but the polish had faded years ago.

The world around her was still shaking. It wasn't a big world but even here the metal of the platform groaned under the strain in the alternating power struggle between gravity and the station's engines.

It was amazing that they were still keeping the place in the air at all. Too bad they weren't managing to keep things steady as well, especially consid-ering where she was.

The door she'd thought would lead her out from the insides of the station had indeed done so. But rather than placing her "up on top" and close to the open space of the landing area it had deposited her on a narrow shelf which made up the lower end of the edge running part way around the station.

Here, the edge of the platform had thinned out enough that, with the cor-responding overhang above her, it wasn't that much thicker than the average person was tall. The "ceiling" here was close enough to touch. It didn't extend all the way though, so most of the place consisted of floor and the occasional bit of wall.

Despite that, the design meant that there was unfortunately no chance of climbing up. Gaile had discovered that the hard way. She'd nearly caught her heart blasting through her chest from it thumping so hard. Also, it was difficult to climb something when you were having your eyes closed.

Not that she'd have had much of a chance anyway. Even if there had been something to climb, the sudden shakes of the station meant that trying to do so would be little more than suicide. Too bad she wasn't able to fly.

The access hatch that had led her here had had another drawback aside from dumping her out here. To her dismay, Gaile had discovered that once it was closed there was no way of opening it from the outside; anyone working out here relied strictly on their colleagues in terms of getting back in again. That was probably a legacy from its time in space … but it was a real pain.

It had shut on her before she'd had a chance to stop it, slammed into place as one nasty tremble had tossed the station about.

She wasn't sure how long she'd been out here by now. Gaile was trying to alternately think of a way out and of staying put, to say nothing about trying to *not* think about what lay just beyond these few feet of plastasteel plating.

The bit that lay right in front of her she couldn't stop thinking about no matter how hard she tried. It consisted of nothing … nothing but air and an indiscriminate view of the clouds and, unfortunately, the ground, way, way down below.

This wasn't fun. It wasn't how it was supposed to be. She couldn't be meant to end here.

Gaile pushed against the door panels again. Why did it do this to her? Why couldn't the universe give her a break? Once … just *once…*

Wait … what was that?

Her ears perked up. There had been something else, just for a moment. Her heart began to race … but not out of fear this time. Tiny tendrils of hope rose from the dark ocean she'd been submerged in.

Had she imagined it?

No, there it was again.

Yes … there was something … a voice. At least, she thought it was a voice. It was faint and she couldn't really make out what it was saying, if it was saying anything.

That was when, over the sounds of the disintegrating structure, it came again. It was closer this time. But, it was too far away, or the noise was too loud, to make out what it said.

Just a little closer, Gaile thought. Come a little closer. Just a little closer … and you'll be able to hear me too, if I can get enough courage to actually raise my voice out here. It was an empowering thought and she tried with all her being to will that into existence.

The voice came again, even closer this time. She could almost make out what it was saying now. There were words, in there, somewhere, she was sure of it. It just sounded like a jumble though it was getting louder.

Yes … good … a little closer…

Gaile tried to fight the nerves that had taken up residence in the pit of her stomach. Gulping air like a goldfish, no sound coming out, her mouth was opening and closing, without reason.

Say something, Gaile mentally kicked herself. Come on. You're being a fool. They won't know you're here if you don't make some sort of noise. Do you want to be stuck here forever? Go on. DO something already!

She screamed against her limbs which would not move without sound, for her tongue had tied up and rolled back into her throat. Starched and broken, every piece of her wanted to go but she couldn't.

Please. Please let them notice me.

But how could they? From above she was completely concealed from view. And by the sounds of it, they were moving away.

Mustering every reserve she had left, Gaile whimpered. Then, the barrier of silence overcome, she cried out again and again, louder each time. Breathing heavily she had to stop, her throat hoarse already, her stomach turned into a wild knot.

'Gaile?'

The voice came from somewhere above. It sounded oddly familiar…

'Where are you?'

'He … ere … down here,' Gaile croaked.

'Where? What? Just hold on a moment, I think there might be a way down.'

Down? What did he want to go "down" for? It was "up" that was the important part … in particular, her going up. Oh, and what did he think she'd been doing up until now? Dropping off just for the fun of it?

'Sera?' she asked of the invisible voice.

What was *he* doing here? Gaile swallowed. She hadn't realized it was him at first. Hadn't expected it to be either. After the Final Exam she hadn't thought he'd ever even want to speak to her again, having, surely, moved on to new and more interesting things in life, even if she hadn't seen him there.

'I still can't see you,' he had to shout to be heard over the increasing noise between the storm and the station. The engines were whining, screaming under the strain. Their power was cutting out at intervals only to rush into overdrive to compensate once it came back on again. The metal that surrounded them didn't much care for that nor did the rest of the station...

'Down here,' Gaile tried to force her own voice into making a noise above a mousy squeak. 'Down here. I'm down here.'

The station shook again, like an angry terrier with an unusually stubborn rat. It nearly dislodged her this time, banging her head against the metal plating.

'Ow...'

Gaile tried to keep steady even with her eyes spinning or maybe it was the world that was doing so. Her hands were hurting from holding on so hard.

'Whoah. Easy there.'

Somewhere above, Sera struggled to keep his balance as the once so firm "ground" beneath his feet bucked and creaked like a galleon in a hurricane. The moment it stopped, he stepped closer to the edge.

'Can you climb up?' he asked. 'No wait ... stupid question. Forget I asked.'

Sera berated himself for even having had the thought. How insensitive of him ... what did he think she was ... some sort of catmonkey? He should have remembered about Gaile and heights. Guess he'd gotten so used to her not having so much trouble around them when he was around that it'd slipped his mind.

'Think ... think... If I could get a rope? No, that wouldn't work. Damnit!' he swore out loud.

'What's going on up there?' Gaile called up.

'Ok, just hang on a moment, ok,' Sera told her. 'I'll think of something.'

'No… I'll just let go and hand in my entry form for the arcane choir early. What do you *think* I'm doing? *You* hurry up and *DO* something.'

Well, if she could still berate him like that, she couldn't be too far gone. That was something at least. Sera winced. It wasn't as if he liked getting yelled at. He was trying to help here … was it too much to ask for just a little bit of understanding?

'Tell me something I don't know,' he said out loud. 'Now … hush, don't talk to me. This isn't as easy as it looks.'

Gaile stayed silent. While she did indeed feel better now that she knew someone else was here, she wasn't happy enough to let go of her handhold. Also, it didn't "look" anything. Not only was he out of sight … she wasn't really going to be looking even if he hadn't been.

However, a few moments later, the clank made by boots landing on metal forced her eyes wide open.

Had he just done what she thought he had? Was he nuts? Was he *trying* to get himself killed?

It wasn't like Sera to be careless, she thought. Swinging yourself over and in like that, as if the fact that there were immeasurable meters between here and the ground … all too happy to aide you in falling all the way until the very bottom meant nothing, was nothing short of insane.

It would have been one thing if they'd just been a few meters above ground or even a few floors, but up here?

Gaile's wide-eyed stare flickered between her friend and the way he had used to come down.

Sera was never careless. Never. That's what she had always thought anyway.

He's bloody insane, she thought now between the bouts of vertigo. That would have been mad to try even if this place *wasn't* falling apart around them.

Her friend knelt down, reached out and pried her fingers away from where they'd latched on to the slightly raised surface.

That wasn't as easy as it sounded. Gaile's fingers didn't come quietly. Her mind might have worried less now that she wasn't alone but her fingers, well … they had their own ideas on that.

'This would be easier if you let go,' Sera pulled at one of her hands.

'You let go!'

'Stop that. I'm just trying to help.'

'Well you're not doing a very good job,' Gaile snapped.

Instead of responding in kind Sera suddenly bent forwards, pulling her close, shielding her from the view of the ether beyond. 'I'm sorry,' he whispered.

'Uh?' she replied, confused. What was going on here? Gaile wasn't altogether sure what he was apologizing for but she was in no state to argue. It was kind of hard to make any coherent sense when your face was buried in fluff.

'I'm sorry,' Sera repeated again.

Still confused, Gaile tried to get her breathing back under control. What was this? Some sort of apologising rally? Well, one things was sure ... Sera apparently didn't have much sense of timing.

Maybe she was over-thinking things. Heck, was she even making sense herself right now? She did feel better now that she wasn't on her own but she seemed to have gone from one uncomfortable situation to another.

Still ... she was all tense and shivering from the ordeal of being stuck out here and now *this*. Maybe some people could make light of it but when you were afraid of heights, being here was more than just nerve-wracking and *this* on top of everything else?

It was just so ... so...

Finally it just grew too much and Gaile buried her face in the one stable thing in this whole trembling world. This way she didn't have to look anywhere. That was good but god, how embarrassing... Shouldn't she be stronger than this?

Also, there was one more thing bothering her...

'Why weren't you there?' Gaile whispered hoarsely. 'I thought you'd be there. *Everyone* thought you'd be there.'

'Where?'

'At the Exam. You were supposed to be there... It was supposed to be *your* day...'

'I know...' Sera held her closer. He'd felt bad enough about it at the time.

Now he felt even worse.

'Everyone thought … you, the king … would be a cinch to get a partner. That the dragons'd line up to accept you. That's what everyone was saying and you weren't even there. Why weren't you even there?'

Gaile's voice was muffled but he could still hear her despite the noise from the station. It had somehow filtered into the background, as if his ears were just ignoring it. Somehow it wasn't important.

'Is that why you were there?' Sera asked gently, a little surprised. 'I know that you were going as part of the staff. Was that why you went? Did you come to the exam just because of that?'

'Uh, hu,' Gaile nodded.

'I didn't realize that. I'm sorry,' he apologized again. It somehow didn't feel like it was enough.

'They thought … *I* thought … that if there ever was someone that'd be made a partner, that it was you.'

Sera wondered what trembled the most right now; the platform breaking apart around them or him. Well, technically it was Gaile that was shivering but she was so close it was like holding on tightly to a small rumbling engine.

Actually, he'd never been this close to her. It was slightly … uncomfortable. Was he feeling embarrassed? How ridiculous.

'I'm sorry. It was just too much. The expectations… I ran away – again. I'm sorry … I'm so, so sorry…' he mumbled.

Whatever Gaile was going to say next was interrupted by a loud screeching of metal against metal as a piece of a nearby section broke free. It screamed metallic death words as it tore loose from its moorings and tumbled into the void below. It managed to avoid the railing but didn't quite manage the same without striking some of the trailing tendrils that gave the station its name on its way down.

The impact knocked them both side-ways, into the door. They struck it with a thud that sent pain all throughout the areas of their bodies that it hit and then some.

Sera struggled to keep them steady. With one hand he took hold of Gaile's shoulders while the other one reached out to use the wall as a point of refer-ence. For the first time in a long while he forced himself to actually meet her eyes.

'No more running. For either of us, agreed? I made my choice a long time ago. I just never had the courage to face it. I should have told them that. I should have told you,' Sera said.

'Huh? What are you talking about?' Gaile used her free hand to wipe her salty eyes.

'After everything you kept telling me about keeping going, now you're giving up?'

Sera shook his head. It wasn't important. Gaile's voice was still not its usual self but the hurt in it was enough to twist his insides into a painful knot. She sounded confused. He really should pick his words more carefully around her ... he should know that by now.

'No, not giving up,' he said. 'Merely stopping trying to be something I'm not. Don't you think it's about time I started being honest to myself? Maybe having a normal life would be good for me?'

'I think ... you might be a little late for that,' Gaile suggested.

Her voice was steadier now that she was no longer alone, once she'd gotten used to it. She nodded at what was left of their surroundings.

'Take a look around you. If you want to stop working to be a rider you couldn't have picked a worse time if you'd tried. You're a fool, Sera. You should never have come here looking for me. How are we supposed to get back up? Now we're both going to end up dead.'

A particularly large bang sent the surface they were standing on rocking even more than before. At the other end of Tendril, a whole sector was breaking loose, disappearing from view (not that they could actually see it from where they were).

They did see it as it had dropped further down though. All too soon did it crash into the ground below, driving the front deep into the earth and scattering bits of itself far and wide. It disappeared in a cloud of earth and dust.

They weren't even that high anymore and over the terrain here it was only a matter of time before it became even less.

This wasn't good. Sera surveyed what he could see. At this rate this place wasn't going to be safe for much longer. It wasn't safe now.

If the station didn't come apart on its own then soon its nether regions would smack into any of the hills or mountains below and the whole thing would come crashing down out of the sky like an overstuffed pastry and spill its guts all over the land.

That was provided that the storm didn't bring it down first. He could see that it was increasing in intensity. He could hear it. That was going to be a problem … even if they weren't going to be leaving in the conventional way.

Looking at the churning storm, it would be prudent *not* to be here as soon as possible, he thought. 'Listen Gaile. Do you trust me?' he asked.

'What? Well … I…' Gaile hesitated. 'I suppose.'

That didn't sound encouraging. Guess he shouldn't have expected anything different with how things had been. It was his own fault really. It would have been so simple to avoid this whole mess if he hadn't been such a stubborn idiot. Yet, here they were. Some day this was turning out to be…

'Listen to me. This is important. Do you trust me? *Really* trust me? Trust me enough to do something even if you think it's insane?'

'I… I don't know…'

'Do you trust me enough to do something even if it's something that'll terrify you if I ask you to? If I promise you that it'll be alright. Would you do that?'

Gaile tried to shove the fuzziness in her head away. It was one thing that certainly wasn't working all that well right now. Her normally analytical mind was being battered from all sides … and it wasn't going to take any first places for coherent thoughts either, not here and now.

Half the time she had no idea what on earth he was going on about. Guess that hadn't changed. Wasn't staring death in the face supposed to bring incredible clarity to your final moments? Hah…

'I… I don't know. I don't want to fall down. Promise me will you … promise me that you won't let me fall and go splat,' Gaile pleaded.

'I promise,' Sera assured her. 'I won't let you fall. Not alone.'

Alone? Well, that didn't sound encouraging. What was he going on about now?

'This place isn't going to stay up much longer,' Sera announced. 'If the explosions don't do it in, the terrain below us will.'

'Your point?'

Sera tried to clear his mind. Now *he* was the one that was avoiding the issue. He took a deep breath and tried to steady his own nerves, for both their sakes.

Holding on tightly he lead them to the very end of the lower ledge. That meant staring down into the void. Gaile pressed closer, more out of desire to get as far away from the edge as possible, than anything else.

'Wait,' Gaile protested, struggling in his arms. 'What are you doing?'

'I need you to jump, just don't nose dive. Hold out your arms and feel the wind in your face, against your body,' Sera turned her around so that she faced the right way. 'Think about nothing else. Empty your mind. There is no pain. There is no fear. There is only the wind. Let it carry you.'

'What? No. No way. You're bloody insane.'

Rather than responding to her protests with force, Sera bent forwards and whispered in her ear. 'I promise you I won't let you go splat,' he said.

A second later he gave her a push, sending her tumbling into the air below.

'SeeeeeeeeerAAAAA!' Gaile cried out as she fell.

The scream reached his keen ears all too clearly. He was going to pay for that, he just knew it. He also knew that if he'd held out for her making the jump on her own they'd still be here even if the platform's decay had been due to slowly spreading rust. He wasn't the one to ask that of her.

Sera spread his own arms wide and pushing off from the world crumbling around him he leapt into the very same sky, following her downwards.

The cold air blasted against her face, whipping every strand of hair from their usual disobedient selves into an army of madmen lashing out at everything in their way. Tumbling over and over it took a while before Gaile managed to bring herself together and stabilize enough to at least be facing downwards.

It probably would have been easier if she'd had her eyes open.

Far above, the great dragon's wings snapped open and turned what had looked like a sure-fire win for the championship in "how to elegantly plum-met to your death, now in five easy steps" into an effortless dive.

It was but mere moments work to close the space between them.

'Ouff,' Gaile grunted as she had the wind knocked out of her along with her current train of thought when her body slammed into the dragon's back.

The impact wasn't nearly as painful as she'd thought it'd be. Considering the height she'd been falling from, she'd expected something a little more … well … terminal.

As a nervous eye slowly peered open, it was apparent that there was still a considerable amount of sky around her. There was almost just as much dragon.

'What the..?' Gaile breathed. 'What's going on here? Silber?'

'Where you expecting someone else?'

'But, we … can't just… We've got to…' Gaile looked around wildly for a moment before realization dawned.

I'm gonna kill him, she thought next. When I get my hands on him, I'm going to wring that pretty boy long neck of his until…'

* * *

Time could move quickly when it was causing trouble. Actually, it probably moved faster right when you didn't want it to just because it could.

The storm that had engulfed the land here was doing much the same. It had moved in quicker than anyone had expected when they'd first noticed it and now it was being stubborn and was refusing to leave.

At least, that's what it felt like.

It wasn't like he'd had a lot of time to think about it. The last ten minutes he'd spent in an ever growing battle against winds and crosswinds and up-winds and downwinds and more air-pockets than he thought could exist in such a small space.

His wing-muscles ached with the strain but Nightwraith managed to gather enough remaining power to put them both down on the small ledge he'd caught sight of. It was just in time.

The crags around them were dark, pointed and scattered all over the place. Not that either of them could see much of them. It wasn't just wind that was blowing around out there.

The dragon folded his wings before they got him blown away and turned his eyes in the direction they'd come from. He could have sworn he'd felt someone following them but up there he hadn't had a chance of catching sight of whatever it was. Nightwraith narrowed his eyes. The last thing he wanted right now was having to fight something.

New Retmia didn't have much that would bother a dragon, as long as they stayed out of the deep ocean, but there were things that just didn't see sense. Under normal circumstances they wouldn't be a problem but right now…

There was something out there, he was sure of it. The massive black dragon strained against the wind that battered him, his eyes set on a fixed point in the distance.

Yes, there *was* something out there … and it was coming closer.

At this distance it was hard to tell what it was. It could be something big or it could be lots of small things very close together. Right now it was just a darker shadow appearing and disappearing depending on how much sand, dust, small bushes and other things that the storm was spinning 'round and 'round as it went along.

Tam had managed to get down and was now standing in the darker opening that announced the cave beyond. In there, it should be relatively quiet and they'd have time to rest and get their strength back. They weren't going to be of any use to anyone in the state they were now.

'Ditch the saddle and get inside,' Tam ordered his partner. 'Come on … this is no time to be stubborn, Wraith.'

Nightwraith would have shaken his head had he not feared losing focus. He was right. Whatever it was, it *was* coming closer; a flash of form hinted at from within the wind.

'Something's coming,' he growled.

Tam didn't try to follow his partner's gaze. For one thing, he knew that his eyes were no match for the sight of a dragon. Secondly, he was squinting hard already, trying not to let any more of the sand in. His eyes stung from the last half-hour of flying.

That's what you got for losing your goggles, he thought. They'd been a casualty of the storm, literally having been ripped from his hands as he'd tried to retrieve them from the saddle pack.

A few moments later and the weird shadowy creature dissolved into two shapes, not one. Now there were two dragons, both struggling to stay on course, to stay horizontal and to *not* be blown away.

Had it been a little longer and they might have lost that battle. As it was, two young and tired looking creatures flopped downwards increasingly fast.

Actually, they were coming in a little too fast and they were both aiming for the same ledge that Tam and Nightwraith had landed on. There wasn't a whole lot of room there.

'No no no…' Tam waved his arms. 'Not here, *not* here!'

'Move it Tam, they're not gonna stop,' Nightwraith shoved him inside. At least he'd be out of the way.

'What the…' Tam exclaimed as the two dragons materialized out of the haze. They grew big really quickly.

The next thirty seconds was a flurry of awkward wings, talons, legs and bodies all trying to stay alive, everyone trying to exist in the same space. What they did couldn't possibly be called "landing". "Crashing" maybe, but certainly not landing.

There wasn't a whole lot of space up here and both of the newcomers ended up bumping into Nightwraith, who was stoically keeping the wind from the rest of the party by shielding them, merely by standing in its way.

'Never mind,' Tam yelled over the wind.

It was almost impossible to hear your own voice out here. Hearing the wind on the other hand was no trouble at all, though the designation "wind" was doing it no favours. It was the windy equivalent of a raging hoard of mad crustaceans attacking in formation over cliffs shattering beneath their "feet".

'Get changed and get into the cave,' he shouted at the new arrivals. 'Hurry up, before it gets worse!'

The red dragon that was the closest to the cave-mouth knelt down, trying to put their shoulders as close to the ground as possible. The rider didn't at first make much attempt at getting off despite the extra assistance.

What was wrong with them? Why didn't they move? Tam gnashed his teeth. What did they think they were doing just staying put like that? Even the dragon was trying to tell them to get off.

This was *not* the kind of place where you wanted to slip and fall. If you missed what little ground there was, there *were*, as if somehow seeking to make up for the lack of horizontal surfaces, plenty of vertical ones. Aside from the wiry path that led upwards, it was a *long* way down.

The reason for the crouching became evident as the "rider" slid off ungracefully and landed with a thump on the rock-hard surface.

'What in the name of all the heavens?' Tam exclaimed. Shielding his eyes, he stared at the assortment of ropes, belts and general clothing that had been tied together around the dragon's neck.

Wait … was that a pair of *trousers*?

Not sure if to believe his eyes or what it meant, he decided to move beyond it for the time being.

Then his eyes turned to the second party to arrive. They didn't look a whole lot better. What had these people been doing? You couldn't go flying like that. It was crazy, that's what it was.

He waved at them both to hurry up. The storm was definitely getting worse in this area. Was it doubling back on itself? He could have sworn that it should have been clearing out of this area by now if it had been a normal storm.

Shivering, the first rider tried to pry loose the knot around his waistline with stiff, unfeeling fingers. He stumbled as he made his way into the cave, trailing the make-shift "rope" behind him. His fingers were like ice and about as useful.

It took only a couple of steps for Tam to get to his side and help him. The older rider struggled with the frozen creation before ending up having to cut it completely.

Why in the world hadn't they used a proper saddle? Even an old one would have been better than this. What a mess.

Tam collected the wildly flapping end before it escaped. He'd been right … it *was* a pair of trousers.

There was another thump behind as a second, not quite as undressed, body struck the ground.

'Could … could I have those, Sir?'

'Oh,' Tam couldn't help but stare at the young man who looked distinctly uncomfortable with the scrutiny, though he might just be cold. Was he crazy? Trying to ride a dragon like that?

'Into the cave, both of you,' Tam ushered them forwards as the black dragon returned to a shape more accommodating for getting through the entrance.

The two riders stumbled exhaustedly into the interior and collapsed in a heap once they were out of the wind. They were followed a moment later by the two dragons, who didn't look too happy about suddenly being both cold and in a serious state of undress.

'That … was … the worst … idea … ever!' Akia muttered almost inaudibly while pulling at various bits of icy clothing. 'Let's … *never* … do that … again.'

Shivering from exhaustion more than cold she selected a shirt and pulling it over her head concentrated on trying to get enough oxygen into her starved limbs to make them move properly. The blood pumping through them caused them to ache something awful. She'd never had to struggle that much to stay in the air before.

Close behind her and trying to separate several pieces of clothing that seemed to have almost permanently fused together so that he too could get something to wear, Jim Walker looked distinctly bedraggled and equally exhausted.

This wasn't anything like what they were used to handling. Students weren't supposed to be out in this kind of weather.

Jim didn't get much further before he too buckled at the knees but he did manage to pull some of the stiff material onto his body. The young dragon decided that this was definitely *not* the weather for flying. Cripes … someone should design better storms; this one was definitely going way overboard.

Tiosh gave him an encouraging nod and helped the two of them to sort through the rest even if Akia at first looked a little uncomfortable at the older dragon's presence … almost as if she anticipated a scolding.

They shouldn't have been out in this…

He didn't say anything at first but he was also the one who gave the sorry looking youngsters a quizzical look once they'd pulled themselves together a bit more.

'Now, I know that neither of you were at the Final Exam, so what in the name of all the insanities are you doing out in this?' Tiosh made a circular motion with his hand. 'Have you *no* sense at all? This thing is dangerous. You could all have been killed.'

'Yes, Sir,' Dayu responded meekly from a little further away. 'That's why we were trying to get out of it.'

'And you two,' Tiosh turned his eyes on the second set of the quartet. 'Have you no sense at all either? Trying to ride a dragon with no saddle, no clothes? What were you trying to do? Win the award for "The Most Stupid Idea of the Century" or something?'

'No, Sir.'

Drak wasn't sure if he should agree or disagree with that. He wasn't sure he'd actually caught what the older guy had said in the first place. His ears were ringing from getting battered about so much.

'It wasn't a very good idea to stay where we were,' Akia filled in.

'What? You should have been at the Academy. I'll have…'

'Now, now, Wraithy,' Tam interrupted things before they got out of hand. 'Before we start telling them off, why don't we let them tell us what we should be telling them off for, eh?'

'Oh, alright,' Tiosh grumbled reluctantly. He had always considered that dragons should be held to higher standards than riders. 'They should still have known better.'

'Well?' Tam queried as they moved further into the cave, away (or at least with a reduced closeness) from the storm.

Now that they'd moved in here there was a very satisfying outside (where the storm was holding court) and an inside (where it wasn't).

Oddly enough, as they continued to head deeper it turned lighter, not darker.

That was odd.

Wasn't the deep end of a cave supposed to be shrouded in darkness? It was only in stories that they were filled with glowing fungus and shining crystals turning what should have been night into something more akin to day.

Tam frowned. What was going on here?

'Stay behind me,' he ordered the rest of them.

The group slowed down, edging closer to the small cavern where the faint light was coming from.

'What d'you think it could be?' Dayu whispered. He wasn't usually the most cautious of people but he was having trouble moving. The young man didn't fancy the idea of trying to run anywhere after today.

'That's what I'll find out,' Tam said and motioned to them to stay put while he investigated.

There hadn't passed more than a minute before Tam was back again, looking much relieved at what he'd found. Turned out that their small impromptu group wasn't the first one that had taken shelter in this place.

It appeared that the storm was making the strangest people come together and seek shelter in the same spot, like a catmonkey and a rach sharing the same waterhole; a truce declared, if only for a few minutes.

Looked like more than a few minutes here to him, but since neither of the two people he'd found gathered around the small artificial light source were in a speaking mood, he wasn't getting any wiser by asking questions.

For now, they were both ignoring him and the rest of the group as they shuffled in, finding somewhere uncomfortable to sit down and just being thankful for not having to move any more.

Actually, they seemed to be ignoring each other too now that he thought about it. Tam shrugged. He could deal with that later. It wasn't as if any of them were going anywhere after all.

Instead, he turned to the four youngsters who had so unceremoniously dropped in on him, almost literally in the case of Akia.

'So, care to tell us what happened now?'

There passed a quick glance between the four of them, then Jim shrugged and took the plunge.

'It was after the exam,' he admitted. 'The year's almost up and everyone was celebrating so we thought we'd have some fun too and kind of *liberated* a couple of the flight-models from storage. We'd got a bit side-tracked along the way and ended up way further away from the Academy than we were supposed to be. The coast was really nice. Lots of beaches and rocks to play on. And then the weather changed and the tide came in and we had to leave, fast. That's it basically.'

He shuddered at the memory. It sounded so simplistic but he sure didn't care to do it again. If he had to, he'd prefer it to be on purpose so that he at least knew exactly who to blame for getting into the whole sticky situation in the first place.

'Are you certain that's all there is to it?' Tam pressed.

Jim shrugged … it was kind of hard to condense what had happened, but he tried his best…

* * *

It had seemed like such a nice day to start with.

Ok, so there had been some rather peculiar weather around mid-morning (you *never* saw clouds at the Academy during the day. Doing so was so unusual that it'd be talked about for weeks, among those who had nothing better to talk about anyway) but who cared about that.

The whole place had been in an uproar, celebrating the new partnerships that the Final Exam had brought about.

Some of them hadn't been all that surprising from the staff's perspective but for the students of the non-draconic persuasion it was always quite the shock (mostly in a good way) to find out which students were actually in possession of wings. But, overall, everyone was throwing themselves into the parties that had sprouted everywhere.

There were everything from small private gatherings of just a few people to whole chambers filled with excited folk.

No matter how excited though, some students had sought their fun elsewhere.

Jim couldn't' recall exactly who's idea it had been now to go model-flying but it had seemed like a good idea at the time.

They hadn't meant to go so far either … but once they took off they'd had no choice but to move out of range from the Academy.

Today was one day when there was so much fluttering around, both in the air and on the ground, that the control-room probably wouldn't waste too much time thinking about them. If they did find out it'd hopefully just be put down to youthful high spirits.

As long as nothing happened that was.

As it turned out … something did.

It didn't help that it was something completely out of their control. If they hadn't been out there in the first place, they wouldn't have gotten into trouble, now would they?

Then, suddenly, being by the side of a sheer cliff and getting hammered by the wind and rain and the sea alike had turned what had been fun into something so far opposite it that it met itself coming out on the other side.

'Well, do something,' Drak had called out. It's freaking hell here.'

'I'm trying, I'm trying,' Jim had shouted back. 'Just hold on.'

Jim had been desperately trying to get any kind of reception on his diom but there was nothing but static. It had worked fine when they set out but now it was as if the DRC wasn't even there.

He'd slapped it a couple of times to see if that helped. Nothing. It was like there wasn't anything out there at all. He'd tried every place he could think of, every setting, but there was nothing but buzzing and whirring and the thing making odd pluck-pluck noises at him when he tried upping the power.

It had looked like they were stranded out here. Any hope of being picked up were beyond farfetched. If they couldn't reach anyone, how were they supposed to let them know they were out here?

This wasn't good. The weather was getting worse. Drak had been right, Jim had thought. This was no time to be out in the open. What the hell was going on here?

By the time the water was high enough to cover them in suds and powerful throws they had been completely cut off from any *normal* way out.

* * *

'So, we decided to try and get back ourselves. Anything was better than staying where we were.'

'And in the process breaking the statute,' Tiosh admonished them, though not too harshly. After all, he'd been out in this too, he knew it could be a pretty frightening experience.

'We didn't have much choice,' Akia protested. 'It was the only way of getting out of there.'

'Holding on with nothing but a makeshift neck strap at that. That's impressive,' Tam interjected, '*and* foolish.'

'Yes, Sir,' Dayu nodded. He was still shivering from the cold but at least his teeth had stopped chattering long enough for him to be able to speak more or less coherently.

'I mean, it was kind of surprising, finding yourself alongside a dragon all of a sudden. But we decided to chance it … Sir,' he added the last, just in case their teacher felt he was taking too many liberties.

'The same goes for you two, I suppose?' Tiosh ran his eyes over the second pair, who nodded.

'We saw them after we'd been flying a while, sir. Figured it made sense to team up. They seemed to know where they were going.'

This raised a couple of eyebrows.

'I'm curious. Just *how* did you decide this? Neither of you can speak to the dragons, can you?' Tam didn't wait for an answer. He knew it already. 'And even if you could, the equipment from our end is shot. The storm knocked it right out.'

The four of them nodded.

Well, that *was* impressive, he had to admit; not only managing to stay on the dragon in this weather but also being able to sort themselves out. He'd never expected it and he told them so.

'Well, I didn't much care for the option, Sir,' Dayu admitted and looked over at Drak, who agreed.

'We were running out of ground,' the large young man offered up as an explanation.

At that Tiosh excused himself and went to bring in the equipment further into the cave. The saddle and the attached packs had almost been lost when he'd changed back there. The second they were loose the wind had threatened to steal them. The straps whipping like mad, he'd received several painful "slaps" from them before he'd managed to tug the whole lot into calmer environments.

It was a good thing they'd ended up having to use an old fashioned one seated leather saddle after all, Tiosh thought. There was no way they would, even all of them together, have managed to get a modern one strapped back on out here. In fact, they probably wouldn't even have been able to lift it. Now, it would still be there when they could go back out again. In other words, it made it tricky, but not impossible, to get suited up.

He unlatched the bags, threw two of them over his shoulders and tucked the saddle itself up against some rocks.

It was already going stiff. It hadn't like getting lashed with water after all, and some of that rain had been outright vicious. He'd hoped to avoid that experience, but it looked like that hope had been in vain.

After a while, none of them were certain how long they'd been in that cave. One thing was sure though, by then it was a cave which, despite having ample physical room, still managed to somehow seem cramped. Maybe it wasn't the space, Tiosh thought, but the awkwardness.

All four of the most recently arrived quartet stayed subdued to begin with and not just because they were busy trying to stay warm and were too tired to cause trouble. Thankfully, by now, they were at least once more dry.

There were plenty of people who weren't riders who knew dragons in both their forms working in the DRC and in the DragonCorps itself. There weren't quite as many who knew the non-commissioned ones; those who were still considered students or in training and even fewer who were familiar with juvenile dragons.

For various reasons, many draconic families preferred to rear their offspring in the less cumbersome human form and not just because that's what their quarters were designed for.

A baby dragon could cause quite the havoc and, once they could be made to understand to switch between them (which sometimes could take several years after hatching), they were encouraged to remain in that form except for special occasions or training (of which there were plenty).

The parents were often unwilling (and the DRC too for that matter) to allow the youngsters the run of the place.

Hence why those outside of those responsible for any direct interaction with, and the training of, very young dragons, rarely, if ever, caught sight of a really young one, not even at the DRC.

They had their own, separate study program and it was only when they'd been deemed fit to join the Corps, even if only as trainees, that they were given the choice to attend the riders program. Not everyone chose that option, some preferred watching from afar because there was one big drawback to working side by side with "ordinary" students.

Because, once a dragon (regardless of age, and even if they'd already been through it once) began the course along with all the other rider candidates, they were expected to remain in human form at *all* times as to not cause suspicion or to give away their status (which would kind of have ruined the reason for their presence there in the first place).

It had not been an easy choice to break that "promise" any more than it could be said that the two humans weren't still reeling somewhat from the revelations.

And if that wasn't enough, the aura surrounding the two who'd already been here when Tam and Nightwraith had arrived, was positively gloomy. Both parties were still content to ignore each other completely.

Even so, Tam realized, now that he was actually noticing, it wasn't as if they were ignoring each other from opposite ends of the cave. In fact, they were sitting in, more or less, the same location that they'd been back then when he and the others had come here. They didn't sit too far apart either, staying close to the source of light and heat. They just weren't acknowledging that the other was there.

Now, there was a story and a half, he thought. How the blazers had they'd gotten here? There *was* a path down, true … but what would they have been doing all the way out here in the first place?

Sera he might have expected it from. He did sometimes go off on his own after all but why would someone like Ashworthey be out here all on their own? It didn't make any sense.

'Hey, I'm getting something…'

Dayu, who'd been playing around with the comm equipment waved at them. It had been practically dead, without power, for some time, so the crackle as of fireworks for a gnat's festival caused them to jump when it suddenly erupted into the echoing confines of the stone chamber.

It was broken and barely sensible but there was something there.

While the rest of them crowded around the poorly received communication, neither of the two sitting by the light showed much interest in it. They remained quiet and introspective.

Whatever went on in those heads was hard to tell. It was like something had built up that was just waiting to explode. It could only be hoped that it wasn't something that would blow up everything around them as well, Tam thought.

Gaile wasn't sure why they were here. Ok, that wasn't strictly the truth.

She was pretty sure they were *here,* here because they'd needed to get out of the storm, but she wasn't certain why they were here, so to speak.

Ok, that didn't make any sense at all.

So, what should she do now? It wasn't like she could just ignore it, was it? And did those people have to be so loud? They were making it hard to think straight and she was having enough trouble on that end already.

Meanwhile, Dayu strained his ears to the max.

'What is it?' Tiosh wanted to know, coming over from where he'd been handing out some food bars salvaged from the saddle pack.

Good thing they always stuffed some of these in there, he thought. It'd be terrible to be out here and not having something to eat. Besides, he didn't fly well on an empty stomach.

'Not sure,' Dayu replied. 'It's kind of hard to make out. Something about a wall and locks … the rest is pretty garbled. It repeats … kind of.'

'Let me see,' Tam asked for the equipment.

Dayu handed it to him without hesitation. 'If this is beginning to work again, the storm's effects must be abating somewhat,' he said.

Several pairs of eyes and ears turned towards the part closest to the entrance. Had the storm really started to die down out there?

'Still sounds pretty windy to me,' Drak offered.

'Shush,' Tam told him.

Now, he was trying to make some sense of the message. The younger man had been right, he decided. The message definitely played on some kind of loop. Or it did, until he lost it. Either it broke off or the signal just wasn't strong enough to get through completely.

'Well?' Tiosh inquired of his partner.

Tam shook his head. 'I'm not sure,' he admitted. 'But I *think* it's coming from Hilo Research Station. They're in some sort of trouble.'

'Does it say what kind?'

'It's hard to tell without an accurate transcript.'

'Why didn't you keep listening then?'

'The battery died.'

'What?' Tiosh exclaimed. 'That was fully charged before we left.'

This time it was the diom that got a small shake, just in case that might actually help. It didn't.

'I think the storm drained it, just like everything else. That's all it had left, just residual energy really. They did say something about locks though. Do you think they're trapped? Hilo RS is, or was, in the path of the storm, just like the DRC. Perhaps they lost their power too?'

'Locks or lochs, it's bad news either way.'

'Lochs... I hadn't thought of that,' Tam frowned as he, again, started pacing.

'I suppose we better find out,' Tiosh suggested. 'It's bad news, lochs.'

Tam didn't argue. 'It sounds like the wind *has* died down a little bit now. It's merely howling out there, not trying to tear the mountain apart. We should be able to risk it. It'll be a mighty bumpy ride though.'

'What else is new,' Tiosh scoffed. 'I'll get the gear ready then, if you'll give me a hand with the last bits.'

It didn't take long to get organized and they would have been able to leave shortly afterwards except that, before they'd gotten quite finished, they were interrupted by one of the younger members of their little makeshift group.

'Sir? What's so bad about lochs?' Drak asked. 'They're nice places – good for fishing.'

Tiosh let out a huffed laugh, slightly annoyed at the interruption but not entirely unfriendly. 'Don't think you'd have much luck in this one,' he said. 'Heavens knows why they even call it a loch. Someone's idea of humour perhaps?'

Tam, setting down the bag he was packing, decided to explain further now that the rest of them had drifted over as well. No, drifting over was the wrong word. It was more deliberate than that.

'It's best described as a small icebound sea ... if seas are that small. Or a very large lake. Its southern end is right at the top end of the canyon which should give you an idea of *where* it is.'

'The research station is built into the canyon wall, just below it,' Jim suddenly said. 'Isn't that right, Sir?'

'It is,' Tam agreed.'

'But didn't you just say it was surrounded by rock?' Drak asked, tagging a 'Sir,' somewhat belatedly to the end of it.

'That's right. All except for this one bit which is basically just a wall of ice. Most of the loch is actually just ice, making it more of a glacier. Actually, it's the lower offshoot of one of the mountain glaciers. That's why you'd have trouble fishing in it.'

'Oh,' Drak looked disappointed. He still wasn't sure what the problem was.

'But you think they're in some sort of trouble,' Jim asked as he got back on his feet.

'That's what it sounded like.'

'And you're going to find out what it is?'

'Aye.'

'Then we're coming too,' Jim announced, his jaw thrust out stubbornly.

A glance passed between the second pair. Then they too added their voices to the discussion.

'Us too,' they said, almost in unison.

Tam took a moment but, almost at the same time as Tiosh, he exploded outwards. 'Absolutely not!' 'Out of the question!'

'But if they're in trouble, shouldn't you utilize *all* available resources to aid them?' Akia spoke calmly yet decisively in the face of their teacher. 'Aren't we resources in this? *We*'re here, no one else is. You said yourself, Sir, that the Armoury was down. So there won't be many of *us* available at all.'

She sounded so reasonable, as if what she was discussing was merely an intellectual debate in a lecture theatre. Yet there could be no denying the seriousness in her face and thereby in her suggestion.

'Absolutely ludicrous,' Tam countered. 'May I remind you that even if we had two extra saddles, which we don't, neither of you can speak with each other once you're in the air *or* with me thanks to our equipment being on the fritz.'

'May *I* point out that we managed to reach here without any of those,' Akia replied.

'We still have all limbs attached,' Dayu added, though he privately thought that it had been a close call in some cases.

'I won't deny that that was quite the feat,' Tam acknowledged, gnashing his teeth. 'I've already said so. But thinking you can go on a rescue mission like that? Have you any idea how important communication is out there? How fatal it can be if you get it wrong?'

'But we don't know it *is* a rescue mission yet, Sir. We don't know anything until we get there. And, right now, we're all you've got,' Akia reminded him again.

'I'm not...'

A hand on his shoulder stopped Tam from finishing whatever he was going to say. Tiosh shook his head at him. 'As much as I hate to admit it, the little lady's got a point,' Tiosh said. 'You heard the DRC, there's no backup for those that managed to get out here. For now, we're on our own. Maybe a few extra hands, even inexperienced ones, could come in handy.'

'You were all for telling them they weren't experienced enough for this sort of thing not five minutes ago,' Tam accused.

Tiosh just shrugged. 'I can change my mind, can't I?' While his expression might *look* hurtful, he was trying hard *not* to grin. He knew his partner. 'Aww ... come on Tam. Have a heart will you.'

'I'm supposed to be responsible here,' Tam returned. 'They're just youngsters.'

'Hey, I'm no kid,' Akia protested.

'Um ... I meant...'

'I'm older than I look too,' Jim piped up. 'Though not by much,' he admitted a second or so later.

'That's not what...'

'And I'm old enough to make my own choices,' Dayu joined the other voices of protest. 'I'm no child you know. Just because I'm not built like a brick wall like someone else we know...'

'Hey, I heard that,' Drak muttered, his hands shoved into his pockets again. 'I'm older than you.'

'Quiet!' Tam erupted.

Surprised at the outburst, the four of them settled down, still looking rebellious as they did so.

Muttering something under his breath about mutiny in the ranks, Tam started taking some of the equipment apart.

'Well, are you going to help or not?' Tam asked pointedly after a moment.

Tiosh, in turn, winked at them.

'Let's see if we can salvage some extra straps and gear from the saddle for you guys. I think Dayu might prefer keeping his clothes *on* for this next flight.'

River of Fire and Ice

While the storm was far from over, it had calmed down enough that they would once more be able to take flight relatively safely; not even a dragon liked getting thrown about by something even more powerful than it was.

Although, considering the state of some of the "riders", "safely" was in this case very much a relative term. There was something distinctly undignified about holding on with nothing but some braces and getting stripped down to your underwear … aside from that you were freezing your ass off, that was.

This time though, they might not have to go quite that far to make it work. By now they were all rested enough to give it a try and had already started making preparations.

'You two had better stay here,' Tam instructed the only remaining people that *weren't* doing anything, as the dragons were being prepared. 'Don't worry. As soon as we're able, we'll make sure someone comes out here to bring you back.'

He didn't get a response. He hadn't really expected one either.

Now, why did he say that? Did they *look* worried? No, not really. They still didn't bother with either each other or anyone else, beyond a few mumbled words when someone had gotten around to handing each of them some food.

Had either of them said even as much as a proper word since they'd come here? Tam doubted it. Still…

'Stand still Ai! You keep making me lose these things,' Dayu scolded Akia as, every time she moved, he ended up getting tugged along by the sole strap of leather he was trying to drag around to where he could fasten it. As he did

~ 387 ~

so, the wind grabbed hold of it instead and smacked him right in the face with it. 'Ouch!'

The crimson dragon fidgeted. Her head held high and defiant against the weather, she kept starting to flex her wings, remembering she wasn't alone and changing her mind again. Every minute or so she turned her head and quite a bit of herself, to see what he was doing.

There wasn't much room to do either here, outside the cave. Still, it wasn't like they could go anywhere else. To get there they had to leave and to leave they had to get themselves equipped. It was about as much a catch-22 as it was possible to get. So they buckled down and got through with it despite everything...

It was no wonder she was nervous, Tiosh thought. The younger dragon had carried riders before, you weren't allowed to join the "hopefuls", the selection of dragons actively looking for a partner, if you didn't already possess the basic skills.

But that was all part of training and with an experienced person on their back (and in a saddle at that). If something went wrong or if you weren't doing something right, they or someone else there would tell you (or would tell you off as it might well be).

This wasn't training. There was no one here to pick up the pieces if something went wrong. Well, he and Tam were here, but considering the situation, that could hardly count. There were only two of them and no matter how hard they might try they couldn't be in more than one place at a time; not as a team. Better than nothing he supposed though.

All *her* rider had to hold on to was a makeshift strap secured as well as it could be in the circumstances. There was that and any part of the dragon he could grab. Thankfully, Akia's built wasn't nearly as smooth as some dragons he knew so there were things that he *could* hold on to.

That boy sure isn't short on nerve, I have to give him that, Tiosh thought as he watched the two of them. And as for the second pair...

'Jim, *stop* trying to be helpful!' Drak told his friend quite forcefully. 'I can do this. You're just making it take longer.'

The teeth of the azure dragon showed for a moment, before, sulking as he did so, he allowed the other young man to finish up.

They didn't, this time, need to resort to clothing. Instead, the equipment that had belonged to Nightwraith had been stripped down to its bare bones. Of course, that left Tam with a seriously sorry looking bundle to hang on to himself. He only hoped that they hadn't made the wrong choice about all this.

He still thought it was an absolutely crazy idea but he couldn't see anything he could do about it short of tying up the students and leaving them here and that just wasn't a safe option either; no matter how well intentioned.

'Everyone ready?' Tam called out not long after.

He had to shout to be heard. While no longer a proper storm, it was evident that the afterthought of it wasn't finished with them. In addition, they'd be catching up to it as they were moving, he reminded himself. Wonderful.

The four he was looking at gave him an affirmation of their status, in four different ways at that, but he got the point. They were as ready as they were ever going to be.

'Ok. Now, remember – the only proper communication up there will be what Wraith can tell me. The comm's still isn't working and there is limited information conveyed between the dragons. So take things slowly and be careful, because there won't be time for any second chances. Ok?'

Again they agreed. It had been rhetorical anyway, but what the heck. It was followed a moment later by a loud 'harumpph' from Nightwraith.

Then, once more, Tam turned to the people they were leaving behind. He wasn't sure when they'd walked up to the mouth of the cave, as if to see them off, but here they were.

'We'll send someone back for you as soon as we can. In the meantime, sit tight,' he said. It felt so inadequate but he couldn't think of anything else to say.

Tam gave a nod to the others and then braced himself. He knew his partner, he knew what to expect.

With a mighty heave (and a totally unnecessary one, seeing as they were having ample room below to catch flight, but there you go), the black dragon beneath him launched himself into the sky.

The two younger, less experienced, dragons soon followed in a far less dramatic fashion. Climbing into the wind, allowing it to do their work for them, the three of them rose rapidly and were soon nothing but specks in the distance; to human eyes.

It was difficult to tell if those left out of this "rescue mission" were relieved at not having to go, or annoyed at not having been invited. It wasn't as if their faces showed much expression...

What was certain was that their conversation hadn't improved. The only difference was that now, instead of the both of them sitting opposite each other and not talking, they were now standing beside each other and not talking. If this was a step forwards was hard to tell.

For a while they just watched the three dragons and their riders disappear off into the distance.

'You did hear what your teacher said,' Sera's voice finally broke the silence. 'We were to stay here and wait to be "rescued".'

There was an unmistakable sneer to those last words. Rescued? Hah! What nerve... Of all the things...

'We can't just sit here,' Gaile said. She jousted with the idea and wrestled it to the ground. She hadn't liked what they'd said any better than he had. Insulting, that's what it was.

'That is what we're expected to do.'

'Since when did you bother with what was *expected* of you?'

'Since when did *you*?'

Gaile drew back her head, eyes gleaming almost maliciously. Those words had really annoyed her. Rescued indeed. Hah.

She watched him for a few minutes, her expression alternating between cold distance and ... something else.

'There might be others.'

'I know.'

'There will be trouble.'

'I know.'

'You really ok with that?'

Sera nodded; an unusually diminutive gesture in this particular case. Reaching into a pocket he pulled out a hairband with which he proceeded to tie back his hair, which had been flopping all over the place.

The band was actually made out of his own hair, woven together. It had to be. That way, it didn't cause any trouble.

'You sure?' Gaile asked.

He nodded again almost absentmindedly, his eyes already fastened on the horizon. 'Let's do this,' he said.

* * *

It wasn't that far into the flight that Tam pulled the hood tighter around his head. He'd have preferred a mask to shield him against … well … *everything* … up here, but that had been an early casualty of the storm.

He shouldn't be complaining though and instead adjust to the experience. That was the sensible thing to do. He had to be warmer than the two other riders but somehow that didn't help much.

As they were climbing higher, it was, as you might have expected, getting colder. They weren't actually all that high over the ground; it was just that what counted for *ground* around here had climbed quite high above sea level all on its own.

Admittedly it had done so a lot slower than the dragons … but when you were freezing your unmentionables off that was little comfort.

The two young men in the formation beside him had tried to cover up the best they could. The truth though was that neither of them were dressed for this. Chillbites might well be the least of the problems if they stayed like this for too long.

Of course, he'd known that when setting out. Maybe he shouldn't have let them talk him into letting them come or Wraith for that matter. He was just as guilty of that, now that he thought about it.

Life was getting more and more complicated these days. Wonder what he might do to make it go back to the simple old days? Had there ever actually been such? Maybe it was just that time culled the memories of the bad things and just remembered the good parts? That'd be just like it, playing tricks on him at a time like this.

'You wouldn't have been able to stop them,' Wraith's voice interrupted his thoughts.

The dragon's speech was as clear as always. At least the freak weather, if that was what it was, hadn't messed that up. Maybe it was because the comm-units were somewhat biological in origin? Tam had to admit he didn't really understand the workings of it, but he consoled himself with that few did, even of those that worked on them.

Tam hadn't said anything himself though. The comms from his end weren't working. Those were pure technology, no corners cut there. It was at times like this that it was almost as if the dragon had been able to read his mind, which was ridiculous of course.

The truth was far simpler; they'd just been partners for a long time, that was all. They didn't *need* to hear the other to know what they were thinking. In some situations they just knew it.

'They chose this,' Nightwraith continued. 'And we might need them. We'll just have to settle this quickly. Just get over the next set of peaks ahead and we should be right there. From there it'll be downwards all the way.'

The black dragon was right of course, Tam knew that. But that didn't mean he could stop paying attention or stop worrying for that matter. Too bad they weren't "visiting" in better circumstances. It was spectacular up here, he thought. It had been quite a while since they'd come this way.

The Cracked Peaks rose here from the flatlands of the dry plains. Almost entirely devoid of foothills in this area (and a very wide area that was) the landscape went from horizontal to vertical with practically nothing in between.

Despite the increased height, this side didn't see much in terms of snow, not even up here. Therefore much of the mountains were bare and devoid of anything other than cracked rocks exposed by the winds that passed through here on their way south, and being slowly ground down by the minute grains within them.

There was no snow here for pretty much the same reason why there was no rain out on the dry plains. The entire mountain range backed against a thin sliver of land on the other side and beyond that was the ocean. That side was green, very green and quite moist too. They got to see a lot of fog. They also got to see a lot of trees, very big trees and some not very friendly wildlife among them.

This side on the other hand, where the rain shadow ruled with an iron fist, only tiny wisps of clouds managed to sneak past the tall sentinels standing guard. Here it was a forbidding place. Dark, exposed, even rugged, it didn't look any more inviting to Tam than a pool of molten rock would to a lost fish. It was, at best, admired from a distance.

Besides, they hadn't earned their name "The Cracked Peaks" for no reason. Bits of the mountains were treacherously coming loose when you least expected it and the closer to the peaks, the greater the likelihood of receiving a rock bashing your brains out.

Considering how much they were eroding they should have been worn down to mere stumps long ago, but not so. The continuous uplift caused by the same powers that had given rise to them in the first place, pushed them ever upwards.

The sky and its wind wore it down and the earth and its movements pushed it up again. It had been going on for eons and wasn't likely to stop any time soon.

Brought out of his reverie by something that glittered up ahead, Tam caught a sparkle between the shadows of the mountains. A stray ray of light where there was no sun.

Ah, good … they were here.

When they said that no snow fell on the Cracked Peaks that was true. But all the more snow fell on the other side of the dividing glacial lake that divided the mountain range into two neat, if not very equal, halves and part of that snow, folded, pressed and compacted together, millions and millions of snowflakes made their way down from the higher reaches in the form of rivers of ice.

They snaked their way through valleys dug out for millennia until some of them reached a very broad, very expansive and above all, very low valley which it continued to feed into to this day.

They did not, however, move beyond it. When you thought about it, that was a little strange. Perhaps more than a little strange even.

Perhaps it was because here it ceased to be a proper glacier and merely became glacial; ice cold on the surface, but not quite so deep within.

There was a lake deep down there, filling a once circular expanse. It only appeared here, right near where Hilo had been located. Vast as it was it didn't expand beyond this section of the valley.

There was also, between it and the air, lots and lots of ice pressing ever downwards, thousands of tons of ice. It was pretty to look at though, Tam gave it that. It was also, after all the greyness of the flight, very blinding.

He averted his eyes from the glittering panorama. Instead he focused them on a spot further ahead. That was where they were going, Hilo Research Station or just plain Hilo to most.

It wasn't much, not like an outpost or even remotely resembling any kind of settlement. If you wanted to live here permanently you probably weren't the type who wanted to live right in the middle of a vibrant city or felt a deep connection to the depths of space.

In its own way it was peaceful to look at.

Usually when someone from the DRC came up here they just followed the great canyon which cut into the mountains all the way up to where the glacial lake "ended". The valley that it occupied, the valley that broke the great mountain range into two was really just an extension of it.

There would come a time, in the far distant future, when the separation between the two would be more than just a rift. It would become new land ... or, depending on the sea levels, perhaps a new ocean.

That was far ahead though and neither of those alive today were likely to see it become so.

As such the truth was that neither of them really ended per se or so it could be argued. The canyon certainly didn't end, you just couldn't go any further, that was all. Once it reached the ice lake it had narrowed considerably compared to what it looked like out on the plains. But it was still plenty wide, for a hole in the ground.

The reason why people argued that it ended at all was the wall of ice that, at that point, prevented any further passage.

It stood, several kilometres high (or thick, depending on how you saw it). It wasn't smooth, especially not up near the top, and it had a habit of creaking as if it was trying to move forwards but couldn't.

The three dragons drew close to the end of the white expanse. They crossed from the side, effectively coming in the long way, swinging around in a wide arch.

Two of the riders looked around trying to identify any kind of structure that would indicate the presence of the place they were looking for. But there wasn't even as much as a piece of scrap metal up here.

No wait, that wasn't entirely true. They could see, as they got closer, some sort of pyramid shape that looked as if it was made solely out of wires off to the left. But that couldn't be it, could it?

As they passed it, they realized that now that they knew what to look for, they could see other, similar structures at regular intervals, very far apart.

Dayu and Drak glanced at each other where they flew side by side. Each shrugged, suggesting that they didn't know any better than the other. Tam *had* said that what they were looking for was located inside the rock at the bottom, right? The bottom of what exactly? Apart from the mountains, everything around here was just flat.

Turning to Tam, their teacher made several stabbing motions downwards.

Down? There couldn't be any down here, could there? The place was as flat as the proverbial pancake (a real one not being very flat at all, and the smaller you were, the less flat it would be) assuming that pancakes came with a frosty sugary coating that was.

It was difficult to make out any kind of individual feature from up here. It all looked white to them, just lots and lots of white.

A little later and the three of them drifted over the top of the "wall". The updraft caught them unexpectedly, making the dragons wobble in the air.

'Woah!' Dayu exclaimed. 'Easy there…' He held on tight as he, unsteadily, struggled to stay the right way up on the dragon's back.

Jim was moving around easier, but was, for once, happy to stay behind Nightwraith, following the older dragon's lead.

Suspecting they were in a hurry, Tam and Wraith would normally have dived straight down; not bothered by such an abrupt steep descent. Neither the cold, wind, vertigo or acceleration bothered either of them. They'd done similar actions many times before, sometimes under a great deal of pressure.

With the two inexperienced riders in tow, this time they instead descended in a series of spirals until at last the three of them reached the very ice-free bottom (ice-free where they landed anyway). The wall that this place was famous for wasn't that far away and it towered above them like a crystal ornament left behind by a visiting giant.

That was another phenomenon of this area that the scientists had yet to be able to explain. Why did it just stop there? The very laws of nature suggested that the ice, the force behind it, should make it move, but no, it just sat there, occasionally creaking. It stood, like an ancient guardian upon the land; cold, quiet and eerie.

Down here there was little to see though. There was nothing, just walls of rock in two directions, a wall of ice in the other. A fourth one provided more distant rocks down the canyon and a fifth one showed rocks that were very close to them (on account of being the ground) and the last, which would normally have shown a brilliant blue, was now trailing the still seething mass of remnant clouds running so low that they were almost hugging the mountains; the supercell's outer limiters, the last memories of its main body. It effectively blocked out any decent view of the sky by having replaced it with another.

'This place is bloody freezing,' Dayu commented dryly, throwing his arms around himself. He tried to stop his teeth chattering and failed. How could it be colder down here than up there?

Of course, now he was parted from the dragon. Maybe that made a difference? He'd never really thought of them as "warm" but maybe they were? Certainly in comparison with the air around them anyway.

Why couldn't dragons breathe fire? That would have been so useful, especially right now. A nice little flame that they could all gather around … maybe toast a couple of boulders or four; turning them into slag would keep them warm for ages.

The three of them had quietly dismounted once they'd landed. They'd tried to avoid the central area, but that was the best place to land if you were a dragon. However, if you were a human being and not wearing a full on body suit, it was the place where a shallow, but wide, expanse of melt water splashed up all around you.

Thankfully, most of it had avoided them, but the few drops that had scored direct hits had practically burned. It left a sting that burrowed straight into the marrow.

'Is that supposed to do that?' Drak asked, pointing at where the slow trickle of water was coming from.

Tam turned his attention away from surveying the structure that had been built into the rock wall. It had a similar appearance to that of the old DRC, if on a much smaller scale, and had probably been constructed around the same time. It was distinctly devoid of aesthetic charm, he decided.

'Oh, that,' he said. 'Don't worry about it.'

Tam tried to focus on the task at hand, but the younger man interrupted again.

'Are you *really* sure about that … Sir?'

'Very,' Tam replied in a somewhat tired voice. How was he supposed to think if people kept asking him questions and expecting answers? 'All glaciers do that. Think of it as lubricant that helps them move.'

'But this isn't a glacier,' Drak insisted.

'And it's not *moving* anywhere,' Dayu chipped in.

That, Tam had to admit, was a bit strange. As far as he knew, not even experts in the field could explain exactly why this part glacier part lake wasn't behaving like it was expected too.

Well, if they had been able to, there would have been no reason to maintain the research station here, now would there? Well, almost no reason... And that would have meant *they* wouldn't have needed to be here either.

Actually, that last bit he wouldn't have minded. He didn't like being cold and the sights weren't anything to write home about, that was for sure. Had *all* of the early structures on this planet been able to double as a fort?

It made sense, he supposed, but what were they expecting? An invading army to lay siege to them?

He'd seen the old DRC … well, the parts that were still visible from the outside anyway. This place had clearly been designed by the same person or someone who was walking in their footsteps. Very unimaginative all around really.

It was, thankfully, scaled down quite a bit so it didn't make you feel quite so small. Out here, all that was really visible were some protruding steel beams, quite a bit of metal wall and, of course, the door frame they supported. It reached barely higher than a large adult dragon; even the blast doors.

There was only one problem with this whole thing. The door, which more resembled a security bulkhead from a starship than anything else, remained closed, regardless of what he tried.

It had, in fact, been sealed shut.

Well, they'd just have to see about that, he made an unhappy noise. Tam hoped, really, seriously hoped, that it was sealed because of a fault and not because there was something on the inside that it was a very, very bad idea to let out.

Logically he knew that monsters didn't just appear out of nowhere … but he had an agile mind. Right now, he wished he didn't. If nothing else, it was distracting.

At first the rest of them just watched but soon, under Tam's instructions, the two younger dragons took up station on either side of the door, grabbed hold best they could and heaved.

There was a grating sound as claws scraped against metal; a metal that protested loudly at being handled with so little care.

The three humans winced noticeably, quickly covering their ears. Trying to block it out completely was futile but at least now it wasn't turning their stomachs inside out.

But the doors still didn't come apart.

All that happened was that, after all that screeching, the claws left indentations behind; long, jagged funnels dug deep into the thick doors. Now it really *did* look like a horde of ravaging monsters had stopped by and been balked by the sheer power of the doors.

As impressive as the doors were to humans they didn't quite match up to the brute strength of the dragons. They tried again, putting everything they had into getting a decent grip to pull the things apart.

It resulted in nothing but another set of imprints, but now there was something to brace against. Once more the front paws of the red and blue dragons took hold, their hind legs straining against the locks and this time, slowly, and not yet willing to give up the fight, the two sections slid apart, groaning as they did so.

It would have been easier to just bash them in, but then they'd have had the trouble of actually making their way through the debris. All in all, this made more sense, to Tam at least.

As soon as there was enough space, the two of them quickly shifted their grips. Rather than trying to hold it with their claws, now their hands could grip the solid chunks of metal directly.

The two dragons forced the now broken and twisted doors apart the rest of the way until they'd been either pushed back into the wall or been bent violently outwards. The doors couldn't have slid all the way into their housing for the parts where the dragons had held on had twisted out of shape, bending outwards. Those doors would not close again. Not until someone got around to fixing them.

Judging from the sounds, both from doors and dragons, it hadn't been as easy as it looked. It didn't look like they'd completely given up trying to close either. Whatever motors that powered the doors must still be running, Tam decided. That was rather peculiar, since almost everything else had shut down. Did that mean that there were some kinds of power that the storm *didn't* affect?

That was the obvious deduction or Tendril would have dropped right out of the sky the moment the storm hit. So, some power sources were more affected than others … just how typical of the world to make things more complicated than they needed to be.

Now those motors were still trying to force the doors shut and had started complaining quite loudly somewhere inside that they weren't being allowed to do so. It wasn't like they could; there was very little left in the middle *to* close. Most of it was all bent sideways.

The dragons weren't willing to concede the battle to some stupid old engine and kept putting pressure on them, allowing a little more to slide out so that, once they'd caught on to what they should do, the two of them, one at a time, pulled at the piece of metal until it was so out of shape that there was no way that it could have been closed no matter what..

That still left a reasonable hole for the humans to get through and if need be, they could always force them back into something resembling a blocked passage.

It was with careful steps that Tam approached that newly created opening.

'Hey, anyone there?' Tam called.

It wasn't a very inviting opening now that he got a good look at it. Obviously they'd suffered the same power outage as the DRC for when he poked his head through only the emergency signs glowed and those didn't rely on conventional power.

They did lend a ghostly light to the premises though. Light should *not* be cold and green, Tam thought ... it gave the mind ideas.

You'd have thought that being buried in rock would have offered some protection from the strange effects of what had been going on but evidently not.

'You three, stay here,' Tam instructed the dragons who were too big to follow anyway. 'You two,' he gave his two companions a nod, 'come with me.'

Tam moved his shoulders and took another step in through the discarded door. He looked around and wished that at least the intercoms were operational. It would have been nice to know where everyone was or even if they were actually still here, without having to look through everything the old-fashioned way. But apparently the universe wasn't going to make things easy for him.

Hesitatingly the two others followed him as he made his way inwards. They weren't too keen on this place either now that they were actually here. It had sounded like such a cool thing to do when all they'd done was talk about it, but now that they were here... Normally they'd have been anything but sedate, but here and now they were sticking close together watching everything around them intently.

'Wonder what the difference between what happened here and the trouble that Tendril was in was,' Tam mused. Of course, the platform's engines were a bit different from the power used in most everyday life items and the doors were probably shut because the power to open them had been switched off, not the other way around, but it still didn't entirely make sense to him.

Something was *eating* the power, somehow? Was that it? Storms weren't sentient, so it was unlikely that it was doing it on purpose ... but what could a natural weather phenomenon want with an artificially generated force?

The platform's QDEM or Q-dems as they were often referred to as (it being easier to say) were usually reserved for craft that needed to expend tremendous amounts of energy. Their "main ingredient" was rare and so the power packs were usually only found in heavy duty starships and similar structures of importance. It certainly wasn't something that'd turn up in a small time research station, that was for sure.

Hilo was fairly small Tam recalled, so it shouldn't be *too* hard to find someone who could tell them what was going on, especially if they were wanting to get out. They should have gathered somewhere close to the exit; or so he hoped.

He tried to remember the layout, but couldn't. There were several floors, he did remember that. But did they go up or down? And how many were there?

Back outside, most of the dragons had settled down, content to wait until the others returned but Jim, no matter what form he was in, soon got too restless to just lie there (nervous energy could be such a pain) and he was soon scampering around exploring nearby.

Nightwraith, in the meantime, was trying to keep one eye on the both of them, another one on the sky, one on the door and two more in either direction of the canyon. Unfortunately, to do that successfully, he came up short of about three sets of eyes. Very inconvenient.

It didn't help that it was still pretty windy, though down here below ground level it wasn't actually so bad. In comparison to what was still blowing about a bit further upstairs it was a veritable breeze, as long as you were talking metaphorically.

Good thing the chill didn't bother him when he was like this, he thought. That was one thing he liked about it. Being a dragon allowed you to enjoy things that would have seriously inconvenienced a normal human being; as long as you remained in draconic form.

Of course, it also had drawbacks. It was very hard to get your hands on cutlery for instance and trying to fit into a normal apartment was just out of the question.

He swivelled an eye in the direction that his partner had disappeared in. He hoped that they'd be able to finish their business here quickly. For some reason the place made him feel uneasy.

It wasn't anything logical that caused concern, it went deeper than that. Some long forgotten instinct that rarely raised its head above the level of the consciousness that was controlling it.

It still made him uneasy … and it showed in his motions, as his tail twitched.

As there was another sound, one he knew all too well, Nightwraith raised his head to watch the sky. Something was coming. No, make that *someone*…

The only other remaining dragon of the three of them that had landed here earlier, and who'd been *not* so patiently waiting for something to happen, scuttled out of the way of the new arrival as the bright shadow descended from the sky.

* * *

The inside of the research station was just as cold as the outside, Dayu thought. Guess the climate control had gone down south along with the rest of things.

It also wasn't terribly inspiring in here, quite the contrary. Somehow, when you called something a "research station" it created an image of a place that was clean and bright and generally just more, well, inspiring. Whomever had designed this place hadn't bothered about aesthetics … at all.

It was, in another word … dreary and that was *with* the light working.

Therefore it wasn't strange that after a period of poking their heads into dark spaces and rooms that were distinctly deserted, that they hadn't found anything other than what seemed to be left-over storage space. There weren't, so far, much in terms of equipment up here.

Guess they didn't use the place much, Tam thought. So, they worked downstairs somewhere? That just left one problem … where was the way down? There had to be one, right?

Also, if there weren't any equipment around… there certainly weren't any people. That had *one* advantage, mind you; there weren't any bodies lying about either…

Another thing on the positive side, there hadn't been any interlocking corridors, strange staircases leading goodness knew where or strange multi-layered walkways, so getting lost was out of the question.

It stayed like that until they reached the next set of doors. These didn't have any more of a resemblance to an ordinary door than the one they'd already been through.

It had another thing in common with it. This one too, was closed.

Tam took a few moments to examine the control panel but it looked like the thing was as powerless as the rest of the place.

'Wonderful,' Tam rubbed at his temples. 'Looks like we'll have to find another way of opening this.'

'Can you do that?' Drak asked. He couldn't see anything that they could pry it open with.

'These doors usually have a secondary opening mechanism,' Tam explained while he felt around the areas close to the wall. 'It's a sort of fail-safe back-up and it should be around here somewhere... Ah, got it!'

He pulled aside a thin plate revealing an old-fashioned gauge behind it. 'Come on, give me a hand with this Drak ... it seems to be ... stuck,' Tam yanked at it.

'Yes, Sir,' the younger man responded and putting their backs into it the two of them managed to turn the wheel, slowly, straining.

As they did so, the doors came apart even slower, complaining every step of the way. They stepped through cautiously.

So far there was no sign of any people. If they were still here, they had to be deeper in or more accurately, deeper down.

Once inside, now the actual station opened up. That meant that all those things that had been lacking before now came into their own. It still didn't mean it turned into a clinical representation of a lab though.

Even with that, a few false starts later (to say nothing about Dayu getting told off for poking something he shouldn't have) and they finally found what they were looking for.

Actually, they heard them long before they actually saw anyone. And what they heard turned out to be a room filled with busy looking people.

'Oh, about time,' one of the researchers exclaimed when they caught sight of Tam in the doorway.

'We didn't think *anyone* would hear us,' another one said, his tone much more friendly, just like his expression.

'And then the equipment died completely,' a third one of them added. The stress in his voice was getting the better of him.

'We tried opening the outer doors but they wouldn't budge. Ira and a couple of the guys are busy rigging some sort of drill but now that you're here, I guess we won't need it.'

'You *did* leave the door open, didn't you?'

'Oh yes, we did,' Tam answered. 'It's open. Very open. That I can promise.' He hoped they didn't want to close it again behind them once they left…

'Good. We should leave right away,' the original speaker announced firmly. 'Before anything *else* happens.'

'Agreed,' the others responded.

'What do you mean?' Tam frowned. 'What *else*?'

Not that Tam got an answer. The researchers were all too busy collecting all sorts of old fashioned files and equipment.

Paper, good old paper, was strewn everywhere now that Tam actually took the moment to look around. This place looked like some sort of control room but at the moment it resembled more one giant wastepaper basket.

A lot of it was scrunched up but more than enough were sheets filled with what looked like calculations or just columns after columns of hand written data; neat rows of numbers that, to an outsider, made no sense what so ever.

There was no heating down here either. Dayu had been right, it had been lost along with the power no doubt. The same must have gone for the oxygen recyclers. Good thing they'd left the main doors open. No wonder if felt so stuffy in here.

Despite the lack of warmth, none of the researchers seemed to be bothered by that little fact. Instead, they wore heavy, outdoorsy, attire, along with fur lined hoods and interiors. Of course, they'd be using those when out and about up above so they had probably not had to go very far for them. Good thing or they'd have been frozen by now.

Bet they'd never thought they'd need them in here, Tam thought.

'Before we go, if there is nothing else and no one's injured, do you have some warm, spare clothing for my two young friends?' Tam asked, indicating the two people behind him.

That *had* been behind him.

'Dayu, stop that!' the older rider ordered. The young man was bent over something complicated looking and looked just like he was about to poke it.

Dayu jerked upwards and turned around, a guilty expression on his face.

Hopeless … that's what this was, Tam barely avoided rolling his eyes at it all.

'Of course,' the first one who'd noticed them spoke again. He eyed Tam's companions warily. To him they looked rather out of place. 'Please don't touch that,' he ordered Dayu, his eyes narrowing. Most people didn't like telling riders off but these two didn't look anything like what he'd expected.

Some rescue party this was… They couldn't even send someone reasonable for them. Instead they were stuck with these *second-raters*.

'Aagni, you go fetch the others. Tell them we don't need them to create us a way out of here anymore. We'll be leaving right away. Lexi, you take these two riders and get them some suitable gear. They look cold. I'll gather the rest of the material and meet you outside.'

Taking their cue from Tam, both Dayu and Drak disappeared after the tall woman. They weren't sure why these people were so anxious to leave, they must have worked here for quite some time after all, but neither of them imagined it could be anything good.

But if they didn't need to go flying again in their bare skin (or what felt like it, the wind blowing through their clothing like it wasn't there) that'd be appreciated and they weren't going to be complaining. Also, those outfits looked nice and warm. A bit on the bulky side compared to what riders normally wore, but warm. That was the main thing right now … well, that and not getting trapped down here.

'Sorry about this,' the head of the station made a sweeping gesture through the room. 'We tried to get as much of the important data down onto paper as we could remember. The machines *are completely* totalled. We've been having trouble with them for some time. The storm was just the last straw. A lot of the old material should be logged already, so this is just the new items – the most important ones anyway. Lexi's got an eidetic memory, but she can't remember things she hasn't worked on. Too bad. I'm Pieter Oort by the way. Sorry about the greeting earlier. You weren't exactly what we expected.'

Oort dumped another lot of paperwork into a large bag and zipped it close. 'It's not five minutes to twelve yet,' he said. 'At least, we don't think it is. It's kind of a situation built on a lot of guesswork at the moment. But it'd be prudent to depart before it becomes so for definite even *without* accurate measurements.'

'What do you think will be happening?' Tam asked.

He didn't like the sound of what he'd been hearing so far. And there was something about the way the big man said it. If there was *more* trouble ahead, he'd prefer to know about it in advance this time.

What had they been doing here anyway? He seriously hoped it wasn't something that they shouldn't have been doing.

Tam eyed the shadows in the corners warily. There wasn't something he should know about this place that wasn't in its official description, was there?

'Possibly,' the researcher replied to his earlier question, picking up the bag and hefting it to gage its weight. There were several other bags, already full, where it had come from.

'Perhaps you'd care to elaborate?'

'Later,' Oort said. 'Let's just say that we don't want to be here when it does, ok? How much of this stuff can your dragons carry?'

'Wait a minute. We're not someone to just haul around your cargo for you!' Tam objected sharply.

'These things are important,' Oort countered, his voice returning more to the gruff state in which he'd first greeted them.

'So, *you* carry it then!' Tam shot back.

The argument had just headed into that stage where neither was listening to the other when the world around them stopped being nice and stable.

'Woah!'

'It's started already,' Aagni shouted over the rumbling. 'We need to get out of here.'

'No kidding,' came a couple of agreeing voices from a nearby doorway.

Drak and Dayu, along with most of the staff, not that there were that many, had just about returned from where they'd been putting on their new outfits. They were doubly grateful for them now. Not only did they keep them warm but they insulated them from the bouncing on the walls and corners that they were doing as they were trying to get through to the outside world still in one piece.

Dayu looked almost twice his usual size while you would have been for-given for mistaking Drak for a small bear or a long haired cat with all its fur burred up.

Neither they, nor the rest of them, were particularly happy about the way the world was moving, which, at the moment, was quite a lot.

They weren't the only ones unhappy about what was happening either...

'Tam, get your sorry ass out of there ... this place is falling apart up here,' Nightwraith's voice was agitated, a quality that was never pleasant to experience from within. He didn't know what was going on down there. He *did* know what was threatening to become reality up here, and it wasn't good.

Tam wished he could reassure the dragon they were on their way. Curse this stupid equipment that kept him from talking to his friend.

'Get out the nets,' Oort ordered. 'We're leaving.'

They could have gotten out of there faster, but with none of the powered lifts working they were forced to make their way up via the stairs.

They didn't look inspiring when they first laid eyes on them and after running up them for five minutes straight the riders' idea of them didn't improve one bit. As if the world around them falling apart wasn't bad enough ... if the staircase did the same they were all going to be down here for a very long time.

The only good thing about that was that they would probably never know.

'What about the others?'

'No use. The ceiling plates collapsed on level one. Timmarin and Jeremiah were still down there,' Lexi shook her head amidst the confusion. 'There's nothing we can do for them.'

'You can't be serious? We can't just leave them down there.'

'What do you suggest we do? They're already gone. Dying ourselves isn't going to help anyone.'

'But...'

'Quiet!' Oort ordered. 'We keep moving. Let's go.'

There were a fair amount of rebellious glances. Those stopped when the next large tremble caused the latter half of the ceiling in the room behind them to fall in.

'Alright. Then let's get out of here,' Oort called out, leading them ever upwards.

It was true that it was easier with someone in the lead who knew where they were going even when the place was coming apart at the seams. That didn't mean they had to like him; quite the contrary.

They just had to hope that there weren't any more collapses between here and the outside. That'd be … inconvenient.

'Watch your step … looks like there's a leak somewhere,' Aagni shouted from up ahead.

The information was somewhat redundant. They could all see the side of the stairwell that had turned into a small waterfall.

'Think it's one of the pipes?' Lexi called back from behind.

'Let's hope so. We're in trouble if the lake comes bursting through,' someone else answered.

It was a small favour that the climb didn't last forever, but they didn't get to rest long. As they rushed up the last part of the staircase and turned a corner, where there should have been a long stretch of access passages opening up before them, there was nothing but solid metal.

Almost nothing but solid metal ... but the rest of the bits paled into insignificance when considering that the door that had been so open when Tam and the others had walked through it earlier on their way down was now very much closed.

'Now what do we do?'

'Look for a way through.'

'Well, ain't this just swell,' Drak growled as another violent tremble caused him to crash right into the wall, balance lost. He grabbed a nearby bar, trying to stay upright.

'Can't you open it?' Tam shouted over the noise.

'Did you close it?' Oort yelled back, accusingly, as a couple of people from his team got to work.

'No,' Tam shouted back again. 'It was wide open after we got through.'

'The quake must have triggered something,' Lexi decided. 'Pieter, can we get through it?'

Someone on the right banged on the door. It didn't sound very hollow to anyone. Of course, the researchers already knew that.

'Hey! Anyone!'

'Can you hear us?'

One of the remaining researchers turned to Tam, a question in their eyes. 'Can't your dragons dig us out?'

'Not a chance,' Tam shook his head, while trying to remain upright himself. 'They're too big for the entrance.'

'Hey! Get us out of here! Anyone!'

'See if you can piece together the manual operating wheel. We'll have to move it by hand.'

'There's no use, Pieter. They wouldn't be able to get us out even if they could hear...'

'Heeeelp! We're in here! Heeeeelp!'

Aagni was interrupted by the dull thud of metal. It bounced around their eardrums, even among the rest of the noise in here.

'Stop banging on the door,' he shouted. 'It's not helping.'

'I'm not doing anything,' Ira protested.

'You're not? Then who is?'

'No one is, Pieter...'

'Are the rocks falling on it?'

'I don't know.'

The doors rang out again; louder this time.

'What's doing that?'

'I don't know ... but these doors are several feet thick. Whatever is behind this is making them ring like if they're nothing but an eggshell bell.'

Noise wasn't the only thing they were making either. At each ring the door shuddered at the impact.

'Look, they're not...'

'Watch out!'

Unlike Oort, the rest of them had already taken a few tentative stumbling steps backwards and as another, even louder noise rang through, this time accompanied by a distinct dent in the thick metal, they scrambled out of the way completely, falling ceilings or not.

Whatever was on the other side was coming through and they weren't bothering about being careful about it either.

They'd barely managed to get out of the way when the doors suddenly exploded inwards. They weren't even just bent out of shape, the thick metal sheets were literally ripped apart by the sheer force of the impact, tearing them from their housing and blasting them into the space beyond.

It was nothing but a minor miracle that it didn't crush them all in the process. Their arrival became noise among noise.

What did it matter how they'd become a hole? What did matter was that there was a hole … a big, gaping, inviting hole, that lead out. The world around them didn't stop shaking because the opening was now clear; if you didn't count the rock dust; the outer areas not being dressed, the rock there was still bare, and now it was coming apart.

It wasn't *completely* empty though…

'Well,' the voice of whatever had been on the other side, spoke. 'Are you lot going to stand there all day?'

'What the hell?' Tam shaded his eyes, trying to see better.

He wasn't normally the type to swear. Now though, he couldn't think of anything better to get his mind off things. He stared at the figure up ahead not believing his eyes.

'How did *you* get here?' Tam wanted to know.

'Never mind about that rider,' Oort pushed past him. 'Let's just get out of here while we still can.'

The rest of them, agreeing down to the last man and woman, barrelled down the access passage as fast as their legs could carry them. It would have been quite speedy, if the ground hadn't kept trying to become an ocean.

Some couldn't move all that fast in the first place. The last bunch of people were carrying (or dragging at times) a large, oval kind of pod, that had, once, been white but was now red or brown with rock dust.

They hadn't told Tam what was in it, but it didn't look like paperwork to him.

The small group burst out of the rockwall to a scene that contained plenty of boulders and smaller rocks, just in a bigger setting. It also contained three frantic dragons.

No. Wait… *Four* dragons? Where had that one come from?

What was going on here?

Tam, even in the middle of trying to direct everyone who was milling about or weren't moving at all (having several large creatures moving about none too careful about where they put their feet could to that to a person) stared, for a moment, as the large silver dragon rose up on his hind legs, a great roar erupting from his throat.

The two younger dragons settled down, though they still fidgeted. They didn't want to be here either.

Neither did the humans for that matter ... they just weren't keen on getting closer to the big "brutes" that could help them escape.

It wasn't quiet out here. If anything the world seemed to have been thrown into a permanent rumble.

It wasn't anything big ... just enough to dislodge things that were already inclined to become dislodged. Here that meant everything from pebbles to thousands of years old bits of rookery (or something that could pass for it if you squinted and covered your left eye with your hand).

While waiting for the humans to return, the dragons had moved out into the middle of the canyon. Out there things were at least not dropping on their heads.

At least, they thought that things wouldn't be dropping on them since there wasn't technically anything out there for them to drop from.

Despite that, Nightwraith had already been struck by something bouncing off his skull and the black dragon was now trying to keep an eye on the low level clouds as well. He was certain that clouds did not bounce...

Coming back down, the silver-skinned dragon shook his head to clear off the lump of ice that had struck it. It shattered as he did so and scattered thousands of crystals as a short-lived waterfall around him, refracting the light as it did so.

This was not going to be a pleasant journey, he thought.

The researchers weren't thinking as much about the journey ahead, not any more. While they'd been thinking quite casually about getting a lift out of here by dragon, they'd never actually been this close to one of the beasts before.

Crikey, those things were huge.

Watch it ... those were ... claws. Ouch, don't want to get scratched by one of those.

So ... exactly how were they going to do this?

It had been easy to talk about dragons or to dismiss the idea that riding them or even just being around them was not being anything much to be all high and mighty about – but it was a whole different thing when you got to see them in person; a whole different thing even if the world around you was crumbling.

'What is that?' one of them exclaimed when they caught sight of what remained of the black dragon's saddle.

'How are we supposed to hold on to that?'

'Never mind... What about *that*?' another one breathed (or coughed), aghast at seeing the sole strap that made up the gear of the approaching red dragon.

How were they supposed to ride *that*?

Akia turned her head, managing to look affronted even as she spread her wings. She wanted out of here, but even so, she didn't care for the insult.

'You can't expect to convey us with just that, can you? I mean, what would we hold on to?'

'Oh shut up! Just get on will you,' Drak growled at the first speaker, urging them on.

As he clambered up, dragged and pushed by others, Oort muttered something that they only caught the last half of.

'...standards must be slipping,' he griped. 'Those have got to be some of the most ridiculous looking saddles I've ever seen.'

His tone couldn't be accused of being jovial. In fact, it had quite a bit of sneer to it. Now that he was "safe" this wasn't the kind of rescue party he'd expected from the renowned DragonCorps, who were well known for their professionalism in all (well, almost all) situations.

This was ridiculous. If it hadn't been for the clutter of stones that made him eye the surrounding walls of rock warily he would never have suffered the indignity of having to scramble up a dragon like some half-baked muffin.

He'd thought it odd to see riders so badly dressed for flying, but this was another level above even that.

Jim, who'd been the one furthest away, came galloping up to them at speed, screeching to an undignified stop, bellowing as he did so.

'We! Go! Now!' Nightwraith's voice suddenly filled Tam's entire world, transporting an urgency with it that burrowed itself right into his very body.

Jim wasn't the only one who wanted to be out of here in a hurry, but the loud noises he was making was enough to get anyone's urgency into overdrive; except possibly for Oort himself.

'Spill it Turing. What's going on? Are the DC so stretched that they send trainees out to do a rider's job?'

It was, for all intents and purposes, a direct challenge. He expected the other man to take him up on it; to defend the DragonCorps. He had *not* expected him to explode into a dry laughter

'Trainees?' Tam grabbed hold of what remained of his dragon's gear as Nightwraith prepared to get off the ground in the speediest manner he could think of. 'These aren't *trainees*. These guys are students!'

'*Students*?' Oort's gasp erupted into an 'aaaaaaah!' drowning out the rest of what he might have said as the dragon beneath him spread his wings and clawed his way into the air.

They were quickly followed by the rest of the troupe and for a moment the immediate air was filled with nothing but wings and wind as the dragons fought to gain altitude along with establishing just where they were.

One good thing though … at least now there were no rocks falling on their heads anymore.

'Ouch,' Drak exclaimed. 'What the hell was that?'

Oort wasn't going to let go of the little red thread he'd bitten into though and he pursued it even while trying to grab himself a better handhold. 'They send *students* on rescue missions these days?'

'*They* didn't send *anyone*,' Tam counted, barely managing to dodge something else whizzing past his left ear. 'We just happened to catch one of your transmissions and came to see what was wrong.'

'No rescue mission?'

Tam shook his head. 'Right now, we're about it in this sector. Don't know about the other ones, since we can't talk to them. The DRC blacked out completely right after we left.'

Tam chose his words more carefully than one might have thought if you didn't examine them with a looking glass. It "sounded" like they'd all come together. Well, that should forestall some inconvenient questions, for now.

'So we weren't the only ones affected then. Guess it can't be helped. We'll just have to make the best of it then,' Oort said philosophically, still not entirely happy about the whole thing.

'Hold on tight now. Everyone's got their bearings? Alright, good then let's… Akia! Watch your passengers!' Tam suddenly shouted.

The red dragon let out an upset squawk, struggling as her load was slipping.

'Down … move down!' Tam tried to signal the upset dragon. Too bad she couldn't hear him.

Nightwraith didn't have that problem with *his* voice. He put it to good work now, directing the younger one to a spot on a nearby slope.

Actually, slope was a too kind a word for it. It was merely a slightly horizontally challenged vertical wall … with rocks on it.

It wasn't pretty and she nearly lost her balance on the way down (forcing her passengers into a series of mad howls) but Akia managed to set down on the slope just above the canyon itself.

For a moment it rained gravel as her large clawed feet struggled for purchase on the loose ground. As she gained hold of herself, Akia tried to pull herself together. She felt better now … as did the people on her back, even if the two extra people she'd had to pick up on the fly had to be set down first … though "dropped" might have covered what happened better.

That was a lucky thing, because it was quite steep and not at all stable even when the earthquake wasn't in the middle of still happening.

Were they supposed to last this long? Earthquakes were quick affairs, weren't they? Akia's experience of earthquakes was entirely from books … this was the first time she been out in one. They didn't usually bother dragons, who could always take wing if they needed to.

She eyed where she'd ended up. Yipes … this wasn't the place to take a rest. If you lost your footing here, you'd tumble right down into the ravine below, at which point you'd end up falling very fast but not for very long. Best to stay close. Akia pushed herself against the slope, hoping not to lose her grip.

Her passengers hadn't been the only thing that had come down along with her. In fact, the main reason for why she'd been struggling was now back on the ground as well.

The only reason it was still "up here" and not "down there" seeing how it was all smooth and slippery, was because Akia kept trying to hold it in place and it kept trying to escape.

The other three dragons were hovering nearby, watching anxiously. Well, some of them were watching anxiously, the rest of them were just watching.

'What *is* that thing?' Drak called out over the noise as they watched the once white oblong. It was a little over seven feet long and several feet wide around the thickest part of the middle. A seam ran right along the elongated equatorial edge giving the thing the impression of being a very polished and technological sarcophagus.

'It's a medical pod. Haven't you ever seen one before?'

'We know what it is,' Tam intervened. 'What he meant was … what is it doing here?'

'We can't well leave it behind.'

'The power's out, but it should still last until we reach somewhere and we can transfer it.'

'You mean there's someone *in* there?'

'Yes.'

'Those things aren't meant to be transported.'

'I know.'

Oh well, Tam shrugged. It wasn't the *craziest* thing he'd ever heard of, not by far. This wasn't the craziest thing he'd been a part of either. They did have a point; leaving whoever was in there behind to be retrieved later would, probably, have been a very bad idea.

In hindsight, it would prove to have been a very bad idea indeed.

'Alright, alright. I see the point,' Tam conceded and instead proceeded to instruct Akia how to best hold it without it slipping through her claws.

They might be out of the canyon but the mountainside was still no place to be right now. Bits and pieces of it kept shaking loose and bouncing around all the way down, putting them right in their path. Not the best place to stop for a rest no, but they needed to get reorganized and some of the new "passengers" had to have a few moments to get used to the sensation of being a dragonback.

Even so, it had been touch and go setting down here … and if the motions of the ground was anything to go by, getting out of here quickly would *not* be a bad idea.

Good thing that only a handful of people were down here in the first place. Those in the air were nice and safe now that the storm had ceased and desisted and gone on to bother someone else.

At least you'd have thought it was safe.

Dayu complained loudly as he swatted off another piece that had nearly burned a whole in his dragon's wing. Where did this stuff come from? All the ice he could see was most certainly *beneath* them not above.

'Ok, everyone ready to go *now*?' Tam called out.

Akia's wings snapped open and, with less grace than usual but no less power, the red dragon pushed into the air once more.

A moment later and she turned and went back to the mountainside. She hovered, flapping her wings furiously to stay off the ground and picked up the pod as it was sliding downwards, with a hind foot, carefully closing around it without ripping into it.

Finally having managed to gather them all together, Tam signalled for the draconic quartet to move out. This whole lack of communication was seriously getting to him; it made a difficult job even more difficult. 'Ouch!' he called out and batted away the burning bit of *something*. 'What's going on here?'

They swung out, making a half circle over the lake of ice before turning and heading right past the ice-wall on their way back.

It didn't look nearly as big from up here. Difficult to imagine it was over a kilometre tall when you weren't looking "up" at it. Guess perspective really did change things, Dayu thought.

It was tall … but it wasn't looking like it was going to stay that way for much longer. The earthquake had already forced big chunks out of the top, not to mention the cracks it had created.

A sharp pitched noise made some of them look back over their shoulders.

'Looks like we got away just in time,' Aagni cupped his hands trying to make himself heard.

'Look!'

Beneath them, the ground rumbled again and great fountains of steam shot out from cracks in the rock where they'd just been. No wonder it had had felt so warm.

It wasn't just there either … everywhere along the ridge they could see and hear whistling pockets of steam venting.

Needless to say, steam and ice didn't mix very well.

There followed a closer and much louder 'crack' as if something was splitting, then another and another, each louder than the last.

Thinking it prudent to make their escape, the dragons began to ascend but before they'd climbed even five more feet there was a deafening noise, as from a giant blender.

It wasn't the steam this time nor the ice. It wasn't even coming out of the ground. It was coming from above.

'Go!' Tam yelled at the top of his lungs. 'Get us out of here you flying rat!'

Nightwraith wasn't about to complain about that … the sooner the better he thought as he forced himself forward.

It really was coming out of the sky. Like an avenging angel of old descending from above, the last ounces of power gone, Tendril station closed in over the nearest peaks. Its hull screamed as the mountains tore into its underbelly, ripping huge chunks out of the structure and sending the rest into a nosedive.

Coming down on its side the station crashed its least bulky section into the middle of the lake punching right through the ice.

The lake reacted violently.

It must already have been bubbling under the surface because there was no way the station alone could have caused such a thing to happen.

Beneath them, the ground gave another heave. Thankfully they were no longer having to be concerned about it shaking them around with it but that was the least of their worries now as it was followed a moment later by an even louder rumble.

Then, a mixture of red, orange and burning yellow, shot into the sky from the middle of the lake, right around where the station had punched through. It coloured the grey metal in flames and fire, some of it already beginning to melt.

Against a background of hissing vapours as the ice was turned to steam without bothering to become water in between, its voice erupted as the pillar of molten rock broke through what was left of the surface ice.

It climbed higher and higher, until, like a great fountain of fire, the spout of earth and magma tossed its body towards the sky as it had offended it. The top began raining down on the nearby ice, melting through it and breaking the ice sheet apart.

The ice wasn't the only thing that small, and large, droplets of lava were raining down on now.

Jim dodged out of the way, jigged this way, then that, as a rapidly increasing amount was heading towards them. If one of those things hit his wing membranes they'd burn right through...

It wasn't long before the wall, already weakened by the earthquake, fell to the onslaught of the fire.

The ice tumbled, in blocks and pieces, pushed out by the free flowing water behind it which now shot out between the openings before the whole thing collapsed. Ice rolled over and over as the white waters of the now almost completely defrosted lake behind it emptied into the canyon like a power hose.

With a mighty roar that blocked out any other sound as effectively as if they'd all just been affected by the worst case of tinnitus in the galaxy, the whole glacial lake broke free of its prison, a raging torrent engulfing everything in its path.

In mere seconds it had reached the research station.

Leaping and frothing, the wall of water standing taller than it was possible to even imagine, swept away everything that stood before it while bits of metal and lava rained down around them.

Akia, forgetting what she was doing for just a moment, lost her grip on the pod. In seconds it was a white shell against the white waters of the fall. Moments before it had been mere water, what it was now, was wild. The once so placid lake had become an enraged beast from the nether realms. The torrent surging forwards beneath them.

The pod, unlike a person, had no chance of trying to grip on to anything. Akia cried out and started to dive after it.

'AKIA! NO!' Tam screamed at her, followed by a commanding bellow from Wraith, who, undercutting the younger dragon forced her to pull up.

'Leave it,' their teacher ordered. 'You can't catch it now.'

'No...'

'I said *leave* it!'

Despite what was happening around them, they watched the pod as it fell.

Already flying higher up than any of the others and having not so much refused to carry any passengers as having been too intimidating to approach, the silver dragon rolled over and dove into the world beneath chasing the disappearing pod like a flash of silver lightning.

Afterwards, everyone described what had happened in the next few heartbeats differently. The only thing that they all did agree on was that it all happened fast, very fast.

Tiosh, who'd had the best view, said that, at that point, it was as if a pale white light fell from the sky. He didn't have words to describe it, but that's what it looked like he said; a glowing light moving faster than any dragon he'd ever heard of, faster than any dragon should be able to fly.

The draft from the passing body, if it was at that point a body at all, slammed into Akia, sending both her and Nightwraith struggling to stay in flight and not to be blown away completely.

By the time everyone had gotten hold of themselves again, whatever it was that had passed by them as if they were standing still, had vanished into the fray below. Tam was waving frantically at the rest of them, trying to get their attention.

What had that been? Tam couldn't recall having seen anything like it. Heck, he couldn't recall ever having *read* anything about anything like it. It had moved *so* fast that by the time your eyes realized that you were supposed to be looking, it had already passed by, little more than a blur in the eye's memory.

A jet of fire in the centre of an icy lake seemed almost normal in comparison. What had just happened? Where had they gone? That *was* the fourth dragon he'd seen? But how had they been able to move like that? If no dragon could, then a dragon and rider combo certainly couldn't. All dragons put curbs on their powers of flight when they weren't alone; the human body just wasn't made for something like what they were capable of.

He didn't have time to think too much about it, not here … not now. 'Go! Go! Warn the ones downstream!' Tam called out as Nightwraith fought to stay steady in the middle of a world turned savage.

They couldn't hope to keep dodging the rain of fire forever. Spurred on by a second pillar of solid flame, they jinxed and dodged as they winged their way out of there. Trying to put some distance between what was happening and themselves, the dragons climbed steadily. Between the wind, the half-molten droplets of plastasteele, the really molten miniature lavabombs *and* their passengers, it was a battle in which the odds weren't in their favour.

It was at that point, just when they thought that everything that could hit them that day had done so already and they had begun to settle into a calm flight pattern out of the general area and back to the DRC, that something else rocked their entire world.

The earthfire that had been eating away at the station had finally reached something volatile and did what volatile things usually do when heated up unexpectedly and rapidly; it exploded.

It wasn't just the noise that washed over them… The shockwave soon followed, sending the dragons and their passengers struggling to stay in the air once again.

A moment later and something whistled past that *wasn't* a mere droplet. Several pairs of eyes followed it as it slammed into the ground with a mighty explosion, a chunk the size of a dragon. If they were hit by that a hole in a wing would be the least of their worries.

'What was that?'

'Did you see it?'

'Yeah.'

'What the hell was that?'

Heads turned, trying to identify what had just happened. Even the dragons stopped their forward motions, casting about for what it might have been.

Then something else screamed through the sky and smacked into a slope behind them. It looked like … metal?

Something else, much larger, whistled through the air, dove right past them, missing them by a breath and dug itself a deep pit in the ground beside the canyon.

'That wasn't what I think it was, was it?'

'I hope not. I really, *really* hope not!'

'Alright everyone. No time for sightseeing. We need to put more distance between this thing and us,' Tam ordered.

Nightwraith didn't need any further encouragement nor did the others. They steadied themselves the best they could and made their wings work for them.

The three of them set a course as straight as an arrow, the shortest distance between here and anywhere else, though the terrain meant this largely consisted of following the canyon below them as it twisted through the last of the mountains.

Soon enough it wasn't very straight either.

It was a good thing they weren't running on the ground or they'd never get out of the way in time ... should this new-born disaster decide it wanted to expand even more.

The pillars of flame behind them had grown as well ... though by now they were further away so they still *looked* the same. Thankfully, it didn't seem inclined to shower anything except the immediate vicinity with anything that burnt and dodging and jinking whatever it was that was falling out of the sky, they sped out of range.

Now they just needed to outpace the torrent beneath them.

The water below moved rapidly. It danced and frothed its way down the canyon. By now it also had a quite a lead on them. But the dragons too could move quickly. And *they* didn't need to go the long way around.

Somewhere down there, wherever the silver dragon and his rider were, they had to hope that they could take care of themselves. It didn't look very friendly. Between the churning waters and the rocks, even a dragon would be in trouble.

Eventually the comms scraped and spluttered back into life. Whatever had blocked them seemed to be gone or at least gone enough for the signal to get through and the power to come back on. It was filled with static, but it *was* there.

After listening to some garbled noises and trying to make himself heard on the other end, Tam eventually managed to get a general message out. One of those who had heard him acknowledged it and promised to make sure it was relayed, making sure that no one would be in the path of the wall of water that was now sweeping the canyon floor clean.

Not that it was likely that there *would* be anyone, Tam thought. It wasn't the kind of place that you sought shelter in even in an emergency and it certainly wasn't what you'd call populated in normal times either.

Still, he'd learnt that it paid to not take chances with things like that. There was always someone, somewhere, who'd be in the wrong place at the wrong time. The universe seemed to be like that. Better to be one step ahead. To anticipate the trouble *before* it happened.

But while the panorama behind them was impressive enough, it was what was approaching them from the front that caught them off guard.

As the other dragon approached, Tam was lost for words. He wasn't the only one either.

Dayu bent forward, leaning his whole body against the scales supporting him. He wasn't sure if his heart was ever going to come down out of his throat, it seemed to have lodged itself there permanently.

But if that was where it was, then why was there something pounding so hard behind his ribs that it felt like he'd trapped a small powerful engine in there? It even pounded in his ears. Was anyone else calling out? He couldn't hear them, the blood's song was too strong.

The others were trying to get their own adrenalin under control as well. Even the researchers or perhaps even more so the researchers, who'd not been able to do anything but hang on and hope like the blazers, were trying to calm down. The last few minutes had been rather a lot to take in.

The dragon before them seemed to stand motionless in the air for a moment, the wings holding him up almost leisurely.

'You dropped something I believe,' the rider said.

'Uh … what?' Tam couldn't do anything but stare. He still had trouble believing they'd actually escaped. It was as if what was appearing before him was an apparition; not a real thing at all.

'It's yours. *You* carry it,' the other rider told him rather pointedly.

The pod, washed clean by the water and shining brilliantly in the now once again cloudless sky was flicked unceremoniously in their direction. Nightwraith caught it effortlessly in a gentle grip.

'Thanks, Missy,' one of the researchers called out.

His exclamation was followed by several others along the same lines. The rider merely shrugged.

Nightwraith came as close to chuckling as a dragon could. It wasn't *quite* the discreet event it might have been if he'd been in human form.

Well, well, well, the black dragon thought. As I live and breathe... He hadn't seen *that* coming.

'I … you … how? I mean … how… Where did you come from?' Tam finally managed to arrange the words in his mouth to at least partially reflect the questions in his mind.

His opposite number patted the dragon neck before them with firm slaps, though the dragon was unlikely to have felt it.

'When you're moving at that speed it's kind of hard to stop. Well … other than ramming yourself into something hard and spending the rest of your point zero seconds of your life as a pancake,' Gaile grinned at him. 'We didn't like that second option much, so we came back the long way.'

'But?'

'I think you might want to hurry and get out of here,' she added as the silver dragon dodged another piece of goodness knew what as it streaked past them.

Tam thought they'd have gotten out of range by now, but apparently it must have grown in intensity since he last looked over his shoulder. It wasn't something that he enjoyed having behind his back but at least it wasn't in front of him. And it was a lot smaller than the last ones.

'The eruption, yes,' Tam agreed. He looked up into the sky. Death by steel rain wasn't his idea of a way to go, even if they had now seemed to have gotten out from underneath its shadow. 'Very well. Forwards then. Back to the DRC for all of us,' he commanded.

Onwards, Upwards and Sideways

They were already out of the mountains but there was still quite a bit to go before they reached the DRC.

The experience they'd just been through had shaken up the researchers no little bit and not just because flying on a dragon was a whole different thing than taking a casual flight on a powered vehicle. Flying on a dragon dodging a rain of fire was a whole different thing to a casual ride on a dragon at any other time for that matter. Right now, while grateful they hadn't drowned, they'd really like to see some solid ground underneath their feet.

Even so, one or two of them were even beginning to take an interest in what was happening down below.

The storm had moved on and the wind that followed in its wake seemed tame in comparison. Its feeble flutters did little to discourage anyone, whether in the sky or on the ground.

Creatures that were similar enough (or who at least seemed to share a similar enough function) to be thought of as birds, and who'd weathered out the storm somewhere out of the way where they *weren't* likely to be blown to pieces, crushed against a mooring mountainside or swept miles out over the ocean, were returning to their natural habitat.

Some were going forth more boldly than others, exhilarated over still being alive. Most avoided getting too close to the dragons but a few of them fluttered around them, chattering excitedly.

While the dragons might be a new part of the fauna of the planet, those that didn't live in reasonable proximity to them, tended to give them a bit of a wide space. They weren't known for appreciating hitchhikers for instance and those teeth weren't *just* for show.

Down on the ground itself it was a different matter. Life was returning, but mostly that which had been able to run away and hide as the storm had passed.

As their wings took the dragons and their passengers past what little foothills there were it was all too easy to see the damage that the peculiar weather had left behind.

Here it didn't matter if there was any power to steal or not, ordinary blows of gusts racing at many miles per hour had been more than enough to wreak havoc in the area.

It'd take decades, if not more, before the landscape returned to what they were used to seeing, Tam thought as they passed over it.

Nothing was static though, you have to remember that, he chided himself. It was part of the natural cycle to change, just as it seemed part of the human condition to dislike such disruptions to their expected equilibrium, no matter what planet they were on.

It looked messy down there though. The forests had been especially hard hit. They only caught sight of the outskirts though, from way up here. The actual forests didn't stretch out into the area near the canyon or the plains that surrounded it.

It wasn't surprising though, seeing as it was by far the most exposed element out here. He'd have to remember to mention that in his report. There was a lot of timber down there that could be used now. Not all though – leaving enough to provide a new springboard for whatever would come next made sense.

By the time they reached the plains proper, dry and desolate as they always appeared from this altitude (not that any of them thought it was any more hospitable when down on the ground) there was little change from before. What had been lots of rocks and dust were still lots of rocks and dust. Some of it might be in different places from before but that was about it.

Here it wasn't the storm that had been responsible for the greatest change. Instead that could be directly attributed to the white and blue snake that now wound forth below them.

How odd it looked, several of them thought, to see anything other than pale dust and shadows down there. It would have been a welcome sight if the water hadn't nearly drowned them in the process of getting there.

Ok, so that might be a gross exaggeration, but that was what it had felt like even if they had only been watching.

Tam sneaked a glance over to his right where, some distance away and slightly above, the silver dragon was flying as steady and as unperturbed as a rock.

How *had* he done that, Tam wondered? How *had* both dragon and rider managed to escape unscathed from something that by all rights should have caught and swept away both of them? While a dragon was powerful, a raging torrent of water that big would have been way too much for one of them to handle.

And while you were at it ... what *was* that girl holding on to? It wasn't like he'd seen even as much as a neck strap on that dragon. It didn't make *any* sense.

Yet, he could hardly deny the evidence of his own eyes, now could he? Not in this.

'I know what you're probably thinking – or thought – or are about to think,' Wraith told him. 'I suggest waiting with the questions. I don't' think they're in the mood for explanations.'

True. That was the second part of this whole oddness, Tam realized. He wasn't the only one who thought it odd ... but being a teacher rather than a student, even a dragon student, did leave him with more of a history to draw upon which just added a magnitude of odd to the whole thing, probably not as much as Nightwraith though, he'd been there when...

Never mind. Regardless of the reason, it was hard to shake the feeling of how peculiar it felt to have the silver dragon at their side. What the blazers was going on there ... really ... Tam asked himself.

It was some time later, before they actually even reached the DRC itself, that they encountered several other dragons and riders.

These ones were clustered around what looked like one of the Academy's shuttles. The poor thing was lying on its side, angled halfway downwards and looking distinctly battered compared to the last time anyone here had seen it.

'Foolish people. What did they expect trying to outfly a storm when already in the middle of it?' Silber snorted disgustedly.

It was the first actual comment he'd made for quite some time, aside from giving orders, and no one could persuade Gaile that that counted.

'I suppose they expected not to crash,' Gaile responded, though she wasn't sure how he'd hear her as they were right now.

Silber merely huffed again. He was *not* impressed.

A couple of the riders glanced up and waved at them when they saw who it was that were passing by overhead. The dragons that weren't occupied raised their heads and bellowed in recognition, happy to see them all back safely.

They'd soon passed them by and it was only a little while later that they came upon the Dragon Research Centre or, more accurately, they caught sight of it, in the distance. Guess the shuttle hadn't managed to get very far.

'Well, there goes the lair,' Gaile sighed as she gazed downwards.

That was probably true, Silber thought. The floodwaters *had* done a job sweeping anything already lying loose (or not so loose even) that it could shove before it as it had thundered down the canyon. By the time it had reached here there had been a veritable dam of debris being pushed ahead of it like a battering-ram.

Quite a bit of that ram had been shoved, slammed or just plain wedged into the opening of the old DRC that was one of Silber's hideouts. It had been such a convenient place for it to get stuck in.

Such a shame they'd never been able to close the doors to that place. Even just having the place overrun by water would have been preferential to *this*. Gaile winced. This would take *forever* to clean up.

The water hadn't stayed of course. It had, mostly, continued onwards, until it had come up against the end of the canyon, where, the level being slightly lower, it was now busy collecting and trying out a new life as a rather oddly shaped lake with thin arms spread in all directions.

How long it would stay there was anyone's guess. The hot sun of the day would probably soon dry it up. In the meantime it was going to be nice to have something sparkling and glittering around.

They'd need to wait for the silt to settle first though. The ground looked pretty soaked. At the moment there were so many other things in the water that the once clear H2O from the glacier had taken on a colour nearly identical to the rock that surrounded it, it was merely slightly more runny.

By now there was at least one impromptu dragon and rider pair that was hesitating about getting closer to the DRC. What had made sense in the middle of all the action, looked like it could get them into quite a bit of trouble now that the action was over.

Here there were quite a few dragons in the air around the buildings themselves. They were easy enough to spot as they were moving about quite a bit.

Must be doing damage surveying, Tam figured. That was the only thing he could think of since they didn't seem to be either coming or going.

One of the closer ones spied the approaching newcomers and moved to intercept them. Coming in over the DRC it became obvious that the place was busy. It was literally bustling with activity and out in the open too.

The reason for that wasn't hard to realize. For one thing it looked like the storm had done quite a number on some of the buildings. As such, a lot of what looked like scurrying ant activity were people and dragons along with some impromptu construction scaffolding.

The second reason was that any large gathering of dragons weren't going to fit into the Armoury.

There weren't just dragons out here though. There were people … and machines … and plenty of them too.

The group circled once or twice while searching for a suitable spot to land in. From up here it looked like that by the time they'd been able to get the Armoury functioning again, the requests for help from areas abandoned by the storm had already been coming in.

It was quite surprising how many dragons actually remained, though they probably numbered less than you thought if you actually counted them, dragons usually did. They had quite a bit of presence to them, to say nothing about size.

There were a lot of other people around as well (the majority falling into that category actually, there were always more people than dragons). From the air, it looked a bit like a convention crossed with a command central with a snap of casualty thrown in for good measure, much of it still in the process of being built.

Eventually they were directed to land somewhere towards the left edge, in what looked like what had been set up as an arrivals area.

Touching down in a flurry of flapping wings, the dragons were quick to relieve themselves of their respective burdens.

The researchers in turn couldn't wait to get off, especially those that had made a large part of the journey other than on the dragon's back. They were slightly weak at the knees. Being down on ground that wasn't shaking was an added bonus.

Several assistants surged forwards to aid them in getting themselves and their belongings out of the way.

The researchers, despite their wobbly knees, waved away the medical team, instead indicating the pod with their injured friend, which Nightwraith had set down as carefully as he could manage, before landing himself.

The whole exchange between the passengers and those that greeted them happened so quickly that those that had brought them here were at a bit of a loss. One moment they were there, you turned your head and suddenly they'd been swallowed up by the mass of people.

A tired looking official who was overseeing the "meeting & greeting" heaved a much put upon sigh, pinched his nose and answered their query as to what they should do now with a put upon expression.

'Report back to your unit, of course,' he said in a very matter of fact voice. 'They'll give you any further assignments, as you should well know. They do drill for these sorts of eventualities.'

The official peered at the bewildered looking lot, as if not able to believe they really didn't know what to do, shook his head and pointed vaguely in the direction of the mains. Then he turned his attention back to more, in his mind, pressing matters.

Silber had already begun to draw both one and two odd glances and was the first to vanish. Just how he managed neither of them were sure of. One minute he was standing behind them, the next he wasn't.

There weren't any shouts, so it was doubtful that he'd switched form, wasn't it? There was the little issue about clothes, after all. That was one of the downsides of moving between forms, you didn't get to keep your clothes.

'Which exactly *is* your unit?' someone nearby suddenly asked, sounding suspicious of the confused expression on both dragons and riders.

Before either of them could think of an answer the official was distracted by an incoming arrival that sent a lot of the medical staff scurrying forwards.

'Let's get out of here,' Tam ushered the other three riders before him, keen to get out of any spotlight.

He tried to stay on top of things but one by one they drifted off from the trail he was making and by the time he'd actually reached the main doors, he was the only one left.

Tam sighed. Oh well, that was his own fault for taking his eyes of them. He should have kept them in front of him, not behind. At least he knew where to find them, that was something at least.

For now, the best thing he could do was to get himself up to speed on what was happening.

* * *

The impromptu grouping of dragons and riders didn't get the rest they thought they'd be getting though, for only a few hours later and they were all together again. Only, this time, it hadn't been entirely by choice.

One by one, or together, they'd been approached, summoned and escorted to their current location. It hadn't been a hostile summoning. But it had been one where the very act suggested that refusing was really *not* in their best interest.

Now they were standing side by side, some looking more uncomfortable with the situation than others. Some of them were merely looking around wondering where they were and trying not to get noticed doing so.

This wasn't a room that many of them had been in before. It didn't look like most of the offices in the DRC. It was almost old-fashioned. No, actually it *was* old-fashioned, at least in appearance.

Question was … was that a good thing or a bad thing?

The man sitting before them calmly set aside the diom he'd been consulting and let his grey eyes play over them. He wasn't giving away anything going by the expression on his face.

'It would appear that you have been quite busy,' he commented almost serenely.

It was hard to tell it he was being ironic, but either way they felt that it was a gross understatement.

'Sir,' Tam replied, followed a heartbeat later by Tiosh.

'Please,' Dr Cosgrove winced. 'Not that. *Anything* but that.'

Tam had been in the showers when the message had come for him. He'd been towelling his hair when he'd picked it up and had made displeased grumbling sounds at it after having read it.

He had a pretty good idea of why they were here and he wasn't looking forward to it. As it turned out, he would prove to have been quite wrong about that.

A very similar sound to the one that had been made by Tam had been expressed by Tiosh after reading the one he'd received (which, when compared, was pretty much identical save for the change of names). His girlfriend had wondered what he was so gruff about – it had been a long day for her too. But she'd taken it in stride when it came to accepting it as a fact of being in the DragonCorps.

They'd been the only ones that had received a written message. Everyone else had been brought here in person. That might have been because Tam and Tiosh were the only actual full members out of the lot of them. Some had been less willing to come along than others but in the end, they'd all arrived here.

Up until they'd reached their destination and seen the others, there had still been the offhand chance that the whole thing had been about something else entirely. At that point however, all such hopes had gone right down one of those elusive drains that everyone was always pouring it down. No one had ever seen one, which was possibly why it was so hard to retrieve it once lost; hope that was.

Tam regarded the older man who'd just spoken with a steady gaze. He wasn't the only one looking but the other eyes might be doing a lot of other things as well. He'd never heard of Dr Cosgrove being averse to being addressed as "Sir". Was there something here he was missing? If he managed to keep the question from showing on his face, he was one of the few that did.

'Please,' Dr Cosgrove pleaded. 'I've had more than enough of people "Sir-ing" me and then staring vacantly ahead of them than I can take for one day. It's been a long day for me too you should know.'

'Sorry, Sir. I didn't mean...'

Dr Cosgrove waved his objection away. 'No matter. It's not important. Now, perhaps we should skip right ahead to why you're all here?'

Dr Cosgrove carefully surveyed the eight people that were standing before him.

They weren't uniform. No one in their right mind could call them that. Even if something as simple as height was used, they were still all over the place. The rest, well, that came even less close.

Actually, there was one thing about them that stood out now that he was thinking about it clearly, but it wasn't something as evident as how they stood or what they looked like. They were *all* stubborn, persistently so in fact. They weren't all stubborn in quite the same way but it was something they had in common alright. It wasn't the *only* thing they had in common either.

'I've had a talk with the people from Hilo,' Dr Cosgrove continued where he'd left off. 'It suits both of us to keep certain parts of their "rescue" quiet. For instance, the identity of those involved. Your arrival back at the DRC appears to have come at such a turbulent time that I'm sure that few will ques-tion the official version of events with more than a shrug or two. It was a busy and confused day for all. Who is to say who saw what.'

Several glances passed between those assembled. Neither of them was en-tirely certain where this was leading.

Were they in trouble? They'd expected that from the start. But if so, why go through all the trouble of keeping their involvement a secret? If they were going to be punished, wouldn't people start asking questions about it after all?

There were plenty of questions that were left unanswered already but would making this unofficial give answers or just close the door on further questions?

'I'm not sure we follow you, Dr Cosgrove,' Tiosh admitted, putting into words what pretty much everyone was thinking.

'Tam. Tiosh,' the Doctor addressed them both. 'You two represent the most stable element before me. You've been working together for some time and while you don't always see eye to eye, you are a good team.'

'Thank you, Sir,' they chorused automatically and without thinking what it might get them into.

'Sir? Couldn't you just *tell* us what you're thinking?' Tam pleaded. Dr Cosgrove's explanations were notorious and for good reason. It was like getting your brain slowly stewed, then scrambled only to be put into a blender afterwards. There was a red thread in there somewhere, usually. As a mere mortal, it was just a question of finding it and then hanging on to it for dear life.

It remained unclear if the good doctor paid any attention to this as he continued without worrying about the interruption.

'That's good. It means that, for the time being, I'm putting you in charge.'

'In charge? In charge of what?' Tam wanted to know.

'As for you four,' Dr Cosgrove turned to the people that made up the centre of their little row. 'You still have *much* to learn. I expect you will make the most of the rest of your time at the Academy?'

'Umm … yes, Sir,' one or two of them answered a little uncertainly followed by some mumbles along the same lines from the others.

'Good. Good,' Dr Cosgrove nodded. 'And you won't tell *anyone* of this little *adventure* of yours?'

'No, Sir.'

This time they shook their heads along with the reply. They seemed to be going around in circles. Where they in trouble or weren't they?

'I think you'll find that these two here,' the older man indicated Tam and Tiosh, 'won't be averse to giving you some extracurricular lessons if you want them.'

He couldn't help but smile at the shine that suddenly grew in their young eyes. 'It will be strictly confidential of course,' he winked at them. 'So don't let anyone catch wind of your little secret.'

'No, Sir.'

The shaking of the heads came much more forcefully this time and a whole lot more enthusiastically.

'If you will want to keep the pairings anything official will, of course, have to wait until *after* you graduate, but otherwise, say hello to your new partners.'

He'd expected a bit of commotion at that point, but most of what he did get was stunned silence.

'Partners, Sir?'

'If that's what you want, then yes. If you're willing to commit to it here and now, I'll even arrange for some D-Comm crystals to come your way. Can't have a partner and not be able to speak to them, now can we?'

'Seriously?'

Dr Cosgrove nodded. 'Yes. In fact, once you've had time to adjust to that and Turing and Nightwraith have been able to give you some training, I'll expect you to be able to take on some small assignments. All unofficial of course. Assuming that you are interested?'

'Sure.'

'Yes, Sir.'

'Absolutely.'

'You bet.'

Now the commotion he'd predicted earlier broke out. So, stubborn but also suspicious of what their ears told them. Not a bad combination overall. Dr Cosgrove silently congratulated himself.

'Umm..?' one of them briefly raised their hand.

'Yes, Dayu. What is it?'

'Sir? What about them?' Dayu pointed at the two people to his far right, who'd so far been left out of the conversation. 'They're the same as us.'

Dr Cosgrove sat back and steepled his fingers, giving them all a very studying "look".

'Not quite,' he finally said.

'Dr Cosgrove,' Tiosh objected. 'They're definitely the same as these guys. How else...' he quieted down as the doctor raised an answering gesture in his direction.

'Ah, but appearances can be deceptive. They might not be aware of it themselves, but those two are actually *already* partners.'

'WHAT?'

They all fastened their eyes on the pair, who, in turn, blinked surprisedly at the whole thing. They were? When had that happened? Wouldn't they have … you know … noticed?

'Err... I'm not sure if...' Sera stuttered over the words. 'I mean... I...'

'And still in denial about it or so it would appear,' Dr Cosgrove sighed. 'Da Silva, you do know that your partner can hear you, do you not? I doubt you would be standing here if you had not, either of you.'

'Well ... yes ... Sir,' Sera replied hesitatingly, as if he wasn't sure what that had to do with it.

'Turing, why don't you remind us all how a dragon is able to speak to his, or her, rider?'

Startled by the question, Tam started up on automatic before his brain engaged properly and he was able to answer.

'Everyone here should know that, Sir. It's on the curriculum. A D-Comm crystal is selected and allowed to soak up a small amount of the dragon's blood after which it is implanted in the rider. A bit like an internal one-way radio attuned to a single biological signal.'

'Indeed,' Dr Cosgrove agreed. 'It would appear that there was a bit of a mix up after miss Ashworthey's accident at First Flight and instead of receiving an ordinary repair replacement in lieu of what she had lost, a D-Comm crystal was used instead.'

'But,' Tam looked as bewildered as the others. 'Even if she did, that alone wouldn't have been enough. They wouldn't have mistaken an infused crystal for a clear one.'

'They didn't,' Dr Cosgrove agreed again. 'What they implanted was a perfectly ordinary crystal. The infusion of dragon's blood came later. An unusual arrangement, certainly.'

'What?' Tiosh exclaimed.

'So that *was* it,' Sera gasped. He'd suspected it. In fact, he'd done more than just suspect it but this was the first time he'd heard anyone backing up the theory. It wasn't like he'd been able to share it with anyone, after all.

That time in the underworld. There had been so much blood the crystal must have been able to soak up some, somehow. No wonder things had looked the way they had. Such a simple, elegant answer. It had been right in front of him this whole time.

'How ... how did you know?' Sera turned his attention to the man before them. 'How could you possibly have known?'

'I have eyes and ears,' Dr Cosgrove smiled benignly at him. 'And I know how to use them. Also, you are not the only one proficient in finding your way around the network without leaving any trace behind.'

'Yes, Sir,' Sera had the decency to look embarrassed about that point.

'Wait a minute here,' Tiosh interrupted and proceeded in putting into words what they were all thinking. 'Even the small amount locked up in the crystals is enough to drive some riders to the brink. Despite their common origins, humans and dragons aren't compatible *at all*. That's why there's no children from such relationships. A small amount of blood is bad enough. A full transfusion would kill the recipient in no time at all and not in a very pleasant way either.'

He'd once seen what had happened with such a mix-up. It wasn't a memory he enjoyed dredging up from the murky bottom of his mind but now it rose up unbidden all the same. He shook himself, trying to dislodge it.

'If that really happened, she'd be dead,' Tiosh said.

'In ordinary circumstances, then yes, I would certainly agree with you Rimwald. It would appear however that whatever else she is, perhaps ordinary is not the word I would choose to describe Miss Ashworthey.'

He offered the unhappy looking young woman an encouraging smile. 'Obviously we can all see that she is, in fact, quite alive. Though, I understand that it was a close call,' he turned his eyes on Sera who nodded. He looked more uncomfortable with things than unhappy about them but he was, despite that, giving the impression of being rather protective of his diminutive partner whether he acknowledged the fact or not.

'I don't know what came over me,' he admitted. 'I should have remembered … about the blood. By the time I did, it was already too late.'

'Indeed,' Dr Cosgrove intoned. 'However, it would seem that fortune has favoured the unprepared this time. As such, I take it that you two won't have any objections to joining this little impromptu ensemble?'

Not hearing any protests, possibly because the parties were too stunned to offer them, Dr Cosgrove allowed a satisfied smile to grace his somewhat wrinkled features.

'Umm,' Sera looked slightly uncomfortable at attracting all the attention he was. Whatever he was going to say was obviously causing him some anguish.

The pause between him clearing his throat and a coherent sound actually coming out of his mouth suggested to several of those in range that he wasn't entirely certain he should be saying anything at all.

'I probably should have told you this earlier,' he confessed. 'But since we are on the topic anyway, I should tell you that it was me. Back then, I mean … who helped you.'

It all came out in a rush, as if the sooner he got the words out the sooner they'd stop causing him trouble. It didn't elicit quite the response he had expected.

Crossing her arms and with an almost indignant huff, Gaile looked unimpressed.

'You're a little too late for that!'

'Sorry? I didn't think… What?'

'I figured *that* out ages ago,' she shrugged.

'You did?' Sera looked surprised and more than a little confused. 'You never said…'

'Well, you never brought it up, so I figured you didn't want me to know.'

'But … but … how?'

'You do have a rather distinct voice you know. You might have bound my eyes under that little arrangement of yours but my ears were still working just fine.'

'Oh.' Sera looked positively crestfallen. All that worry. All that effort. For this?

They couldn't help but to chuckle at the whole thing.

'She's got you there,' Tiosh slapped him on the back. 'Should have disguised your voice if you were that keen to stay an unknown.'

'It slipped my mind.'

'And let that be a lesson to you," Dr Cosgrove interjected. "One can never be too careful.'

'Yes, Sir,' Sera acknowledged

'I think all of you will make a fine team, with some practice. You're all more individualists than team players, but with the right incentives that should prove to work just fine. Our established system is working fine. However, it is unwise to trust ones entire future to a single system. You will be one of the balancing pieces on the board and I'm sure that you will be a good one. You might want to think of a name for yourselves, though there is no hurry. The designations they use and reuse here, Team A, Team Green and so on can get very boring to say nothing about confusing when you have to read all the reports.'

'Yes, Sir.'

'Well then. I'll let you all be on your way.'

It was obvious that it was a dismissal and should be taken as such. Despite that, Tam hung back as the rest of them headed out the door. One question still burned on his mind.

'Dr Cosgrove? About ... in Hilo. There were ... umm ... a couple of things that happened...'

'Yes? I read the report, Turing. *Both* reports in fact.'

'About that. The places I highlighted. I just wanted to ask you about them ... are ... are they even possible?'

'It would appear so. We've seen small tendencies before but nothing even approaching this scale. A very unusual pair indeed.'

That was all he said. Apparently Dr Cosgrove wasn't inclined to make further statements without having a bit more evidence to back it up.

Tam decided not to push the issue but he did resolve to keep a close eye on those two to see if he could figure it out on his own.

* * *

Not everything around the Academy had quite such a serious feel to it as what was transpiring between the new members of the impromptu thrown together team; something that the participants were sure to be grateful for, had they known.

'So," Kalim nudged Pol in the side. 'What's up?'

They were both waiting in the lobby for one of the interconnecting shuttles coming from the city. There weren't really any regularly scheduled services out here. Most of the time anyone from the DRC used the facility's own shuttle buses, which moved regularly between the two sites, but there wasn't anything commercial on this stretch of "road". Those weren't particularly large and could only carry a limited number of people and certainly weren't comfortable if you wanted to haul a whole section of luggage along with you.

Due to the large number of students and staff leaving during this period however, there had been special ones requisitioned. That wasn't anything strange but it did mean there was quite a bit of competition for places on the individual vehicles.

Because of that, Kalim and Pol weren't the only ones waiting here; not by far. Quite a number of others; students and staff both, had gathered even for this early morning transfer.

'Ready to head off?' Kalim asked casually.

'No, I'm standing here because it's my new hobby,' Pol rolled his eyes at him. 'What d'you think?'

'Pol, you can be such a bore sometimes, you know.'

'That isn't being boring. That's making something boring interesting. Quite different. *This*,' he indicated what was going on around them with a sweep of his arm. 'This, now *this* is boring. Just how much longer do we have to wait for this stupid thing anyway?'

'You know, you're just sour because your head hurts. You know, you wouldn't be having so much of a headache today it you hadn't left the party until, like, five AM in the morning.'

'Oh, shut up,' Pol grumbled.

They weren't the only ones there who were feeling a bit under the weather, but there was, however, a remarkably small amount of students, beyond those in the same year that was.

When Pol remarked on this, someone behind them suggested that this might be because a lot of them had already left.

Someone else then suggested it was just as likely that, this time around, they weren't actually leaving to begin with.

It was true that a large number from the senior years had volunteered to stay on and help with the "clean-up" as they called it, both at the DRC itself and out in the field. They figured that it not only benefited others, but it worked in their favour too, earning them experience. As such, many saw it as the best of both worlds and the one positive thing to come out of this whole disaster.

Neither Kalim nor Pol knew anyone in their year that was sticking around rather than having a well-earned rest away from it all; which only proved that they weren't the complete know-it-alls that they were, often, inclined to think of themselves as.

Others, such as Teran, had already left, much to the surprise of his class-mates. A private shuttle had come in to pick him up earlier, the very morning after the term had officially ended.

What that said about how seriously those people were actually perusing their interests in becoming a dragon-rider was anyone's guess but the sudden exit of some had caused quite a few raised eyebrows and no small amount of grumbling on behalf of those students left behind.

Would they be back? Well, that was anyone's guess really.

* * *

Yet others were taking the time to enjoy the reduced amount of competition for some of the prime relaxing locations in the Academy.

'Hey! Hey! Over here,' Dayu waved enthusiastically at the rest of them through the trees. 'Here! I've found a great spot!'

Making their way through a small set of bushes, when they saw it, the others couldn't but agree with his assessment. Even before they passed the last of the trees, they could see the light opening up before them. It scattered throughout the leaves, leaving a dazzled pattern all over the grass-clad ground, moving with the artificial breeze. It was an emerald treasure deep within the forest.

'Wow … this is absolutely gorgeous,' Akia exclaimed, her eyes moving from one dazzling piece to the next.

'It sure is nice,' Tam agreed. He didn't usually spend much time in the Hive and rarely explored beyond the immediate area around the entrance, so this was a new experience for him.

The Hive was home to plenty of different places. This one wasn't actually all that far from one of the set paths. In fact, you could still see the pale brown snake winding its way through the forest from here. So, from that you'd think that it wasn't exactly "out of the way" but since this section of the path wasn't attracting much in terms of visitors, it itself being quite some distance from the more frequented areas, it was nice and private. You could almost feel like it was your own personal forest that you were taking a picnic in.

Being around midday right now, there were a number of people taking advantage of the Hive. However, the fact that the term for the students was over meant that there were less people than usual. The Hive was one of the more popular locations to "hang out".

Here, on the other hand, it was perfectly quiet. You couldn't even hear anyone else … well, not anyone else *human* anyway. There was the occasional flash of colour among the trees and gentle chitter suggested that a number of the resident dragonlings were watching the visitors intently.

In other words, it suited their little outing very well.

Drak looked about. He wasn't really the type to bother about these sorts of things at all and he was feeling a bit out of place. Still, he had to admit it was good not to have the whole world under his feet for a change.

They were all here, weren't they? Well, actually, no, they weren't, he thought. There were still a few people missing.

Jim still wasn't here and Sera had said there was something he needed to take care of and had disappeared shortly after they'd entered the Hive.

What that could be, Drak had no idea. He couldn't think of anything anyone would need to do in the Hive on such short notice.

Still, Sera was the one that had suggested they'd head deeper into the woods than usual. That was something that had had Tiosh nodding in agreement.

Annoying guy, just going off on his own like that. Acting all high and mighty too… Drak didn't much like the young man who was so frequently referred to as "the silver haired god" by a good number of people *or* the people who referred to him like that, but even back in the day something had told him *not* to pick a fight with him.

Now that he knew the reason, he still didn't like it much. Wonder if it's because he's stronger than me? Drak wondered.

He wasn't altogether certain where the third year had disappeared off to, but he sure wasn't going to follow him. The guy had eyes on him that could sure stop you dead in your tracks. That's what it had always felt like. Even when he smiled there was something incredibly cold and calculating in there.

It had been less than a week since the "incident" and the guy still gave him the creeps. They hadn't seen much of him around either, despite the fact that they were supposed to be a team.

So, who *was* here then?

Drak looked around again and stifled a sigh. Now that he thought about it, the only ones here were him, that little guy, Dayu, and the two instructors. What were their names again? Ti … something, wasn't it? Oh, and Tam. He could remember that one, if only because it rhymed with "ham".

That left them, about, yes seven people short. No, wait, five people. There were only four of each of them; four dragons and four riders. Why did he keep getting confused and thinking there were five? There wasn't some invisible ones around, were there?

'Oight, watch it!' a voice suddenly exploded from behind him. 'Don't just stop like that.'

Akia shook her head at the way he just stood there and proceeded to step around him and help the others set things up.

They'd already placed the blanket (not like that was rocket science anyway) along with several wire baskets and containers, each one of them having carried at least one of them with them. A number of items had already been unpacked, mostly by Tiosh, who was already shooing Dayu away from a selection of cakes and pastries for the second time.

She set down the basket that she'd brought along among them, returning the friendly greeting with a small wave and a smile.

As a dragon, she'd known Tiosh for quite some time. To her, he was the person she was the most comfortable being around of their present company.

'Did Jim say how long he'd be?' Drak pounced on her.

Akia shook her head. 'Sorry. I haven't heard a thing. I'm sure he'll be along. Relax will you.'

To this there was a rather grumbled reply. Drak hated to wait.

'Gaile didn't say either, did she?' Akia stated firmly. 'She *is* coming, isn't she? It'd be just like her to skip out.'

'Now, now, no need for that,' Tam admonished her.

'I suppose she's with Sera,' Akia shrugged.

Even if, as a dragon herself, she'd never held any illusions about becoming his rider or having known him at all really, Akia was still a bit miffed over the whole thing. Never in a thousand years had she (or anyone else, she defended that thought with) dreamt that the silver dragon would choose someone like *that* as a partner. What in the world did he see in her anyway?

'Actually,' Dayu interrupted her inner world. 'Sera's here already … *somewhere*. He just went into the forest. He said he had something he needed to do.'

'Here?' Akia looked around, then shrugged. Just one more thing that didn't make sense.

With the clinking of earthenware and the soft thuds of plastic and glass, Dayu was compiling a small section in the centre of the tartan blanket.

'Do? Do what?' Gaile asked curiously, blinking at them.

Her voice made them all jump. How had she gotten here without them noticing?

'Oh well, I'm sure he'll be back,' she shrugged at their lack of reply and put her own offering down and took off the lid, starting to rummaging through it. A moment later she held up a small box triumphantly. It made a noise when she shook it, so there had to be something in there.

'Did you bring cookies?' Dayu asked, trying to sniff out the scent.

Gaile chuckled at the sight. 'Sorry, these ones aren't for you,' she held the box aloft, out of reach. Dayu was one of the few people she actually outranked in terms of height.

'These ones are already promised to a friend of mine,' she said. 'There should be plenty of munchies left though. I tried to bring more today-stuff than plain sweets. I'm sure it'll taste alright.'

'Oh,' disappointment radiated from him like a small sun.

'Don't worry. There's plenty here for everyone,' Tam nudged him with a plate.

'Yeah, better dig in before someone else gets all the best bits.'

'Aww, that's so unfair of you to say,' Akia pouted.

'It would be better if *everyone* was here,' Tiosh muttered.

'Oh, do lighten up, will you,' Tam put something cold and brisk in his partner's hand. 'They'll be along eventually.'

'Yes, well…'

'Try one of these,' Akia smiled and offered him what looked like a white

'Must have been something drastic.'

'I think I heard something about cookies, but, honestly, that didn't make much sense.'

'Hell, if they don't want any of these, more for me,' Drak said and crammed a whole creamed bun into his mouth. 'Oeil osh…'

'You're a louse,' Gaile mumbled.

She tried keeping her breathing normal, to force it back into something other than the mad gulping of some oxygen starved fish thrown unceremoniously onto dry land. Her legs hurt.

'Could we decide that you will be sensible about this?' Sera asked.

He'd drawn closer but he still wasn't too anxious to get within reach, just in case.

'Bugger sensible.'

'I *was* going to tell you. I promise,' he pleaded. 'I just hadn't … eh … gotten around to it yet.'

'You should be strung up and slowly halstered over an open fire,' was Gaile's muttered reply to this latest offering.

Though, while her words were perhaps less than friendly, the tone of voice suggested to him that she'd calmed down considerably.

With effort, Gaile pulled herself up until she was sitting rather than sprawling on the grass.

'Any *other* little secrets you'd care to share, while we're at it?' she asked, every word dripping with irony.

Sera looked uncomfortable, but shook his head. 'Umm … no, not any that I can think of right now,' he replied.

The recipient narrowed her eyes. Well, maybe she shouldn't be too harsh with him. After all, she had plenty of secrets of her own. And it wasn't like she was in a hurry to share those, now was it? It'd be a bit strong, asking to know his, while not sharing hers. Still, *that* one had caught her *completely* off guard. What a rascal. Guess that was to be expected, now that she *did* know and all.

Maybe she should let him off the hook, just this once? Even so, it *had* been quite a shock. Ok, maybe half a hook?

'Does any of the others know?' Gaile asked, as she accepted a hands up.

'No,' Sera said. 'And if possible, I would prefer if it remained that way.'

'Suit yourself. It's not like anyone's likely to guess anyway.' For who in the seven stars had ever heard of a dragon having more than two forms? Wasn't that one of those set impossibilities in the existence of everything?

It was one of those things that no one, nowhere, would believe if you told them, even if you kept knocking them over the head with the evidence. It was, in other words, one of those things that everyone, and that meant *everyone*, knew wasn't possible. Almost as if, if it *was* possible, it'd upset the order of the universe or something.

That was perhaps taking it a bit far, Gaile thought. But it certainly would upset a lot of people and their view of how the world worked.

Obviously, she concluded, in this case, what everyone knew and what actually was, were two very different things. Well, it wasn't like it was the first time she'd come up against something like that.

Who'd have suspected it? She certainly hadn't seen it coming, that's for sure. It did explain a lot though, especially answering that question she'd always had about how the blazers her friend had been able to get around like he did or even get out of the Hive in the first place.

It did make you wonder though. What on earth was he doing, running around the Academy like that?

Gaile still remembered how they'd met. What possible interest could he have had for sneaking around the Armoury, when he'd obviously been able to just walk in there normally whenever he pleased.

She also wasn't all that keen on trying to figure out just why he'd been dropping nuts and bolts on her even if admittedly she *had* been trying to capture him. Why hadn't he just flown away? What was in it for him? Indulging a mischievous streak or something, maybe?

It could be useful though, now that she was able to view the whole thing objectively. A dragon that could pretend to be a dragonling had all sorts of possibilities. No wonder that his features as a dragonling didn't match theirs.

Also, on a brighter note, it made him easier to carry around. She couldn't help but giggle at that thought. Now that she knew … it *was* kind of amusing, even if she wasn't quite ready to forgive him for the whole thing, not just yet.

'Say … remember that really cool move Jim pulled out at First Flight?'

Dayu asked Tam. 'Think we could do that? Akia and me?'

Tam looked thoughtful for a moment, but he was beaten to the answer by Jim himself.

'It's not something you can just learn overnight, you know? It took a lot of practice to get it right,' Jim said. And a whole lot of bruises, he added silently to himself.

'Aww, come on. It can't be that hard, can it?'

'It's not that *easy* either.'

'When did you get the chance to practice it anyway?' Drak wanted to know. 'Did you skip class?'

'Nah,' Jim waved that thought away! We learnt that ages ago.'

'Don't go giving Dayu here any more ideas, do you hear?' Tam suddenly looked stern. 'One is more than enough.'

'One what?'

'And I bet I could do it too,' Dayu looked eager, as if he couldn't wait to try it out.

'Forget it. Thomas and I practiced a lot to get it right,' Jim insisted.

'You shouldn't have been practising it at all,' Tiosh admonished him.

'Tommy didn't have a problem teaching me that.'

'That's because your brother is a lunatic,' Tiosh stated firmly.

'Aww ... come on ...'

'Say, Akia?'

'Hmm ... yes?' Akia replied. She hadn't really been paying attention. She'd been busy with her own conversation.

'You know that move Jim pulled up at the station. Want to try it?'

'No thanks,' Akia flat out refused, turning back to where she'd left off describing something from her hometown to her listeners.

Looking distinctly dejected, for about five seconds, Dayu quickly perked up. Maybe he could ask her again, later?

Tam tried not to shake his head at the whole thing. Dayu was like a two-way floater in a bowl of soup. Push down on one end and the other would bob up as sure as the sun rose in the west.

Next week would be the start of the yearly intermission. A significant break at the end of one year and the beginning of another. Wonder what *we're* supposed to do?

Normally, it was a time when students returned home or went travelling, teachers focused on other things and the Academy (but not the DRC) grew somewhat deserted.

It was a time for relaxing. For holidays. For expanding your horizons. Gaile sighed. Somehow she suspected that they were going to get all the "expanding your horizons" that you could possibly ask for and then some, but that there wouldn't be any relaxation involved in the whole thing. Guess they were going to be busy, whether they wanted to be so or not.

Well, that was up to Dr Cosgrove, wasn't it? Nothing she could do about it, short of getting up and leaving anyway. Gaile mumbled something incoherent and settled down for seeing if there was "anything" left among what they'd brought that she actually wanted to eat.

Epilogue:

One thing the storm had done was to clear the air. It felt lighter and sharper than ever.

Of course, when the wind came in from the north, north-west, it also carried a distinct sulphuric smell with it. The eruption at Loch Lod which wasn't a lake any more, at least not one of water and ice, had quieted down. There wasn't much rumbling of the earth in that area any more. It hadn't stopped completely, hence the faint scent in the wind as you drew near.

Not that they were near. At least, here, above the clouds that formed a thickset landscape of their very own, it was difficult to tell what lay below it.

That was alright. It was better that way. Well, it was better when you didn't actually have a location that you needed to find and were paying attention to any guidance system. In fact, if you were just enjoying the sensation of freedom, carefree freedom, among the mountains and valleys and plains of fluffy white and grey and blue then you couldn't really ask for more.

Gaile tugged at the mask. She still hadn't gotten used to it but it was very difficult to remain anonymous if your face was visible. She knew it wasn't likely to stay that way forever but for now, the identity of the silver rider would remain a secret. And with it, going flying in the daytime was no longer an obstacle.

Like now.

They were drifting lazily, without a goal. Just experiencing themselves up here, where the clouds came to play.

Here, the wind, harsh in its performance as always, buffered the cotton balls as it pleased, evolving and revolving every moment. The same wind carried the dragon and rider effortlessly.

His vast wings fully stretched out. His legs tucked up tight. Silber's eyes were, almost, closed. He was enjoying this late afternoon flight. It felt a little like it somehow wasn't real, as if, at any moment, he would wake up and find out it had all been just a dream after all.

'Hey, you're not nodding off, are you?'

'What? Of course not,' he replied guiltily, having almost been caught red-handed, or should that be red-winged?

'Sleep on your own time. I'll lend you a pillow even. It's a long way down.'

That was true, it *was* a long way down. It was also true he had a habit of curling up on pillows and snoozing. It was very comfortable.

No pillows up here though, unless you counted the clouds.

There was no one else here, just the two of them.

It was nice not being alone.

*** THE END ***

www.ingramcontent.com/pod-product-compliance
Lightning Source LLC
Chambersburg PA
CBHW020828030726
47496CB00001B/137